love, ever so painfully, a manipulative media man . . . a literary romance featuring the sophisticated English abroad in France' Fay Weldon, *Mail on Sunday*

'Cunningly plotted, extremely well-written and compulsively readable' Beryl Bainbridge

'The authentic tang of human emotion at every level' Claire Rayner

'A cleverly-plotted, witty black comedy, modern storytelling at its most enjoyable. The throwaway observations made me laugh out loud' *The Literary Review*

'Grand guignol in a gite – shockingly readable' *New Statesman*

PEARLS

'Absorbing, entertaining, its grammar impeccable, its theme the sufferings and eventual triumphs of a pair of beautiful sisters . . . Her Malaya is exactly rendered, her women sound and act like real women. Readers will devour it, as I did' Anthony Burgess, *Independent*

'A triumph – Celia Brayfield's first novel is a complex and delicious amalgamation of glamour and sensitivity, sensuality and betrayal, sweeping from war-torn Malaysia through the England of the Beatles. A rich, multi-faceted story, her plot is a masterpiece of construction, her prose literate, insightful and frequently witty' *Rave Reviews*

'A great adventure of our times' *Le Meridional*

D1578742

Amanda

Celia Brayfield grew up in the London suburbs and was educated at St Paul's Girls' School and at university in France. She graduated from _The Times'_ typing pool to become first the _Evening Standard'_s TV critic and later a journalist who still writes for _The Times_ and other media. Her first novel, _Pearls_, was an international bestseller; she followed with two more, _The Prince_ and _White Ice_, before concentrating on modern social comedies: _Harvest_, _Getting Home_, _Sunset_ and _Heartswap_. Among her non-fiction titles is _Bestseller_, about writing popular fiction. A single parent with one daughter, she now lives mostly in West London.

Praise for Celia Brayfield

GETTING HOME

'Brayfield, with lightning flashes of wit and scalpel-sharp observations, pokes fun at a host of targets – rich mothers, community action groups, class prejudice, property tycoons, live TV audiences, precocious children and nouvelle cuisine. Gloriously vicious and compulsively readable' _Daily Mail_

'Her eye for the irritating minutiae of contemporary life is enjoyably sharp' _The Times_

'I couldn't be wrested away from it, though they tried' Fay Weldon

'Wonderfully funny' _Woman & Home_

'A juicy exercise in literary curtain-twitching. You wonder whether Brayfield achieved the madcap climax by dipping her pen in Viagra' _Evening Standard_

'A sparkling satire about the suburban dream' *Evening Herald*

'With sharp wit and snappy dialogue, Brayfield has produced a very funny, cleverly plotted novel that displays Fay Weldon's understanding of the pleasure to be derived from seeing the bad get their just deserts' *Daily Telegraph*

'A writer of enormous intelligence with the widest possible common touch' *Mail on Sunday*

'At once a biting social satire and a passionate denouncement of mindless environmental vandalism' *Good Housekeeping*

'A witty, dark tale of suburban lives going wrong . . . superbly readable' *Sunday Times*

'Brayfield's writing glitters: the humour is as sharp as a Sabatier knife, the satire immaculately honed, her observations precise down to the last shell-pink toenail. And under the wicked wit, some hard home truths' *Image*

HEARTSWAP

'Delicious – a laugh-out-loud book' *Evening Herald*

SUNSET

'Celia Brayfield's style is as exuberant as it is poetic' *Daily Express*

'Brayfield is a fine prose stylist' *Sunday Times*

HARVEST

'Heaven knows, a good read, but far from trivial. A brilliantly-textured "proper" novel about the women who surround and

Mister Fabulous and Friends

CELIA BRAYFIELD

timewarner paperbacks

A *Time Warner* Paperback

First published in Great Britain in 2003
by Time Warner Paperbacks

Copyright © Celia Brayfield 2003

The moral right of the author has been asserted.

*All characters in this publication are fictitious and any
resemblance to real persons, living or dead, is purely coincidental.*

A CIP catalogue record for this book
is available from the British Library.

ISBN 0 7515 3138 3

Typeset in Garamond by M Rules
Printed and bound in Great Britain by
Clays Ltd, St Ives plc

Time Warner Paperbacks
An imprint of
Time Warner Books UK
Brettenham House
Lancaster Place
London WC2E 7EN

www.TimeWarnerBooks.co.uk
www.celiabrayfield.com

To almost all the men I know — with love

No matter what anybody says, it all comes down
to the same thing: a man and a woman,
a broken heart and a broken home.

John Lee Hooker 1920–2001

Introducing . . .

ANDY 'Mr Fabulous' FORREST: Vox/bass.
   Married to Laura; daughters Lily and Daisy

Percy GEORGE HODSOLL: Guitar.

MICKEY 'Blue' RYDER: Guitar.
   Married to Mo; son Joe

SAM 'Fingers' CHUDLEIGH: Keyboards.
   Living with Alice Waters; children Melanie and Jon

RHYS 'The Gas' PRITCHARD: Drums.
   Married to Barbara; children Emma and Toby

Mister Fabulous
and Friends

CHAPTER 1

The Intro And The Outro

Andy Forrest was a big man. He was six foot three, as his wife would delicately boast when she was sure he wasn't around to hear her. She would say it with a twitch of her lips downwards and to the left, to show that she knew she was sounding smug but what was a woman to do, married to a man who was *tall*, at least, if he was nothing else of much interest.

Andy Forrest was getting love handles, as his daughter had pointed out when she really wanted to tell him that she knew why love handles were called that, a message his father-filter had automatically deleted. The love handles themselves didn't worry him. He told himself they'd just melt away as soon as he had a couple of busy weeks, or maybe a holiday somewhere it was too hot to eat. Middle-age spread? Something that happened to your parents. And the funky old Hawaiian shirt covered up well.

Andy Forrest had a safe pair of hands, as his old friends in advertising used to say after they'd handed him a poisoned chalice and watched him simply down it in one and let his relentless good nature metabolise the toxins without harm. And he had broad shoulders, as he would admit himself when people pointed out to him that others were taking liberties. Taken all round, which was the only way to take him nowadays, Andy Forrest was a man whom people expected to stand tall.

High, wide and handsome was how God had made Andy, but men (and women, who are, of course, worse than the men) had messed up the plan so that he had no real sense of his stature. Most of the time he experienced himself as of average height and insignificant build. Until he got behind a microphone.

Then, no matter how poxy the dive, how unsalubrious its environs and how ludicrous the basic idea of a one-time student band that refused to die, when Andy jumped on stage, took up his spot at the centre front and lifted the mike off the stand, everything that diminished him day-to-day just blurred into the smoke behind the spotlights. His chest swelled like Superman, his head felt close to the ceiling. His hands engulfed the mike and his feet, planted solidly on the boards, felt longer and wider and not likely to let him down in an emergency.

Four friends jumped up on the stage behind him. With one mighty bound they were free of their other selves. They jumped because, years ago, George, the lead guitar, had heard Keith Richards say in a TV interview that The Rolling Stones had taken the decision to jump up on stage so that the audience knew they really wanted to be up there. And these five men, playing a fairly classic R&B set in a pub in West London on the second Friday of every month, really,

really wanted to be up there too. Even after all those years.

At the start, the ignorant portion of the audience, those who did not know what to expect, dismissed them as the usual bunch of losers cranking out somebody else's greatest hits. They weren't interested in music; they had another agenda. In a long-hours metropolis, the purpose of a Friday night is to apply alcohol to the pain of living.

A scattering of regulars turned away from the bar to listen, but the work-weary stress junkies, passing through irony on their way to oblivion, kept their backs to the stage, even after George lobbed in a couple of cheeky chords to let them know the set was starting.

Then Andy heaved in a breath, bounced it on his diaphragm, squeezed it with his ribs and let it out as a voice. And what a voice. Unreal. A voice made of poetry, soaked in testosterone, coated with honey, roasted in rage and hurled out under the smoke-stained polystyrene ceiling tiles, a couple of hours after the bruised-looking autumn sun had set over junction four of the M4.

They began with 'You Give Love a Bad Name'. It was a concept they could all get behind, these five men whose hormones were raising hell in the Last Chance Saloon, roaring through their arteries, touching off desires they'd never known they had. Love had conned them all and now the most credible romantic gesture they could make was to blame women in general. In addition, Andy had, as near as dammit, the voice of Jon Bon Jovi in his early days.

Out in the audience, people who remembered the early days of Bon Jovi yelled, 'Fuckin' ringer for Bon Jovi!' at nobody in particular. Others who thought they heard a whisper of the young Rod Stewart kept silent, because they knew from bitter experience that there was no point trying to tell anyone that Rod Stewart had ever been either young or worth hearing.

Through the lights and the smoke Andy saw the flash of teeth as he started to make people happy, and he smiled himself. He liked making people happy, and he stubbornly refused to understand that this was a terrible mistake in life.

Andy was not now, and had never been, rangy, shaggy, blond or long in the jaw like Jon Bon Jovi. His accent was more Somerset than *Sopranos*. His hair was half a centimetre long all over, which made the least of the grey. He was an R&B man, hardcore. He was a successful multimedia entrepreneur with a remote office in The Terrace, Westwick. So the Bon Jovi thing was only a matter of sound. One hell of a sound.

If Andy was, as the French would say, a solidly carpentered kind of man, the figure at the front beside him had been knocked up out of a couple of offcuts. A thin, rickety kind of a structure was George, with skeletal fingers that seemed to hardly touch the guitar strings, and worn jeans that flapped against his bones. His nose jutted out from his concave cheeks, his sharp jaw overhung his bony throat, his teeth leaned at crazy angles like old grave stones. On stage, George Hodsoll, dispatch rider to the gentry and instinctive musician, whom the world had treated harshly and to whom Lady Luck acted like a slut, could feel like a king and enjoy a warm state of euphoria without necessarily doing any drugs or running the risk of falling off his bike. Once people were past the wonder of Andy's voice, they noticed that the lead guitar wasn't bad either. Actually, quite like the early Gary Moore.

At the keyboards, holding down the far corner of the stage, was a round, short, dark-haired individual with sweat standing in beads on his smooth olive skin, stabbing at the keys with conical fingers and bouncing with the rhythm. Sam Chudleigh wore black; a black polo-neck, even. You would have thought he thought he was in a jazz band, and you would have thought right. Jazz, in Sam's opinion, was the intellectual's proper choice. In this band, he was only indulging the others for old times' sake. With his equipment plugged in, Sam Chudleigh of Chudleigh Estate Services, a property lawyer about to enter the business stratosphere, could be admired for his sensitive phrasing. Especially by himself.

Mickey Ryder, rhythm guitar, skittered around between the others, gyrating on the heels of his tan cowboy boots, which added a useful inch or two to his height. His hair flew away from his forehead, not quite curling but not yet grizzled, and his humorous eyes, startlingly blue, glinted from a maze of laughter-lines. While he ricocheted from one player to another, some instinct kept him away from the drums. In his business, Mickey was a bit of a legend. They called him The Man, and if he'd still had a show-reel it would have included about fifty per cent of the world's award-winning TV commercials. But, of course, The Man didn't need a show-reel, hadn't had one for years. And here, on stage, this legendary director strummed along amiably enough and sometimes said to George, 'Ready when you are, Mr De Mille.'

Behind the drums sat Rhys Pritchard, a figure who appeared too neat for this primitive trade, too fresh-faced, floppy-haired and generally boyish to throw a TV set off a hotel balcony or drive a car into a swimming pool or back up even this bunch of reprobates. In short, this was a man whose black leather waistcoat didn't fool anyone and who quite likely had creases in his jeans. Safe behind his instruments, Rhys Pritchard, a good doctor, a good father and a good-enough husband (whatever his wife said), felt free to hit things hard enough to bruise his hands.

These were the five leisure musicians who now and then played rock and roll in the function room of an out-of-town pub called the Beehive, a place with low ceilings and lower aspirations.

West London has had its moments in the history of British rock and roll. In Shepherd's Bush there is a mouldering ex-youth club where Pete Townshend is supposed to have met Roger Daltrey before they formed The Who. In Hammersmith, Paul Cook of the Sex Pistols still lives on the street where he grew up. People were even saying that the mother of Ant, the actual Ant of Ant and Dec, had once lived on Westwick High Street, over a dry cleaner's shop. The kind of people that people in Clerkenwell called Great West Chauvinists made that claim.

The Beehive had no historical pretensions. It clung on to the Thames embankment on the south side and looked enviously over the scummy water to the trailing willows of Westwick, cowering behind a fast and dirty road that roared with traffic until past closing time. It kept its punters happy and it gave a stage to part-time guitarists who just about deserved the opportunity.

On the second Friday of each month, these five immigrants from reality arrived at the Beehive in search of a better quality of life. They got there in time to argue about the running order and they enjoyed having these small choices to make, because mostly they were men who made big decisions, got paid big money to do it and sweated bricks in the small hours of the morning when they thought about what they were doing.

When they had agreed, Andy borrowed a biro and scrawled the song titles on the back of a beer mat or an envelope or an old piece of card picked up in the street. Andy Forrest, who in his real life was a gizmo king unnaturally fascinated by the relative merits of Psions and palmtops, would default to words written on paper; enjoy defaulting, even.

Being at least three-fifths intelligent and three-fifths sensitive, they knew they were a bunch of lucky white men who were still obsessed with ghetto music because their own language had no words for pain. Their combined age was now over 222 and they still had fond feelings for the Ikettes.

They had names for this other life, names created by George, who would take over the mike for the last-but-one song, rasp out some verboid transmission like 'thangyouvairmuchlyladesandgentlemones', start squelching his wah-wah pedal, and then announce his fellow musicians in homage to the Bonzo Dog Doo Dah Band, a long-forgotten prankster combo of the Sixties whose creative heritage includes a satire on traditional jazz practice titled 'The Intro And The Outro'.

'Like to introduce to you this evening . . . Rhys "The Gas" Pritchard on drums!'

A frenzy of cymbals. Rhys had his secret shame. He admired Dire Straits. He kept quiet about it in case the others rubbished him. It had been bad enough the night he'd said that 'Lady in Red' was really quite a good song. So that nobody would suspect his heart of kitsch, Rhys set up an excessive number of cymbals and belted the shit out of them.

'Come in Mickey "Blue" O'Ryder, on guitar!'

Throb, throb, thro-thro-throbb! Mickey's issue was the volume. He'd once said he wanted music so loud you could hear it with your bones. A whole sentence was an achievement for Mickey, who worked only with visuals.

'And . . . Sam "Fingers" Chudleigh, over there on keyboards.'

Many notes. Too many notes. If he didn't get his full five minutes at this point, Sam would sulk immediately, throw a tantrum later, walk out of the bar and stomp off into the night saying he didn't know why he bothered. Three weeks later, Andy would get the job of calling him up and talking him round.

'And on vocals, ladiesandgendlemones, Andy Forrest! We call him Mr Fabulous!'

A bit of a frenzy from the audience at that point, then Andy would step forward, a shade too soon because applause always embarrassed him, with, 'Let's hear it now for Percy George Hodsoll, guitar!', after which George threw in a ker-rang or two, pulled the band together and, if he was feeling mellow, took the opportunity to introduce a few fantasy musicians for good luck: 'And looking very relaxed here – Adolf Hitler on vibes! Ni--i–i–ice!'

In their other lives they had all given George opportunities, at one time or another, as year followed year and they found themselves evolving into four solid citizens and a screw-up artist. The band was their freemasonry, these actions were expected. The original three, George, Mickey and Andy, met at their art school in the Midlands. In the second year, when their drummer dropped out, they recruited from the wider student population and added first Rhys, and a little later, when George had said they needed a keyboard man, Sam.

Wealth had found Mickey for keeps, Andy for quite a while and was about to discover Sam. Rhys had married comfortably. One after another, four of them got rich while George was making other plans.

He picked up each opportunity and contrived circumstances in which it would trickle through his fingers. Then he would grin, revealing the leaning teeth for which they had all, at one time or another, offered to pay the orthodontist of his choice, and say something like, 'Old George does it again, eh?'

Take any five men playing in a pub on a Friday night. Their music will not bring harmony to the universe but it keeps them sane. They're in the first days of the Indian Summer of their endocrine systems, twenty per cent of their muscle power has already gone and their chickens are coming home to roost.

One of them will be blind-sided by a Corvette Stingray. One will be caught out by love when he least expects it. Two of them have no idea that their wives are cheating on them. Three of them will shortly cheat on their wives. The same number have thought seriously about L'Oréal for Men. Four of them have already counted up the maximum possible number of times they can have sex before they die. One of them will die sooner than expected. The combined number of times the four who had counted expected to have sex before death was 14,563. None of them thought that was enough.

The Beehive was the last pub in West London to sail under its own name. The rest had become gastrodomes or Internet cafés or taken to fusion cooking, with new names that George misread generically as the Fart and Swizzle.

That same Friday morning at five, Andy had been woken by noises on the street. A bang, a shout. A vehicle's engine in labour.

The Terrace was called 'Westwick's Georgian Gem'. A run of white villas with pillared porches overlooking the one-time village green, The Terrace was not Georgian, only Regency, but out in Westwick the English language had been sadly degraded with the patois of estate agents.

Streets like The Terrace seldom hear banging, shouting and labouring engines at 5 a.m. Apart from the distant hum of the first commuters of the day snaking towards central London on the motorway, Westwick was normally silent at the break of day. Carefully, so as not to wake his wife, who had draped herself along the far side of the marital mattress, Andy sat up, put his feet on the floor, then rose and padded downstairs to the room which was now his office.

The house had the original shutters. In a planet ruled by estate agents there was no higher symbol of status. He unbarred these shutters and folded them back to see what had disturbed his sleep.

Next door, a big green penis was coming up the garden path. The penis was six feet high. At least. Maybe eight? Taller than the men who were carrying it. His disconnected early morning mind struggled to make sense of the sight.

The penis was green. Four men were carrying it. The base was stuck in a pot. It was obviously heavy, and the men were carrying it cautiously. The penis had pricks on the outside.

It was a cactus. Four men were carrying a giant vegetable phallus into the house next door. A removal van was parked outside. New neighbours.

Neighbours, a house next door – I must be in a suburb. Every day this fact surprised Andy and every day he wondered, just for a nano-second, how he had ever come to live in a suburb, even if Westwick was the first and finest suburb in the world. His soul belonged to the ghetto. It was only his body that had moved on up.

George would have liked the sight of the cactus. He heard George in his mind's ear: 'What's the difference between a cactus and The Groucho Club? With a cactus, the pricks are on the outside.' George's tragedy was that he had been born too early for stand-up. Born when rock and roll was the new rock and roll.

Andy rubbed his eyes. It was too early. His T-shirt was sweaty. He slept in a white Fruit of the Loom T-shirt and cotton boxers, fresh every day. Laura, his wife, used to find them sexy.

He went to the kitchen, made himself tea and sorted Weetabix for his daughters. In the downstairs bathroom he showered and wrapped a towel round his waist. From the dressing room upstairs he put on Dockers and a grey fleece, then went back to the raised ground floor and the room that was his office. 'The remote office' he styled it. Self-employment was a work-life choice, not a euphemism for unemployment. Just like redundancy didn't mean the sack.

Now the removal men were carrying round objects swathed in bubble-wrap. Followed by an etched glass table with chrome legs. Then an Arne Jacobson Egg chair in classic black leather. Hello, young style victim, whoever you are. Welcome to The Terrace, Westwick's 'Georgian Gem'. Of course, it's really Regency. He could hear himself saying it.

Laura had never looked as happy as she had on the day their own moving van had fouled up the traffic on The Terrace. She came from the caste that liked a house to be as old as possible. If you were really posh, living in a suburb didn't worry you as long as your house was at least two hundred years old.

They had waited three years to buy a home that would express their precise social trajectory and the full integrity of their personal taste. Post-Nina Campbell and posh to meritocracy for her, post-Conran and upper working to middle class for him.

A second removal van lurched up the pavement and a second gang of men began carrying boxes in, leaving tracks of dark footprints in the heavy autumn dew on next-door's lawn. Fingers tickled Andy around the love handles. Daisy, his younger daughter.

She yawned into his lightly padded ribs. 'Do they always move in so early?'

'Do you think we should offer them a cup of tea?'

'Oh, Dad, you're such a girl.'

'It's the neighbourly thing to do.'

'They'll have stopped off on the motorway.'

'Just a thought.'

'But it could be cover for asking them who's moving in.'

That's my girl.

She went out to investigate, neat in her school clothes. Jeans suitable for school wear, as specified on the clothing list of St Nicholas's High School. Suitable meaning not ripped, slashed, cut-off or embroidered with political or other slogans. A sight to glad a removal man's heart. All eight of them stopped work to have a word.

'Yes, they did stop at a caff,' she reported, skipping up their desirable front steps, the stone treads worn by centuries of up and down. 'And he's someone called Charles Holderness and they're moving him from Hackney.'

An hour or so later when Laura appeared, lipstick-perfect and ready for work, he relayed the information.

'Bit of a culture shock for him, leafy Westwick,' she said dryly, helping herself to coffee from the filter machine her husband had primed for her. 'Are you going to shave today?'

'I was waiting until you guys were out of the bathrooms.'

'Just asking.'

Every woman I wanted, every woman I really need. Taller, blonder, smarter. And with an edge. She made him feel grateful. People, mostly on his side of the family, thought he'd married above himself.

Sixteen years of marriage and her silences were like the rock pools of his childhood, full of wonders waiting to be discovered. She kissed the air under his ear and placed her coffee mug on the draining board for him to wash. Then Laura left for work through the glass kitchen door and crossed their neo-Tuscan back garden, beyond which lay the garage and their cars.

Andy had no meetings that day. Friday is a good day to move house but a bad day to do business. He sent e-mails, tinkered with spreadsheets, researched his prospects for the month to come, surfed the Net for news of the dot.com recovery in the States and thanked God or whoever that he'd started his own business with a better mousetrap to market. He had built his house in the forest and people really were beating a path to his door. Music software. The designers were in Utrecht, customer care in Kilmarnock, and he, in his remote office at The Terrace, Westwick, London, UK, was sales, marketing and corporate development. And they prospered. Not as lavishly as he had prospered as a senior account executive at KKDW, but not far off. After all, advertising was a young industry. And life was good.

At eleven or so, a startling yellow Lamborghini purred in from the opposite direction and parked nose-to-nose with the moving trucks. A man in combats and a leather jacket sprang out, holding a roll of charts.

Would a man with a yellow Lamborghini enjoy tea? Andy merged a spreadsheet with Kilmarnock's database and left the two computers to sort it. In the master en-suite bathroom he shaved, watching the street below between the slats of the venetian blinds.

Charles Holderness, in the brown leather jacket, was agitated. Leaping, pointing, up and down his new front steps. Charles? Charlie. Charlie-boy. Chaz. Chazza. Chuck? Time to find out.

Andy set off next door. He could not avoid seeing that an oversize bottle of champagne lay across the passenger seat of the yellow car. Would a man with champagne in the car really care for a cup of tea? Was he going to be rumbled straight off and written down as Nosy Neighbour No. 1?

The front door was open. In the hall, a chart had been hung on the wall and covered with coloured markers, coded to match the labels on the furniture. Charles Holderness was standing beside it, running the fingers of his free hand through his short hair. The other hand clutched a clipboard.

'I'm Andy, I'm your neighbour. Welcome to The Terrace. Anything you need, just give me a shout.'

'Oh, cheers.' The handshake was short and sticky with styling product. It said don't bother me now. 'I'm Charles. That's very kind of you. No, not upstairs . . .' His eyelids flickered with exasperation. The gang, who were struggling with a handsome birch bookcase, paused on the staircase. 'In the study, down there. Sorry.' His attention switched to Andy. 'Bit of a nightmare just at the moment.'

'I'll leave you to it. Just – anything at all. I'm next door. That way.'

The unloading of the furniture went on all day. No matter where he was in the house, Andy had a view of it. He hoped the curtains hid his curiosity. Laura did not call them curtains. She liked to talk about window treatments. In her World of Interiors phase, Laura had called in Mickey's wife, who had a design business called La Maison. Between them, they had stuffed the house with French country antiques and turned the spare room into a nightmare of red wallpaper with tiny little Chinese people on it. Toile de Whatsit.

Their own bedroom windows were hung with fluffy muslin and some sad, floppy blue drapes which the invoice claimed to be woad-dyed French linen sheets. Neither Laura nor Andy had ever figured out how to close these curtains. Laura claimed that they were not intended to be closed at all. They stayed as they were, their blue stylishness flopping just-so, the perfect camouflage for neighbourly nosiness.

It was twilight when the bell rang. Charles was boyish now, charm circuits connected. Beside him stood a living Botticelli, a portrait of a young man, taller, willowy, face framed by glossy black curls. He hung back and flipped the hem of his T-shirt, watching the conversation sidelong.

'You wouldn't have a screwdriver?' Charles suggested. 'We need to fix our sofa together. This is Pascal, by the way.'

Pascal had the biggest eyes Andy had ever seen on a man. A hand had floated forward and was appealing to be shaken. His grip was fierce and dry. Well, why should it be anything else? 'We had to put it into two pieces to go upstairs,' Pascal explained. An exotic accent, American-plus.

'Charles and Pascal,' Andy informed Laura when she got home, exactly as he was about to leave for the gig.

'A couple?'

'Both male.'

She giggled briefly. 'Well, here comes the neighbour-hood.'

That Friday, George had set out on the road with good intentions and a load of fat envelopes in the top box of his Motoguzzi. He wheeled down Cheyne Walk, wanting to feel as free as the seagulls swooping over the Thames. Instead he felt a touch lonely. That was the trouble with dispatch work. One of the troubles with dispatch work.

He peeled off the river at Lots Road and took documents to an auctioneers' showroom. He sped over The Bush and took video tapes to the BBC. Out West, more papers went to some glass palace of a pharmaceutical firm off the Great West Road. At Acorn Junction some bitch in a 4×4 jumped the lights and nearly totalled him.

He stormed back eastwards to leave a packet at a private house in Putney, then over the river again for a drop in Chelsea and back to the West End to another corporate HQ with a marble atrium.

By then, George was more than lonely. He felt mummified by the lack of human contact, as if no one had touched him for millions of years, as if his skin was all leathery and cracked over his cheekbones and his guts had been taken out and put in a jar somewhere. His leather suit was heavy on his shoulders and cold on his thighs. He was down to his last 50 pence and could have done with lunch.

'I could murder a cup of tea,' he told himself.

In Bar Italia they were watching football, for a change. George did not follow football but he had nothing against it. He didn't follow anything; his mind wasn't up to following. His chains of thought were short, although there were a lot of them and many were amusing.

'Did you hear that Arsene Wenger?' he asked the room in general. 'What'd he say? "My man was the ball in the net putting and the question asking afterward?" I ask you. Deep stress for the earlobes, hearing the English language get all murdery like that.'

'That's English football,' said a listless voice.

'Amazing they can understand each other,' George agreed.

'Who says they understand each other?' asked someone else. 'The way Arsenal's been playing.' George poured sugar into his tea and so an hour slipped away. He left his radio on his bike. It was perfectly safe, out there on the street with all the other bikes lined up outside the bar.

After an hour, somebody he knew came in. A man he knew well, in fact. A man who was looking for him, because in this man's back room George kept three Gro-bags with four marijuana plants growing in each. George had a number of men around town looking after his gardens like that. Every month or so he'd go round and give them new light bulbs, and every two months it was time to harvest. A nice little business. When TV shows asked you to call in, George voted against legalisation.

There was a bit of a problem, because the man had split up with some woman and his rent was due. George agreed to take the crop early. By then it was nearly five in the afternoon and time to get motoring if the packets left in the top box were to be delivered by the end of the day.

The new girl came in just as he was leaving. 'Do you believe in love at first sight, or shall I walk by again?' he asked her conversationally.

'Take it easy,' she said in a bright Aussie accent. 'I wouldn't want to put you to any trouble on my account.'

'Some of those lazy bastards in offices stop work at five,' he said, meaning that he didn't want to leave but he had a job to do. Then a van trying to squeeze through the narrow Soho street clipped his bike and knocked it over, leading to a bit of a row on the pavement, which, if it hadn't been for the boys from the bar behind him, could have turned nasty.

At the end of the day he went to the office to collect his wages and the boss said to him, 'George, come here a minute. I want to talk to you.'

This was an approach with which George was familiar. The rest of the story was also stuff he had heard before.

'You're a good laugh, George. It's not that we don't get on with you. And you've had warnings. I've tried to be fair. But I don't know what I've got for you.'

'That's it, is it?' The way they did it annoyed him. They were always so short about it, like they wanted to get it over with and be buggered to it.

'I'm sorry. As I say, I like you, we all do. But I can't rely on you, can I? And that's what this business is about, isn't it? Just being reliable.'

'Right then. Fair enough.'

'I'm paying you an extra week's money, just to tide you over. Mind how you go, eh?'

They always said that too. As if it made any difference.

George had often toyed with the idea of putting all his eggs in one basket and taking up gardening full-time. Other geezers made a living at it; more than a living. It was just a question of getting organised.

That Friday morning Rhys drove his wife out of London to their son's new school, and as she heaved her seat belt around her belly she said, 'Why in hell I married a stupid Welsh anaesthetist I'll never know,' as if it had been his nationality and profession that had made her fat.

He watched the road. Sometimes he considered himself Welsh, sometimes not. His father now lived in Wales but was English. His mother, now dead, had been Welsh. His childhood had been spent in West Africa, in the bungalow compounds housing European technical experts and their families. He was not stupid, and it would have been stupid to waste breath arguing with his wife when she was on her broomstick.

Intelligence, his golden blessing; Rhys had built his life on it, and the life of his family. Ten years of his youth dedicated to breezing through exams, and then – that was it. He really thought he'd made it. Out the other side, into a world of making a difference, of saving lives. He had intended to take his intelligence somewhere where he was needed.

He really had intended to go back to Africa. Every day he thought of it, and felt a smothering cloud of guilt because he had never returned. His father's last posting had been Sierra Leone. Once, he went out with him to inspect forestry projects, and out of the car window he saw boys his age standing at the roadside selling wild birds they had snared in the bush, waving their flapping, living wares in the dusty slipstream.

He had met Barbara as soon as he graduated. The woman now rolling in the passenger seat beside him like an angry cow walrus had once been a sprite with white-blonde hair flopping into her eyes and an adoring father ready to apply his cheque book to the wound she tore in his son-in-law's conscience.

They decided on four children. A daughter came first and she too was blessed with intelligence and it transported her to a far-off medical school, well out of the family fix.

After the daughter – nothing. Or rather, no one, because Rhys was seeing their children as real beings well before they were born. He revelled in parenthood; Barbara did not. You could say she had panicked. She took to suffering with enthusiasm. She had, so she accused him, endometriosis, pelvic inflammatory disease and chronic back pain.

Her waist disappeared, her belly ballooned. Long deserts of celibacy were punctuated by fervent reconciliations in which she would want sex whenever she saw him. One by one, the specialists who treated her elected to break their oaths and tell him no physical cause could be found for her misery. And then, in their thirties, they got Toby. The whining turned to aggression.

In ten more years, Rhys found he was using half his intelligence just to stay sane. He empathised: she was suffering. He rationalised: she had a bad relationship with her own mother. He displaced: his patients needed him, 24/7. If he let up for a day with these procedures, his thoughts fell apart like spillikins and he found himself up to his chin in a swamp of depression.

Perhaps stupidity was the best hope for Toby. A little wave of tenderness washed over Rhys at the thought of his son. Their destination tonight was the parents' evening at Toby's school, a new school, a last resort, a struggling college an hour's drive from Westwick which claimed a good reputation for the arts.

Last June, Toby had had an accident with some matches in the library at St Nicholas's. St Nicholas's did not expel pupils. Its staff knew all the tricks of staying high in educational league tables. The head had merely recommended that Toby should not return the next year.

'Toby seems to be settling down,' Rhys suggested. Barbara heaved her handbag on to her lap, rummaged for a comb and pulled down the vanity mirror to fluff up her hair.

'You mean he hasn't set fire to anything yet.'

'No, I mean he seems more contented.'

'Or stolen any cars, or run away, or taken to having a pint of lager for breakfast and spewing it up in assembly. We haven't been asked to take him away yet, is that what you mean?'

'He's never deliberately set fire to anything at school, has he?' Rhys dug in his defensive position. 'When I talk to him he sounds happy.'

'You shouldn't talk to him all the time. Leave him alone. You're always obsessing about him.'

'The point of this evening is to talk about him.'

'You're such a fool. The point of this evening is for the teachers to put on a show so we'll shut up, fuck off and keep paying the fees. They don't care about the kids any more than we do.'

It would have been stupid to affirm his feelings for his son, so Rhys did the clever thing and kept driving in silence.

'Toby is taking time to find his niche in the class.' 'Toby? He's a quiet boy, isn't he?' 'I'm still trying to find out exactly what Toby is interested in.' One after another the teachers twitched their lips, buried themselves in their files, struggled to find Toby's grades, avoided his parents' eyes. Impending disaster, they were signalling. The most optimistic, bullied into a box by Barbara, confessed that it might be possible to get Toby to university with a careful choice of course.

'They all go to university now. Don't tell me my son's going to have a problem,' said Barbara. On the way back, she said, 'Though why we should bother, I don't know. These degrees they get don't mean anything. He can get a job. He'll do much better in the real world.'

Rhys watched the road. He was on call. He wished that his bleeper would go off and give him an excuse to step out of his life for a few hours.

That Friday, Sam Chudleigh took a call from a client who was having some difficulty in settling her bill. Her name was Mrs Larsen and she had a most attractive accent, which he assumed to be Swedish since she was, so she said, the daughter of a Swedish millionaire steel magnate.

'I'm so embarrassed,' lisped Mrs Larsen. 'I – just – don't – know – what . . .' A pause, an intake of breath – 'What to do. I just hate owing money. I never intended this to happen. My life is – so difficult. I just can't – I don't . . .'

Another breath. Mrs Larsen did a lot of breathing. To listen to her better, Sam swivelled around in his CEO-style chair, making himself more or less invisible to Pats, his assistant, who was, in his judgement, too much given to peering around his office door. The prestigious flagship premises of Chudleigh Estate Services were not quite spacious enough for total executive privacy.

Sam put his feet on the windowsill and let his eyes occupy themselves with the yellowing autumn leaves of Westwick's forest canopy. Soaring plane trees lined the High Street. Their leaves would start dropping any day now, costing the council a bomb in street-sweepers' wages.

As he listened to Mrs Larsen, Sam visualised the consequences of breathing in a woman with a small rib cage and round breasts. He could not forget that she wore a gold star on a gold chain around her neck, and he imagined it lying on the brown, petal-like skin over her sternum, twinkling over the valley between her breasts, winking at him with every breath.

He felt that his heart was touched. Sam was a man who got mixed messages from his bodily organs. It was not, of course, his heart that was responding to Mrs Larsen.

She owed his business £8,557, the fees for the legal work on her proposed purchase of a riverside penthouse, from which she had withdrawn, giving no reasons, two years ago. The money had been owing since then.

Normal practice at Chudleigh Estate Services was to

arraign a bad payer at Helford County Court after six months, using the delightfully cost-effective small claims procedure. From the moment he saw her, however, perching cross-legged on one of his Corbusier-style chairs in reception, Sam hoped to be able to make exceptions for Mrs Larsen.

'Sam, I'm holding Ted Parsons for you,' Pats called to him over the speakerphone. Pats was the new assistant. He had acquired her along with a rival conveyancing partnership in Westwick, the One-Stop Home Shop, formerly of Station Road, whose proprietor had driven to the airport one morning and never been seen again. Thus one man's mid-life crisis became another's business opportunity.

Sam had hoped to be able to make exceptions for Pats, as he had succeeded in doing for most of his assistants except the occasional feminist who slipped through the net. Pats had been playing a waiting game. She had insisted that all her attention was needed to install the One-Stop files in the only possible place, the room beyond his own office which he designated The Boardroom.

The files now hung there on steel racks, protected by security shutters. He felt that they diminished the status of The Boardroom, even though they represented tens of millions of pounds' worth of business and the commission was going to propel him into the financial stratosphere.

Having invaded The Boardroom in this unnecessary manner, Pats had thrown herself into the operation of transferring their data to the office system. Nothing if not dedicated to the business, Pats.

And what business she created. Pats now sat in the outer office, always on the telephone, writing new mortgages at a magnificent rate. Perhaps she thought she was entitled to bonuses. Cross that bridge when they got to it. Twenty, thirty, even forty new mortgages a week she handled. She was sleek, pert, bright-eyed, contented, self-contained and busy; she had the air of a spinster's cosseted cat. Sam had felt drawn to her, definitely, and had been impatient for her schedule to allow lunch. Now that Mrs Larsen was on the line, however, Pats looked like cold potatoes and he had forgotten that he ever had ambitions towards her.

'I'll get back to him,' Sam snapped. 'No more calls, Pats.'

In a way, Pats had done him a favour. If he'd got tangled up with her, he wouldn't have been free now for Mrs Larsen. Ta muchly, Pats, for holding me off with your frosty little mannerisms, your selective deafness and your political announcements about your boyfriend. The boyfriend who had actually appeared in the reception area one afternoon, dressed for tennis and flaunting intimidating lengths of muscular, brown hairy legs. Until ten minutes ago, this strategy had annoyed Sam severely. Now he saw the hand of destiny lobbing a greater prize in his direction.

'Would it help to talk about it?' he asked Mrs Larsen, tenderly cradling his telephone to his cheek while he reached for his diary. 'Would you like to meet for lunch, perhaps?'

She breathed oh-so-deeply. 'You're – so – kind.'

His arteries teeming with hormones, Sam did not ask himself why the so-called daughter of a Swedish millionaire steel magnate might be short of money.

There is a tide in the affairs of men which, taken at the flood, can lead straight to a fucking disaster.

The tide came in for Mickey in the middle of the Buxton Building Society shoot, when he had a herd of a thousand non-speaking extras, in Day-Glo green boiler suits, penned in a film studio in Buckinghamshire. The agency was Kaplan Krieger Donohue Wallace, known as KKDW. Until that moment, the tide of fortune had been flooding in his direction for twenty years, which was why Mickey Ryder, in the world of advertising, was The Man.

'They just ain't got it,' he told the casting director, a kind woman who worried about the grey hairs she was getting in commercials. 'They're not giving me any emotion. It's like a pile of dead fish out there. They don't look like real people.'

It was already 5 p.m. on the first day in the studio.

The role of the herd was to wave their arms and smile while being filmed. Their images would be blended into a shot of blades of grass, then shown with a voice-over raving about customer care at the Buxton Building Society. It would not disclose that they outsourced their customer services to a call centre in Indonesia.

Shooting the grass had been tough. Not until you needed vibrant, dynamic, thrusting grass to symbolise the energy of a modern financial institution did you realise how hard it was to find the right kind of grass for the job. Five different seed blends had been specially grown at a turf farm in Suffolk. But if grass had been a problem, the people were a fucking nightmare.

'We can do the people with computers,' the account director had said.

'Yeah, we *can*,' Mickey had responded.

'Fucking Wembley Stadium, double-click, there you go.'

'I dunno.' Mickey had some indefinable feeling about a computer-generated crowd. His face started to get wrinkly.

'We want 'em to look peopley, don't we?' The account director had worked with Mickey for a long time. He could deduce a world of meaning from just three syllables. The Man was not going to be happy with computer-generated people. 'We'll get it costed, yeah?'

Calls were made, calculations were done, a decision was taken, Mickey's face smoothed out. Now the casting director had put a thousand people in the studio, but to Mickey's eyes the general effect was still not what he'd have called peopley.

'That one.' Mickey pointed at a tall, thin man with black hair and thick eyebrows. 'And the woman behind him.' A full-bosomed woman with a lined face and bright eyes. 'They're what I want. Get me some more like that.'

'They're Russian,' the casting director told him. 'Actors from Moscow. We took a chance on them.'

'Well then, I need Russians. Get me some Russians for tomorrow.'

The effort of composing two sentences left him with a sense of trauma. Mickey had his driver take him to The Groucho Club and passed a few hours in the depths of a sag-bottomed wing chair, having a crack with some mates. When the Club closed, he had his driver take him back to the studio and got a couple of hours' shut-eye in a dressing room.

He woke up thinking about the piano. In a career of great peaks, the piano was his personal K2. The piano had taken place at the end of a tyre shoot in Turkey, when they'd got a Steinway on to this awesome aqueduct over a gorge up in the mountains.

To Mickey, if there is a piano on a bridge, it's begging to

be pushed off. It wasn't in the script, it wasn't on the story-board, but nothing Mickey did ever was. His way was to plan like fuck, then throw the plan away.

So he had them push the piano off the bridge and shoot it as it fell. Ready when you are, Mr De Mille. Until you've actually seen a piano falling through the air, you don't know what it does, how it spirals around but still goes down with decorum, feet first, lid down. The shiny black top reflected the sky. Finally the keys cascaded off the keyboard. It landed in a bank of violet flowers. His homage to Antonioni.

He never used the sequence. It was a legend in the business. He'd been asked to enter it for some video festival. Fuck that. Art is art, ads are ads. He was clear about that. Some other guy, some director, thought he was an artist and stood outside the Tate Modern with a digi-cam, showing people one of his commercials and asking them if they thought it was art. Fuck that. When he created a work of art – and that was a definite when, art was on his life's agenda somewhere – he wouldn't need anyone to tell him.

The casting director, the line producer and all their associates, their assistants and their gofers went out into London to find Russians. They took cash in sports bags and they visited the Russian church in Westwick, the Ukrainian Club in Holland Park, the Polish Club in Hammersmith, the Daquise café in Kensington, the Belarus Social Centre in Helford, the Anglo-Serbian Society in Acton, the Baltic Trading Co. in Brondesbury, the Friends of Estonia in Fulham and the Croatian delicatessen in Queen's Park.

By 5 a.m., when the coaches left the pick-up point outside Harrods, 981 people who could pass for Russian were on board, including a complete wedding party. Among the first to arrive were thirteen men from Macedonia who had been greeted by a relative at the Ashford freight terminal when he opened the container in which they had hidden to cross the Channel.

The new people looked real and Mickey was delighted with them. They waved their arms, they smiled, they filled his lens with human warmth. The Macedonians, who were euphoric at the chance to earn their first sterling wages, he put up front. It took the rest of the week to get The Shot and by the second day, when word had thoroughly got around the Eastern European community in London, the crowd control problems outside Harrods began.

On Thursday an elderly Latvian man had a heart attack, but the studio nurse got him to hospital in time. That same day the line producer made the studio barmen lock up their stock. On Friday, when there were quite a few fights on the buses, a young Serbian woman was stabbed, but not fatally.

On Saturday morning, after the film crew had left, the cleaners found the body of a boy of about fourteen in a dark corner of the studio. He was the youngest of the Macedonians, and it seemed he had died on the first day, but had not been noticed. The cause of his death was TB. The police, pleased to be able to share the glamour shed by all things filmic, even a TV commercial, fed this news to the local paper. That was how the client, the CEO of the Buxton Building Society, who by chance lived in a mock-Tudor mansion a few miles from the studio, got to hear about it.

There were stories about Mickey Ryder. He was that big a name in commercials, he had his own mythology. The piano story was most often told.

After these incidents, another legend was born. Mickey

had been The Man a long time. Most people could reckon seven years at the top, then they were finished. Mickey was on borrowed time. 'He was bussing in Russians,' the story went, 'and the client found out.'

The moral of this story was that Mickey Ryder had gone too far.

CHAPTER 2

Further On Down The Road

On that same Friday, about the time that Sam was letting his mind rest lightly on the question of Mrs Larsen, and Mickey was getting that nice fat sense of justified euphoria that came from having got The Shot, their partners were travelling into central London for a meeting. Mo Ryder was driving, as she always did in every sense. Alice Waters Chudleigh looked wonderingly up at the high buildings as they passed.

Their meeting was with Ted Parsons, a man notorious in Westwick for having walked away from the Oak Hill Business Park scandal with clean hands and a new wife. The walking away was what worried Westwick the most. One might get mixed up in the occasional distasteful fraud, these things happened, especially in a property hotspot; one might practise serial monogamy, that was the way of the world. But one did not *leave* the most desirable suburb in the country, thereby casting doubt on its property prices.

Ted Parsons was metropolitan now, an inner-city developer, lucky with low interest rates and high prices and with a fine eye for a brownfield site in the right location. And a marble atrium which impressed Alice Waters Chudleigh greatly.

'Oh my God, it's enormous,' she whispered as they began to cross the slippery sea of shine.

'For heaven's sake,' murmured her business partner, her high-heeled mules clicking confidently on the marble. 'It's only an atrium.'

She signed them in. Mo and Alice, La Maison. Home of toile de Jouy, old bird cages, worn French tea towels, bent weathervanes, chipped enamel coffee pots and rusted Provençal milk churns. Address: Grove Parade, Westwick, between Parsley & Thyme, the deli, and Pot Pourri, the florist.

For a Westwick wife, La Maison was a good business. It passed the time pleasantly. It gave their lives a purpose and it didn't rattle their men. It created the reassuring but completely false illusion that, in the event of a recession, they had a little enterprise that would keep the family afloat. It brought them the occasional ego-boost of a profile in a design magazine and it sent Mo on buying trips to France several times a year.

It didn't stop Sam from calling Alice a useless creature who brought nothing into the house except her endless demands and her idle children who were even lazier and more demanding than she was, but it did give Mo the evidence to prove to Alice that Sam was wrong.

Financially, therefore, La Maison needed only to wash its own face. Their meeting with Ted Parsons had been called on a misunderstanding. His property company sent many clients to Sam's flagship office in Westwick and Ted had assumed that Sam would be happy if his wife's business landed a large order. Having a good heart, Ted often misread the motives of others.

'Take the lift to the twelfth floor,' the receptionist instructed. 'Mr Parsons will meet you.'

'Well . . . hello . . . er . . .' Mo saw that Ted still had to stop himself from calling them 'girls'. He was looking almost handsome. Maybe that was what leaving Westwick did for a man.

'Well,' he began again, once they were in the safety of his office, 'the good news is, we're going for it.'

'Excellent,' said Mo. She heard a squeak from Alice.

'Exactly as your quotation,' he confirmed. 'The six show-homes, fully decorated with curtains, carpets, fittings, furniture, decorative antiques and accessories, as per – er – your quotation.'

Mo heard Alice gulp and swallow. She could picture her round eyes popping. There were times when you could have sworn Alice was a Loony Tunes character, digitally inserted into real life.

'What's our deadline?' Mo asked.

'The contractors . . .' A shadow of pain crossed his face. 'In the real world, I think they'll be finished in about six months.'

'But we can work from the plans.'

'Of course.'

'Right. Right. Well, ah – we should agree a payment schedule.'

'Mo.' Alice's feathery hand tweaked her sleeve.

'What?'

'Can we have a word?'

Ted said, 'I'll get us some coffee,' and scuttled out of his own office.

'We can't possibly do this,' Alice squeaked. 'He can't accept that quote.'

'Darling, he has accepted it.'

'But it was outrageous. We made it outrageous on purpose, don't you remember? We don't want this job.'

'We thought we didn't want it because we thought we'd never get it. Now we've got it, it's different.'

'No, it isn't. We can't do it. Don't you remember? We worked out we'd be running flat-out for six months. We didn't want that.' Alice was a woman whose glass was always half empty. Mo, on the other hand, was a woman whose glass was usually half full. With Jack Daniel's, cleverly disguised as Diet Coke. She said, patiently, 'But Alice, it's silly money.'

Now Alice had to get out of her chair and walk to and fro in front of Ted's desk. 'But that's it. It's silly money because it's a silly job. We're a little shop. We do people's homes. We don't do commercial design projects, Mo.'

'We do now.'

'But it'll kill us.' Now Alice was darting about the room like a distressed goldfish.

'Look, it will be OK,' Mo assured her. 'It's just a bigger job. I'll take responsibility.'

Alice stopped darting. 'Well, if you're happy to do that, to take the responsibility . . .'

'Yes, if you're OK with it.'

'Oh, well. Yes, I'm OK.'

'Right.' Mo unfolded her legs and stalked to the door to call back their biggest-ever client.

'Have you ever thought that life is like a pool table?' Mo asked Alice in the car on their way back. 'People are like the balls, they just kind of roll about in that random sort of way, and you can be trying like all hell to get one down but it'll be another one, way over on the other side of the table, that'll just get shoved into the perfect place. This'll be good for us, you'll see.'

A pool table! How like Mo to use some raunchy rock-chick image like that. Alice always felt more secure when she had someone to admire. 'I suppose I'd look on it the other way,' she said, by way of apology. Alice had a way of placing words neatly, as if she was putting down coasters. 'I'd look on it that you could try so hard to get one ball in a pocket that you wouldn't even realise that you'd be setting up all these problems for yourself with the others.'

'What problems could we possibly have? We can do this standing on our heads, you know we can.'

That same Friday, in the early evening, a woman and a man sat in a bar on Baker Street that was mostly used by tourists. The walls were decorated with a dusty tweed deerstalker, a cobwebbed violin and, in frames, some fake Victorian news-paper pages telling of the exploits of Mr Sherlock Holmes. The name etched in the frosted glass door was Elementary, and in her own real life the woman would not have been caught dead in a gutter within a thousand metres of such a place. That Friday, however, its merit was precisely that it was a long way from where she really lived.

They chose a table at the back, away from the windows. He said, 'Have you used them before, these Around Midnight people?'

The woman smiled at his question. 'Why, are you worried about them?'

'The ad says "discretion assured", doesn't it?'

'It also says "stimulating meetings with attractive people just like you".'

They thought about this one. In the man's eyes she was nothing like him. She was the upmarket type; blonde, expensive, a decisive manner. Also perfectly relaxed about the situation. He had fantasised about picking out someone rather like her and, so far, he had indeed found their meeting stimulating.

In the woman's eyes he was attractive in a rather young way; curly haired, gangly, genuine, quite sweet really. Not a person just like her, but attractive. She always liked them to some degree because, she was beginning to understand, it wasn't really the men she found exciting, or the sex or even this sleazy procedure. The real thrill was getting back at her husband.

'I saw it on the back of a bus,' he told her, still talking about the ad.

'I saw it in a newspaper,' she told him, 'a couple of years ago. I've met five people so far. Not all of them I liked, but a couple I did. We had some good times.'

'And nobody finds out?'

'Not so far.' She had learned that it was important never to let them talk about their wives. A bit of story, a couple of sentences to explain why they were there, that was OK, but nothing too personal. 'So what do you reckon, then? Are we going to meet again?'

'You're very . . .' He paused, trying to find a good word. 'Very calm about this.'

'It's the best way. I would like us to meet again.'

'Well, yes. So would I.'

'Good. Shall we do a hotel? There must be a nice one around here somewhere. I can book something, if that's easier. You tell me what you'd like.'

He had no diary with him. She told him to e-mail her at work. 'That's quite safe, nobody reads them except me.'

'Mine's safe too,' he told her, smiling at last. And then he had to spoil it. 'So,' he asked, drawing the word out as if that would soften the impact, 'where's your husband this evening?'

'In a pub, I suppose.'

'Having a few beers with the lads?'

'Worse than that. He's singing. With a band. One of those student bands that nobody grew out of.'

There was the green flash lighting up the young eyes and the rangy shoulders settled with respect. Another one who probably still played air guitar. She wondered why she always seemed to get them.

CHAPTER 3

If Loving You Is Wrong, I Don't Want To Be Right

Montreuil-sur-Mer is a little town in Normandy on which the sea ran out many centuries ago. It still has a sea wall, a grassy embankment that curls protectively around the backs of the houses on the coastal side of the main square, but it stands high and dry, overlooking grassland.

Where watchmen once patrolled, looking for English pirates, the elderly citizens of Montreuil go to walk their pugs and poodles. Marauders still come over the Channel, but their booty is in the cheap wine warehouses at Calais.

Beyond the sea wall, the muddy flatness of northern France stretches away almost to the horizon, dotted with scrubby trees, survivors of ancient hedges. Only on a bright day, when the air is clear and there is sunlight to catch the faraway waves, would you know you were anywhere near the English Channel.

Rhys imagined Montreuil as a town painted in a medi-aeval book of hours, houses rolled up in the walls, roofs peeking out at the top, a bouquet of architectural flowers.

The walls were gold, the roofs red, the sky cerulean and the people, just one couple, eyeballing each other with the lust-crazed glare that monks always painted on lovers in the age of chivalry.

Imagining things was a dangerous sport. Some people went paragliding, some took skiing holidays, Rhys had holidays with his imagination. Most of the time, if he allowed himself to dream, he could be putting a patient at risk. A good doctor, a responsible father, a life compromised even into the second level of his mind. Sometimes in England he felt as if he couldn't breathe. In France he was a different man, a free man. As for what kind of husband he was – well, he'd tried. You had to know when to give up.

Twice a year Rhys argued plausibly to Barbara, who never listened anyway, that a booze cruise was still good house-keeping. It really was worthwhile to buy French wine at French prices. Then he held his breath, booked a ferry ticket and when the day came drove off to the coast and took the catamaran from Folkestone in England to Boulogne in France. A joyful half hour away from Boulogne he turned off the route nationale and on to the twisting little road to Montreuil and paradise.

Mo had no need to make excuses. Keeping La Maison stocked with rusty garden chairs and chipped enamelware meant buying trips six or seven times a year, as well as a base, a place to store her acquisitions. He would find her sitting at a table outside the Café du Port, the front left-hand table which got the most sun. 'Darling,' she would greet him, turning up her face for a kiss and taking off her shades.

He would have been content with just that, a dry kiss and an extravagant word. It had become a pilgrimage, a crusade to capture peace. The quest would call him through territories that were lovelier, more dangerous and more distant, one after the other in pre-ordained sequence. He would enter France, he would enter Montreuil, he would enter her apartment and finally he would enter Mo, holding her close to him in their squeaking carved bed. Afterwards they would tangle their legs and arms and lie together for a long time, tracing patterns on bare skin with fingertips. The smell in the apartment was sweet and dusty, the smell of sunshine in empty space, the smell of possibility. Each would open up the trunk of thoughts that had been stored away since the last time, and one by one pull them out and look at them.

This is heaven, was Rhys's first thought. I wish I could live like this. If I left Barbara now, she would get the children. She's a mess, Barbara; she could have a breakdown. Either way, the children would suffer. It will have to be when they're older. I don't care what it costs. Why did it turn out this way? She was normal when I married her, what happened? Would she leave me if she found out? It's a thought. I'd still be cheating the kids. Mo could never cope with Toby – could she? What's in this for Mo? Why is she here anyway? I don't deserve this. This is heaven.

On top of Mo's trunk was: this is nice. Do I like this better than the sex? That would be so suburban, wouldn't it? This is like being twenty again, being free, nowhere I ought to be, nobody I have to think about. I hope he isn't going to get clingy. Poor man. Stuck with that harpy. What would Mickey do, if he ever found out? There's no harm this way, nobody gets hurt. We go home and our marriages are stronger. I've paid too much for those sconces, I should have just left. Never buy when you're getting tired, that's when you make mistakes. Oh. Mmm. This is good.

The soft, cold light of a Normandy afternoon filled the room. Little noises of contentment echoed between the creamy walls.

'I'm going to have to come over again next month,' she told him, tracing the lines on the palm of his hand, her head pillowed in his arm. 'We've landed this mega commission.'

'Well done. What is it?'

'Alice doesn't think it's well done, she's in a right two-and-eight. It's for Ted Parsons, Maple Grove Estates.'

'That crook.'

'He's not a crook, he's a property developer. God, Rhys, sometimes you are just so public sector.' He felt the laugh flutter inside her ribs. 'He's commissioned us to do six show-houses. It'll clean out our stock. More than clean us out. I was thinking of doing the vide-grenier at Saucisson-le-Mauconfit. It's about the last one of the season. I could check out some other places in the Caux on the way. There are a lot of little dealers down there, I haven't been for a while.'

He wasn't sure if she was inviting him or not. 'Where is that exactly?'

'South of here. South of Dieppe. It's pretty. The Alabaster Coast they call it, because of the white cliffs. Bloody cold.'

'I've never been there,' he said, hoping for an invitation.

Instead, Mo murmured into his forearm, 'I'm going to make a lot of money this year. Almost as much as Mickey. If this deal works out like it should.'

'That's great,' he said, 'isn't it?'

'We didn't want the job so we overquoted something unmerciful.' He had not understood, but she let it go. Part of the luxury of the affair was that nothing was political. A little misunderstanding could be left to flicker out by itself instead of smouldering for years in the hotbed of a marriage.

'Why didn't you just turn it down?'

'Because we're women, you fucking idiot. We didn't want to be rude. That's another mistake I keep making.'

'Don't tell me you've got a problem with being rude,' he dared, stroking the peak of her hip.

Later, as they were getting dressed for their ritual meal in the restaurant down the alley on the far side of the square, as he pulled his shirt over his chest to button it, she felt a good belt of desire. He was a fine-looking man, Rhys. Still fine-looking. Wasted. She translated that into vague thoughts of the plunder to be had in the Caux, of old oak farmhouse tables and slipware bowls. It was Mo's way to attach her more troublesome feelings to objects; her shop alone represented decades of emotional struggle.

'It'd be good to have a strong man along,' she told him, speaking the bare truth as usual. 'Vide-grenier, you never know what you'll get. I've seen wardrobes, even; bloody great armoires. Do you think you can get away?'

'I'll see what I can do,' he promised.

Later, she said another thing that he didn't really understand. 'Mickey doesn't have to find out.'

'About us?' All at once, they were stuck in a moment they couldn't get out of. Then it passed.

'No, dummy, about what Ted's going to pay us. He doesn't have to know unless I tell him.'

What would happen to them, where they were going — she never went there, even in her inner conversations. An affair, she felt, should have the romance of despair. Then it was safe. She had hoped Rhys never went there either. Another mistake.

In London, the smallest living unit in the rattiest area rented for ten times what George earned in a year, the weed included. The best his luck had been was when he found this room. A big old space in a Victorian mansion block in Battersea, rented by a housing association. Plenty of room for his stuff. He'd built a sleeping platform for his mattress. Quentin Crisp was right about dust; after four years it didn't get any worse. The only thing missing was a window, but who wanted to see the rotten world anyway?

George elaborated the design of his life around rickety towers of reasons. The room had a commodious skylight – but the plants did better with the daylight-spectrum grow-bulbs. Why, he'd had good crops in rooms with no windows at all. But the association were sneaky and sent people round to check you out at all sorts of times. Well, he'd spent too long dossing with strangers to risk making himself homeless again. So he talked other people into growing his gardens of weed.

All he had was a map on the wall, with markers showing the places where his gardens grew. Sometimes he amused himself by pretending to be an actor in a World War II film, Jack Hawkins or Trevor Howard, marching up and down and pointing with a swagger stick. 'Our men are deployed he-ah and he-ah in Ongar, and over he-ah in Hackney Marshes. We've also got J Division up he-ah in Stoke Newington. Enemy patrols are active in all areahs but so far they haven't been on to us. Reinforcements, the Twenty-first Sheepshaggers, will be sent in he-ah in Kentish Town, and will make their way up the Great North Road at night to meet up with F Division he-ah at Brent Crawss. Any questions, anybody? Right, men. Good luck and may God bless you.'

Over a couple of beers in Bar Italia, he confided to the potential commander of the reinforcements: 'My dream is to be like them toffs in that film, whatsit, *Two Smokin' Barrels*. Have a fucking great warehouse full of plants, have so much money you need a machine to count it.'

'Go on,' she agreed, gulping half her pint in one. 'What kind of space are you looking for?'

'Big.' George was no good at measurements. He had had a good stab at working out how many plants he needed to grow to make a living, covered the back of an envelope with laboriously written arithmetic, then broken the lead in the pencil and given up. All he had retained were the visions of a forest of weed and bags stuffed with banknotes.

'I might know somewhere,' she told him. She was still working for the bastard company who'd just fired him. He'd shown her around a bit, when they'd taken her on almost straight from the airport. Bar Italia, the place in Covent Garden, the Brick Lane Caff, the night garages, all the spots the wise dispatch rider needed to know. She was an Aussie. He thought he liked Aussie women; he believed they had loads of guts and no attitude crap. The tattoo worried him slightly, sexy as it was.

'Well done, Sheepshagger.'

'I can see this empty building from where I live. I'll check it out.'

'Recce and Sitrep, Sheepshagger. Carry on.'

'It looks like it shouldn't be too hard to get in over the roofs at the back.'

A few days later, on a good rainy afternoon when nobody would even bother looking out of their windows, especially not in a hell-hole like Kentish Town Road, she led him out of the back window of her room, along a couple of walls and over some easy flat roofs, via an efficiently broken window into a derelict office suite.

'Perfeck,' he told her, looking around the light, dry, empty rooms. Curling notices on a board in the corridor still proclaimed this to be a community arts centre. 'It's a council place. It'll probably be empty for years.'

'Looks like it's been empty for years already,' she said, pulling down a notice advising clients that the women's storytelling club had moved to Tuesday nights. 'This is dated nineteen ninety-seven.'

'It must be one of them buildings they don't even know they've got any more.'

They paced out the floor area in yards, George because he despised the metric system as Eurobollocks and Sheep-shagger because she knew only imperial measurements anyway.

'Twenty-two times seventeen,' he proposed.

She had a calculator on her keyring. 'Three hundred and seventy-four. We'd better have a space to walk down the middle. Take away twenty-two, leaves three hundred and fifty-two. One bag per square yard, is that enough?'

'Plenty.'

'That gives us three hundred and fifty-two bags. Have you got enough seed? Four plants a bag, three hundred and fifty-two bags, one thousand, four hundred and eight seeds.'

'And some extra because they won't all start. I got plenty of seeds. I pick 'em out every time we harvest. Takes ages.'

'Great, you've got the seed.'

'We have fertility.'

'Then we need the bags, at what? Two pounds sixty-five each? Makes nine hundred and thirty-two pounds, eighty. Blimey, that's a lot of money, George.'

'Correct, Sheepshagger. We'll have to rob a bank.'

She started and gave him a look of downright alarm. 'Only joking,' he said quickly. 'You didn't think I was that kind of guy, did you?'

'I don't know, do I? I'm new in town. Growing a bit of pot's no problem, but I ain't getting into anything major, you hear what I'm saying?'

'Roger, Wilco. Message received. Don't worry, Sheep-shagger, I'll think of something.'

'I'm not selling my bike.'

'I'm not selling my bike either. So we got that settled.'

On Sunday the first noise Andy heard was the brisk toot of a car horn at their gate, the soft, rapid footfalls of Daisy on the stairs and the discreet closing of the front door as she left to get her lift to the stables. This would be at about six in the morning.

Daisy was fifteen. Like her father, she had a strong body and a considerate character. Her sport demanded boots, a hard hat, all-weather clothing and armfuls of stuff that jingled and rattled and thumped on the floor, but she managed the stairs so quietly that her parents were rarely disturbed. If his sleep patterns hadn't been wrecked by his resurging hormones, he would never have heard Daisy leave the house at all.

A couple of hours later their elder daughter went to

church. Lily was slender and fair, like her mother, and carried only a Bible and a prayer book, but she made a lot more noise. Andy heard her feet stomp on the floor of her room, the water splash in the upstairs shower, then footsteps crashing down the stairs and the front door slamming hard enough to make the wall shudder.

This told her parents that Lily believed she was putting Sunday morning to its proper use, and thought her family ought to be doing the same. The church was a quarter of an hour's walk away, in an old youth club building in Helford; The Church of Christ in Glory, a member of the London League of Charismatic Churches. It was raining heavily; sheets of water rippled on the road surfaces.

Andy lay beside his sleeping wife and thought about showering, then bringing her coffee in bed, then making a move on her. The window of opportunity for that was small, between her regaining consciousness and starting to think about her work. Could be as little as thirty seconds. She worked on Sunday morning in the same spirit that Lily went to church: to shame the onlookers.

Since when had sex become a matter of foxing about with optimal timing and mood management? Since long before Daisy, if Andy told himself the truth. After they had got married it had all been fine for a couple of years. Then, Sunday was a day to get up at three in the afternoon. Fucking in bed was almost an admission of failure, when the bath, the table, the kitchen worktops, the sofa, the floor and the walls were available. And the car. And, after they first bought this house, the garage. That smell of old oil and dampness – it still made the hairs on the back of his neck prickle thinking about it.

Then something shifted. Andy never wanted her less but he began to pick up subliminal messages from Laura which made him hesitate. She used embarrassed looks, as if she didn't want other people to know they had sex. Her movements became crisp instead of urgent, suggesting that this was a task. When they finished she breathed a faint sigh, as if it was another thing done. Then the girls came, bringing a period of deep, chaotic parenthood, and so the planning began.

That morning, Andy was not successful. When he reached the bedroom with the coffee Laura was already climbing into her clothes. He figured out that she had heard him shower and had known what was coming. Years they had spent manoeuvring around each other like warships in fog, blindly evading each other's desires.

Laura had drifted back into public relations when her decorating phase expired, just a couple of weeks after his outplacement from KKDW. Two younger men she'd once worked with asked her to come in on a new company. It had prospered, wrapping her in another layer of defences against him. She had her phone and strangers to talk to on it, an office in the house that had once been the au-pair's room, a door to close and a far-off look in her eyes.

In the kitchen, he prepared lunch, a traditional meal – chicken, potatoes, beans, a tart bought yesterday from Parsley & Thyme. When he had been able to tie the teatowel around his waist, cooking had been a gift to Laura and he had enjoyed the work. Now he had to tuck the tea towel into the waistband of his trousers and cooking meals was an operational necessity. If he didn't visit the supermarket, the fridge would be empty. If he didn't cook, there would be no

Sunday lunch. He seemed to be at the front line of a war to keep the family running. The day when he bought his own apron was coming soon.

'Hello! Andy and Laura? Are you at home?' Outside, trainers leaped up the front steps.

When he opened the door, Andy found Pascal in a blue and black Lycra running suit, panting on the doormat. He was wet; water was standing in drops on his cheeks. His eyes were shining. He said, 'We're having a little party next Saturday for Charles's birthday and we hope very much you can come.'

'Great. Yeah. Sure.' Laura's diary, he'd have to ask.

'You're cooking. That's so sweet.'

'Sweet? Ah, I don't know. Would you like some coffee?' Am I a fucking housewife or what? Andy asked himself. As he led the way to the kitchen he pulled the tea towel out of the top of his trousers and wiped his hands with it.

In the kitchen, Pascal fingered the CDs and picked out some new jazz, saying, 'This is good. I don't know anyone else who's into this. Can we play it?'

'Why not?'

'I always have music on when I'm at home. I can't con-centrate without it.'

'I've never played that. It's a compilation, isn't it? Somebody gave it to me.'

'Oh, you should play it.' He read some artists' names from the label. 'This is quite a line-up.'

'I wouldn't know. Sad thing about getting to my age, you can't read the tiny print on CD covers any more.' Andy immediately wished he had not said that.

Pascal simply said, 'I can't read it anyway,' and pressed

Play. Then he moved to the pinboard and inspected the photographs there. 'These are your children. I've seen them coming in and out.'

'Two daughters. Daisy and Lily.'

'Which is which?'

'Daisy is the younger one but she's taller and darker.'

'Looks more like you.'

Andy ran his hands over his head. The close-cropped look, the tactful Number Two. Minimised the grey, camouflaged the thinning. 'I'm not so dark any more.'

'Yes, you are. I think so.'

It seemed like a very personal conversation. The beans needed topping and tailing, but Andy didn't want to do it while Pascal was watching him. A gender crisis was looming. He dealt out a brace of manly espressos and sat down at the table.

'I'd better stand,' Pascal told him. 'I'll make your chairs wet if I sit down.' On his shoulders and thighs, where the running suit had soaked up rain, there were shiny patches.

After they had been talking for an hour or so, Laura appeared in the doorway saying, 'I thought I heard music.'

'Blame me,' Pascal suggested, holding out his hand to shake hers.

'Pascal came over to ask us to a party next Saturday. It's Charles's birthday.'

'Well, how nice. We'd love to, wouldn't we, Andy? Were you out running?'

'I don't call it running. I just go to the park and scare the ducks on the lake.'

Pascal flicked his fingers through his hair and became teasing – flirtatious, even. Laura began to laugh more and more readily. Andy threw in a few remarks but nobody picked up on them. He felt the shadow of envy. Laura rejected coffee and instead pulled a bottle of wine out of the fridge, for which Andy had to supply the glasses because she was no longer sure where he kept them.

The front door slamming indicated that Lily was back. She thumped upstairs to her room without greeting them. A little later Daisy also returned, plastered with mud. She eased off her boots at the door and left her anorak with them. The unusual sound of adult chatter drew her to the kitchen.

'Well, hello – but what has happened to you?' Pascal's face expressed compassionate horror when her mud-splashed face peered around the door.

'He tried to roll on me. I won't shake hands.' She held up grimy palms.

'Who did? Oh, your horse did. I didn't know they did that, horses.' Pascal seemed impressed.

'This one does when there are puddles. He likes water. If we go near a stream he's terrible.'

'But you show him who's boss, eh?'

'Well, you have to.'

'Lunch in twenty minutes,' Andy told her.

'Will you stay?' Laura asked Pascal.

He wavered like a sapling in a breeze. 'Better not,' he said. 'Charles is at home today. Another time, maybe. But thanks anyway.'

After he had gone Andy began to assemble their lunch, pulling the roasted bird out of the oven and leaving it to settle while he made gravy. Daisy reappeared in clean clothes.

'Lily says she isn't eating with us,' she announced.

'Why?' demanded Laura.

'Um – maybe you should go and ask her.'

In the end it was Andy who climbed the stairs. The girls' rooms were under the roof, side by side, with dormer windows in sloping ceilings. He found Lily sitting at her desk, writing something that looked like poetry in a notebook which he'd seen before. Briefly. She kept it in a locked drawer.

'Daisy says you aren't coming to lunch,' he began, as softly as a person can when they have spent half the morning cooking.

'You can't expect me to eat with him,' she said, keeping her eyes on her composition.

'Who? Our new neighbour? Pascal?'

'Whatever his name is, he's an abomination.'

'He's gone home, you're quite safe.'

'It makes me sick to think of them.' She had put down her pen and was twisting a piece of her long pale hair and rocking a little on her chair. Andy remembered her doing the same thing when she was struggling with her sums at the age of seven or eight. Then he'd spent Sunday afternoons patiently showing her the magic of numbers, counting out bits of pasta on the kitchen table. Now he was sure there was an equally simple way to show her the magic of tolerance.

'Then don't think of them,' he suggested.

'You have to live with the consciousness of good and evil.'

'Yes, but you also have to eat. You didn't have any breakfast.'

'We eat too much.'

Andy held in a sigh, which he knew would also annoy her, and decided to wind up the conversation. 'Look, sweetheart,

I'd like you to come to lunch. So would Daisy and your mother. We'll be starting in a few minutes, you're welcome any time, your place is laid. Any time.'

'He pollutes the house just by being there.' Lily seemed not to have heard him. 'I'm writing a prayer. I might come when I've finished.'

The three of them ate without her. Conversation, which had bubbled effortlessly while Pascal was there, was a struggle. When Daisy started a story about her horse, Laura shoved away her half-eaten dessert and said, 'I keep wondering when you're going to give up riding, Daisy. Most girls have dumped horses and taken up boyfriends at your age. You're wasting good dating time.'

'When I find a boyfriend who's as much fun as riding I promise I'll be right there,' their daughter answered without a trace of ill will.

'You'll never find anyone if you spend all your spare time with bloody animals,' Laura persisted. 'You're just ruining your skin and avoiding getting any social skills.'

'It counts towards my Duke of Edinburgh award and when I get my exams I'll be paid to teach,' Daisy pointed out.

'She has social skills,' Andy defended his daughter who, like him, was the smiling sort who made friends easily.

To his surprise, Laura took this badly. The light snapped off in her eyes; her face settled and filled with grey shadows. She took some coffee and went back to her office. The woman who had been laughing with Pascal was a different person, the new Laura, the executive model he hadn't met before.

*

'I am an heiress – that is the right word, isn't it? My father in Sweden is a millionaire. Multi-multi, maybe billionaire; I don't know what he's worth actually. I adore him, of course, and he adores me. But sometimes we fight.' Mrs Larsen spoke tumultuously, the words scrambling to get out as her tongue pressed them to the roof of her mouth behind teeth that protruded the smallest, most appealing, degree. There seemed to be tears in her eyes. Sam did not ask himself why a millionaire's daughter should still have crooked teeth.

Sam perceived her eyes to be a deep violet, like the eyes of the young Elizabeth Taylor. She had a slight Scandinavian accent, the breathy 'o's and 'a's, the slurry 'v's and 'j's, which to a man of Sam's vintage and pretensions would for ever evoke intense and tragic passion as filmed by Ingmar Bergman.

In his diary, he had cleared the afternoon for this lunch. Pats was holding the fort at the office. Earning her wages for once. That'd show her.

'My father, he has . . .' Mrs Larsen took another breath, and the gold pentacle on its gold chain glittered just as Sam had imagined it would. 'No love to give me, only money. It's not his fault, I'm not saying that – it's just the way he is, that's all. He gives me money, it's all he knows to do. But when he is angry with me, no money.'

'And he's angry with you now,' Sam deduced.

'My mother died when I was a little girl,' she went on. One of the tears overflowed on to her cheek and dropped without a sound into her salad of chargrilled calamari on a bed of wild rucola. 'I am the only child. For many years he loved no other woman but now . . .'

'A new girlfriend.'

Another tear dripped into the squid.

'I don't know what to do. I tried to be nice, I was happy for him, really I was. She won't even let him speak to me, you know. I can hear her, when I call home; she's there in the room screaming at him not to talk to me . . .' Delicately, she patted her cheeks with her napkin.

Sam wished he still carried a handkerchief. 'And this happened back when you were about to complete your purchase?'

'I feel so bad about this.' A waiter removed her watery salad, then took away Sam's polished and empty plate. Mrs Larsen lit a cigarette and blew the smoke into the air above their heads. The gold pentacle at her throat gleamed with implication.

'I don't know what to do,' she said again. 'He's not like you. Not sophisticated or cultivated or, you know, a man of the world. We owned a steel works. Of course that's all over now, he got out at the right time, but sometimes I think he only understands something if it's made of metal.'

'Building a business is always a struggle. A man has to fight, to get up early, make a lot of tough calls. He has to work very hard, do so many things he doesn't like doing – you have to be ruthless, even if you don't want to be.'

'This is so strange. Somehow I knew you would understand.' She fired up another cigarette.

'Suddenly you wake up twenty years later and find you're supposed to be this heartless bastard.' Sam made this statement in a self-righteous tone which, though he would never have believed it, told Mrs Larsen exactly how his wife felt about him, and for that matter how he felt about his wife's opinion.

'He must have been so lonely,' she suggested, her breasts somehow rising like dough above the neckline of her pink cashmere sweater. She achieved this effect by squeezing her arms to her sides. Sam noticed the rising, but not the squeezing.

'It is lonely, being the main man. You can't talk to anyone, not anyone who can understand.'

'I was just a little girl, all this must have been happening and I just didn't know it.'

'Do you think that, in time of course, this – er – situation is going to change? I mean, what's she like, this woman?'

'Well, I think she's very nice, really. Very good for him. She's just a little insecure, you know; they have first got together, she loves him, she doesn't know me at all, I'm working here in London . . .'

'What is it that you do, exactly?'

'I work in the hotel business. European Development Manager for the Embassy Group, actually. Here . . .'

She undid the gilt trappings of her handbag and found him a card. Mrs E. S. Larsen, European Development Manager, Embassy Hotels Group. A red crest, too small to see properly without taking out his glasses. Sam thought his glasses were an insult to his manhood and used them only if there was no hope for it. He could just about make out that the address was in Mayfair, home of premium rents and Arab money, and to Sam the very choicest part of town.

The waiter reappeared bearing plates of fish. 'Mrs Larsen, here's what I'm going to propose to my partners.' Sam thought it would be kindest to put her mind at rest so she could enjoy the rest of her lunch. Of his own enjoyment there was no question. 'I'll explain your circumstances. I'll say you've agreed to make us a small payment every month – perhaps fifty pounds, would that be reasonable? And then we can meet like this, every now and then, and you can tell me how things are going.'

'Ah!' Her lips went everywhere and for a moment he thought she was going to cry. Instead she stood up, reached over the table and brushed his cheek with a kiss. Her breath rustled in his ear. A few forks hit the floor and the edge of her pink tweed jacket dipped into her champagne sauce.

She dabbed the lipstick off his cheek with her napkin. 'I can't believe you really understand, you're so very kind. I can't begin to tell you how wonderful it is, what you've just said – I can sleep at night now, I feel I can breathe again.'

Sam began to feel substantial.

'You must call me Elizabeth now,' she proposed.

Sam felt himself blushing. She twittered on, exclaiming more thanks. Other people in the restaurant looked at them. Sam felt important. This had once been a familiar sensation. The trouble with Pats was her attitude. The trouble with Alice was that she was a self-centred woman. They'd been getting worse, both of them. It was time for action.

Mickey woke up feeling wet. He had been sweating so much in his sleep that the duvet cover was clinging clammily to his chest. The sheet and pillow were soaking. The room was stuffy; he felt hot all over. He sat up and poured himself a glass of water, but it slipped straight through his sweaty hands and hit the floor.

When he kicked off the duvet and got out of bed, he saw that where he had been lying a damp stain measured the length of his body. Disgusted but still curious, he reached for the quilt, twisted a corner of it and squeezed. A few drops fell to the carpet. Yes, it was wet enough to wring out. The effort of wringing made him sweat even more.

In the bathroom mirror he saw that his face was as red as if he'd been out running and his skin shone with the perspiration that was still streaming from his pores. His hair, which normally waved vigorously off his scalp, was plastered to his skull in lank bunches. He ran a cool shower and stepped into it.

After a while he stopped feeling like a woodburning stove at full blast and turned off the water. Wet and naked, enjoying the fresh air on his body, he went downstairs to find the central heating thermostat. The house was like a sauna. Mo must have turned up the temperature; she was always complaining she felt cold.

The heating had been turned off. Mystified, he went to the kitchen and opened doors, expecting to find a rogue boiler roaring away on its own. He had no idea where to find the boiler or anything else domestic. The house was Mo's business – in every sense, since she had moved them through five homes in nine years, profiting immensely each time. Normally he was quite proud of having married a woman who could double the value of any given portion of real estate just by stripping the floorboards and painting the walls gardenia.

He began to feel blessedly chilly. It was over. This was not the first time. He couldn't remember the first time. He had noticed himself sweating on a flight home from LA, earlier in the year. Then again after he got back, several times. Most recent occurrence, last week.

Mickey was not a hypochondriac but nor did he take care

of his health. This sweating thing was so bizarre you couldn't ignore it.

A few hours later he was sitting with Dr Joshua Carman in his Hyatt-style consulting suite on Elm Bank Avenue. Dr Carman was a wiry, energetic man with very little hair. Pictures of his wife and two sons, thickly framed in silver, beamed from the side of his desk.

'Hyperhidrosis, which is just the medical name for excessive sweating, can have several causes. It can, for instance, be an emotional or stress-related condition. Is there anything in your life at present . . . ?'

Am I stressed? Mickey asked himself. No. Quite the opposite. He shook his head.

'Work under control?'

'Between shoots at the moment so nothing going on there to wind me up. Company's in good shape. Shortlisted for all the awards this year as usual.'

Dr Carman coughed to indicate professional curiosity only. 'And things at home?'

'Good. Marriage is in good shape. Son's in good shape, or so he says when he gets in touch . . .' Their son, Joe, had been born even more self-contained than his father. He was working on an educational project in Mexico City and sent infrequent text messages saying: AM OK. RUOK? PLS MMD +£S. LUV.

Dr Carman looked relieved. 'I'm going to ask for some blood tests. I'd like to find out some more about your thyroid activity.' His relief now transformed itself into tension. A ligament flickered in his cheek. 'And there is one other test that is recommended for this condition.'

'Oh?' Mickey picked up the vibe instantly.

'It's for HIV. I need your permission to ask for it.'

'Long shot, isn't it?' A huge black hand of terror seized Mickey's heart and began to crush it.

'Oh, yes. But while we're taking blood, we might as well exhaust all the potential diagnoses.'

'This is HIV as in AIDS, yeah?'

'Yes. It would be helpful to be able to exclude it straight-away. Just a precaution.'

'Well, sure, that's fine. Do I have to sign anything?'

He could see that Dr Carman was relieved, and so must have been expecting an argument. In another ten minutes Mickey was driving away from Elm Bank Avenue with a tiny circle of sticking plaster in the hollow of his left elbow, resolutely refusing to think about all the women he'd had sex with in the last twenty years. Unprotected sex, as the kids would say. Somehow he couldn't put sex and protection together in his mind. Conceptually, they cancelled each other out. The test was just a precaution. Nothing to worry about. The sweating was probably stress. Or emotion.

He felt warm. He felt warmer. The disc of plaster peeled off his arm. His shirt was sticking to his back. It was happening again.

CHAPTER 4

Slippery When Wet

Their Friday came and they played the Beehive as usual. In the autumn night Westwick was just a sparse necklace of lights twinkling across the dark water of the Thames. A few lights meaning a lot of drawn curtains. Westwick families enjoyed their privacy.

Location, location. South of the river, in a different world, another planet, a parallel universe. The Beehive was only a few kilometres downstream from the multi-occupied stews of south London. People who drank there had too much on their minds to remember to draw their curtains. Most of them didn't have curtains anyway. They had lives that were worth forgetting with a lot of alcohol and friendly noise. A good gig, always full; and an audience who appreciated the standards.

Tonight the band had not been in the groove. Not that anyone but themselves had noticed. 'Come back any time,' the landlord invited Andy while he bought the first round after the set. 'This bar does double normal business when you're playing. I've had people buying champagne, even.'

'That'll be one of the wives, I expect.'

'Wives, eh? You're lucky they let you out to do this. My old lady'd have a fit.'

'Anything to get us out of the house. That's it with them.'

It was close enough to home for Mo to come over if she'd been working late. Sometimes she dragged Alice with her. Laura used to come, but soon got bored with playing the over-age groupie.

Barbara – well, they were all glad Barbara stayed away. For once she was doing the right thing. The band was not at all a couple activity. The men wished the women were not so accepting. It was a wife's job to gripe, not to arrive mid-set, swinging a Prada handbag, ready to make the landlord happy by buying champagne.

Andy took the beers back to the table. If George had lost his way in his last solo, and Andy himself had blanked on the second verse of 'Mr Pitiful', and if Rhys had played as if someone had dropped Valium in his beer, their audience had not noticed. They were now stuck in for the rest of the night, crammed shoulder to shoulder, laughing and grinning and splashing vodka down each other's necks.

The band was wedged around a table on the fringe of the mob. No, they were not going to admit to their shame, not yet. They looked at George. George was present in body only; he was gazing into the smoky distance with sunken eyes. They badly needed diversion. They were craving. Sam cleared his throat.

'Here's a thing,' he announced. 'What do you think of this? There's this company in America that makes, like, luxury quality life-size sex dolls.'

'Is that a fact?' Mickey put in as a first-round bet. The circle drew tighter around the table.

'Completely life-like; you know, soft when you touch 'em, and heavy. You can pose them, they've got jointed limbs. People – I mean couples – save up for years to buy them and then have them in their homes and treat them like one of the family.'

'They don't do the business?' Mickey raised his stake to curiosity.

'Oh yeah, they fuck 'em. But it's like three-in-a-bed, you know what I'm saying?'

'What are they made of?'

'Some kind of silicone, looks just like flesh. Beautiful breasts, beautiful nipples – very life-like. I've seen pictures; they've got lovely hair and everything. They buy them all the clothes, lace underwear, little shoes. You can specify the measurements – how big the tits are, that sort of thing.'

'That is really sad,' suggested Rhys. He did two days of aesthetic surgery a week. Things like that changed the way you thought about a woman's body, even the body of an all-silicone gynoid. 'Shows you how we're all obsessed with image.'

'But it's the wives that love 'em to bits,' Sam protested. 'They just love dressing them up in beautiful lingerie, doing their hair.'

'How much?' Mickey raised him.

'Six thousand dollars. What's that, four thousand quid? And – here's the thing, the thing that's really touching – if a couple gets bored with its doll, they have her adopted by another couple. They don't just chuck 'em in the bin.'

Some men went into the nearest wilderness, built sweat

lodges and beat drums together to buttress their masculinity against the erosion of civilisation. This was not the way in Westwick. Hereabouts men took their sons to football, grew ponderous as school governors or dedicated themselves to raising money for a new pavilion for the Helford Green Cricket Club. Mickey, Andy, Rhys and even Sam looked on these pastimes with contempt. Music was all they needed to feel like men.

Putrid humour, bitching about women, some dodgy chat about sex toys – these were the sanctioned adventures for the socialised male. Three of them had daughters. It cramped your style. And someone would blow the whistle when it was time to go home.

'Four thousand a throw, you'd expect a re-sale market,' Andy suggested. 'How do they do it, then? What's the actual process? An adoption agency, to make sure they go to a good home, or just a small ad in the local paper?'

'Well, I expect it begins with an ad,' Sam theorised, wanting to look as if his knowledge was boundless. 'Maybe in one of those contact magazines. Then perhaps the two couples meet up.'

'Have a bit of a group session with the doll, make sure they know how to use her right?'

'Yeah,' Sam agreed. Daft prat, he didn't realise he'd lost them. 'Make it an occasion. That'd be the way to do it.'

'No timewasters, eh?'

'Obviously, you'd have to screen people.'

Mickey was following attentively and keeping schtum. He divided the world into creatives and civilians. Civilians were audience; they were consumers, there to be scored. When he was with civilians, and he classified Rhys and Sam as civilians, and it was necessary to spend time with them to avert the danger of disappearing up your own arse, it was down time. No need to be The Man. No point, actually.

Any other night, George would have got them all howling with laughter just by using the word 'orifice', but George was still absent. He sat in silence, swallowing his beer twice as fast as the others, periodically biting the side of one of his fingernails, unattracted by the notion of dismembering a life-size human doll.

They waited, all of them, even Sam, for George to weigh in and ride this dodgy subject off in a wacky, hilarious, surreal direction, somewhere way out beyond the edge of taste, in the way that only George could. But tonight he wasn't playing. He got up and headed for the lavatory door on the far side of the room.

Rhys decided that if George wasn't going to stop the rot, it was down to him to knock the giant sex toys out of their orbit. 'They're washable, I suppose?' he enquired with an earnest face.

'Washable? I don't know.' Sam spoke as if offended.

'You'd have to wash them,' Rhys reasoned.

Unpleasant images flashed through their minds. Andy drained his glass. 'Your round, isn't it, Sam?'

Once Sam was out of earshot, he said to Rhys, 'Thanks for that. It was getting weird. I thought if I pushed him a bit he'd give it a rest, but he wasn't getting it.'

'He never does, old Sam, does he?'

George returned and it was Mickey who then began the process of making him better.

'All right?' he asked with a twitch of his Irish eyebrows. His face had the meandering lines that made up what the

Anglo-Saxon world considered an Irish face, but it was the eyebrows, thick, curled and unswept, that gave him the crazy Celtic edge. The older he got, the quieter he got, the wilder his eyebrows became. It could have been that all the wildness in Mickey was slowly growing out into those fantastical brows.

'Yeah,' George responded. 'I'm all right.'

'Gardening business going well?' Mickey bought from George occasionally. They went back a long way, it was the proper thing.

'Yeah, mustn't grumble, you know how it is.'

'You're a bit quiet.'

'Am I?' Now this conversation too was falling into a ritual pattern.

'Not saying much. Got something on your mind?'

'It's the bike,' George confessed. 'Got knocked over in Soho a couple of weeks back, cracked the fascia. Knocked out the clocks, speedo, revs, all that.'

'Bummer.'

'Yeah. Expensive, too.'

'You need your instruments.'

'That's right, Moriarty. A man needs his instruments.'

'No, you know.'

'Yeah, but they want twelve hundred quid.'

'Christ, that's a bit harsh.'

'All in one piece with the windshield. Gotta replace the lot.'

'You've had a second opinion?'

'Oh yeah, that was the garage the firm uses and I checked it out with the place I usually go to. It's all kosher, they showed me the price list.'

It went without saying that George didn't have the money. Question was, had Mickey got the message? From George's viewpoint the other four were wrapped in the fog of comfort that stopped them seeing his world clearly. None of them had had an easy start in life, but George knew that he was the superior being among them and he put the status they had achieved down to a mysterious good-luck deficit that had victimised him alone. In the mists of wealth, the others could forget that he hadn't been lucky like them. An event like this, properly managed, would bring home the fact that he lived hand-to-mouth. Over the years he'd trained them to respond pretty well.

'I can help you out,' said Mickey quietly, for these arrangements were always kept quiet. 'Come around some time in the week, I'll have the cash.'

'Thanks, mate. 'Preciate it.' They nodded at each other. Sam returned with full glasses and George felt empowered to rejoin the conversation.

'Of course, you could have a lot more fun with one of them dolls if you got a chainsaw and cut it up,' he suggested. 'Isn't it in the Bible, some geezer did that?'

'Not with a chainsaw,' suggested Sam, jealous of the moving spotlight.

'You leave recognisable portions all over town, causing mayhem and public alarm. "Local policicles admit they bafflode by the terrible outraging."'

'Oh God,' appealed Rhys, but the rest laughed.

'You could lop off the hands and conceal them in your local municipal shrubbery, among fallen leaves, in a place where people walk dogs. Little Fido could make a few gruesome discoveries. Deep joy, happy doggy. "Here boy, c'm 'ere, boy, that's a good doggie, has he found a nice new bone then . . .'" He imitated the kind of woman he imagined to have an IQ as high as her bust measurement in centimetres. "'Ooh, Fido, what have you got there . . . ?'" They laughed some more.

'And the head.' George rolled his eyes and slugged back some beer while his brain changed gear. 'You could put the head in a block of concrete in the foundations of a new municipal flabberblock with up and down lift shafties. Or be like that Japanese nutter and chuck it in the sea, deep down in Davy Jones's locky-locky until it all wash up on the beachitude for the amusement of the old coastguards.' He became a newsreader. 'A grisly secret was uncovered this morning at Old-Slapper-on-Sea in Northamptonshire, where children playing on the beach discovered a block of concrete which appeared to contain human remains. Forensic experts are now examining the find while the children are receiving counselling to help them come to terms with their experience.'

'You're mad, George,' Sam told him, not wholly kindly.

'The counsellors would be specially trained in the effect of unsolicited contact with plastic dolly parts. There'd be a school of plastic dolly studies at some university, with some fancy name and some beardy old professor.' George became a TV presenter. 'In the studio with me tonight is Professor Norbert Beelzebub Bumfluff, Professor of Sex-Toy Studies of the University of Central Rutland, formerly Rutland Polytechnic. Tell me, Professor, what lies behind the sudden increase in macabre sex toy crimes being reported today?'

George was well in the groove. The other four began to sprawl happily and enjoy themselves. "'My research indicates that the collapse of the Indonesian economy, leading to a glut of cheap silicone beavers from Sumatra flooding the market, has brought the price of a premium-grade sex toy within the reach of the ordinary consumer. Whereas a sex toy was once a major household investment, something to be cherished, treated as one of the family and dressed in expensive lingerie and designer fetish shoes, she has now become a disposable item which consumers are ready to discard when a new model comes out." Oh, folly! folly! Western civilisatilode all gone infernal.'

They all laughed heartily, and not one asked himself if he too would be ready to discard a major household investment in favour of a new model in the right circumstances.

'But why are people cutting them up with chainsaws and leaving them around the country in public open spaces?' George demanded with inquisitorial vehemence. '"Well, it's more fun than waiting for the dead of night and sneaking them on to your neighbour's skip under cover of darkness, isn't it?" "I wouldn't know, Professor." "Oh yes you would. I can spot a dirty bastard like you in ten seconds. Middle-aged, middle class, outwardly successful but secretly sexually dysfunctional – the classic profile of a closet skip-abuser. Own up or I'll out you, you slimy pervert."'

Even Rhys was with them now. 'But isn't pop music to blame?'

'"Of course. Pop music today is a load of pitiful hype for two-year-olds wot don't know any better, enacted by juvenile retards wot cannot sing or play their supposed instruments. Reaching for a chainsaw and cutting up some silicone-breasted lady robot is a normal human response to this shite."'

The great beauty of a George-ologue was that there was always a moral argument in the madness.

'What happened to "Mr Pitiful"?' Mickey asked Andy a few moments later, when the tears of laughter were drying on their faces.

'I dunno,' Andy admitted. 'I just checked out there for a moment. Lost the words.'

'Yeah, I checked out and all,' George nodded, as if mystified by this finding. 'Plink, plonk – goodliebylode everybody. Senile dementia. Whaddya think?'

They created the space for Rhys to own his share of the disaster but Rhys, at that moment, appeared to have checked out also.

'You were well zombied,' Sam suggested to him.

'Was I?' he asked, not as anxious as he should have been.

'You'd have been fine for J. J. Cale, with his bass line strong and male,' George minced, drag queen style, 'but we are the Roedean girls.'

'Meaning?'

'Meaning what fuckin' solar system were you in, Rhys? You were playing like the great slime monster from planet Zog that forgot to switch on the auxiliary brain in its arse.'

'Sorry,' said Rhys. 'I've got a lot on right now. Must've let it get to me.'

This was considered an honourable recompense, and Rhys was allowed to get the next round. While he waited at the bar, images attacked him, kamikaze-style, flying in at all angles like moths bombing a lantern in the tropical night. First a breast sliced open, the breast of a twenty-two-year-old patient that day, a breast whose fullness ballooned inside the white skin, almost ready to pop.

Normally, his place behind the patient's head meant he couldn't see much of the operation, but today he'd had a

72

view of the first incision as it was made. The picture pestered him. Smooth white flesh, flesh to be adored, cherished, caressed in intimacy, had been lifted by the surgeon's plastic-sheathed fingers as impersonally as a butcher lifts a steak. Half-severed, flopping like a bag of milk, it was still a breast, and it made those secret, semi-solid movements only a breast can make, as if it was accepting the touch of the fingers in love, not hanging from them like a piece of meat.

Rhys had felt something, a twinge of desire. Then a flush of horror: a severed breast, for Christ's sake. Rhys Pritchard and Jack the Ripper, brothers under the skin? Then a crack of fear, because his concentration had snapped while he had removed his patient's consciousness.

Now at the bar, while he was still shuddering, he was also seeing Mo in one of her T-shirts sitting opposite him in the café, and the response of her breasts as she moved her arm. Then he saw her lying beside him, the velvety surfaces falling convex and concave, stirring with every breath.

Then he saw her lying beside Mickey. He couldn't switch this picture off, and it was coming up more and more often. Did Mickey know? Surely, after all this time, Mickey must have an inkling. He was sharp, he knew what was going on. Didn't he?

That Saturday, in his highly desirable Maple Grove house, a house by the renowned architect Tudor Wilde, the creator of the Maple Grove aesthetic, Sam started the process of checking out in real life. This house was complete with the signature Dutch-farmhouse-style gables of Maple Grove and a double garage for which planning permission had been most immaculately applied for and obtained; it had a hand-built farmhouse kitchen and a living room with a minstrel gallery balustraded in dark oak. On the first floor was the master bedroom and four further bedrooms with ensuites, while above that were further offices and a sixth bedroom/study.

This house was not merely imposing but also a deal, a business stroke which to Sam had a Zen-like beauty. When the original owner, the very same Ted Parsons, had been temporarily disoriented, in the time after his first dingbat wife had deserted him and Ted had been anxious to marry the second, he had allowed Sam to buy the place cheap. Therefore, the whole three-storey forty-foot-high red brick edifice was a monument to Sam's acumen, which was synonymous with his virility, and Sam felt like a world-beater every time he opened his own front door.

The feeling never lasted past the doormat. Inside the house were people – Alice, at times their children, Melanie and Jon, and the whole damn caravan of friends and neighbours and cleaners and relatives and outworkers and shop people and Alice's bloody mother, all of whom Alice was too stupid to get rid of. Plus the bloody great dog and the cats and whatever other animals she was giving house-room to, because Alice was a sucker for anything homeless. They were always there, in his house, eating his food, occupying his space, costing him money.

Now that, as he put it, Elizabeth was in his life, Sam felt like a world-beater constantly, except when he was in his own home. So things had to change. Here, in his family's major asset, Sam began to make arrangements to check out.

For good.

It was, as he saw it, Alice's fault. Always trying to make

74

more of their relationship than what it really was. And now, insult to injury, she was letting someone else finish her sentences.

He had given her twenty-two years. Sam had never wanted to marry Alice and had disguised it by saying he did not believe in pieces of paper, which indeed he did not unless they defined commitments to his advantage. Sam felt that all this was understood, that Alice knew he was staying with her and raising their children only on that basis, the basis that none of it was really happening because it was not what he had desired. The prime function of the universe, after all, was to give Sam whatever he desired.

If Alice did not understand it was because she was stupid. After twenty-two years with Sam, Alice shared this vision of herself. A stupid woman, that was the picture. First of all, the adorable fool who had ensnared him. Then the no-brain who had got pregnant. The idiot who could not understand that none of this was real. The wally who assumed, because Sam had quite often given the appearance of contentment in this arrangement, that he was happy and really wanted to live this way.

If Alice was stupid inside her home, she was nothing but a retard outside it. She could not manage her family so that she earned enough to take the pressure off Sam, she spent her life puttering through part-time jobs that hardly paid for the groceries while she and all the rest of them were spending his money, and now, the final idiocy, she was messing around in that stupid shop with Mo.

Mo, in Sam's eyes, was a tough cookie, probably a feminist or something. Even though Mickey kept her under control, any fool could see that Mo was going to be trouble and only a fool would have gone into business with her. A fool such as Alice.

The entire symphony that was Alice had been written on this theme, with the big goofy eyes and the flyaway fair hair and the habit of shrugging and giving a little gasp when she needed someone else to end a sentence for her. For twenty-two years the sentence-ender had been Sam.

Now there was Mo. My goodness, how right Sam had been about Mo. Dangerous! Mo had proposed to Alice that she become a partner in La Maison, and Alice, thinking she would please Sam, had agreed, thus placing her husband in a double-bind. That was her first mistake.

Unaware that she was already in error, Alice began to see Mo through her own eyes. Her vision no longer tinted by her husband's plenteously delivered opinions, soon Mo was ending her sentences instead of Sam. Sometimes, Mo had this scary little trick of letting Alice end a sentence for herself. Madness!

Alice's second fatal fault had been to succeed. 'I'll take responsibility,' Mo had said. The earth hadn't opened and swallowed her, nor had the hand of God come down from heaven to smite her with lightning. Alice's eyes had popped in wonder, half-terrified, like a child watching grown-ups fight.

All that had happened was that a tidal wave of paper had hit Alice's cosy desk at La Maison. While she struggled to keep her head above the cash flows and the costings and the budgets and the filing – she was really quite good at filing – Mo had sorted the schemes and the contractors and the suppliers and the buying and the ordering and then – good heavens! Walls were painted and fittings fitted and they were going to finish their first house that week as ever was.

It was easy, goddammit. It was no trouble at all. And they'd made so much money! Alice was terrified of money; she felt banknotes would burn her hands if she touched too many of them. Those long, long figures in the budgets hissed at her like snakes. Thirteen-thousand-two-hundred-and-fifty-six-poundssssssssssssssssss! Her heart turned over every time she saw a figure like that.

Sam had suffered, she couldn't deny it. She had been worried, snappy, preoccupied, late home and heaven knew what other wifely no-nos. She'd been getting skinny and her boobs were disappearing, one of them faster than the other. Alice assumed that Sam had seen these lapses and been wounded by them; they lay on her conscience.

Then the perfect solution occurred to her. That menacing credit balance in her bank could be applied to making Sam happy. He who loved jazz – she would take him to one of those festivals for which he had, from time to time, expressed a yearning.

Alice telephoned and made notes, she surfed and downloaded, she assembled brochures, she compared prices. The day before she had called him. 'Will you bring your diary home, Sammy? I was thinking it would be nice to plan a little holiday for us, since we've both been working so hard.'

But here was Saturday and he had not remembered his diary. 'You shouldn't ask me that kind of thing,' he informed her when she approached him with brochures in the morning. 'I have enough to remember without that sort of trivia.'

'It doesn't matter,' she placated him automatically. 'I can call the office on Monday and Pats can find a date for us.'

Now, however, it was Sam's turn to freeze over and evade. 'What's this idea you're obsessed with?' he began.

Even a woman as stupid as Sam believed that Alice was would have caught the uncooperative tone of this opening and realised that a pleasurable hour of holiday planning was not on the cards. Being far more intelligent than her partner estimated, and far more sensitive than he could possibly imagine, Alice felt an immediate drenching of dread. Being also more courageous than Sam understood, she persevered.

'Look,' she appealed to him brightly. 'All those lovely jazz festivals you've told me about. We could go to Umbria. Or Montreux. Or to Marciac, look . . . You're always saying you've never been to Marciac.'

'You don't want to go to some jazz festival,' he told her.

'I used to enjoy those clubs we went to,' she argued. Alice felt that her husband must be reasonable because he was a man, and men were reasonable because Sam said so and her mother and father, backed by a considerable body of informed opinion, had said so even before him. She could not quite believe that arguing with Sam, on any grounds at all, was just suicide. 'In Soho. Like Scottie Ron's.'

'*Ronnie Scott's,*' he scoffed. 'That was years ago. Before the children.' With Sam, it was always 'the children', or even 'your children', never anything that indicated joint interest in the two people for whom they had chosen the names Melanie and Jon.

'But they still play the same music, don't they? Standards? Classics?'

'What do you know about the new jazz?' he demanded from the great height of listening to Jazz FM in the car.

'I'd like to learn. I'd like to find out. I'd like us to do

something together, Sammy. Something nice. Just us.'

'If I wanted to waste money going to one of those rip-off jazz festivals, don't you think I'd have done it by now?'

'But you always . . .' She could see that holding him to his idly spoken words was not going to work. 'And anyway, Sammy, I want to pay for this. This contract we're doing for Ted, it's been the making of the shop. We've got more money than we know what to do with and I realise I've been so bound up with it that I've neglected you. Well, I feel I have, anyway. So I thought it'd be so nice to—'

'—pay your own way here for a change. You have more money than you know what to do with because you don't know what to do with money,' he informed her, seeing his exit opening wide and invitingly before him. 'The proper thing to do with it is to make a contribution to the household, not fritter it away on enjoyment.'

He paused to think. Sam had devised a housekeeping scheme which ensured that Alice's income, such as it was, was spent on items that were legally invisible. Alice bought the food, the children's things, the kitchen appliances, the fuel and the entertainment. He paid for the utilities, the council tax, the savings plan and the mortgage. They each made these payments from their own bank accounts. When the day came that they would separate, as Sam had always planned in theory and now looked forward to in reality, Alice would be able to make only the feeblest claim on their assets, which were in his name alone.

Rapidly, Sam computed items for which Alice could pay without compromising his capital gains. 'BUPA,' he said. 'Health insurance for the whole fucking family. Have you any idea what that costs? If you've got so much money, you can pay for that from now on. See how much you've got left when you've taken care of a few family responsibilities.'

'Sammy, are you sure?'

'Never been so sure of anything in my life. Pay the BUPA. Make my day.'

'Well, if you're really sure . . .' It wasn't quite a weekend break at a great jazz festival, but Alice felt honoured to be allowed to take this responsibility.

'Just do it. And all this rubbish,' he picked up her brochures, her price lists and her research and threw them in the wastepaper bin, 'forget it. You're mad if you think I can take time off work for that kind of junk.'

'Silly of me,' she agreed. What kind of wife was she, to have so little understanding? She'd been so busy herself the last few weeks she'd hardly noticed that Sam had been working desperately late too.

The beep was there when he turned his pager on outside Cardiothoracic. If it was CT it was Monday, Tuesday or Wednesday. Aesthetics on Thursday and Friday. Three days' public service, two days' breadwinning. Three days' conscience, two days' prostitution. Thus Rhys earned a good life for Barbara, Emma and Toby.

'Call Barbara,' the screen commanded.

'What's happening?' he asked her when he could use his mobile.

'The school called,' she said. 'They want you to go down.'

'Why?'

'Don't ask me. I can't go, I've got bridge tonight.'

'Didn't they say anything?'

'Well, obviously there's some problem, Rhys. Since I can't

get away, there's not much point me going into it, is there?'

A woman of logic, that was what Barbara posed as. Every conversation with her was suddenly subverted into an orbit that left you circling helplessly around the glowing ball of her ego. She was right, her needs were paramount, you were just cosmic dust, grateful for her gravity to keep you in line.

At the end of the day he drudged towards the school through the commuter crush. In the car, he called Mo.

'What do you think it is?'

'Oh, some bust up with the other boys. Toby is fine. I can feel it, you know.'

'Father's intuition; you're telling me you've got that? Have you felt this before?'

'Yeah, I have. Don't you laugh at me. I just know when he's really acting out. He's basically a good kid. He just gets frustrated.'

'Yeah, right. Then he burns down the school.'

'He did not burn down the school. You know he didn't. He was just playing with matches.'

'And accidentally set fire to the school.'

'He was just watching a piece of paper burn. Like boys do. The flame went up the edge.'

'Then he put the paper in the bin, and the flame went up the edge of hundreds of pieces of paper in the bin. Which was in the library, near billions more pieces of paper.'

'It was an accident.'

There was no stopping Mo, least of all by Rhys. He enjoyed being teased about his fatherly obsession. Much better to be teased by Mo than withered by Barbara and her endless criticism. Sometimes Rhys felt as though his heart was going to stop and he was going to die under that.

'The bin caught fire and set the table alight. The table set the rest of the furniture in the room alight. Then it reached the books. The door caught fire, and the corridor, and the other classrooms, and then the whole old wing of St Nicholas's school was blazing away.'

'He didn't mean that to happen. But enough about me . . .'

'Rhys, you could see the smoke miles away.' She was giggling like a school child herself. 'I could see it at La Maison. Ted could see it in his office in town. Mickey could see it when they stacked his plane at the airport when he was coming back from California. They had nine fire engines out.'

This was how it ended. He would make an attempt to reach her, and she would stop playing and start a safer game.

'Boys experiment,' he told her. 'It's only natural. Didn't yours ever do anything naughty?'

'No. Joe was as good as gold. Funny, isn't it? I never understood him that way, he was just totally good, no trouble at all. I remember looking at him when he had just been born and thinking, My God – who the hell are you?'

'Well, what about you?' he countered. 'When you were at school? Didn't you ever start something you couldn't finish?' Yes, you, Maureen maiden-name-that-was, you with your forever legs, striding through the playground while the boys could only watch and yearn. Rhys believed himself among them, dragging on a crafty fag, watching the girl with the legs and the eyelashes and the wild curly hair blowing in the school-yard wind.

'Yes, I suppose I did. I suppose Mickey was something like that. But not the kind of fire that takes nine fire engines

82

to put out, darling.' So casual, the way she said these things. Such deep sadness; he could hear it even over a half broken mobile line and the purr of the car heater and the drone of the vehicles all around. Protect yourself, defend yourself, don't let anyone near you in case they won't love you. Talk about him, don't talk about you. His heart ached for Mo for a hundred different reasons.

'Are you still at the office?'

'Of course. I've got Mickey under my feet at home, haven't I?'

'Christ, that's a long time.'

'Tell me about it. He's been a few weeks between jobs before but this is months. Two months, anyway. I'm going crazy. Tell me what you did today.'

'Reconstruction this morning, three-month-old baby.'

'Is that with ice-packs?'

'Yup, it's a chiller. Pack the head in ice, induce cryostasis, divert the blood to an oxygenator, the guys go to work on the heart, put right whatever it is, switch back the blood flow, warm up the patient, bingo.'

'Was it bingo?'

'Pretty much. Little fighter went from flatlines back to normal, not a blip, no trouble at all.'

'And your afternoon?'

'Bypasses, three of them. Two emergencies. All old fellas – I give them a couple more years maybe.'

'They'll say that about us one day.' She said the most ridiculous things. That was one of the reasons he adored her.

'And you?'

'I've taken delivery of fourteen pairs of curtains with matching pelmets and tie-backs, sent back a sofa which was too big to fit in the lift or be carried up the stairs, and drawn up a contract with Pot Pourri for eighteen container arrangements to be refreshed twice a week. You need me to keep you grounded, don't you?'

'Don't know how I'd get by without you.' Many true words were spoken in jest when you were talking to Mo. 'Are we on for our Christmas?'

'Don't see why not. La Braderie de Saucisson-le-Mauconfit, a jamboree of junk, a festival of frippery, the second largest brocante fair in northern France, always the first Sunday in Advent. How could I let you miss out on that?'

It was dark when he arrived at the school and the building was as empty as a haunted house, the staff and pupils long gone for half term. Except for Toby and a young assistant matron whom he found in the sitting room of the head teacher's apartment.

'Dad!' said Toby, lurching to his feet. Yes, he was looking guilty. He was tall. Good God, he was nearly as tall as Rhys. Could he have grown that much in two weeks?

'Son,' Rhys answered, wary. OK, so he was tall suddenly, but such a normal-looking boy, so brown-haired, pink-cheeked, straight-backed, clean-limbed. What could possibly be wrong?

Cheerfully, Toby assured him: 'It's OK, Dad, I haven't actually done anything.'

'He just didn't want to go,' the matron said, rising from the sofa in a way that would have made any man think of Venus rising from the waves. 'I'm Miss Sweetling. I don't think I've met you yet.' Sweetling by name. Maybe it was just a trick of the long vanilla-coloured curls tumbling out of the girlish hairslide which was intended to discipline them. She seemed to be all of sixteen. In ten years she and his son would be in dating range.

'I didn't want to go,' Toby echoed her.

'He hid when the rest of them were getting on the bus for the station,' she explained, holding her charge by the shoulders. 'Then sneaked out when there was hardly anyone here. I should have told one of the teachers but they'd all gone. Now you're here though, so there's no harm done.'

Rhys sent his son away to find his suitcase and visit the lavatory. 'Has he had any problems?' he asked.

'Oh no, not at all,' she assured him, shrugging her razor-sharp shoulders. 'Nothing like what happened before. We were told about that, of course. He's just very quiet, isn't he? But he likes his music.'

'Quiet?' Damn schools and their euphemisms. If something was wrong, surely there was a name for it?

'Doesn't seem interested in making friends. But if we can't find him, we always know where to look. In one of the music rooms.'

'When you say he doesn't make friends . . .'

'Well, just that really. But give him time. It's only been half a term. I'm sure he'll settle down. He comes and talks to me sometimes.'

'What about? What does he talk about?'

She was looking anxious now. Something was lurking in this conversation but it wouldn't be tempted into the open. 'Soap operas on the telly, mostly. They all watch *EastEnders*.'

'So what happened exactly?' Rhys asked his son later, when they had stopped for a forlorn travesty of a meal at a motorway service area.

85

'I don't know.' Toby was looking intently at the edge of his pizza and hacking into the rubbery dough with his knife and fork.

'You must know.'

'Well, I don't.' The boy pulled back, not wishing to sound rude. Toby would always retreat into silence rather than risk offending anyone. Rhys could see himself in this behaviour so clearly that it made him angry. 'I was just standing with the others, waiting to get on the bus, and – then – well, I couldn't get on with them. So I went away for a bit and waited till they'd gone, and then I realised I couldn't get home so I went to find the matron but everybody had left. Don't ask me why, Dad. It's a mystery to me. I just don't know what happened.'

It was the best offer he was going to get so Rhys had to take it. His reward, ten minutes later as he settled the car into the fast lane again, was a question whose significance he did not realise.

'Is Mum at home?'

'I should think so. She usually is.'

'But tonight, is she at home?'

'No, wait a minute, she went out to the bridge club. She usually gets back from that at about eleven.'

'Why is she always home?'

'Well, she likes to be an old-fashioned Mummy and stay at home with her family,' Rhys suggested, convincing no one, not even himself.

'I wish she didn't. She ought to go out. Can I borrow your phone?'

He handed it over. His mysterious son curled up around the handset and had a muttered conversation that went on for about ten minutes. Then he let his head flop sideways and fell asleep in the passenger seat.

Laura was not the only woman at Charles's birthday party. There was some female cousin of Jabba the Hut, in green brocade harem pants and a turban, waving arms that clacked with bracelets. There were also two girls with string bean legs and absolutely fleshless bums, and steel spikes through the stiff skin on which their eyebrows were painted.

Apart from these three and Laura, the two hundred guests were all men. Black leather coats lay heaped upon each other on the bed in the main bedroom like the shed skins of a herd of dinosaurs. It was a small double bed with four wrought iron corner posts. Against the wall, where in their own home Laura had positioned a wire-fronted French armoire, Charles and Pascal had installed dark wood panels without handles. Laura boldly smacked one and it opened, revealing a mirrored inside and shelves filled with shiny shoes on shoe trees.

'Imelda Marcos, eat your heart out,' she recommended.

Andy looked down at his own shoes; they were reassuringly dusty.

'This really is the Pink Palace, isn't it?'

Andy winced. Homophobic cracks when your host was gay? No, no, no.

From downstairs came the hearty roar of conversation. From the basement throbbed the beat of a discotheque. People were out in the garden, smoking. The day after the new neighbours had taken possession, a contractor had arrived to recreate the garden in homage to Luis Barragan. It had a pink wall, large pots, pebbles, a rectangle of water and no plants. Andy and Laura went downstairs.

'Better look out for yourself,' she laughed into Andy's ear, leaning against him as they entered the sitting room that was disorientingly identical to their own, architecturally at least. 'If you get into trouble, just give me the nod,' she advised.

Andy walked into the door frame. Embarrassment always made him clumsy.

The hardwood floor amplified the clamour of the guests. The windows were naked holes, their blinds undescended. The space was loosely filled with groups of revellers and the bright lights cast hard shadows on the naked white walls.

The giant cactus had been installed by the window at the far end of the room. It looked more like a penis than ever. There seemed to be some swelling at its tip and the angle at which it leaned was just plain obscene.

In the shadow of the cactus they saw Pascal, swivelling like a leaning weathervane. For his partner's birthday he was wearing a nylon T-shirt, orange, patterned with clouds, which wrinkled over his arms and rode up above the low waistband of his trousers. He was clutching a tall and almost empty glass to his chest and kept turning as if he expected people to speak to him. Instead, those around him seemed to be keeping a safe distance.

'Hammered,' Laura diagnosed. 'Charles'd better watch out.'

'Why?' Andy wondered.

'Haven't you spotted it?' He felt her weight on his arm as she strained up to speak confidentially, and he lowered his head. 'He's got trouble with Pascal,' she hissed in his ear. 'Passive aggressive. Grenade with the pin out. Accident waiting to happen.'

Andy wondered how she knew. It puzzled him that she should instantly divine a problem for Charles in the drunkenness of his partner.

'Why?' he said.

'The way Charles is when he comes back from his office. He takes a deep breath before he puts his key in the door. Haven't you noticed? You must have seen him.'

Pascal, Andy had observed, was in and out at all hours. Charles was the orderly one, keeping a regular schedule, leaving around the time that Laura left for her office.

'Nobody loves a fairy when she's forty,' said a hard, sad voice not far away. It came from a circle of men adjacent to Laura and the speaker was watching Pascal as he stood alone in his indoor desert, swaying in the unfelt wind.

One of the group responded. 'Is he forty? I didn't know.'

'He must be,' the first speaker insisted. He seemed to be the oldest of them, a man with a shiny, pockmarked face. 'Why else go to all this trouble?'

'This is going to a lot of trouble?'

'I know. Hard to tell, isn't it?'

'Well, it's not something you'd necessarily want to make a great fuss about.'

'Pascal's just drunk, isn't he?'

'Looks it to me, but you never really know with Pascal. Probably got stuff all over the house. Or maybe his friends have given him something. You know what his friends are like.'

'Are they here?' There was now some looking about the room, as if they were new arrivals seeking company.

'Can't see any, thank God.'

'No, I can't see any.'

Impersonal as a lighthouse beam, the gaze of the group passed over Laura and Andy.

'Typical, though, isn't it? Typical of Charles, all this.'

'Making like it's all OK, making like nobody's got any problems. Making nice.'

Boldly, Laura breached their circle. Andy felt himself flinch. 'He is nice, Charles,' she told them. 'We think so anyway. We live next door.'

'Oh, so you're the people next door.' The older man tried not to say this with emphasis, but failed.

'Charles's talked about you,' said one of the others. Now they looked again, and looked with interest. Andy felt, for a ridiculous moment, that they looked particularly at him. Being the husband of an alpha female like Laura, he was not used to such attention. Perhaps because he was taller their eyes rested on him that little bit longer.

'I'm Laura,' she was saying, holding out her small and shapely hand.

'And I'm Andy,' he added. The shaking all round was surprised but eager.

'So,' the older man said to them when they stood back in expectation, 'leafy Westwick, eh? How long have you lived here?'

As Andy's heart was shrivelling on the verge of small talk, Pascal lost his balance and fell into the cactus, and the cactus in turn swayed on its terracotta base and toppled over, parting the revellers, causing them to scream, and hitting the floor with a heavy vegetable smack.

'Fuck me,' said the older man.

'It cost a fortune, that thing,' one of the others recalled.

'Is it OK? Will it break its spines?' asked another.

90

'Oh God, the top's fallen off,' reported a man in the front row.

The crowd drew into itself, first in fear, then in amazement and soon, as Andy had no trouble detecting, in reluctance to tackle Pascal, who lay writhing and grimacing on the dark boards.

'Is he bleeding?' asked someone in front of Andy. 'I can't see.'

'Pascal always bleeds, doesn't he?' was the answer.

With a moan and a whimper, Pascal pulled himself up to a sitting position. His mistake was to put out a hand and try to lean on the cactus itself to get up. Then he screamed in his turn, and it was a violent sound.

Now nobody moved. Somebody was going to have to sort this. The boy was actually bleeding, for heaven's sake. Common decency, common sense. Common to whom, exactly? Not very common around here, that was for sure. The boy was lying on the floor whimpering and they were all holding back and making smart cracks. Andy shouldered through the crowd, knelt at Pascal's side and helped him to his feet.

Pascal passed a hand over his eyes as if his vision was cobwebbed and said, 'I'm OK. Leave me alone.'

Blood was seeping in patches through the thin orange T-shirt. 'You're bleeding a bit,' Andy advised him. Here and there the fabric was snagging. 'Looks like you've got some spines stuck in you.'

'Fucking thing,' said Pascal. He turned to kick the fallen mass of the cactus and his boot sank toe-cap-deep into its succulent bulk, and he staggered. If Andy had not been holding him he would have fallen again.

'Oh Jesus.' Charles appeared in the doorway and now the guests made way for him to approach his wounded partner.

'Piss off, you,' Pascal spluttered. An edge of blood appeared hesitantly at the roots of the hair at his forehead.

With many years' experience of George behind him, Andy then foresaw the progress of the night in prismatic detail. For him, the party was over. For the rest, it had just begun. He was going to be spending the night in A&E at Helford, a venue familiar from many of the most anxious moments of fatherhood. The baby fell off the bed, the toddler glugged the greenfly spray, Laura threatened to miscarry, the new baby fell off the bed, the eight-year-old fell off her pony, the ten-year-old perforated an ear-drum, and now the gay neighbour was pissed and had brought a cactus upon himself.

Rapidly, inevitably, it was decided that Pascal should go to hospital. Pascal argued like a cat in the bath. The company overruled him. Pascal hit a few of them, staggered, fell, gashed his head on the corner of a table and passed out.

Several voices advised that no taxi would take him. Nobody else wanted to volunteer their car. Using the yellow Lamborghini as a bloodwagon was out of the question. Andy bowed his rumpsteak shoulders in resignation and volunteered the Volvo.

Pascal came round, launched some kicks in Charles's direction and screamed, 'Leave me alone, you bastard! Get out of my life!'

'I'll be OK with him,' Andy assured Charles.

'He isn't really hurt. And we're your guests and we need you,' argued Laura coyly. 'And it is your birthday.'

'Well, if you're sure,' said Charles.

Andy got ready to drive Pascal to the hospital. In the

doorway, Charles contorted like a Saint Sebastian and said, 'I feel so bad about this. Will you be all right?'

As the nurse gave him a shot of sedative before starting to extract the prickles, Pascal took Andy's hand and smiled like an angel. 'You're like my Dad,' he said. 'Or like my Dad should have been.' His teeth were white and translucent.

At 5 a.m., when Andy drove back, Pascal was mumbling, bandaged and, from the smell, sweating alcohol through every pore. They discovered Laura and Charles propped against each other on the sofa. A drain of Southern Comfort was left in the bottle on the floor.

'How can I ever thank you?' Charles asked him, as a man might if another man had taken his car to the car wash. Pascal then revived sufficiently to take a swing at his partner.

'You really had better go,' said Charles. 'I am OK. He'll be fine, he usually is.'

Pascal spat at him.

They left, and as Andy opened their own front door Laura told him, 'I really enjoyed that.'

'God, you're a weird woman sometimes.' Andy shut out the outside world with a sense of achievement.

'You have to admit they cheer the place up.'

He had to yawn. 'That's not how I'd put it.'

'You poor sod,' she blessed him. 'Good old Andy, always takes care of the shit that nobody else will.'

'They were going to leave him there,' he defended himself.

'Quite right too,' she said. 'Boy, have those two got problems.'

Something about her inflection made him stay with the judgement. They were tired but not sleepy and found a re-run of *On the Town* on a cable channel and watched it with glazing eyes. When Gene Kelly got to pirouetting through dry ice with a daffy roll to his eyes, Andy felt embarrassed. Gene Kelly always came a touch too near the bone for him.

His thoughts turned inward. After a while he said to Laura, 'What about us? What d'you think? Have we got problems?'

'Of course not, sweetie-pie. What kind of a question is that?' She slumped against the thickness of his arm.

Was she up for it now? Before they were married, when they had gone to the cinema, or rather, when he had taken her to the cinema, she had leaned into him that way. Andy sneaked his fingers around the most accessible breast.

She sat up as if she'd been meaning to do that all along. Nothing you could put a finger on, nothing you could call a rejection. But a definite no, all the same.

Mickey had been in the bathroom. There was a razor guard on the edge of the bath, an empty glass that had the air of Jack Daniel's on the windowsill, bloodstains on a towel, splashes of urine on the floor by the lavatory and some of his mouse-coloured pubic hairs on the soap that was poised stickily on the side of the bath while the soap dish itself remained clean and empty. There was no toilet paper.

The top was off the toothpaste. In fact, lots of tops were off lots of toothpastes – Mickey's bog-standard Colgate toothpaste, his American baking powder formula toothpaste, Mo's Sensodyne gel and also her Genevieve whitening toothpaste. Only the tube of Mo's special French homeopathic dentifrice still had a top, but it had no contents left and was squeezed out flat.

Mickey had been in the family room. The TV was immovably tuned to MTV and the sound was muted. The clock on the video, which Mo had been keeping ten minutes fast since her life had suddenly filled with meetings, had been reprogrammed to on-the-nose time. Five newspapers had been unfolded, rustled and fingered, then left in bundles on the coffee table next to a plate on which a pool of ketchup was drying. A leg had come off the decorative nineteenth-century inlaid lacquer baby chair. One of the red velvet bolsters had a stain the size of a big watch-face on it. The new chequered mohair throw had been pushed off the back of the sofa and the cat had been nesting in it. Three glass drops were missing from one of the wall sconces. The stench of old curry filled the room and it took Mo ten full minutes to find the congealed plates on top of some shelves.

Mickey had been in the kitchen. A tap was running. Crumbs surrounded the toaster. A mug was in the washing-up bowl and its handle was on the worktop. The stainless steel frying pan had been scoured with a Brillo pad and scarred for ever. There was no water in the kettle, nor in the filter jug. The microwave had been stopped mid-cycle. He had pushed a six-pack minus one into the fridge and crushed the bag of salad she had been keeping for supper.

In the pool room, the balls were perfectly placed, the cues were all racked, the chalk was in its box and the CDs by the player were all in their cases. It was only possible to tell that Mickey had been there from the well-filled ashtrays he had carried out to the kitchen and left by the fruit bowl. The presence of many hand-crafted roaches suggested that George had been with him.

Something had even drawn Mickey into his wife's office.

The drawing board was horizontal, while she used it at an angle. Several drawers were half open. Her CD case was splayed in front of the monitor, while the keyboard was on the floor. The fax would not transmit. Mo restored her desk to working order and tried to check her e-mails. An avalanche of error messages ran down her screen. Investigating, she found that the modem had been unplugged. Mummy bear deduced that someone had been sitting at her work station.

When Mickey was on a shoot, he was seldom home and lived a lot in hotels. When he was not filming, his house was simultaneously his own home and a strange place. You might as well take in a tramp off the street. He never learned how things worked or where Mo kept stuff. In his mind, there was always a maid imminent to clear up. This time he had been sprawling around the house for six long, messy, disorganised months, and this week their cleaner was on holiday.

It was early in the evening. When she had left the house that morning it had been in a state of perfection and Mickey had still been asleep in bed. She had spent all day at the site of La Maison's first show-home, creating perfection of commercial order for the fantasy buyers who would snap up the investment. All these disturbances had been created by Mickey between the hours of twelve and seven, she estimated, for she knew him too well.

Mo went to fill a glass with Diet Coke and Jack Daniel's. She reconnected her computer, picked up her keyboard and checked her mail. Since the back office at La Maison had disappeared under an avalanche of fabrics and trimmings, it had been easier to do the desk work at home.

Among the dispatch notes and the order confirmations, a message from Joe asked her to forward a petition about human rights in Afghanistan. She was the last name on a list of twenty, and there was no greeting from him. She did as he asked, then replied to him: 'Fighting oppression all very fine but what's happening with you?'

With the help of a refill, she levelled off her drawing table, closed the drawers after reordering their contents, zipped up her CDs and put them away and reprogrammed the fax. Moving on to the bathroom, with a fresh drink to give her strength, she began by washing the soap and cleaning the bath. Fast and practised, she moved through the rest of the house, replacing, restoring, cleaning, putting away.

There was nothing to be done with the velvet cushion except have a drink and let it go. While she was washing the ashtrays she felt that her cheeks were wet.

It was midnight. She took the wet ashtrays to the front door, stood outside the house and hurled them on to the front path. They shattered, and their crumbs glinted on the ground by the sickly yellow glow from the street.

What is this? Mo asked herself. With her glass, her comfort, held around the rim by the tips of her fingers, she folded her legs and sat down on the doormat, her arms around her knees. The soaring trees of Maple Grove blotted out the sky. Not a leaf moved. The glow of the street lights leached their colours. A heavy dew of late autumn was hazing the air.

'What is this?' she asked the empty air, and heard her words go out into the terrible void of a street in the suburbs at night. 'This is not about ashtrays,' she whispered to herself. 'And fuck the soap. Just – fuck it.' The tears which had been seeping out of her eyes' corners now ran to the centre of the lid and spilled boldly down to the edge of her lips. With the inside of each wrist, she wiped them aside.

Do I hate him? After all these years – is there still love underground, under all this irritation on the surface? A secret river of love still running or – nothing? Am I growing to hate him? Did I ever love him? Do I love Rhys? Can I love anyone or am I dried up now and finished with all that? Would it be any different if I'd had another child?

The plan had been a big family. Her body had had other ideas. First – the false sense of success. Joe, their perfect son. Perfect pregnancy, perfect birth, perfect baby. The optimum interval, two years and a bit, then they went for the next one and found their luck had run out.

Two pregnancies ended themselves before twelve weeks, two episodes so hard to remember that she sometimes thought she had imagined them. Mickey orbiting her warily; the creases on his forehead never went away after that. Then – nothing. No more periods. Early menopause. Awful word. She put a HRT patch on her thigh every morning when she brushed her teeth and if Mickey was away it stayed there twenty-four hours, the badge of her failure.

Lately, it felt as if her body was trying to re-start itself. One day her breasts would be blooming, another day she'd get a lurch of libido. Or a craving for chocolate. Or puffy ankles. Or a sudden spot on her face.

No answers were getting through the muddle in her head. Mo drained her glass and leaned against the door jamb. I've got to stop this. I'm going to bed drunk every night.

Finally, the drink had done its work and no more thoughts bubbled through it. She dug her heels into the mat, hauled herself upright, shut the door and went upstairs.

Several hours later, Mickey came back with George. 'What's this, a windscreen?' The glass crunched under their feet. 'Can't be a windscreen in the front garden.'

'I know what it is,' Mickey told him, but said no more.

'Old lady had an episode?' George diagnosed.

'That's what it looks like.' Both then considered the subject fully explored and their way clear to play pool until they were too tired to line up one more shot.

In the morning, Mickey said to his wife, 'Are you trying to tell me I should give up smoking?'

'No.' She was dressing for work. Trousers, twinset, jewellery, her face done first with bright lipstick.

'What's it all about, then? Why is our garden covered in broken glass?'

'Because I smashed the ashtrays, Michael.'

'I twigged to that when I was walking through them on the path, Maureen.' Could the stricken ship be steered into the calm waters of comedy or was it doomed to wreck on the rocks of an argument?

They rarely argued. Arguing is like a pas de deux, much rehearsal is needed for a good performance, and Mickey and Mo were so seldom together they were out of practice.

Mo stopped the process of assembling her outside identity to stand at the end of the bed for one last mission. 'Why won't you understand? I have two lives. One when you're here and we're a couple. Another one when you're working and I'm on my own. Every time you come back, I feel like I'm invaded and you're a stranger. I have to have a new I.D. We have to find out who we are all over again, learn to live with each other all over again. Sometimes it makes me crazy.'

He was wary. Many years earlier he had noticed that Mo could take care of herself. It niggled him, it made him anxious. She could take care of herself. Well, if she could take care of herself, that was it. Nothing for him to do. Nothing for him to worry about. Old Mo could take care of herself. Why should that worry him? Why the hell should that little blade of fear slip in under his heart because his old lady could live without him. Why the hell. Let her get on with it. He had his life, not much he could do about it.

'George swept it all up,' he told her.

'Oh God, not George.'

'He's not here, he went home. Shouldn't have, but he did.'

'Do you get it now?'

'Yeah, I get it,' he admitted. 'I just don't know what to do about it. I have to go away, I have to come back. When I go away, I make a lot of money. If I don't come back, we aren't married any more.'

Mo nodded. Mickey was aware that she was aware of the time and that she had a place to be, and because the time didn't matter to him and he had nowhere to be all day, he was resentful. She moved away and stepped into her shoes. They looked new. Snakeskin, backless, sexy. Why the hell should he worry?

'If you don't get a job soon I'll go mad,' she said, looking inside her handbag to avoid looking at him.

'*You'll* go mad.'

'You don't seem bothered.'

'Well, I am,' he assured her. 'But it's not like I'm on the dole. We do have money.'

'It's not about money.'

Go on, get out of here, get off to work, you've got a job to go to. Instead Mickey said, 'They offered me tampons yesterday, Sanpro, that's what they call it. What d'you want me to do, take it?'

'Don't put it on me. It's your career. You do what you want.'

'You want me to do it?'

'I said, don't put it on me.'

'I'm not doing fucking tampons just to keep the ball in play.' No tampons; it was the golden rule. Ads for the feminine protection market had serious status implications. She knew that. He knew she knew that. He softened. 'It's not just me, love. The industry's having a bad time. Something'll turn up.'

'I thought revenues had never been higher. I read that somewhere.'

'Oh, you're the expert.'

'I'm not getting into this.' Mo made for the door, eager for freedom. 'It's your business. I've got two lives and it drives me crazy. So there'll be a bit of broken glass now and again.'

'You've always liked the money.'

'Who wouldn't? I've paid my way too. With this job, and the way you're going, I'm going to make breadwinner this year.'

'You'd like me to move out,' he told her, wondering how the words spoke themselves.

'It's a lot easier when you're not here,' she agreed. 'Look, I'm late, I have to go.'

From his place in their bed, he watched the door shut and his wife disappear. Should he call the office, see what was happening?

Mickey sat on the edge of the bed, rasping his chin with a thumbnail and weighing up the options. Hang out, call up, drop in, do lunch, keep the air moving. Shit, he hadn't done that routine for years. Made you think of Status Quo reforming, squeezing back into the old Levis, letting out the belt buckles a few more holes, Francis Rossi tying back the receding hair in a ponytail before he flogged the old bones back up on stage. Not a dignified procedure when you'd been at the top for a few years.

Pussy-whipped, for God's sake! What was he thinking, letting Mo get on his case like that? Suddenly she thinks she's a born-again superwoman and starts giving him grief. Maybe the thing to do was just clear out for a few weeks, give her space to cool off.

Space had saved the two of them pretty often over the past two decades. Doing the cha-cha in a haunted ballroom, that was the whole secret of their happiness. When he was away, she was at home. If he took a break, Mo went to France. Forward, back; forward, back; advance, retreat; reach out, withdraw; speak out, clam up; going and coming and meeting in the middle just long enough never to get bored. She was right, it wasn't about money. The best thing about his bloody brilliant career was that it put space between them. It used to work fine. It would work again. All he needed was the next job.

His phone rang. 'We wanted to run through the arrangements for Thursday,' said a bright girl's voice he half-remembered.

'What's Thursday?' The whole thing was something he ought to be able to remember, damn it.

'Thursday. The DADs? Our ad for Hofburg's been nomi-nated?'

'It's Sandy, isn't it?' Now he remembered. In line for the industry's premier award again. The real Mickey suddenly burst out of the shrivelled chrysalis that a few seconds earlier had sat on the bed and wasted thought on its marriage.

'Yes, Mickey, if it's Tuesday it must be Sandy. Now, we're sending the car for your wife and yourself at five, to your home, which is still . . .' She read his address to him. Associates of KKDW relocated frequently. 'Liam and Jerry are hosting a private reception for our tables here first . . .'

The relief! Back to life, back to reality, back in the groove. Mickey was once more The Man. He felt himself life-size again, filling real space in the real world. The other place, the place where he killed time with George and slept until midday and was hassled by his wife about ashtrays and woke up in the night sweating like a pig, the place where he felt only as tall as a toy – that was just a bad dream.

CHAPTER 5

I'll Sleep When I'm Dead

How did the garden grow? In Gro-bags in lines all over the floor of what had once been a community arts centre somewhere off Kentish Town Road. The plants were tall enough to lean over George as he lay down in the aisle between them to get an idea of how they would look in a month or so. When he stood, the tallest ones were up to his knees.

Marijuana plants came barrelling up out of the compost, their rosettes of leaves piling on top of each other like fountains of foliage spouting out of the yellow plastic bags. Nothing else he knew of grew with so much sheer vegetable enthusiasm. They were almost as keen to grow as he would be to cut them down, dry them out, chop them up, mash them and sell them for £120 an ounce. Already the big room was getting that spicy, sappy smell of growing weed.

'Good work, Sheepshagger,' he said, folding his hands over the buckle of his belt. He was flat on his back again, looking at the ceiling through the starry leaves.

'They're storming ahead, aren't they? Little beauties.

Grow on for Mummy now.' She was moving around at the end of the room with the hose pipe. He could see her through the stems, flitting about the place like a parrot. She said she'd dyed her hair pink, but it looked red to him. Her head bobbed above each Gro-bag as she watered it. 'It's so bleedin' cold over here I never thought they'd go, but they have.'

'They don't mind a bit of a chill. Just as long as they don't actually get frosted. And they get plenty of light. They're pretty tough, they'll survive.'

'Too right they will. Doing better than me at the minute, I can tell you.'

'We'll get a couple of heaters. When it gets colder.'

'It gets colder than this?'

The thought came to George that she might be leading up to something. 'Are you suffering, Sheepshagger?'

'I could use that heater at home myself right now.'

'You want to get out more.'

'There's no bloody life over here, is there? What'm I supposed to do when I stop work? Back home I could go to the beach, or hang out in a bar by the water, or somebody might be having a bit of a party. Nothing happens here, does it? People just work and then they go home and sleep.'

'They work, then they go home and do drugs, then they sleep,' he corrected her. 'Thus keeping us garden gnomes, the primary producers, in business and making sure that we don't have to work, in the way they understand it, because our work is just giving them the stuff that keeps them from going mental doing their work.'

'So we should be glad they have rotten meaningless lives because it keeps us in business?'

'You catch my drift.'

'Yes, I got it. You mean people wouldn't buy the weed if they had better lives? Because they buy it back home and have good lives too. And what are we going to run these heaters on, anyway?' She was at the wall now, flicking the light switches on and off to show that there was no electricity.

'Oil or something. Paraffin. Gas. I don't know, whatever they've got.' The conversation had strayed. George resolved to round it up. Red hair or not, she was toothsome. She had those sloshy, freedom-loving breasts that women who liked growing things often had. She was earthy, the way those women usually were, and she had a comfortable kind of arse on her. She had a sort of glow and she was always smiling in a gentle, forgiving kind of way. All together, it was like having a large, soft, benevolent goddess wandering around making ancient green magic with her strong, dirty fingers. George remembered the sight of her backside in black leather, ahead of him in the traffic, bouncing briskly on her saddle, and even then he had thought of how briskly that same feature, peeled and pink, might bounce in a different setting.

Not a lot of goddesses came George's way, not many of them chose to hang around with him, and even fewer of those ever admitted that they needed protection from the climate. In short, he didn't get lucky much. Skinny, broke blokes with mouldy teeth were not at the top of any goddess's wish list. But it really, definitely, absolutely seemed his luck was changing now.

He prompted her. 'So you're finding it a little chilly, old London town?'

'Too right.'

'Come over here,' he suggested, raising an arm to dead vertical above his chest, 'and I'll see what I can do about that.'

'Oh,' she said, pretending she was surprised at the turn the conversation had taken. 'Oh, right. I'll be there in two. Better turn the tap off first, yeah?'

Any other time, he would have been pleased that she'd thought of it.

'So you and Pascal,' Laura began. 'How long have you been together?' They were getting as cosy as a couple can in a high-tech kitchen with metal mesh chairs. The moment had been coming for weeks.

'Popping in for a drink,' Charles had said. 'Isn't that what people do in the suburbs?'

First of all, Charles had started popping into Laura's kitchen, which was awkward because it was now Andy's kitchen and Andy was there a lot, flicking tea towels and pouring their drinks, and Daisy would want to wash boots at the sink and Lily, who took care never to meet or see or come within ten metres of Charles, still emitted toxic gusts of disapproval from behind her Bible upstairs. The Church of Christ in Glory in Helford issued an edition of the Bible published by the International League of Charismatic Churches, a fat book bound in fake red leather with gilded gothic lettering. It wasn't the faith that Laura minded, just the goddamn awful design.

Laura and Charles wanted their privacy. They wanted to bond. They wanted to move from gossip to opinions and from opinions to disclosure, and from there to personal scandal, misplaced trust, saying too much and giving themselves away. Psychologically speaking, each would bare their neck to the other and invite character assassination. Laura especially wanted this. She suddenly found her life an emotional desert in which Charles was an oasis of intimacy. Or maybe he was only a mirage, but what the hell, it'd be fun finding out.

Laura started popping into Charles's kitchen, which was easier because Pascal only rarely manifested himself in it, mournfully drifting to the fridge and surveying it for vodka. The popping-in happened daily. Both lovers of routine, they started to make a habit of each other.

Charles poured the wine and set out olives, oil and bread before her.

'How long have we been together? God, I don't know. Too long.' He coughed out a laugh and took the first sip.

'You must remember when you met.'

'Why must I?'

'It's important, isn't it?'

'I think we just knew each other around.' He waved with the hand that was not holding the glass, as if dispersing a fog of treacherous memories.

'You know perfectly well, you just don't want to talk about it,' she diagnosed. He was sitting on his stool with entwined legs and crossed arms. Such thin limbs; his kneecaps looked sharp enough to cut through his spotless black trousers.

'It's such a freaking mess,' he allowed at last.

'That bad, huh?'

'Even worse, if you want the truth. Here.' He suddenly leaned forward and brushed his glossy dark hair off his forehead. With his index finger he pointed to the hairline, where a red scar snaked along the edge of the follicles. 'He did that with a glass in a bar. Actually, in Quaglino's. We were just having a conversation and I said something he didn't take right so he stuck a glass in my head.'

'God.'

'They threw us out.'

'Well, they would. They really are suburban, Conran restaurants.'

'He's much better than he used to be, actually. I know it's hard to believe.'

'Has he ever seen anybody?'

'Dozens of people. That's his game – get everyone running around after Pascal, trying to work out why he's such a fucked-up mess. He's seen counsellors and mentors and pro-bation officers and social workers and if it's 3 a.m. and nobody's taking any notice of him just for twenty seconds he'll phone up The Samaritans. Not a word of a lie. I woke up one night and he was on the phone to The Samaritans.'

'Saying he wanted to commit suicide?'

'No. Coming on to the guy at the other end, fixing up to meet him at some club somewhere after he got off his shift.'

'I don't believe it.'

'Oh yes. He runs me around, he cats about all over town, he takes off and doesn't come home for days . . .'

'You look like such a devoted couple.'

'Oh, but we are. Devoted to Pascal, both of us.'

'Sling him out, why don't you?'

Charles swirled the wine in his glass. The thought had occurred to him. He probably gave real consideration to throwing Pascal out at least once a week. It was one of those questions that always got the wrong answer. 'He would probably kill himself.'

'Well, that'd be a solution.'

'Whoa! Tough lady.' Charles swirled his wine again, drank it and refilled their glasses. 'Would you say that about Andy?'

'Andy wouldn't make my life hell. Not the way Pascal does yours.'

'I can't imagine Andy making anyone's life hell, anyway.'

'You'd be surprised.'

'Would I?' He waited, but Laura wasn't ready to put her cards on the table yet. There were some rituals of new friendship still to be performed. 'We've been together so long, Pascal and I. He'll always be part of my life, I know that.'

'But not the best part, surely.'

'You won't believe this, but we do have our good times.'

'I'm sure you do.'

'He's much older than me in some ways. I wasn't really sorted about my sexuality when I met him. He sort of helped me decide. Don't give me that old-fashioned look.'

'I wasn't giving you an old-fashioned look. I wouldn't know how to give an old-fashioned look. My looks are totally hot, totally now, totally what's happening.'

'OK, OK. Sorry. Sor-ry.'

'Just thought I'd better make that clear.'

'Right. Got it. Don't give me that totally hot look, then.'

'Hey listen, you were the one thinking about rethinking your sexuality.'

'I was NOT thinking about rethinking anything. Honestly. Women.'

Laura tossed her head to show offence at the mere notion

110

that she could be the sort of sad bitch who regarded every gay man as a sexual challenge. 'But don't you ever?'

'What's the point? It's done now. I went walking in the wood and took the road less travelled. This is my life. Can't find the way back, no exit, keep right on to the end.'

'Would you like a way out?'

'Yeah, sometimes. When I look at you and Andy and your girls, I do think sometimes – things might have been different.'

'No, you don't.'

'You're right, I don't.'

The truth was pressing like a tumour. She had to take it out before it killed her. The words were there, waiting to be spoken. All she needed was the courage to speak. Not yet. 'You could have ended up with Lily,' she told him. 'It's OK, she may be mine but I do know she's a monster.'

'Won't she grow out of it?'

'Only into something just as bad. She's only the symptom, you know. You don't want a family like ours. Something's not right.'

'You're right, something's not right. What's not right with you and Andy, then? Oh, I missed that. You mean he makes your life hell in a different way? Or are you thinking about rethinking yourself?'

Now or never. Time to get real. Time to open up the barrier between her two lives. 'No, I'm sort of taking the Pascal route.'

'Laura, you couldn't. I promise you, you are not a drama queen.'

'No, and I don't sit up all night phoning The Samaritans, and I don't get pissed and fall into the houseplants either.'

'So what are you saying you do? Cat around?'

'You could say that.'

'Laura! You mean you're having an affair?'

'No. I just have meaningless sex with people I don't know.'

He assumed she was joking, then looked at her face. No smile, just appealing eyes. Share this with me, it's getting too heavy. 'What people?'

'Don't sound so shocked. Don't tell me you and Pascal never have sex with anyone else.'

'We only have sex with anyone else. That's the deal. Come on, what people?'

'People like me – people who're happily married but find that isn't enough.'

'Laura, I can't believe what you're telling me here.'

'I can't believe it myself half the time.'

'But why?'

'I couldn't work it out. All I knew was my libido just shot through the roof, but I didn't always want Andy. I wanted someone I could really let go with, you know. Definitely not my husband.'

'When did it start?'

'After he lost his job in advertising. I couldn't stand seeing him enjoying being around the house all the time, making the girls' breakfast and stuff.'

'That was your job.'

'I hated doing it. I was happy for him to do it, but I just didn't fancy him when he did it.'

'You women.'

'You men. The deal was, he went out to work. The house was my business. Now it's the other way around. I wouldn't want it to go back to the way it was; I love my job and I really love my salary. But our marriage just wasn't the same. I had all this anger I couldn't get rid of. It must have showed, because this guy at work made a pass at me.'

'And you fell?'

'No. I didn't do it, not with him. Much too dangerous. But it put me in touch with what was going to fix things. Then I saw this ad in the paper.'

'Miss Lonelyhearts.'

'Mrs Lonelyhearts. Married people only. The first two guys I met were creepy, the third was cute. I'm on the fifth now.'

'And Andy doesn't suspect?'

'I don't think so. He'd be gutted if he found out. He does love me, you know. I know it's a risk, but it kind of equalises things. It sounds bizarre, but it's the best thing for both of us. Like this, our life works.'

'I suppose there's no harm. If he doesn't find out.'

'I'm careful. But you have to tell one person, don't you? If you have a secret.'

'Well. Thanks for choosing me.'

'I thought you'd understand.'

'I won't ask why.'

That was it. Mission accomplished, job done, bond forged, trust in place, intimacy up and running, truth spoken, tumour removed. And the bottle was empty.

'Shall we do another one?' Charles suggested, leaning towards the fridge. They had a double-sided stainless steel American fridge that hummed at the end of the kitchen like an alien spacecraft preparing to take off. 'Are they expecting you at home?'

'Oh, Andy will take care of them,' she said carelessly. 'Go on. I want to hear more about you and Pascal. How come you don't do it? We thought you'd be shagging like crazed weasels. Did you ever?'

'Oh yes. But it was too exhausting, really. Not the shagging, the fighting and arguing before. Life's more manageable this way.'

Seeing his wife in her jewellery made Mickey nostalgic. Going way back to when they had all been foundation students at art school, special occasions had brought out Mo's sparklers – a complete collection of vintage diamanté items, from the four-inch chandelier earrings to the 1927 Cartier cocktail watch whose face was so small none of them had ever been able to read the time from it, even before the lazy lenses of mid-life made it difficult to focus.

The sparklers went with black lace and the black lace had evolved from skinny stretch in the disco days to designer now. This year's model was a seams-out patchwork job featuring red chiffon inserts and it clung wonderfully to the forever legs. Whatever his wife wore did that. As he watched her walk ahead of him to the car, Mickey noted that the legs looked as unchanged as the sparklers, and just as classy.

'You still scrub up OK,' he told her, and all she said was, 'Yeah, I do, don't I?' but she seemed pleased. For a change.

'How many times is this?' she asked in the car.

'God, I don't know.' I am not going to sweat, he told himself. No sweat, no sweat, no sweat. Pores closed, thermostat working, no over-heating. Actually, he hadn't sweated for weeks. Or gone back to the doctor for those test results. No need. Must've been a bug.

'When did you win the first one?'

'The first one was Delux Paints.'

'Was that the Seventies?'

'Eighties, wasn't it?' He couldn't have been in the business nearly thirty years. Well, he could. But not visibly. If people really realised he'd been in the business almost thirty years – well, they didn't realise. Thank God. Thank God it was a fast-moving industry and the average worker had the memory of a goldfish, and that much impaired by the use of alcohol and charlie. Surely nobody really realised Mickey Ryder had been in the business that long.

The DADs were scarcely the Oscars, but the organisers did their best. The dinner was at the Savoy, as good a place as any to eat the rubber chicken. A couple of photographers from the trade press and the agency itself dutifully flashed every couple as they disembarked from their cars at the River Room Entrance. The ballroom, forever duck-egg blue encrusted with gilding, was packed with tables around which people moved without enthusiasm, checking their dinner partners.

The KKDW table was centre front of the ballroom, just the place where it always looked as if the chief among the painted cherubs on the ceiling was ready to drop a major turd on somebody's head. Slowly the chosen posse of people migrated to their places.

Jerry Wallace had come over from California. Like Colonel Sanders or somebody, he was now completely white-haired. He wore a midnight-blue velvet tux and he sat down first, letting his new blonde wife pull out her own chair. Dave Kaplan joined them, his rubbery lips now almost purple and framed in deep, deep nose-to-mouth wrinkles, escorting Marjorie Kelly from the Cape Town office.

Ben Krieger was missing, at home recovering from chemotherapy for his lung cancer. Last of the letters to arrive was Liam Donohue, who heaved into view displaying the red braces that seemed to be holding up his stomach. There was a new wife bobbing along behind him too. A nearby pillar, faced in gilt-crusted mirrors, let Mickey check them all as they settled in for the night. Did he look as old as they did?

Whenever it was, the first time, the agency had been just Kaplan and Krieger, and all three of them had been lean and mean. He'd been the fairest; now, because his hair wasn't greying, he was the darkest. And the leanest. Kaplan was the richest, Krieger spent his money on art, Donohue was a couple of wives down, so was Wallace. And he was still The Man, and in black leather.

'Still with the same wife, Mickey?' Donohue lowered himself into his chair next to Mo and patted her hand.

'Only the best is good enough,' Mickey replied. Nobody was likely to ask what he meant. He couldn't have answered the question. More than twenty years of backchatting the suits, you learned a few tricks.

'What are we up for?' growled Wallace.

'Hofburg,' supplied the account director. At this table for twelve, he was the youngest by a good fifteen years. Why is it all about age tonight? Handsome lad, clean-looking, dark hair, bringing along a feisty girl with a nose ring. No trouble to work with – whatever ideas he had he kept to himself, let people get on with it.

'Have I seen that?'

'We screened it in-house last year.'

'Remind me.'

'Snowboarding.' He wasn't getting through. 'In the Himalayas. Very blue sky.'

'Breakthrough commercial?'

'Uh . . . Mickey was our director.'

'Another breakthrough for Mickey, huh? You know what I've always liked about your work? You flatter the viewers. You're ambitious, you push the envelope, you move the game on. Anybody watching one of your works would always feel good about themselves, you know?'

'I don't think about it,' said Mickey. It was a lie. 'I just think about enjoying myself, having a good time with it.'

'Another breakthrough for Mickey,' Wallace said again and nodded, issuing a premature benediction. They all nodded around the table. Mo unfurled her charming smile in his direction. Mickey's chair was hard. And it was hard to act like he hadn't been hearing this for – well, too long.

The short list was Hofburg, Nike, Fritzies cat food, Ikea and an insurance group. The menu was non-specific mousse, rubber chicken, something chocolate. They still did those little fried potato balls with chopped almonds; delicious. Things seemed to stick in Mickey's teeth more these days, nuts especially. Better not let the camera catch him with a toothpick. They didn't do toothpicks at the Savoy. Better not let Wallace hear him ask the waiter for one.

Mo's hand alighted next to his wine glass, then slipped away, leaving just the item he desired, one of those quill picks in a paper sleeve that she brought back in boxes from France. Did she think he needed to pick his teeth? Did he look like some gummy old dude who was wanting in the oral hygiene department? He let the toothpick lie.

The host had the envelope half-open in his hand and was

reading the citation: '. . . a beautifully observed script, a fresh, eye-grabbing style, an ad which shows you all the raw excitement of being alive. The panel applaud this work for its courage, its ambition, its inspiring take on an eternal theme. We have the greatest pleasure in giving The Director's Award this year to Draco Dracovich for his brilliant work on Fritzies Morsels!'

'Great ad,' intoned Dave Kaplan magnanimously, clapping his hands as slowly as a performing sea lion.

'Have I seen it?' asked Jerry Wallace. He should have frowned in perplexity, but the botox had finally taken and his brow remained serene.

'It's clever, but nine out of ten of the consumers won't be impressed,' joked Liam Donohue, and Mo added a peal of laughter.

'It's shite,' said the account director, looking straight at Mickey. 'Dracovich is just fashionable.'

If there was one thing in the world Mickey hated worse than losing, it was being pitied for it. 'It was good work,' he announced, getting to his feet. 'Draco's a bright boy. He deserves to win.'

At the edge of the room Dracovich was bounding towards the podium steps, a tall, thin man in a pea-green zoot suit which made him look like a jumping cucumber. He came from the table filled by a small new outfit called Bates & Bates, far back in the rear corner of the room.

Time to table-hop. Get over there and congratulate the boy, let the whole room see you do it, grab all the reflected glory that was going. Mickey'd met one of the Bates lads a few years back anyway.

'Great work,' he told the room in general as he started

weaving between tables in the direction of Bates & Bates. 'Great concept. Great script, really great. Wish I'd made it myself, really.'

A chair was in the way. 'Steady,' said a voice to one side. Was it speaking to him? Distracted, he almost walked into a waiter.

Dracovich was up there giving thanks now and the Bates table was on its feet, applauding him. That was the Bates table. Wasn't it?

Another waiter caught him by the elbow and said, 'All right, sir?'

There were parts of the room he could not quite see. It was like being in *Last Year At Marienbad*, walking down black and white corridors that just went on and on. All around him the details were blurry and the distances wrong. The Bates table was ahead of him, he could see it distinctly now, with the figures of the Bates boys hugging each other round the shoulders and the long green shape of Dracovich approaching them, but all around him was a lot of white dazzle.

'Excuse me, excuse me,' he muttered protectively, gripping the backs of chairs as he passed. He could feel the way forward even if he couldn't see it. Christ, this was like going blind! Fucking hell, going blind!

Thank God, Dracovich was close now. The way to him was clear – ten feet around the back of the room, miss out the floral decoration on a plastic pillar, grab the kid around the neck, tell him he done good. The photographer was lurking so Mickey turned around and gave him all the teeth, grinning like a post box and shaking Draco's hand for the record. We are the champions. Last year me, this year him, next year – who knows? Friendly rivalry, healthy competition, spurring each other on. So much talent, such a bad suit. But seriously. You couldn't argue with quality.

For some reason Mo had taken it into her head to follow him, so there they both were at the Bates & Bates table, and a lot of introducing went around, and the room was breaking up now, and there were chairs, so they sat down and had a few laughs with the Bates boys until, thank God, the white dazzle calmed down and the middle-distance came back looking as if it had never been away. He was left with the terror that someone had seen him fuck up.

That was when he noticed the hissing. Around him somewhere, in the general murmur of chat, a sizzling note in the general buzz. And after a while Draco leaned over and said to him, 'I hear you been bussing in Russians, Mickey.'

'Yeah,' he agreed, puzzled. 'That's right. A thousand Russians. Brilliant, they were.' There was some laughter.

'How'd the client find out?' enquired one of the Bates lads.

'Dunno,' Mickey smiled at him. 'Never heard nothing about that.' More laughter. Something wasn't right but he couldn't figure out what it was. Soon the room thinned and they could leave without shame.

From the car window Mickey watched the lights of London twinkling past. He rolled his eyes around their sockets, checking his vision. No more dazzle but he wasn't going to forget that in a hurry. What the hell was coming down? Was it stress? George's home-grown? Was it something to do with the sweating? Nobody in his family had gone blind. What the fuck was happening to him?

*

Sam drew a mighty breath and informed Alice in the drawing room: 'I need some time to myself.'

'Of course,' she agreed with him. 'I can work late at the shop if you like. There's plenty to keep me busy at La Maison.' She was sitting on the sofa with a box of stuff, the sort of stuff that came from that shop, bits of curtain material or some such rubbish. Lately this kind of thing had been spreading from her desk in the hall to every room they had. She obviously couldn't control her business at all. It was invading the house like a fungal growth, colonising windowsills and table tops and spare chairs so that there was nowhere free of it.

Elizabeth's flat was not like that. Elizabeth's flat had crystal bowls of pot pourri and scented candles in silver-topped glasses and pink-striped wallpaper and an onyx sphinx on a little table with a skirt.

'Not here,' he specified irritably. 'Somewhere else.'

'That's no problem,' she assured him. She was so helpful, so eager to please, so pathetically, goddamn stupid it made you want to kick her. A woman who compromised a man's civilisation like that, she deserved everything that was coming to her. 'I'm happy to see you whenever you get back, you know that. I won't wait up or anything, so you can feel free to come in whenever you like. You know I won't be sitting up worrying.'

'You don't get it,' he told her, inhaling mightily again to give his words the force they obviously needed to get through her thick skull. 'I need to be somewhere else. I need to get out of here.'

'But can we get out of here? You always said Westwick was such a good investment . . .'

121

'Not us. Me. Just me. I need to be on my own, by myself, somewhere else. I need to move out. I'm leaving. Now do you get it?'

'You're leaving, Sam?'

'Bingo. The eagle has landed.'

'What do you mean, you're leaving?' Now she was struggling out from under all the stuff and twitching to get up on her feet. Elizabeth never did that. She collected her little elegant legs inside their spotless little skirt and rose out of a sofa with no effort at all. A woman could do that if she took care of herself.

'What do people usually mean? I'm taking my stuff and getting out.' Maddening to have to go through this. It had to be done though. He had a business to protect.

Alice's eyes were starting to bulge and her mouth was opening and closing. Her hands were flapping. She looked like a landed fish. 'Sam, you can't just leave.'

'Yes, I can,' he responded triumphantly, as if he'd just proved a vital point in an argument.

'But where will you go?'

'I've got a place. I'll ring you. You'll be all right.'

'What do you mean, you'll ring me? Where are you going?'

'You don't need to know that sort of thing. I've said I'll ring you.'

'Sam! Of course I need to know where you are.' Now she was starting to twitch. It made her look really ugly, especially since she'd got so many lines. Elizabeth took care of herself. She wore pearls and silk scarves. It made such a difference.

'Nobody at the office is to know. Especially not Pats, I

don't want her gossiping. None of the family either. I don't want people getting involved.'

'But Sam, what about the children?'

'They're hardly children and I've spoken to them already.'

'You've spoken to them already?'

'Do stop repeating everything I say, Alice. The kids are fine, I've spoken to them.' He turned and made for the door. She ran after him.

'Sam! You have to wait! This isn't what I expected. Can't we talk about things?'

'Stop following me around, Alice. There's no point in all this, I need to leave now. I've stayed with you long enough.'

She obeyed him and remained at the bottom of the stairs while he stomped upwards towards his suitcases and freedom. 'But what's brought this on, Sam?' she called after him. Amazing she could sound strident and plaintive at the same time. 'Have you met someone else?'

'No, I have not met someone else,' he bellowed from the landing. 'For Christ's sake, leave me alone. I've got to get packed and out of here.'

Alice went back to the sofa, but sorting the swatches once more seemed the wrong thing to do. Her chest felt tight, her eyes were burning and there seemed to be a rubber band cutting into her throat. She went into the hand-built farmhouse kitchen and turned on the gas. A carton of soup, clam chowder with sweetcorn, extra cream and chives on top, Sam's favourite, was ready in the fridge.

After a while he carried his cases downstairs and out to the car one by one, then returned to find two places laid on the Provençal tablecloth at the table in the kitchen. Alice stood ready with the steaming saucepan.

'I thought you'd like some soup before you went,' she said, amazed that her voice was working when her throat felt choked.

Sam saw that her eyes were still huge. His objective was to get out before the stupid fool started crying.

'That won't be necessary,' he told her coldly, reaching for his wallet. 'Here.' He held out two £50 notes.

She flinched away from the money. 'What are those for?'

'I thought you might need them.'

'I don't need money, Sam. I need you to be sensible. You could at least tell me where you're going and what this is about.'

'You can't be trusted with that sort of information,' he informed her.

It is reckless to insult a woman when she is holding a saucepan of hot soup in her hands. Scalding clam chowder slapped Sam across the face. A split-second later, the saucepan itself missed him by eighteen inches, hit the floor at his feet and splattered more soup on his shoes and trouser legs.

'You've gone mad,' he announced, making a rapid damage report. His face was burning. Chunks of fish and potato were plopping off his belly. Sweetcorn kernels covered in cream were working their way inside his shirt collar. Elizabeth admired his immaculate shirts. She liked men in faultless tailoring and polished shoes. He would have to change. He needed cold water on his face, fast. His clothes were all in the car.

'Get out of my way,' he advised Alice, 'and don't try any more stupid tricks.'

Obediently, she stepped aside and watched him trail

white smears of chowder along the carpet in the corridor to the downstairs shower room. Here he climbed out of his clothes and left them in an appetisingly smelly heap on the floor. Swathing his body in an old bathrobe, he scuttled out to his car in the dank November air and unpacked a clean suit and shirt. After that, he came in again, locked himself in the shower room and set about washing his hair.

Alice stood in the kitchen and looked at the upturned saucepan in its puddle of soup. After a while she turned and picked the phone off the wall behind her. Melanie and Jon were the second and third numbers on the speed dial. Both were out. 'It's Mummy, will you call me back, darling?' She left messages, wondering why her voice sounded so normal, wondering if she really was a mother and really had grown-up children because she felt about five years old.

Eventually she saw Sam emerge from the shower room, clean and clothed. His face, where the soup had splashed it, was fire-engine red. Elizabeth would not be pleased. 'Goodbye.' He faced her to say the word, then swivelled on his heels, performed one of his pompous turns and made for the front door.

Alice watched the door close behind him as if she had never seen it shut before. How finally it fitted into its frame, how emphatically the lock clicked, how hopelessly smooth and solid it was, shut on Sam, on trust, on security, on a life shared, on companionship, on couplehood, on being a family, on being a wife. Or as good as a wife. Just as good as a wife. Better than a wife. No pieces of paper. If her heart could have flown out of her chest and shattered into a thousand pieces on the floor, it would have done it then.

She went to pick up the saucepan and found herself on her knees in the soup.

The phone rang. It was Sam. Had he forgotten something? Was he changing his mind? Carefully, thinking of the slimy floor, she got to her feet and answered it with a sticky hand.

'Yes?'

'Alice?' Mo's voice.

'Oh.'

'Sorry, were you expecting your secret lover?'

'Don't be silly.'

'What's up, Alice? You sound – I don't know. Are you OK?'

'Why shouldn't I be OK?'

'Because you don't sound OK.'

'Well, I'm in the soup.'

'In the soup?'

'It's clam chowder. I made it for Sam. Then it got on the floor and I fell in it.' A sob started swelling in her tight throat.

'Alice, you're not OK. What's happening?'

'Sam just left. Left as in left. You know.'

'Walked out and left?'

The sob was big enough to burst but through it she managed to confirm, 'That's the one.'

'Was it the soup?'

'I don't know. I don't think so. The soup held him up, really.'

'Because he ate it?'

'Because I threw it at him.'

'Well, that's good. Throwing soup at the shitbag is good,

Alice. I'm proud of you. Soup-slingers of the world unite. You have nothing to lose but your croutons.'

'But then it was on the floor and I fell in it. Maybe the floor was slippy.'

'I think I should come over.'

'That would be nice.' Suddenly the sob exploded and yelping took over. Tears were running through the soup smears on her cheeks and spots of diluted chowder appeared on her sweater.

'Hang up the phone, Alice. I'll be there in five.'

It was Sam's night to be a target for unusual missiles. When he laboured out of the lift at Elizabeth's flat, dragging his suitcases one by one, her door crashed open and she appeared in a state of rage and a satin dressing gown. His presence, his embrace, his attempted kisses and the grimy yellow roses for which he had stopped at a petrol station – none of these could pacify her. She slapped his face several times and threw an onyx obelisk engraved with hieroglyphs at him. It hit him on the forehead. Since the flat was exquisitely appointed with a pair of matching Louis-whatever-style gilt-legged sofas that were too narrow to sleep on, he passed the night on the fake Aubusson rug, stitched in a sweatshop in Taiwan and bought from Peter Jones.

Elizabeth, he had noticed, treated that venerable upper-crust department store as a good Muslim might treat a mosque, and performed devotions there several times a day. Her apartment was just a couple of blocks away. Superb duplex penthouse apartment with two roof terraces, convenient for Knightsbridge, Westminster and Belgravia. Sam felt his forehead for the bruise left by the obelisk and closed his eyes in the belief that he would rather have slept on the floor in that nirvana than shared a bed with Alice in any desirable suburb in the world.

It was Friday, and if it was Friday it was aesthetics. This Friday, the Friday before the first Sunday in Advent, Rhys had his travelling bag in his car in the hospital car park and a ferry ticket for Boulogne in his coat pocket. He was on the last sailing, leaving at 7.30 p.m., which meant being on the M25 by 5 p.m., which meant being out of the hospital by 4 p.m., which meant that the last operation for which he was rostered was at three.

Watson was the patient's name. Ms S. F. Watson; the name was on her plastic ID bracelet. Nothing there that could have told him this one was going to be trouble. She arrived before him drowsy from her pre-med. 'Just a small pin-prick,' he warned her as he put a needle into her arm. 'And the next thing you know you'll be waking up with a nice flat tummy.'

'Can't wait, love,' she whispered and gave him a wavy thumbs-up.

Ms S. F. Watson was the Slenderworld South of England Slimmer of the Year. She had lost nine stone, or a hundred and twenty-six pounds, or fifty-seven kilos, however you chose to measure it, over eighteen months and appeared on the cover of *Slenderworld* magazine in hot pants and a crop top, beside her 'before' picture with arms like legs of lamb sticking out of a flower-printed viscose marquee. Her family, half of whom still lived in her native Jamaica, had given her the money for this operation to remove the balloon of belly skin which had once covered most of those fifty-seven kilos.

It was the easiest of all aesthetic procedures. Snip, stitch,

Bob's your uncle. Sagging spinnaker of epidermis replaced by taut new tummy with a hairline scar cunningly concealed in the natural crease below the navel. Fifteen minutes, tops. He prepared enough anaesthetic for half an hour.

Ms Watson sank readily into oblivion. Rhys sank readily into planning the Big Conversation he planned to have with Mo.

Conversations seldom went the way Rhys intended them to go, which is why he avoided starting them. He admired the method of communication that Toby had been getting into lately – the telling statement issued in circumstances which made a comeback impossible.

Toby had issued a number of statements about his mother in the past few weeks, and Rhys had picked them up and decrypted them with growing confidence. Toby was saying that he knew Barbara was a problem and, should his parents separate, he'd be fine. As a result, Rhys had been redesigning his family's future.

A nurse removed the theatre gown and Ms Watson's belly was revealed, wrinkled and deflated. The stretch marks showed white against the brown skin, a swathe of pale lines around the sides of the abdomen. An optimistic red line drawn with a marker showed where the procedure was to be performed.

Rhys ran his eye over the dials and settings on the monitors, alarms and recorders. All OK. Back to the future. It was time to talk to Mo, find out what she wanted. A future together, that was what she wanted. Women weren't like men, thank God. They didn't get involved without their feelings being part of the package.

Operating today was Mr Sydney Debrosser, FRCS Rand,

who was young, energetic and keen on cricket. The radio in the theatre was tuned to the highlights of the day's play in a one-day series in the West Indies. As Ms Watson was wheeled in, a new test match umpire, a young newcomer from Grenada, gave a player out in a disputed decision. The crowd roared with rage. Debrosser listened indignantly, his gloved hands on his gowned hips.

'What d'you think of that? Wall-eyed platypus!'

Rhys mumbled soothing words. The nurses unfolded the green theatre sheets.

'What the hell does he think he's doing?'

'Bit out of line?' Rhys suggested with reluctance. Cricket was not his passion. His passion was probably unlocking their door in Montreuil-sur-Mer at that moment. Should he say something like, 'Let's talk about us?' No, that was desperately Knopfler. He could imagine her nose wrinkling, just the way it did at any mention of a concept like 'us'. And yet there was an 'us'.

Debrosser was deaf to his preoccupation. 'I'll say it's out of line,' he said, grasping scalpel and forceps. 'You sit on your arse out in the West Indies all year picking your nose, then start telling the professionals what they ought to be doing. People are going to think you're a bit of a dong, stands to reason.'

'Yeah,' Rhys assented. Ms Watson's eyelids seemed to have flown up. Her face had a wild, doll-like stare. A nurse reached out to close the lids but after a few seconds they slowly raised themselves again. It happened sometimes, a natural reflex. No harm in upping the dose a little. Rhys adjusted the drip feeding anaesthetic into Ms Watson's arm.

'Ignorant,' Mr Debrosser continued, picking up the flap of

surplus with his forceps and making the first snip. 'Fat-arsed, ignorant little toerag, eh?' Snip, staple, snip, staple. 'Where do they get off with that attitude?' Snip, snip, staple, staple. 'Only been in the game a monkey's fart and thinks he speaks to God.' Snip, snip, staple, staple, all done. 'Just wants to be shaking his arse about all over the newspapers.'

Rhys decided to postpone conversation planning, wind up Debrosser's tirade and get out of the theatre and on to the road as fast as he could. 'It's not going to make a lot of difference either way, is it? The series is nearly over, the tourists have won whatever.'

'No thanks to our West Indian witch doctor,' Mr Debrosser said, letting the sutured skin drop back into line. Ms Watson's belly, though still streaked with stretch marks, now lay smooth between her iliac crests. He threw his instruments at a bowl. A nurse picked them up off the floor. It was only 3.22 p.m. From Rhys's viewpoint, a normal Friday afternoon. And plenty of time to catch the ferry.

'We could really fit this place up,' George mused. Not for nothing was the plant called The Weed. The former office was now a thicket of luscious skunk trees. They were flowering already. The plants were so high he could no longer see Sheepshagger as she went about her watering duties, only track her by the hissing water and rustling leaves. They owned two greenhouse heaters that ran on paraffin now. The garden air was warm and humid; the smell of paraffin mixed with the smell of the weed.

'We could plough back our profits,' he continued grandly, dragging on his sample spliff. 'We could have an automatic watering system with pipes from the bathroom, a cooling system with fans on time switches for the summer and a heating system on a thermostat for the winter, and a ventilation system with ducts an' that all over the ceiling. The big boys even have a carbon dioxide feeder system giving the monsters a little of what they fancy. Well, a lot of what they fancy, to be precise.'

There was a silence from the other end of the forest. Fluffy as his perceptions were getting under the influence of their promising crop, the silence was not lost on George.

Here we go again. Back in the old routine. A woman showed up, you had a few laughs, a few shags, things were looking good and then she turned all moody. Nobody had a row, nobody misbehaved themselves, nobody got drunk and unmentionable, nothing happened that you could point to, but suddenly the silences would start, then the sighs, the 'I suppose so's, the 'if you like's, maybe even a 'whatever you say', or a 'you're the boss'. Straws in the wind at first.

She'd get difficult to amuse. There'd be no more toast in bed and talking about a holiday. Instead he'd get the cold shoulder on the mattress, the hours of miserableness in the pub. Going shopping would get political, she'd start minding about who paid and what for. All the little things, the putting his cheques through her bank account, paying back stuff on her credit card, all of it would suddenly be a great big drag.

George knew the form and at this point he would put Plan B into operation. Plan B would involve getting drunk and unmentionable, or disappearing off in the pub with some other tart, or just disappearing off. Plan B never failed. The purpose of Plan B was to get the party of the first tart to fuck off, returning George to the stable situation that had existed before.

Stable but lonely. Stable but alone. Singular. Isolated. By himself. On his ownsome. At the age of 47 he'd realised that he would never drive through Paris in a sports car with the warm wind in his hair. Or any of the rest of it. It had become painfully clear that the big, fat, juicy satisfactions of life, the things he vaguely imagined would happen to him one day, were in fact not going to come his way at all. This was not George's favourite phase of the cycle.

He had never thought he was going to be the pipe and slippers type. Or the leather jacket and Grand Cherokee type like Mickey, or the Algarve villa type like Sam, or the Georgian terrace type like Andy, or the kids at private school type like Rhys. He had thought there would be something more, somewhere, just around the corner, coming up soon. After operating Plan B, that vague something more appeared to be an illusion. Was it not possible, then, to be the Motoguzzi and mattress on the floor type, such as he was, and still have a good time?

Superior skunk such as that which was sprouting before him did strange things to a man. Some people got the munchies. Some people got stupid. Some people thought there were goblins playing music in their hair. Some people became unstoppable sex machines, some people wrote poetry, some people went to sleep. George got paranoid.

It came with the gift of perfect understanding. He got this complete and utter sense of oneness with the cosmic purpose, this blinding, all-embracing, totally unutterable sense of knowing what it was all about, and what it was all about was unfairness. It wasn't fair. In fact, it was so unfair that there was no point to it all and the best thing you could do was just waste it, all of it, the whole fucking lot. Rip it up, smash it up, tear it . . .

'Are we ready to go then?' Sheepshagger was standing in front of him with her coat on, smiling her forgiving smile.

'Huh?'

'All done. Time to go now.'

'Yessss,' he hissed between his teeth. 'Ready to go.'

'We'd better get going then,' she suggested, most reasonably. The thing about Aussies, he remembered, was that they were reasonable types on the whole. Maybe he had been doing her an injustice. He let her lead him out of the window and across the roofs, back to her place.

CHAPTER 6

I'd Die For You

Rhys never thought of it this way, but his problem began in 1108 when Baudoin the Lame, second viscount of Lower Picardy, granted to the citizens of Saucisson-le-Mauconfit the right to barter their personal belongings on their doorsteps on the first Sunday in Advent.

Baudoin was, obviously, lame and so could not gain Christian kudos by going on a crusade. Instead he decided to pave his way to Paradise by helping his serfs celebrate Christmas so lavishly that his generosity would have come to the attention of St Peter by the time he reached the gates of heaven.

Things were made worse in 1668 when the Count of Auge, an amiable, unmarried man who was a slave to the dictates of his dominating valet-de-chambre, granted in addition to all the valets and ladies' maids of Saucisson-le-Mauconfit the right to stand in the market square in the biting December winds and sell the cast-off clothes, bibelots and fol-de-rols of their employers.

This double dispensation meant that, by the time of the Revolution, the braderie at Saucisson-le-Mauconfit had become the most famous one-day flea market in France. The tradition of cooking apple fritters at the roadside to sustain the buyers and sellers just added to its reputation.

After the Revolution, the departmental Prefect spoiled the fun somewhat by issuing an edict prohibiting the un-citizenly custom of offering unwanted wives or husbands for sale alongside other cast-off household goods. After that only the second World War, during which the Germans half-demolished the market cross, checked the growth of the braderie.

The effect of these events, experienced by Rhys early in the twenty-first century, was to de-rail his plan for happiness. Almost a thousand years after the Christian superstitions of Baudoin the Lame created the fair, Rhys and Mo drove out of Montreuil at 5 a.m. and crossed the wind-scoured plateau of the Caux in La Maison's capacious Renault.

Nothing but a handful of tractors delayed them on the empty roads. Rhys drove, half-asleep. After an hour, he noticed a white van. Then another. Then a horse box. Then a trailer. A stampede of vehicles was bearing down towards Saucisson-le-Mauconfit from all directions.

The way into the village was choked with a line of pick-ups, Transits, trailers, people-carriers, mini-vans and full-size trucks. With alarm, Rhys noted that the outlying streets were lined with parked cars. In Saucisson itself, the municipal parking areas were crammed and gendarmes with fierce faces defended the cobbled pedestrian zones. He was despondently preparing to lose another half-hour finding a space when Mo's finger stabbed him in the biceps.

'Over there!' she ordered, pointing at a school playground where a woman in a fur-hooded parka was about to pull out. The back of her Citroën Xsara was full of purchases bundled in newspaper. 'Quick! The early birds are off already!'

The truth about Mo, as Rhys had to stop himself observing every time he accompanied her on a buying expedition, was that she was in this business mostly because she loved to shop. Buying something, anything, even a yellow plastic ashtray trademarked 'Ricard' in square black letters, always gave her pleasure.

Buying something beautiful made her happy for days. Buying something beautiful and cheap transported her into ecstasy. Rhys was too wise to make the comparison, but he could not avoid registering that she seemed far happier after a successful buying trip than she did after he made love to her. In fact, she always looked sad after sex. He put it down to their circumstances.

So Mo walked fast towards the market square, then faster, and faster still, her nostrils flared, her eyes bright, her narrow feet in their black boots eating up the pavement like the hooves of an eager racehorse cantering down to the start. He found himself getting out of breath at her side.

'Are we looking for anything in particular?' he panted.

'Chandeliers, dining chairs, wirework,' she instructed him, her eyes scanning the road ahead for the first stall. 'Anything pretty. Not a lot left by now. It's only a flea market, not a real brocante. And we're too late, really, for the good stuff.'

The first few streets suggested that she was right to be pessimistic. Tables loaded with outrageously ugly and useless items lined both sides of the roadway. Looking over the dusty souvenirs – chipped plates, garish figurines, old ice skates and plastic toys – her smile disappeared. The heavy-weight dealers were chatting behind their stalls, the major business of the day already behind them.

'Should have got here earlier,' she muttered. Rhys pulled his coat collar around his neck, feeling the Normandy wind stinging his ears. How long before he could suggest cutting into a café?

Finally they reached the main square. The crowd heaved around the gothic grey stone market cross and the smell of apple fritters warmed the air. 'Wow,' he said, astonished by the seething mass of buying and selling before them. 'Now I believe it's the biggest flea market in France.'

No answer. She was gone. She was on a mission. He whirled about, looking for her black fleece hat in the seething mass. Hoping to spot her, he jumped on a buttress of the market cross. Yes! He could see her dear dark shape in the gloom of a side-alley.

With a blast of his whistle and an enraged flourish of his forefinger, a gendarme ordered him down from his look-out. 'Excusez-moi, Monsieur. J'ai perdu ma femme,' he grovelled optimistically. Ma femme! It sounded so sweet. 'Ma femme, Mo.' The words just rang with joy, whereas 'Barbara, my wife,' dinned like a funeral bell. France, the land of never-never, where all your wishes came true.

She had stopped in front of an ancient gateway built for carts and now, from the lingering whiff of oil, leading to a garage. Rhys approached with caution, having learned ear-lier, from her looks like missiles loaded with contempt, not to spoil her buying strategy with inept enthusiasm. A non-committal, 'Ah, there you are,' was the safest opening move.

'Hello,' she responded, lost in thought over a frail wooden chair. Its legs and bars were carved to look like bamboo and the dusty rush seat was fraying underneath.

'That looks bloody uncomfortable.'

'You think so?'

'I know so. Get stuck on that at a dinner party, you'll want to leave before the coffee.' The alley, thank God, was out of the wind. It was really quite pleasant here.

She sighed.

'Might as well sit on a bed of nails,' he went on, delighted to have picked up her signals.

She frowned. Don't overdo it, sweetheart.

The seller, a rotund, confused-looking individual in a corduroy jacket, said he had others.

'Others?' she answered, businesslike, implying that the seller should forget this bozo. He was not dealing with some species of silly tourist, she was a serious client, a dealer, and so he'd better quit faffing and get out his best.

He bowed her through the gateway into a yard which was filled entirely by a horsebox, which in turn was crammed with legs, arms and seats of shabby wooden furniture. Eager to sell, but not eager to exert himself without hope of reward, he pulled a second faux-bamboo chair from the top of the pile.

Mo smiled brightly, encouraging him. He pulled out another chair, then a fourth.

She moved forward to inspect the goods. Rhys knew his role in the negotiation was over and helped the seller unload. Finally nine faux-bamboo dining chairs and two matching carvers stood on the uneven oily ground, looking self-conscious, like guests at a party waiting to be introduced.

Taking her time, Mo inspected for woodworm and rot. Rhys sat in a carver, which creaked under his weight. It was just as uncomfortable as he had predicted. He asked the owner if he kept horses and where he had come from, and the man delivered a long explanation of the journey up from his family home in the Suisse-Normande and how the terrible traffic had delayed him and so he had only just opened his doors when Mo appeared.

His story did not suggest a wealthy man, nor an experienced dealer. Mo preserved her poker face. She found a chair from which a few bars were missing and muttered, 'Beaucoup de travail.' The seller did not attempt to argue.

In a definite tone, Mo offered a thousand francs for the lot. The form was normally for the seller to protest vehemently at this point. Instead the man failed to disguise his expression of relief. He haggled half-heartedly; with a sniff, Mo suggested they call it 170 euros. He paused, trying to look calculating, then gave a grudging nod. They shook hands and started discussing the best method of getting the chairs to her car.

Since the market regulations prohibited traffic in the square, the choices were to wait until the close of business at sunset, say 4 p.m., or carry the stuff through the crowd. It was 8 a.m. The crowd seemed larger and noisier than ever.

The seller pointed out that the tourists would be arriving soon. Mo agreed. They promised to return at four with the Renault.

The day already being out of control, it determined to stay that way. He decided that Mo was on the verge of clinical hysteria. 'Faux-bamboo!' she yelled at him in the café. 'I can't believe it! Do you realise, Rhys, you just don't find stuff like that any more? Carvers and everything!' She gulped her coffee only when it was cold and ignored the apple fritter he bought her to go with it. The café was so crowded that getting their cups to their lips at all was a risky move.

'Are we going on?' he asked her, trying not to show despair.

'Are we ever!' she answered. 'Baby, I'm on a roll!'

She tore off into the crowd again. He knew this mood. The cool, focused, traditional Mo would disappear and a giddy, gabby doppelgänger would rush about in its place, shrieking over trifles and plunging into long gossips with perfect strangers. She swooped about the square like a parrot, finally roosting with a dealer in country slipware, with whom she passed a full hour learning to appreciate the blistered platters and pitchers once thrown for Normandy milk-maids. Weary from the cold, Rhys set his hopes on lunch. Intimate, quiet, *à deux.*

The restaurant occupied all four floors of a half-timbered town house settled drunkenly in a corner of the market square. It was aromatic and blessedly warm but a shout rang out before they had their coats off and Mo was hailed by a whole crew of fellow British dealers. With resignation, Rhys watched the waiters push tables together and transform his intimate dream into a raucous, bibulous, three-hour reality.

When he drove the laden Renault into their courtyard at Montreuil it was six on a cold and dark December evening. Now, he pledged, now they would have the conversation. A day of joy, success and companionship – surely she would agree that being together was bliss, that they had a duty to this magical synergy, that life should be like this always and now was the time to make the move?

By the time he had built the fire in the grate, she was asleep. He drank some brandy and watched her, asking himself what he could have done differently. Somehow life had always blind-sided him.

What grand ambitions he had set out with, and how weakly he had relinquished them. He had wanted to travel, to work in Africa, to dedicate his youth to mitigating the world's inequalities, and instead Barbara had appeared and demanded that he dedicate himself to her.

He had wanted to dismantle the apparatus of medical privilege, to join a co-operative practice in a deprived area. They had children. Barbara got ill. He found himself living in Westwick with the logic of family responsibilities and rising property values ordering his life. And now, as he felt the prison opening and he could move his limbs and stretch towards the tiny glimpse of freedom that remained, the old mojo was still working. He wasn't going to get what he wanted. He was never going to get what he wanted. The lineaments of satisfied desire were not for him in this world.

It happened faster and more finally than George had predicted.

They decided to harvest before Christmas to take advantage of the seasonal demand. On the appointed evening, he went over to her place, banged on the door and got no answer.

'Sheepshagger,' he yelled, thinking she must be asleep. Nothing. No sound, no movement. Just that especially eloquent nothing that you get when you bang on the door of an empty room.

Looking back, he should have sussed then. What annoyed

George most about the events of that week was the part that skunk-madness played in it all. Had he not been breaking the first rule of successful dope dealing, he might have been more aware. The first rule of successful dope dealing is: Never get high on your own supply.

There was another way into the jungle from her building. You could go up to the top of the stairs, disconnect the alarm, bust open the door to the fire escape and climb over the roofs that way. Ideally, your accomplice should reconnect the alarm after you. He'd send her back to do it when she showed up.

The lights were off. Normally they glowed through the blue plastic dust sheets they had taped over the windows. Maybe a fuse. Or they'd flipped the switch by accident yesterday. Not a problem; one day without the gro-lights wasn't going to spoil the crop at this stage. Still skunk-crazy at that point.

Inside the premises, he put on the lights. They illuminated nothing. Nothing worth having, anyway. Or, more vitally, nothing worth selling. That is, there were no plants. There were the Gro-bags, and the compost, and a few mangled yellow leaves here and there, and a lot of muddy footprints, and the hose still attached to the tap. There was a recent addition, the end of a roll of black plastic bin bags with yellow tics. But no plants.

The footprints led to the internal door, which was open. They led down the corridor to the external door of the whole suite, which they had never used because it was comprehensively locked. Now it was open. Calm, undamaged, not locked any more. Open.

For one skunk-insane moment George thought about

going to the office below and asking if anyone had seen a load of stuffed black bin liners coming down the stairs. Instead, he hit the door a few times, until his hand hurt. Then he kicked it until his toes hurt. Then he rattled downstairs and off to the pub over the road.

The next couple of hours became, for a short time, the most painful memory of his life. He spent almost all his cash on Scotch. With Sheepshagger around he had lost the habit of being careful with pennies, because she always seemed to have money. Sitting in the corner of a merry old pub full of righteous nine-to-five citizens getting in training for the office party season, he brooded on how she would take the tragic news.

With paints and brushes scattered around her, Mo sat crosslegged on the floor of the salon in her Montreuil apartment. The faux-bamboo chairs had been restored to within an inch of their lives. Each faux joint had been darkened and each faux stem mottled with tiny dots and embellished with faux knots. She had treated the frames for woodworm and glued the loose joints. For good luck, she'd stripped off the dusty rush seats: Westwick cherished an Armenian wicker-weaver who would renew them for her. Just another coat of varnish, mixed to the ideal aged walnut tone, and they would be ready. The job had taken two days. More details kept suggesting themselves. She didn't want to finish. Once she was finished, she would have to go home.

Thank God for solitude. Maybe she wasn't so different from her son after all. Joe had been a great retreater behind closed doors. After the weekend, she'd been longing to wave goodbye to Rhys and be alone in her own space. Here I am, a woman of forty-mumble, embarrassed with the riches of a husband and a lover, and all I really want is to be by myself. Sometimes.

No way out. She'd finished the second coat of varnish. A third would just look jammy. Time to wash the brushes and pack up ready to go home.

Every antiques dealer has a room like Mo's apartment. Everyone with that combination of an eye for beauty and a nose for a bargain has a place for the things they've acquired when the eye has overruled the nose. Things that are too damaged, things they've paid too much for, things that aren't fashionable any more.

She made a mournful tour of the room, picking up her beautiful losers. The Sèvres plate with the hairline crack, the Lalique vase with the chipped lip, the Daum lampshade with the broken base, the fine linen spotted with mildew. All those things she should never have bought in the first place but still couldn't find the heart to throw out.

She lived her life through things, buying in pain and selling in joy. Sometimes her things advised her. Now they showed her that Rhys belonged here, in this room of cherished rejects. She should never have got into the affair.

It was her fault. And the fault of the Venetian chandelier. Pretty little thing, with turquoise drops among the crystal. She'd liked it so much she'd had to show it off. Into the window it had gone, before she'd had time to get it rewired. Barbara had come straight in and bought it, then sent Rhys to collect it when it was ready.

Such a dear, chivalrous man. Handsome, if he hadn't always looked sad. Wonderful legs. He insisted on climbing the steps to get the thing down. She held the ladder, the least she could do. With one of those beautiful calves just a few centimetres from her nose, and her hormones raising hell in the Last Chance Saloon, she just had to reach out and stroke. Ten seconds to adultery, that was all it took.

Of course, the actual sin came a few days later, after the dropping-in and the stopping-by and the just-passing and the fancy-meeting-you-here. Hell, it was a neighbourhood. If you wanted to avoid all that you had to stay indoors 24/7. And Rhys hadn't wanted to avoid it at all. Nor had she. And Mickey had been on a shoot in Peru.

Fresh flesh after all those years. A posse of hormones had run out of the Last Chance Saloon and started shooting up the whole damn town, whoopin' and hollerin' and carryin' on.

So now it was over five years. He was still beautiful, her skin still tingled at his touch. They talked too much, and she knew more about him than she wanted. When Mickey mentioned Rhys in the band it was always in a certain tone, just a shade dismissive. She understood that. She and Mickey didn't need to talk, they knew they had the same thoughts. With Rhys, she had to translate. Do I love him? In a way. Like I love the cracked plate, which is more beautiful for being hopeless.

Westwick sent out invitations and prepared for Christmas. In a place where consumption was an art form, the season became a frenzy of acquisition every year as buyers and sellers set out to beat their previous best.

The wreaths went up on the front doors. Did we do all-white last year? Shall we do white and silver this year? All red? Red roses? Red apples? Twigs? Eucalyptus? Bows? Or pink? Charles and Pascal did galvanised wire and chilli peppers.

The windows of Parsley & Thyme were crammed with French truffles, Belgian chocolates, German love cakes, Italian panforte, Spanish nougat and an embankment of English Stilton cheeses.

At the same time, in the window of Bon Ton the lone mannequin was rigged up in sequins and chiffon. Catchpole and Forge, suppliers of organic free-range meat and game, opened their order books and filled them rapidly with requests for turkeys, geese, ducks, hams, pheasants, legs of pork, ribs of beef, sausages, bacon and ready-shelled chestnuts.

The Magno supermarket piled high its bumper Christmas packs of everything that could be sold for a few pence more with a lame holly leaf on the label. And at Pot Pourri, Marcia unpacked her orders of red tapering candles, tartan ribbon and aerosol snow and began to design table centres.

The scene was set for the ritual torture of each member of the suburban family. Festival rage was rife. Desperate mothers traded tips for making angel wings and shepherd's crooks. Hung-over fathers hassled through the traffic to carol concerts. Exhausted children fought over the toys they hadn't got yet and frantic nannies escaped to bars and swore that next year they'd get this career thing cracked.

Following established tradition, the parties began in Westwick when all the other parties, the office bashes, the dinner-and-dances and the corporate hospitality, had finally ceased. The Carmans claimed Hanukkah. Andy and Laura had the Sunday before Christmas, when Andy had the odd feeling that Laura was just another guest. Mickey and Mo, who always did Christmas Eve, decided to go to Morocco instead. Mickey made this decision because he'd seen enough of his own four walls that year to last him a lifetime. This year, Christmas Eve went to Charles and Pascal. Pascal wore a jacket and a martyred expression. Their caterer provided sashimi on slate platters and their guests protested too much that everyone ate too many mince pies anyway.

Rhys and Barbara, having an unhappy house, never entertained. And this year the dawning of December had brought home to Alice the complete horror of her new position.

She had mastered getting up and carrying on as normal. She only cried in the evenings. For a deserted wife, she was getting by pretty well. Then Christmas loomed. Christmas Alone.

'Sam won't tell me what he wants to do,' she wailed to Mo as they dressed the window at La Maison with antique glass wych balls on bright satin ribbons. 'We always did Twelfth Night. I don't even know if he's coming home for Christmas.'

Mo sat down on the windowsill with her back to the street and pointed at her partner with her scissors. 'Alice,' she said, 'you can't go on like this.'

'But what can I do? There is nothing I can do, is there?'

Mo put down the scissors and ticked off the alternatives on her fingers. 'See a lawyer. Change the locks. Get a new phone number. Shake things up, make some waves, find the bastard, for God's sake.'

Alice's poor heart began to tremble. 'What about the children? I just want to know what he wants to do about Christmas Day.'

'Stuff what he wants to do. What do you want to do? Go to Barbados or something?'

'We always had a party on Twelfth Night.'

'And if you want to have a party, go and buy the invitations, for Christ's sake. You don't need Sam to show your friends a good time. All he ever did was lurch around the room peering down everyone's cleavage anyway.'

'Did he really?' Alice, desperate to escape the need for action, clutched this straw of distraction. 'I never noticed that.'

'Believe me, Alice, you were the only one who missed it.' Mo, way ahead of her, refused to be diverted from her purpose. The human waste of the spectacle presented by Alice offended her deeply. Over the years she had seen her warm, kind, conscientious and open-hearted friend bullied into a heap of helplessness by Sam, who was now squaring up to deliver the coup de grâce.

'He's taken off, you don't know where he is, and he's desperate to keep up appearances so nobody asks questions. It doesn't stack up, Alice. You have to do something.'

'But he'll be so angry if I don't do what he says.'

'You'll probably be banged up for criminal conspiracy if you do do what he says.'

Alice's eyes seemed to grow to the size of her head. 'You don't really think so, do you?'

'Of course I think so.' Mo grabbed both her partner's hands in hers. 'Wake up, Alice, darling. This is not good. There's something coming down here.'

'But Mo, what can I do? I don't even know where he is.'

'He's with another woman, Alice, that's where he is.'

Alice gulped. 'Oh God, I suppose he must be.'

'What about when he phones? Do you do one-four-seven-one?'

'It's his mobile or the office. He's being really careful.'

'What about from your house? I bet he called her from there. Have you had your phone bill? Are there numbers on it you don't recognise?'

'Oh, Mo – you're so full of ideas.'

Alice surrendered. Mo shut the shop just as it was, with the window half-dressed, and, hell-bent to scandal, drove Alice home to rifle her domestic paperwork. The telephone bill, so neatly filed, indeed revealed repeated calls to a number Alice did not know. Mo called it.

'Voicemail,' she reported. Alice fluttered with relief. 'Automated voice, no clues there.'

Relentless, Mo called directory enquiries but failed to wheedle an address out of the operator. 'There's got to be a way,' she insisted while Alice made coffee.

As if programmed, the phone on Alice's desk rang. It was Ted Parsons, thoughtfully calling to tell them that the contractors were observing the building trade's traditional holiday and the site would be closed completely for a fortnight.

'Ted,' Mo demanded, 'how do you find an address from a phone number?'

'You ask me,' he offered. Ted liked to help where he could. 'I've a coupla mates used to be in the police, they'll know. I'll call you back. What's the number?'

Alice clicked sweeteners into a coffee for Mo. 'Stop wifing around,' her friend ordered sharply. 'It makes me nervous. A person wants sweeteners, they'll sort their own.'

In another ten minutes Ted called and gave them an address. 'It's in Knightsbridge,' Mo announced. 'Flat nine, thirty-six Pont Street, SW1. We're off.'

'Off! Where?' Alice squeaked with dismay. 'We can't just go round there.'

'Why not? I don't think going round there was a problem for Sam, was it?'

In the car, Alice twittered until Mo pulled over and looked her in the eye. 'Look, we're checking out a building. What can possibly happen to us? Unless the building actually falls down while we're looking at it, nothing can go wrong here. It's only a block of flats, Alice. It won't bite you.'

'I'm being silly,' she admitted.

'And you're not a silly person,' Mo pointed out. 'That's what really pisses me off in all this. He's just made you into an idiot.' Alice's eyes filled with tears. 'Sorry. I didn't mean that, exactly.'

'It's OK, I understand,' Alice nodded.

'Will you, for Christ's sake, stop being so understanding!'

They identified an imposing, six-storey red-brick mansion a few doors back from the massed designer boutiques of Sloane Street. Alice stood before it, vibrating with fear.

'We can't go in there,' she protested as Mo approached the front steps.

'Yes, we can,' her friend insisted, holding her firmly by the arm.

They compared the address supplied by Ted with the highly polished brass plates by the entryphone. Each plate bore a number alone, not a name.

'That's it,' sighed Alice, turning to leave. 'We know where it is.'

Mo pressed the bell for number nine. 'She's still out,'

Alice protested from halfway down the steps. Then she turned and walked up again, saying, 'Oh God, I'm being pathetic, aren't I?'

The door opened. In front of them stood a tall, immaculate woman with prominent gold jewellery and glossy, dead-straight hair the colour of dust held back in a suede band.

'I'm the concierge,' she drawled. 'May I help you?'

Mo and Alice, slick at decoding their fellow women's fashion statements, instantly identified a socially mobile aristocrat slithering downwards on a raft of petrodollars. Alice's fears popped like a soap bubble.

'I've got an unusual problem and you may be able to help me,' she announced with her most beguiling smile. The concierge hesitated. 'It won't take long,' Alice promised.

'You'd better come in,' suggested the concierge.

Her office had been hand-painted to look like a Caribbean balcony. 'That's a lovely job,' Mo commented, seating herself in a fat tub chair upholstered in silk damask.

'Pierre Frey, isn't it?' Alice took an identical chair, stroking the precious textile as she sat.

'It is.' The concierge's pale eyes widened with respect. 'Are you . . . ?'

'Oh, yes, we're decorators,' Alice confirmed.

'How marvellous. I've always thought that must be such a lovely thing to do.'

'We like it,' Alice smiled. Bonding was completed over cups of Earl Grey. 'The thing is,' she confided, 'I'm trying to find my husband.'

'Aren't we all? I mean, not your husband necessarily . . .'

'We've been together twenty-two years, our children are nearly adults, and now he's just left.'

'Oh dear.' Expressing sympathy, the concierge looked like a constipated whippet.

Alice rushed through the rest of the story, worried she might start sobbing or become speechless with grief. The concierge's eyes flashed.

'Number nine! Well, we're very interested in her ourselves! Fascinated, even!'

'You know her!'

'Oh, rather. Mrs Larsen, Elizabeth Larsen, she calls herself. She comes in here every week to pay her rent. In cash.'

'In cash – but isn't it . . .'

'Rather a lot! I should say – it's two thousand pounds a week.'

'You're not telling me that my husband . . .'

'No, I certainly am not. Several women's husbands, if you ask me. Mostly Middle-Eastern. Quite a few regulars. We don't see them much, they mostly send cars from their hotels.'

'Cars?'

'To pick her up.'

'To pick her up?'

'You're saying she's a call girl,' Mo interpreted.

'No!' If Alice's eyeballs could have shot out of their sockets on springs, it would have happened then. Boing! Boingg!! 'A call girl?'

'Well, what other business pays in cash at that level and requires a woman to jump into a Roller several times a week for a night at the Dorchester?'

'Good God.' Alice felt herself almost throbbing with shock.

'Is your husband a short, dark man . . . What am I saying,

they're all short, dark men. But he's British, right?'

'Well, yes.' How would you describe Sam? Important-looking, distinguished, always immaculately dressed?

'I've seen him, then. There's only one who's British.'

'Fussy little man with small hands, walks with his bum stuck out like Hitler,' said Mo.

'That's the one.'

'And wandering eyes,' added Alice, now not to be left out if Sam's character was to be trashed. What a thrill! Dissing the master!

'Definitely the one. Always leering at my legs if I leave the door open.'

So, thought Alice, Mo was right. I must be the only woman in London unaware that Sam's become a lecherous creep. One of the only two women. But this Elizabeth Larsen must like him. Or maybe she likes his money.

'And, of course, we've had the police round,' the concierge went on with a happy smirk. 'Oh yes. They don't tell you officially, naturally. But she's got convictions. Credit card fraud, goods by deception, keeping a brothel, that sort of thing. The last time it was this cult she's into that they were checking out.'

'Cult?'

'Well, it was news to me. Apparently she's something to do with a religious cult. There isn't any chanting or fire-walking or anything. I mean, I was quite worried. Fire regulations are terribly strict in a building like this. It's something about ancient Egypt, anyway. They think it's harmless. To the building. And they don't have any meetings here. I'd never have known if they hadn't told me.'

'Why were they interested?' demanded Mo. 'It's not illegal to join a cult, is it?'

Alice regarded her friend with admiration. Trust her to ask the right questions. 'They don't do those mass suicide rituals, do they?' She tried hard not to look hopeful as she asked.

'Oh God, no! You don't really think . . .' At the prospect of body bags on the top floor, the concierge's patrician forehead wrinkled in alarm.

'No, no, no,' Mo reassured her immediately. 'We didn't know anything about this cult until you told us. Don't worry, she was just speculating. Ancient Egypt?'

'Ancient Egypt. She's got pyramids and things all over the flat. That's all I know.'

At that moment a bell rang and the concierge drifted away to deal with a washing machine repair at number three. Out on the street, Mo and Alice gave each other a high five.

'What a prat! A hooker! No wonder he doesn't want anyone to know where he is!'

'But do you suppose he realises she's a hooker?'

Alice! So dyed-in-the-wool nice she was still thinking the best of him! But, wait a minute. Consider the self-importance of Sam. Consider the stupidity of a man who was that far up himself. 'Well,' Mo proposed, 'you'll be able to put him in the picture now, won't you?'

'And I know who she is.'

'You know who she is? Alice! I had no idea you knew such interesting people!'

'I don't know her, but I know the name. She owes them money. The company.'

'Owes them money? What for?'

'She was buying some fantastic luxury penthouse on the river and she backed out at the last moment and didn't pay the bill. I'll never forget how angry Sam was.'

'Hang about. You mean she was a client? He's having an affair with a client?'

'Is that wrong too?'

'Wrong! Alice, it's as wrong as a lawyer can be. And, believe me, that's *wrong*! Oh yes. Wrong, wrong, wrong. No wonder he's trying to bully you into keeping quiet about it. You've got him, Alice, my darling.'

'How've I got him?'

'Obviously, he's let her off the bill and if his partners knew that they'd be livid. If the Law Society knew he'd started an affair with a client they'd have to investigate. And a client with a criminal record! They'd have to chuck him out. Strike him off. Defrock him. Whatever they do to lawyers. The end of his career. With what we've found out today, you can make that happen. Got it?'

'Well,' said Alice. 'That certainly bears thinking about.'

Mo grabbed a lamp-post and pretended to bang her head against it. People turned to stare as they passed. A woman banging her head on a lamp-post was rarely seen around Knightsbridge.

Afterwards, George's blood ran cold when he thought of what he did when he was down to not enough money for one more Scotch. He went to the payphone and called Sheepshagger's mobile.

'Where are you?' She was in a bar too from the sound of it.

'I'm in Soho,' she told him. 'What's it to you?'

'I thought we had a date.'

'We did. I didn't make it.'

'I've got good news and I've got bad news,' he went on, thinking the strop in her voice must be the drink talking.

'What's the good news?' she asked. Yup, must be, she was definitely a few bevvies down.

'The good news is you don't have to do any more watering,' he told her.

'That's right,' she agreed. Excessively cheerful. 'Now, what's the bad news?'

'You are not going to like this,' he warned her. And he felt terrible at that point.

'Try me,' she suggested, 'I'm strong.'

'It's gone.' He whispered it, trying to make it sound less of a disaster. 'The jungle's gone. We've been raided.'

'What do you mean, "raided"?' Poor cow, she wasn't getting it. The full enormity was not sinking in.

'I told you it was bad news. Someone has broken in and stolen the jungle. All of it.'

'Is that right?' If anything, she sounded even more cheerful.

'I suppose you're too pissed to understand,' he sniped, disappointment finally starting to bleed through the alcohol.

'You're supposing erroneously.' She was cackling. He was just about to explain in words that even a drunk Australian could understand when she said, 'I've got worse news.'

'It must have been somebody with a key. They took it all out through the front door and down the stairs.'

'And it took for ever,' she told him.

'Well, there was a whole bleedin' jungle in there. It must have taken hours. Somebody must have seen them.'

'George, you pitiful old bong-brain, you don't get it, do you?'

'Not if it's all been ripped off,' he moaned.

'It was me, you sad old pot-head. I'm the one what done it.'

'It was you?' Hope dawned. It actually fucking dawned. Christ, he'd acted so thick. 'You've got it?'

'Not any more, George old boy, half of London's probably got it by now. I moved the stuff straightaway last night. What I've got now is a wad of wonga and a plane ticket and I'm going home for Christmas. Bye, George. Can't say it was a pleasure but it was surely worth it in the end.'

And she ended the call. The bitch cut him off. And wouldn't pick up when he called her back. She'd left him flat, with less than 20 pence, in Kentish Town, on a cold, wet night in December.

George didn't feel too good. He sat on the staircase by the payphone for he didn't know how long. He felt cold and hot and sick and itchy and utterly, painfully sober.

Lily was out carol-singing to raise money for the church. Daisy was out carol-singing to raise money for the stables. Laura was at her office party. Andy was home alone as usual, wondering what felt wrong about this Christmas.

Perhaps it was that the girls were older and the days when he and Laura had had a few glasses of mulled wine after midnight mass and foxed around the house stuffing stockings in the role of Father Christmas were gone. Perhaps it was that.

Perhaps it was that he and Laura had hardly seen each other since the beginning of the month. He went to parties because in his insecure state, running a small business that needed more clients, networking was a numero uno priority. She went to parties for pretty much the same reason. Once or twice they'd even turned up at the same party, waved across the room and never managed to speak. He'd done the house decorations himself, with help from Daisy, when Laura had casually admitted that she wouldn't have the time until Christmas Eve.

Perhaps it was the lack of mothers. Gone too were the days when Laura sighed and started, in September, the lengthy and delicate negotiation about whose mother would join them this year. His mother had died of a stroke two years ago, swiftly and unexpectedly in her sleep. Her mother, just as fast and surprisingly, had found a third husband and moved to South Africa.

Perhaps it was the money. Back when he was with KKDW, Christmas meant dragging home a tree that would touch the ceiling, filling the entire fridge with champagne and commissioning a new piece of jewellery for Laura. It had also meant voyaging to Knightsbridge to choose an item of silk underwear to go with the jewellery. Now he was earning the same money, but it didn't feel the same when you were the boss.

A rainy day account, an emergency fund, contingency margins – OK, he had them all and they were healthy. Spending the equivalent of a day's pay for a top-line techie on a pair of knickers? Not an option – especially not when Laura seemed to have fallen out of love with lingerie altogether. He could just imagine her face.

So they had a modest, table-top tree which Daisy had still managed to load with most of their beloved decorations, and it didn't look right. And Andy didn't feel right.

Perhaps it's me, he suggested to himself, opening the fridge and wondering if it was too early to test this year's pudding mixture. With just a teaspoon of brandy butter. Nobody would miss just a teaspoon. Who the hell am I kidding that Christmas is for kids? It's for me. I love it, all of it. What's wrong is that there isn't enough of it this year. Yup, that's it. It's me.

A knock at the door. An odd knock, almost like an animal scratching out there. Only certain kinds of people announced themselves with their bare hands when the porch had a state-of-the-art video entryphone and the door itself was adorned with an immense antique French knocker from La Maison. Children knocked like that, and people who were in a state because they had had accidents, and passing lunatics looking for a hand-out.

The caller was all of the above. It was Pascal. He was wearing a bath towel around his waist.

Now what?

'Something terrible has happened,' Pascal declared, clutching at his dripping black curls with both hands.

No, it hasn't. And watch that bath towel.

'Charles is going to be absolutely furious.' Pascal moaned. The goose pimples were standing out all over his incredible Bernini chest. Down the front path he had left a trail of wet footprints.

'What's happened, Pascal? Is it the plumbing?' Kill that smile, don't look like you're patronising your neighbour. However much he invites it.

'Well, it is sort of like plumbing. Come and see, please.' Now Pascal had hold of his arm and was pulling him out of the house. Watch that bath towel, for Christ's sake.

'Let me get my shoes and keys, will you?'

How prissy was that? When the man was standing there in just a bath towel? Andy grabbed his keys. He'd go barefoot too. And what about some tools? It looked like a case for the toolbox.

'Two minutes,' he promised Pascal, and dragged out the toolbox from its cupboard.

'We have to hurry! It's going to be a disaster!' Pascal set off, half running, down the path, with his hands, at last, thank God, holding up the towel around his waist. The towel was blue and his skin was olive, that beautiful, dewy olive skin that was as flawless as new-fallen snow and as soft as the cheeks of a peach. The boy certainly had a body. If he'd been a gay man, Andy reassured himself, he'd have probably put up with Pascal too, just for the sake of that polo-pony butt.

Inside the Pink Palace, a pall of steam was drifting down the stairs.

'It's the bathroom,' Pascal explained. 'I was running a bath and then it just wouldn't stop. I hope it hasn't overflowed everywhere. Charles'll go crazy if I get water coming through the ceiling again.'

So there's been water coming through the ceiling before, huh? Andy got a grip on the toolbox and headed upstairs.

The steam in the bathroom was thick and the tub was brimming. With hot water only. Andy tested it and whipped out his hand. Scalding! Shit!

First objective, turn off the water. He took a towel to the searing taps and found the hot one jammed. Shit, shit, shit!

OK, next objective, stop the tub running over. The room was of a piece with the Pink Palace aesthetic: pale, minimalist and high maintenance. Limestone tiles, matching mosaic, lots and lots of chrome. The tub had a pop-up waste which was operated by a round chrome handle. Which was well under the scalding water and undoubtedly red-hot by now. A wrench would do the job but a wrench would wreck that mirror-perfect finish.

Pascal had followed him and was pacing around the room like a zoo-crazy tiger, firing rhetorical questions. 'How bad is it, really? Do you know how it works? Can you fix it? Is it going to blow up? Can't we do anything?'

'Where's the tank?' Silly question, try again. 'Any idea where the water tank is, Pascal? They're usually at the top of the house somewhere.'

Pascal's eyes widened. 'Water tank? Do we have a water tank? No, I have no idea.'

They were long, narrow houses. Andy ran up the next two flights and arrived, breathless, on the attic landing. To the left the sauna, cold and empty; to the right a room full of junk. Not dusty, higgledy-piggledy, piled-up junk but junk stored as only Charles would have wanted it, packed into labelled boxes and stacked architecturally against a wall. The same rooms that were the girls' bedrooms in his own house.

And the tank, praise be, was in the same place, accessed through a trapdoor in the junk room ceiling. Leaping up the tier of boxes was a doddle, squeezing through the trap a bit tight, and there was the stop-cock. Not a willing stop-cock, but it yielded in the end. Below, in the bathroom, the tumultuous noise of running water stopped.

Pascal regarded him with worshipping eyes. 'How did you do it? It's wonderful, it just stopped.'

162

There remained the problems of the submerged waste handle, the paralysed tap and the steaming heat of the tub. Let out the water. He tried wrapping the wrench in a hand towel but it wouldn't get a grip. 'They make these with rubber grips. If I had one of them I'd be all right,' he told nobody in particular, since Pascal could not be expected to understand. His fleece jacket was covered in dust and was now getting splashed with water, so he took it off.

Pascal watched him. 'I have an idea,' he proposed, flashing a naughty smile. He went over to a cupboard, opened it and picked out a little square packet. The label promised: Fetherlite Ready-Lubed Extra-Strong.

One fast movement – flick-rip-pick! – and Pascal tore open the packet with his teeth and extracted a condom. Then another one. Flick-rip-pick! And there it was. There they were. He held them out to Andy between finger and thumb. 'Go on,' he said with a hint of a giggle, 'take them.'

No doubt about it, condoms were worth a try. Andy gave an uneasy laugh and stretched the pale, slippery rubber over the jaws of his wrench, where it clung promisingly to the serrations. Using a fingernail, Pascal picked a fragment of condom packet out of his teeth.

Now rubberised, the wrench gripped the waste handle precisely and it turned without trouble. Up popped the pop-up and, with a blessed gurgle, the steaming water began to drain from the tub.

'Wonderful! Wonderful!' cried Pascal, jumping up and down like a child until the bath towel came loose and fell to the floor. He stooped to pick it up. Slowly.

Andy peeled the condoms off his tool and let it cool off. The next job was the tap.

'Andy?' The voice was Charles's, from the doorway. Andy turned, and there behind Charles was Laura. On Charles's face detached amusement was being pasted over pain. On Laura's face there was nothing but shock.

Pascal giggled outright. 'This isn't what it looks like,' he assured them in delight. And he wrapped the towel around his loins again, flashily this time for the audience.

Andy realised that he was half-naked, and kneeling in front of Pascal, who was almost completely naked and definitely, in emotional mode only, over-excited. On the floor were two used condoms and their ripped-open packets. The bath, his best witness, was now suspiciously empty. Even the steam had vanished as if it didn't want to get involved. And Laura, his wife, was utterly pale. Under her eyes, the skin was almost green. That only happened when she was really, really churned up. Car crash, childbirth – the first time – death of her father. That bad.

On the other hand, he was innocent. Better than innocent, he was doing these two incompetent style victims a neighbourly favour. As he was always doing for anyone who asked. As Laura herself would have demanded of him, as she had demanded all kinds of favours from Charles and Pascal ever since they'd moved in. And he'd already saved their ceiling. And he was about to repair their plumbing. And he'd pulled something climbing into the loft, and his back hurt, and getting up from kneeling wasn't going to be athletic.

Explain? And sound like a complete wally and probably a liar as well? Fuck it.

Pascal, however, was not going to pass on a cue for drama. 'No, no,' he protested, 'don't think that. We had a problem. I went to take a bath, I turned on the taps . . .' He moved to demonstrate and Andy, forced to get out of the way, heaved himself up with the help of the side of the bath. 'And something happened with the hot one.' Another no-help-for-it giggle. 'It was coming out everywhere, very hot, I couldn't stop it, and I was afraid for the water overflowing, for the ceiling, spoiling the paint, so I went to ask Andy and he came to help.'

Charles, the sour little queen, wasn't buying a word of it. Pascal continued, his English breaking down as he got angry. 'So we came back here and the water was full in the bath and very hot and it was impossible even to open it so the water go away. Don't look like that to me, it's true. And you either, he is your husband, you should know him!' This was to Laura, with a violent stab of the forefinger. Protectively, Charles moved closer and took her hand. A paranoid conspiracy! Well, fuck that too.

'You don't believe me!' Pascal accused Charles, then turned on Laura. 'You think I want to fuck your husband!' His voice changed key. Pascal was shifting from his speaking voice in C up to his making-a-scene voice in F-sharp minor. By now they all knew what that meant.

Andy threw the wrench back into the toolbox and closed the lid, then grabbed his wet shirt from the floor. 'When the taps have cooled off you can try the hot one again. It probably just seized because it was overheating. Faulty design.'

'You never have trust for me,' Pascal complained to Charles. 'Every bad thing that happens, it has to be my fault. And whatever I say, you don't believe it. I can't live like this. It's impossible. You are impossible.'

Charles folded his arms and yawned. Pascal upped his volume. 'You are a man with no intelligence, no heart, nothing. Actually, I don't think you are really a man. You are just a machine.' Pascal turned himself into a robot and started to stagger jerkily about the bathroom, gesticulating. 'Look, this is you, this is how you think. Nothing human with you, you don't have any feelings at all. You're a stupid thing made out of metal.'

He reeled towards the door, causing Charles and Laura to step back out of the doorway. Charles then turned suddenly and ran downstairs. 'I hope you fall down and break into little pieces!' Pascal yelled after him.

'Look, time's getting on,' Andy said, amazed at his own reasonable voice. 'Better get going. The girls will be home wanting dinner.' All the way down to the door he listened for Laura following him but there was nothing to hear.

It was going to be fine. Nobody who knew him would really believe he'd actually been doing anything with Pascal. Straight-arrow, four-square, father-of-two Andy Forrest; nobody could seriously think for one minute he was gay. Not even at the level of fooling around with other boys when he was a kid. The voice of Jon Bon Jovi, the lifestyle of Mr Average, the sexuality of – well, John Wayne, maybe. Nobody had ever hinted he was perceived as anything but 100 per cent hetero.

And there was evidence. Sooner or later, Charles would find it and realise that Pascal had been telling the truth for once. The trap door was still open in the junk room, and the storage crates moved to let him climb up them, and in the rush to stop the bath from running over he'd forgotten to turn out the light in the attic. Charles had an ounce of intelligence; pretty soon he would figure out what had really happened.

It was cold work, carol-singing. He made the girls sausages and baked potatoes. Lily gave thanks to God, ate her share and had enough gratitude left to throw a couple of words at her father. Daisy didn't finish her plate and soon went away to make phone calls. Laura came back after midnight and slept with the tiny red Chinese people in the spare room.

'Your vision seems quite normal for your age,' said the doctor.

What about my age? I'm not even fifty. Sit up, suck in your gut and smile. He'll soon notice that this is nothing about age.

'If it's fine, why did I start seeing white noise everywhere?'

With Hanukkah out of the way, the Carmans were spending Christmas in the Maldives and had left their practice to a locum. This was not a professional who inspired confidence but a skinny young man with thin blond hair. He wore a patterned sweater that would have been improved by washing and seemed to have some kind of rash on his forearms. Running the eye tests had taken for ever with him fussing around, dropping charts. Now he was laboriously reading Mickey's notes.

'The last time Dr Carman saw you, you'd been having a few *sweating problems*.' He dropped his voice to a cloying whisper on the last two words.

'What's that got to do with my eyesight?'

'It looks like some tests were ordered.'

A rush of horror. A horror he hadn't felt since he was at school, when he'd perfected the mind trick of erasing unpalatable homework entirely from his memory. Only a ghost of a scar remained in his consciousness to show where the rejected item had once been. Erased from his mind, the item would seem erased from reality also. And then . . . someone would hit that scar. Yowwwwww. Pain. Guilt. Fear. Rage, because he had imagined he was safe and all the time he had been in danger. Rage because he couldn't bend the world to his will after all. Rage because now he'd have to front up and claim the dog had eaten his homework.

The tests. Including the HIV test. Yowwwwww. And the black hand of terror was reaching out to grab him again. But what right did this pimply brat have to make his world unpleasant? None. The black hand squeezed but missed. Mickey squared up in the patient's comfy chair. No, now he was an adult. More than that, he was a man. More than that even, he was The Man. And if he said something had never happened, then it had never happened. And if he wanted a thing not to be, then it would not be. And anyway, they'd have called him if there was . . . a reason to worry. Wouldn't they?

'I can't see that he's been through the results with you?'

'I assumed he'd have called me if he needed to.' Go on, condescend to the brat. Keep it light but lordly.

'If that's his normal procedure, I'm sure he would.' The file was in two parts. On the screen were the clinic records. While Dr Carman punctiliously kept the screen visible so his patients should feel included in the consultation process, the brat had turned it around so that only he could see the contents. The livid green and mauve glow from the screen made him look like an undiscovered Tretchikoff.

The rest of the file was made up of a few documents, letters to and from the pathology labs and specialists who'd investigated Mickey over the years. There was a pattern to it. He had health problems when he had the time. Nothing short of a tooth abscess would stop him if he was on a shoot. In between jobs, when he had time to worry, he'd log on to the health scare of the moment and decide he needed a check-up.

The brat unfolded every piece of paper in the file, smoothed it out on the desk-top and read it through, beginning to end, in no hurry. People didn't do that with The Man. If he said jump, they said how high? If he said go, they said how far? If he said he had a problem, they sorted it. Mickey leaned back in the patient's chair and clicked his teeth.

'You agreed to the HIV test?' The brat was making it sound as if that alone was some kind of admission.

'Sure, why not?'

'The result was negative.'

'Glad to hear it.'

'Your vision problems are probably hormonal.'

'Come again?'

'The result of a hormonal imbalance.'

No chance. Women were hormonal. Men were not. The Man definitely couldn't be.

The brat had switched back to his unctuous, confidential voice. 'You are showing several classic symptoms of hormonal irregularity. These are quite normal in ageing people, when the production of hormones starts to wind down.'

Ageing? Who's ageing? He's calling me ageing? The brat is calling me ageing? A bit harsh, isn't it? Just a little bit harsh, calling a man ageing when he isn't even fifty. Until next year.

'In women, of course, the phenomenon is recognised by the name menopause. In men, people are starting to call it the viropause. It's basically the same phenomenon although in women, of course, menstruation ceases as well and that is the most obvious effect. But in both sexes, as the glands begin to slow down, the hormone levels start to dip, and the body takes a little while to adjust.'

Slow. Tired. Less. Cease. You talking about me?

'In the process of adjustment you may feel you have less energy, you may feel tired, there may be things like joint pains, muscular stiffness, the changes in vision that you've obviously had, the problems with the body's thermostat that lead to the hot flushes you saw Dr Carman about earlier.'

Hot flushes! Bull – shit!

'And your skin may feel dry, or tight, or itchy. There may be an outbreak of acne. The way your body fat is distributed starts to change. There may be loss of libido, or surges of sexual feeling. The sense of balance may be impaired and there are also mental symptoms – depression, mood swings, sometimes quite violent or distressing feelings.'

'Bollocks.'

The brat smiled at him. Smirked at him, to be exact. All the animal arrogance of a young male facing down an older male was flaunted in the way he pulled the cuffs of his disgusting goddamn sweater down over his ugly red knuckles. 'Dr Carman ordered extensive blood tests and they do show that all your hormone levels are low.'

'What fucking hormones?'

'Principally testosterone in a man, of course. But just as women also naturally produce small quantities of testosterone, so men normally produce small amounts of the hormones that are thought of as female. And in your case the analysis showed that all the levels are normal for an older man, but significantly lower than would be found in a man of twenty or thirty.'

A man as young as you, you mean, you smirking, fucking nerd. Mickey got to his feet. No impaired balance, thank you. No muscular stiffness, no joint pain, no lack of energy. Loss of libido, get out of here. 'I think I'm wasting my time,' he said.

'There is a recommended therapy,' the brat protested.

'I don't think so,' Mickey advised him. 'I think I'll take my chances.'

Women. He'd like to kill them all. George lay on his bed thinking about it. Snotty women. Women in high heels. Young women. Women who thought they were so sexy. Women who thought they were so clever. They could get on their knees and clean his boots and then he'd cut their heads off with a samurai sword and he'd be standing in their blood. Go on!

The radio was mumbling and hissing but he couldn't be bothered to fix the tuning. Besides, it was pumping out the crap of the season. Coming home for Christmas, dah-dee-dah-dee-dah. Strange how cheap music could be so absolutely fucking awful. It made you want to puke. It made you want to die.

Rain streamed down the skylight. It had been streaming for days. He had been lying in bed for days. His skin felt like mummy wrappings. The room smelt of bad milk, from a curdled half-bottle by the kettle.

There had been a plan. He had some mates who'd moved

out to Wales and the plan had been to go and see them for Christmas. She'd killed that off, the bitch. The bike had about a pint of petrol in it; he'd be lucky if he got as far as Basingstoke.

Hungry. He was hungry like people in Dickens or something, hungry like acid in his stomach eating its way through his body. Moving legs or arms made it worse. Closing his eyes made it worse.

Four days he'd been holed up, trying to work out what to do. For four days the options available had been churning around the slurry at the bottom of his brain. Sign on. Go back to courier work. Get some other kind of work. Sell the bike. Sell the guitar. Take the guitar and try busking somewhere. Find someone, bum a loan off them. Find a woman and kill her. Kill them all.

'It's all horribly familiar,' he said aloud. His voice evaporated in the loneliness.

More than hunger, the unfairness of it all ate away at him. Life was like a sadistic teacher who picked on him all the time. He'd been victimised from the day he was born.

He would think of something. If he got off the bed, maybe an answer would come. If he went out on the street, maybe things would look better.

The hallway of the house was littered with junk mail. People kicked it aside when they opened the door and it blew back into the stairwell and lay there, yellowing and curling, for years. Pizza leaflets, home-designed flyers from painters and decorators. Invitations from your local churches. And if you went down there, the old vicar would get up and give you a sermon about how you only went to church on Christmas. Forgetting that Christmas was the only time the fucking church ever got off its arse to invite people.

Somebody picked up the real letters and put them on the stairs. Surprise, surprise. Something for him. Two somethings. A Christmas card. From Andy. Mr & Mrs Andrew Forrest, Lily and Daisy, 29, The Terrace, Westwick. Semi-detached, suburban Mr Jones; trust him to do a pitiful thing like that.

There was also a brown envelope. Brown envelopes bode evil.

A form. A form from the courier company. A tax-like form. A form that meant he was officially and unintentionally unemployed, had been for, what? Five weeks, six weeks. Ah! Yes! Correct! If he went out, something would come. A tax-like form could be taken to the dole office and used to sign on with. Sign on, option one, tick the box. They used to have these emergency grants if you'd been off work six weeks. Maybe, just maybe.

His boots knew the way, they could probably walk to the dole office by themselves. Five minutes later he was there, outside the horrible dirty concrete excrescence down by the fire station and the post office. It was shut. It was raining, it was cold, it was gloomy and getting dark. The notice in the window said: Christmas Opening Hours. What was the point of that, when people didn't know what day it was?

'Excuse me,' he asked the drunk man making an elliptical move towards him. 'What day is it today?'

The drunk man blinked at him, then said, 'It's Christmas Eve, mate.' And he heaved forward and left George behind. Lucky drunk man. George was not drunk and had no money. And it was Christmas Eve. Unfair.

Christmas Eve. No dole office, not for three days. Forget

option one. And options two and three – no jobs going on Christmas Eve. Forget four and five – all the pawn shops and the loan sharks and the offices of *Loot* magazine where all manner of goods could be sold, none of them working. Christmas fucking Eve.

Forget option six – better to starve to death than expose yourself with a guitar on some tube station playing Paul fucking Simon's greatest fucking hits.

Which left option seven – scam some dosh off a mate. Stiffen the sinews, summon up the blood, crank up the bass, get on yer bike and go begging. On Christmas Eve.

The bike, thank Christ, started up OK. George drove over the river. Albert Bridge, its pale ironwork hung with lights, twinkled blurrily through the raindrops on his visor. He turned in the direction of Westwick.

Andy might have sent a Christmas card but you couldn't go to Andy for money because he'd look at you in that smiley, kind way he had and ask you if you were all right. And that snotty cow of a wife of his would be hanging about; he'd like to cut her head off. Same for Rhys – Rhys would hug you round the shoulders and say, 'All right, me old mate?' when there was nobody else he knew to whom you could use an expression like 'me old mate'.

There was a genuine danger that either of those two would ask you to stay for Christmas lunch as well. Ask you to sit down and share the fucking turkey and listen to their wives telling their children to be polite to you. The ultimate in charity, the final patronising frontier. They'd feel that sorry for him, they'd think they were that much better than him, they'd ask him to lunch on Christmas Day. Sam, at least, would be honest. He'd just tell you to fuck off and get a life.

So today's destination was Mickey's house. And Mickey's thing was looking cool, so he'd most likely find a way to do the bunging without making it painful. This was because Mickey did not wish to appear to be a lame suburban eunuch like the others. He'd be gratified with the opportunity to behave like an authentic man. So George would be guaranteeing Mickey's cred for another month or so. Letting him pretend he still had balls.

All of this he knew from previous experience. George and Christmas, they never had got along. Once Andy had said, 'Who needs Crisis at Christmas when you've got George?'

Twenty-whatever years since he founded the fucking band, he'd borrowed money off every one of them. Or tried to. Sam had always been a tight-arsed shit. Mickey and Andy had brought Sam in, said he was good and they needed keyboards, but personally George had never seen the point of Sam.

Twenty-whatever years ago, they were all boracic. They had all been skinny, they had all had long hair and they had all borrowed money off each other. There used to be the migratory fiver that just went round and round between them and as soon as one person had it somebody else would borrow it off him. Back then, buying a pint had been an investment in pleasure.

Now it was pints and chasers, bottles of champagne, booze cruises to Calais, fucking wine cellars. It was poncey great four-by-fours, not waiting for the bus, and egregious great houses, not rancid little rooms. He was the only one who could still count his ribs and cut his own hair. The rest of them had the power shaves and that good-living upholstery, looked like they'd been cladded in steak.

Except for him. None of the money had happened to him. He'd tried. He'd ducked and dived and bobbed and weaved and, as it seemed to him, grafted his fucking arse off. He had talent, he still had talent — he could play the rest of them into a hole in the ground — but they were rich and he was still on the fucking bottom and they'd be so fucking gracious they'd invite him for Christmas lunch like he was their personal charity. Unfair, unfair, unfair.

'What's the point?' he asked himself as he swooped up the flyover that led to the stretch of six-lane highway that led to the Acorn roundabout and the Westwick slip-road. 'What is the fucking point?'

Los Angeles had smog. Westwick had smug. The smug of Westwick had risen out of the leafy streets and was creeping down the highway towards him. Everyone indoors doing their fucking Christmas trees and getting drunk so they didn't have to talk to each other. Unfair, unfair. What was the fucking point?

Coming the other way on the eastbound carriageway he saw a mighty truck, lights blazing all around the cab and an illuminated sign on top screaming 'Merry Christmas!'. Coming home for Christmas. What was the point, in a world where people actually listened to songs like that?

'Bang. Wallop. Bye, bye, old George,' he said to himself, and shoved at the handlebars just enough to send him over the central barrier but not enough to make him skid.

Bang.

Andy went to midnight mass at St Nicholas's. Daisy went with him and put her hand through his arm as they walked over the green and through the echoing streets towards

Maple Grove. From far away they could hear sirens and the throb of a helicopter. From the direction of the city they saw the aurora borealis of a metropolis, a flicker of blue emergency lights against the red sky. Over there, people got drunk and stabbed each other. Over here, families wrapped presents and went to church.

In the past year St Nicholas's had become a stronghold of bells-and-smells, everything-and-jam-on-it Anglicanism. They sat contentedly together, coughing when the censer swung in their direction trailing clouds of incense. He tried not to sing too loud. Nothing more embarrassing than having your father belt it out in church. But at the end he had to let rip in 'Hark the Herald Angels Sing'. That long high C. Magic.

When the service was finished, Daisy went to light a candle at the crib. Andy watched his daughter sink gracefully to her knees, her pink petal lips moving as she muttered a prayer. She was blushing as she returned to his side and she wouldn't look at him. Were they going to have two happy-clappy daughters? Something was afoot. Twelve inches, George would have said. But something was afoot all the same.

'That police car is outside our house,' she said as they crossed the green.

'It's the easiest place to park,' he reassured her.

'I've got a feeling,' she insisted. He hugged her. Course you have, sweetheart. You're Daddy's big girl with Daddy's big heart. You get feelings all the time.

In the porch, they found a police sergeant. In the sitting room, she stood with her back to the fire, looking over their Christmas tree as if she was going to give it marks out of ten.

Lily was still at church. Laura was speaking with her absence, as usual.

'Sergeant Clegg,' she introduced herself. 'I'm from over in Helford.' Helford was Westwick's less desirable neighbour, an area in which all the unpleasant necessities of community life, including the hospital, the sewage works, the local government offices and the main police station, were installed. Westwick's purity was compromised only by an outpost police office fit for traffic offences and servicing the Neighbourhood Watch schemes.

Daisy threw off her coat and dived suddenly into hostess mode. 'Can I get you a cup of tea? Would you like a mince pie?'

'Very kind but I can't stay. Busy night for us. This won't take long. Can I have a word, sir?'

'I'll be in the kitchen,' promised Daisy, now whisking out of the door as if she had an appointment.

'Would you know someone called Mr Percy George Hodsoll? It seems you sent him a Christmas card, anyway.' As the police sergeant said this she looked around the room, appraising the furniture and the paintings with bewildered curiosity. No one would put George together with a man who looked prosperous even if he didn't feel it and lived in The Terrace, Westwick.

'George, that's the name he prefers. I've known him for – oh – more than twenty years, must be.' How to describe their relationship? What had George done now? 'We went to the same art college. We've got a bit of a band going, get together sometimes to play some music.' Did that sound pathetic? She had a pitying look on her face. 'Rhythm and blues, mostly. Has he – has there been any trouble?'

'I'm sorry to have to tell you that Mr Hodsoll died in a road accident near here tonight.'

Poor George. So, something had been afoot. Poor old George. He would have hated anyone to say that.

'What happened?'

'We're not certain. He was on a motorbike and it seems he crossed the central barrier into the path of oncoming traffic. We found your address at his home. It was the only address we could find there. Would you know how we could contact his family?'

'I wouldn't, no.' A twenty-something-year-old picture popped up of a fierce, white-blonde woman with George's bony nose and a shrieking voice, beside a silent fat man with a long beard. George's parents, who'd come to see his graduation art show and walked around it as if the whole display was something George had done on purpose to offend them. 'He hadn't seen his family in years. They used to live in London.'

'Was he a bit eccentric? Were there any brothers or sisters?' Now the sergeant had the unmistakable look of a woman trying not to get lumbered. George's philosophy had always been to give authority more trouble than he was worth.

'I think there is a sister. You can leave it with me,' he told her. 'I can contact people.'

She trusted him, people always trusted him, especially to take on a thankless responsibility. 'We can give you the names of funeral directors in the area.'

'Where is he now?' Stupid question, most of him was smeared all over the A31, east of junction two for Westwick. Marc Bolan is dead but he's still on the radio. And on the dashboard, and on the steering wheel.

'In the mortuary in Helford. There will be an inquest, but the coroner will usually allow burial before that if we agree to it. If you want to go to his place, the landlord can send someone over with a key. Their office is open all over the holiday.'

After she had gone he went down to the kitchen. Daisy was curled up in a corner chair, talking into her mobile. When she saw him, she finished the call.

There on the table was a small tray, and on the tray was a plate, and on the plate a mince pie, a glass of sherry and a carrot. Fifteen years old and she was still putting out a mid-night snack for Father Christmas and Rudolf the Red-nosed Reindeer. He wanted to cry. It was half past two in the morning.

'Hello, Dad,' she greeted him brightly. 'Was it bad news?'

'Yes. You know our band? One of them. Our lead guitar. Car crash.'

'Bummer.' She put her arms around him, her perfect, milk-white fairy princess arms that still just about met around where his waist used to be. 'Christmas, too. That is so sad. Was he badly hurt?'

'Well. He died, sweetheart.'

'Oh Daddy, I'm so sorry.'

'I don't know what to do about telling the others. I can't call them now.'

'Yes, you can. They're all big, bad, up-all-night rock and roll boys like you.'

He had to laugh at that. 'If I call them in the morning I'll mess up their Christmas Day.'

'Dad, nobody cares about Christmas as much as you do. They'll all be bored out of their minds with their families.

You won't be messing up anything that isn't messed up already.'

'You think?'

'Dad, I know. Tell them tomorrow. Nobody wants bad news in the middle of the night at Christmas. Go to bed now and do it in the morning.'

The stockings were ready wrapped and ready stuffed and ready decorated, hidden in his secret hiding place in the garage roof which the girls had never been able to find, with the rest of the presents.

'I'm going to bed then,' he said. 'But you might want to rethink the sherry. Father Christmas could use a large brandy this year.'

CHAPTER 7

Blaze Of Glory

Alice was being babied by her own offspring. Where had these children come from? And who exactly was the child here? They had fluttered back to the nest, first son, then daughter, taking up their old bedrooms, fussing around her as a team. She had had no idea they too believed that she was just some loveable ditz.

Loveable, ageing ditz. A contradiction in terms. Alice had thought about asserting herself, but thought again and played along.

On Christmas morning she woke up in a room full of red balloons. Pinned to the wall facing her was a ridiculous hand-made paper stocking, decorated with spangles and plastic blossom in the funky style that her daughter currently found pleasing.

'Don't get up,' Melanie and Jon ordered her. So she stayed in bed while her son brought up breakfast on a tray, the best china, a fresh red flower, a double-choc choc-chip muffin, a glass of Buck's Fizz and coffee that was really good and only a little gritty.

'Since Dad's being a total arse, we can have fun without him,' he announced. 'When you're ready, I can give you an Indian head massage. I learned it from this bloke at uni. It'll make you feel fantastic.'

'And I'm going to give you a pedicure.' Melanie sat on the end of the bed like a real girlfriend. 'And we don't have to run around cooking a bloody great turkey, so you don't have to go near the kitchen all day. We can do it all.'

The stocking contained a rubber brick for throwing at annoying people, a dartboard with Sam's face laminated on it and a little blue book entitled *The Truth About Men*. Outrageous! They watched her carefully, evaluating her reaction, so she looked pleased. Well, she was pleased. Just a bit shocked, that's all. A year ago she'd have been teaching them to treat their father with respect.

'What is the smallest book in the world?' Melanie read out.

'Oh God. This is like a test. I hate tests. I don't know.'

'The man's book of knowledge.'

'Uh-oh, I'd better leave,' Jon suggested. 'Don't go into the garden, OK? I'm just cleaning up a few things, burning rubbish and stuff. You don't want to get smoke in your hair. Better stay indoors, yeah?'

'I don't mind a bit of smoke, I like the smell,' Alice protested. Cleaning up the garden? And this was her son?

'No, you don't. Stay in bed, Mum. You can trust me. I'll be back in an hour for the massage.'

A tall young man with freckles and a perpetual bright-eyed grin – why, he'd make some girl a quite acceptable boyfriend. He was charming, he was practically urbane, he could do the Indian head massage. What had happened to the scrawny pustulent kid who had gone off to university just a little while ago?

And was this really her daughter, this elegant, self-possessed woman with her own job, her own salary and her own flat? And she looked like one of those glossy young things who were photographed in glossy old magazines, with her two necklaces and neat earrings and a smart little cardigan to wear with embroidered jeans. What had become of the resentful, pale-faced stress bunny, revising herself into a migraine before every exam?

'What is the definition of gross stupidity?' demanded Melanie.

'Oh help! I can't think.'

'It's a hundred and forty-four men in a room. How many men does it take to screw in a lightbulb?'

'I can't do lightbulb jokes, you know I can't.'

'Only one. They'll screw anything.'

Then she had to laugh. And laugh and laugh. Even when she caught Melanie looking at her with that patronising, go-on-dear, let-it-all-out expression. Maybe she should tell her. Maybe not. It could wait. What exactly would it do to a girl to find out that her father had left home to live with a pros-titute, even if he had done it in all stupidity? When was the right time to hurt your children?

Alice started filling up with panic. The thought of Sam just opened up a tap and all her terrors gushed out. With nowhere to go, because nobody else knew the full story except Mo. And how could she tell Melanie and Jon?

Party after party she had been to this Christmas, with a

fresh smile-graft bandaged up with politeness. She had lied about Sam according to his instructions. She had taken her place with the women who gathered at one end of the room to talk about their children while the men flocked to the other to talk about their work, and had said nothing. She had carried around the plates of bruschetta and the crudités from Parsley & Thyme, from time to time feeling a colossal compulsion to jump up on a sofa and yell at the whole room that her husband wasn't with her because he was with a cult-following call girl in Knightsbridge. But she had resisted. The silence was killing her.

'So about this pedicure,' she smiled at her daughter. 'Have I got to choose a colour?'

Maybe the Indian head massage would open her energy sources just the way Jon had promised. When the call came, she was sitting in the kitchen admiring her newly blue toes while he was tapping her scalp and saying, 'This is supposed to feel like raindrops.' Melanie was sitting at the end of the table, gouging the peel off a parsnip. The faint smell of smoke from the burning rubbish in the garden mingled with the enticing steam from the oven.

The phone rang. It's Sam, he isn't coming at all, she predicted to herself.

'It's Andy,' said the caller. Much better. She'd always liked Andy. 'Is Sam around?'

Something overflowed inside her, probably pain. 'No, Sam's left us,' she told him, amazed that she could say it so easily. The raindrops stopped. There was a silence from Andy on the phone.

'Sam left us, oh, a month ago now. He's living in Knightsbridge with a call girl.' From behind her, she felt

Jon react. She took one of his hands and held it. Melanie was now lopping leaves off sprouts. She looked up, eyes narrowing.

'Alice, are you all right?'

'Yes. You must think I've gone mad, mustn't you? He told me not to tell anybody. I'm sorry to dump this on you on Christmas morning, Andy, but it seems ridiculous just going on with nobody knowing.'

'I'm so sorry, Alice. I had no idea.'

All these years in Westwick, Alice had seen the pack turn on the weakest too often. Watch them take sides now. Watch all the men side with the man, all the women side with . . . well, Mo was on her side anyway. The rest of the women would probably side with Sam too. Nothing worse than a wife out of control in a suburb.

'Is there anything—'

'You can do? I don't know, Andy, maybe next time you all meet up for a rehearsal you could try to get some sense out of him, I suppose.'

'Why did he tell you not to tell anyone?'

'Well, Andy, it seems the woman he's living with is not only a prostitute but also a client of his firm, so it's all a bit unprofessional. If not actually criminal. Anyway,' she was frightened now, like a woman in a soap opera, she'd Said Too Much, 'he is supposed to be coming here at eleven, so if you call back then you'll catch him. If he actually turns up. He's not bothered about keeping his promises to his family, as you can understand.'

Sam had informed her that he would visit them on Christmas Day but return to Elizabeth, who preferred to have a proper lunch at a hotel. She had said 'an hotel', which

Sam thought very refined, so he said it too. Alice thought '*an* hotel' was vulgar and pretentious, and she found herself repeating it back to him with a sarcastic inflection.

But at the bottom of her heart, Alice was hoping that her home would look so inviting, and the children so creditable, and the food so delicious – for never let it be said that Sam's stomach was not, until lately, the most frequently indulged of his bodily organs – and most of all, of course, that she herself would look desirable enough that, well, he would change his mind and stay for lunch. And then – who knew what else? Maybe there'd be some special emotional alchemy and they'd all be a family again.

Andy said again, 'Alice, I'm so sorry.'

'Well, you know, Andy – what can I say?'

'It's just a thing he's going through, maybe. It'll all be all right.'

'Dear Andy, don't come out with that kind of stuff, it'll make me cry.'

When she ended the call, Jon said, 'He told us there wasn't anyone else.'

'I know, I know.' Oh God, I should have told them before. Now they're angry with me too. 'He told me the same thing. But we traced his phone calls and he's living with this – woman.' Briefly, she ran through the essentials of her visit to Pont Street.

'Disgusting, lying little creep,' said Melanie, who had had issues with her father.

'Pathetic tabloid cliché,' said Jon. 'I can't stand any more of this, I'm going to get on with the garden.'

They decided to open champagne. Jon took his glass outside. He came back for firelighters. Soon thick clouds of smoke blew up from behind the big Mexican orange bush that screened most of the lawn from the house. Such a practical chap, able to start a roaring bonfire when it had been raining for weeks and all the leaves and the rose prunings must have been wet.

Sam arrived an hour or so late, to hand out fifty-pound notes and dry pecks on the cheek to the three of them.

'You're putting on weight,' Melanie observed, flinching from her father's kiss. He wore a suit and a white shirt, as if today was just another business day, and his neck had moved into jowls that overflowed his collar a clear centimetre or two.

Aggrieved, he said, 'You could be more polite, on Christmas Day.'

'Oh could she?' Jon waded in. 'Do tell. How polite should we be when our father's run off to live with a tart?'

'Don't be rude about Elizabeth. I won't allow it.'

'I'm not being rude, I'm being accurate. She's a prostitute. What else should I call her? Incidentally, does that make you a pimp? I never know what that word really means.'

'Where on earth did you get that idea?'

'Jon!' Alice squeaked in warning, but Too Late.

'Mum told us. She's been there. Everyone in the building knows what she does for a living. Everyone except you, it seems.'

'Elizabeth is from a wealthy family. She has no need to work. Alice, how dare you tell the children these lies? Just because I prefer to be with Elizabeth, you shouldn't take out your jealousy on her. I'm . . . well, I'm shocked. You've been to her apartment?'

'It's just a flat, Sam, and why on earth shouldn't I go there?'

'It's trespass. It's harassment. There's a law against it, though I suppose I can't expect you to know that. How can you be so stupid? I'll get an injunction to stop you. If you dare . . .'

'Oh for God's sake, Dad.' Melanie squared up, bristling with her newly acquired knowledge of tort and precedent. 'It's nothing of the kind. One visit to a public place, you couldn't begin to make a case out of it. The judge would laugh you out of court.'

'She told me I shouldn't have come here today. She didn't want me to come. I said I had to see my children on Christmas Day, so I've made her unhappy and this is the thanks I get. I'm not standing for any more of this. You're a pair of nasty, demanding, ungrateful brats and that's the last money you'll ever see from me. I'm going to get the rest of my things now and that'll be it. This chapter of my life is closed.'

A hissing noise issued from Jon, first the sound of breath exhaled with contempt, then the effect of a laugh bitten down between his back teeth. Sam rolled his bulk out of the door. His feet stomped upon the stairs.

Floorboards above them creaked. They heard a muffled curse. Heavy things began to hit the floor, probably drawers. Several doors slammed. His footsteps agitated with violence. Soon the impact of Sam descending the stairs shook the wall. He burst into the kitchen.

'What the fuck's going on? Where's my stuff?'

'In the garden,' Jon said immediately, standing aside to let his father through.

'What the hell — what have you done?' Sam flung open the back door and rushed out on to the lawn. A trickle of smoke was still rising from the site of the bonfire.

As soon as he was out of sight, they heard roars of rage building into a crescendo. Above the dark foliage of the Mexican orange bush they saw things flung into the air: a piece of shirt with flames still licking at its edge, some blackened CD cases.

'Jon.' Alice turned to her son, half fearful, half delighted. 'What have you done?'

'Put his stuff on the fire,' said Jon.

'What stuff? How much stuff?'

'All of it. All I could find, anyway. I went through the cupboards last night while you were at that party. Suits and shirts and things. Shoes. All his ghastly jazz CDs. The stereo. His pathetic golf stuff. Lots of boxes and files and junk in his desk. Old school photo. If he's out of here, well, he's out of here, isn't he?'

'Good one,' Melanie admitted. 'Smart thinking.'

Sam came charging round the shrub like a rhino lumbering out of the bush. He was snorting and heading straight for his son.

Jon moved away from the table and, when his father was in range, he hit him.

It was a beautiful punch. A punch to make a mother proud. A punch even a sister could admire. It curved through the air in a perfect arc and landed with the most wonderful clean smack. Blood actually spattered on the floor. Sam squealed like a stomped poodle and staggered in his tracks.

'Nice work, Jon,' said Melanie.

Sam clutched his face and mumbled. Blood began to drip through his fingers. Top-heavy with obesity and self-importance, he teetered on his shiny little feet and slumped against the wall.

The telephone rang and Alice answered it. 'Oh Andy. Yes, he's here. I'll pass you over to him.'

Jon was looking at his hand as if amazed by its supernatural powers. 'It was a good one, wasn't it?' he marvelled. 'I've never hit anyone before. This could be the best Christmas I've ever had.'

'Can't we get him out of here?' asked Melanie, clattering saucepan lids. 'Everything's ready, I'm starving and it'll be overcooked soon.'

Sam, now a pallid grey colour except for the bloodstains, was barking embarrassed monosyllables into the receiver. 'Oh. Right. OK. Thanks. Yeah. OK. Bye.' He turned to his family, his threatening son, his elaborately uninterested daughter, his anxious wife. Not wife. Former partner, merely.

Alice felt suddenly feeble. She sat down on the nearest chair. Her hands had gone all silly. He'd hit his father. Jon had punched his father and, yes, there was Sam, swaying where he stood, rolling his eyes like an anxious bullock – Sam was afraid of him, afraid of his own son. And the sky hadn't fallen and the clock on the oven timing their Christmas lunch was still ticking on regardless. He was getting blood on the telephone. And her plan to tempt Sam to stay with a vision of domestic bliss was pretty much finished.

'You haven't heard the last of this,' Sam mumbled, gesticulating with the non-gory hand. 'Appalling behaviour. Absolutely disgraceful. You think you've been very clever, don't you?'

'Have you finished, Dad?' Melanie was overdoing the drawl a bit. 'If you've finished you can go now and we can get on with enjoying ourselves.'

*

'We're not really equipped for Christmas, are we?' Mickey wriggled on his sun lounger, trying to find a way of lying that felt as comfortable as it ought to be under a palm tree by a swimming pool in the miraculous heat of midday in Marrakech.

The Sheltering Sky this was not. No distant drumming, no ululating from the dark mediaeval alleys, no Blue Men on camels dusty from the ancient road to Timbuktu. Casablanca this was not either, no Sydney Greenstreet in a fez doing dodgy deals in a café. Instead there were padded Beverly Hills-style pool loungers and waiters in white mess jackets dawdling between them, picking out the clients who'd be good for extortion and buggery in the shrubbery after dark.

'What do you mean, not equipped?'

'We ought to have somewhere to go.'

'I thought you wanted to go to Morocco?' Just a tiny bit niggled, Mo sounded. Her niggle on top of his niggle was an exponential rise in their joint level of dissatisfaction.

'I do, I do. I do like Morocco. But we shouldn't be in a hotel.'

'What else could we have done? Bit strong to rent a villa, just for the two of us. Everybody's in a hotel, that's the way it is here.'

'It's all the people.'

'Yeah, that was bad luck.'

Mo sighed. She would have felt for Mickey if he would have accepted her empathy. Things had gone wrong on the flight. The minute the pilot sanctioned movement, a child of two or so had toddled down the aisle towards them and after her, horror of horrors, had come her adoring father, Draco Dracovich.

Draco: taller and darker and handsomer than they had remembered, cool in his low-slung baggy pants and his frameless sunglasses, and so natural with his baby. Natural as men in bestselling posters are, natural as an Anglo–Saxon man can never be, a fine arm holding the infant to his chest, those white teeth bared in a fatherly grin. Draco, ten points.

Yet more horror: Draco and his elfin wife, her brassy mother, plus, of course, their gorgeous child, were with them at the airport, behind them in the shuttle bus and just a few doors away from them in the hotel. Wherever they had gone in the ancient alleyways of Marrakech they'd found him, and whatever he'd been doing, he'd been doing it better than Mickey.

Another ten points to Draco for spotting the antique Berber rug in the carpet shop, plus ten for haggling so mercilessly, and ten for finding the testicle in the whole-lamb roast, plus ten for joking about it so becomingly, and ten for picking the fiacre pulled by the white horse, and ten more for his gracious refusal of a joint after dinner. 'When you don't do tobacco, the smoke is too much, you know?' No, Mickey did not know – nobody who'd smoked since they were nine years old would know. Draco was well ahead now.

He wriggled on the sun lounger. 'No. No. That's not it.' The agony of communicating without a camera. Having to struggle with cold, slippery, ugly, deceitful words, horrible things that scattered like scared fish every time he tried to grab one. Mickey writhed into a sitting position. 'I mean, our own place. We should buy somewhere.'

'Buy somewhere?' Now she was anxious. Buying some-where was her territory. She had Montreuil, she had a home for her secret self. Why did they need a second home when they hardly occupied the one they already had?

'The French say that a man with two houses loses his soul.'

Typical, that was. Mickey reached for his cigarettes. She'd never come out and say she didn't like what he'd suggested. She'd make one of those pointless comments, the sort of comments women made, that girls made, that girls like Mo probably learned to make at school when they preened around the playground being superior. Comments that didn't mean anything but implied that if you didn't understand you must be stupid.

'Is that supposed to be an answer?'

'I didn't think there was a question.'

'I'm asking if you want to buy a place. For holidays. For us.'

'Where?'

'I don't know. Where do people have places? Italy? Spain? No, that's where all the old crims go, isn't it? And people who play golf. France, maybe.'

'I'm OK with France already,' she warned him.

'You may be, but what about me?'

'There's never been any point having a place for holidays because you're always working,' she pointed out, trying to keep it light. 'You never have time to go anywhere. And our son never wants to be with us. We're not that type of family.'

'So you're saying I'm a bad father? That I was never around?'

'No, I'm not, Mickey. Joe doesn't need us, does he? He's never needed us. Our son was born sorted. He liked us around, all right, but he never wanted to be fussed over.

194

He'd have died if I carried on with him the way Alice carried on with her kids. There was never anything to do except just be there.'

'So what's your point?'

Mo turned over. She was getting soft. Her body, that was. Where the edge of her swimsuit pulled against the rise of her breast, it cut so easily into the flesh. Younger women had bouncing flesh that strained against their clothes instead of giving in to them. Mickey got through quite a few younger women, at least one on every shoot. In the sun their skin tanned evenly. Mo had freckles now. She never used to have freckles.

He saw that she saw that he was watching her. The shutters came down behind her eyes; suddenly she looked as blank as a doll.

'My point,' she said in that dreamy voice she used when she didn't want him to think she was being offensive, 'is that if we had a second home we'd never go there. What do you think, Mickey? That we're going to do the corporate retirement thing? That you're going to go down the golf club and I'm going to waft around in floral chiffon being a hands-on granny?'

'There's no need to get in a strop. I just thought another house would be nice.'

'I think we've got enough things already.'

'Who're we talking about here? You're the one who buys stuff. You spend your whole life running around looking for things to buy.'

'That's my business.'

'But what about me? What do I get?'

'What do you get? You get your freedom, Mickey. As

195

much as you want, whenever you want. Most men would envy you.'

'So you don't want us to buy another house?'

'You don't want to relax. You don't want to be with me all the time. You want to be out there, Mickey. That's the way you are.'

'You don't want a house somewhere?'

'Not if all the time we spend in it we're going to be rowing with each other.'

'Are you calling this a row?'

'All these questions! It's like you're in one of those TV games where you have to answer every question with another question.'

She looked comfortable, lying on her front in the sun, while he was walking around now, pacing to and fro in a pocket of shade. She was smiling a little. The sun caught the downy hairs on her lip. So unmoved. So laid back. So bloody uninterested. So goddamn superior.

On the far side of the pool, the Dracovich womenfolk were packing up and taking the baby indoors out of the heat. Draco himself was in the pool doing lengths. Up, down, up, down. Gliding through the water, sending out a bow-wave that washed over the sides. Power, control, motion. Fuck him.

'All right?' Mickey greeted Draco as he got out of the water. Smooth bastard probably didn't even drink. But no, he could be persuaded to the shade of the bar for a beer.

'You got a lot lined up when you get back?' Of course he has. He's The Man now, Draco is. He'll be flavour of the month, of the year, of the next bloody decade.

'A few things. I don't want to be doing too much, you

know. While she's a baby. You don't get that time again. I don't have to tell you that.'

'No. Uh – no.' So unfair, this new-father crap. There was no retrospective faking it. You could buy a car or a phone or some other gizmo, you could trade in your wife for a babe, but you couldn't be a new-father hero if you'd been born too soon.

'I've been meaning to ask you.' Draco leaned his toned torso forward in a confidential motion. 'That story about the Russians . . .'

'Oh yeah. That.'

'It was true, then? You bussed in Russians?'

'They weren't all Russian.'

'The boy who died was from the Ukraine, I heard.'

So unfair, this rainbow nation crap. Once it had been oh-so-hot to be a Northern working-class lad, just like him. Now all that was oh-so-over and the Eastern Europe thing was hot, just like Draco. You couldn't do the European thing if you'd been born in the wrong place.

'People are talking about that?'

'Somebody told me about it, so I suppose they must be. Very sad.'

'Uh – yes.'

Then his phone rang. Absolutely totally spooky, it rang at that very moment. Who the hell . . . it was Andy. How like Andy to call and wish them a good Christmas.

George. George was dead. That fucking bike. Leader of the pack, rebel without a cause, dead.

'Thanks, mate. I appreciate you telling me.'

'Bad news?' asked Draco. His eyes were practically brimming with tears. So unfair this manly feelings crap. You couldn't do feelings if you hadn't started early. Like the guitar. You have to start young, you can't just pick it up some time in your forties.

'Somebody's been killed. A friend of ours. Road accident.'

'That's bad. I'm sorry.'

'Yeah.' What to say? Crack a gag, old George would have done that. But his head was empty, no gags came.

'Had you been friends a long time?'

'Yeah. A long time.' How long? Art school and beyond. Twenty years, twenty-five? More? Better not say that. Make yourself sound old. To a kid like Draco twenty years was a lifetime. 'Yeah. We went back a long way.' Just leave it there.

He thought of George sitting on a bar stool, one leg crossed over the other, the rim of his kneecap sharp through his jeans, his shins hanging parallel as if the weight of his boots was pulling them straight. Elbow on knee, arm held vertical, a roach squeezed between first and second finger. His back curved over and his nose curved out and his cheeks curved inwards and his hair, the only thick and healthy thing about him, curved over his forehead, the old Ronnie Wood chop that he never changed.

George had once said, 'If I go to a cocktail party and people ask me what I do, I tell them I'm a failurist. Failure is my art. Some artists get out of bed and that's their thing. Me, I fuck up my life and that's my thing. "If at first you don't succeed, maybe failure is your thing." Old Quentin Crisp, he said that. People think it looks easy but being a failurist requires total commitment. Not everyone can do it. You have to work at being absolutely bleedin' hopeless. The great failurists can't even turn on a light without blowing the place up. For a failurist, you see, getting out of bed in the first place is a compromise with bourgeois society. That may be where I've gone wrong.' The grin. The festering teeth.

'You want to be by yourself,' Draco told him. 'I'll go in now. See you later.'

So fucking unfair, this feelings crap. And people were talking about the Russians. Fucking, fucking unfair. What exactly was the difference between throwing a piano off a bridge and bussing in a few Russians? Why was one a work of art and the other career suicide?

If Rhys ever wished he were richer, his father-in-law was there to show him the folly of his yearning. A one-man study in the evils of wealth, Barbara's father bought art for investment and lived alone in Hampstead. His house itself was an investment – a white concrete mansion designed by a famous architect of the Sixties, on a street of mansions on a hill, protected from the rest of the city by high walls, enormous trees and the man's unshakeable faith in his own intellectual superiority.

'I hope he's not going to be mean with the booze this year,' said Barbara as the gates opened before them. 'Stingy old bastard. I told him, I'm your only child and I want a damn good drink on Christmas Day.'

'I'm on call, don't forget,' Rhys warned her, anticipating her outburst when he refused the first glass.

'Oh really, Rhys! You're the most boring man I've ever met. Why the fuck couldn't you arrange things better than that?'

He felt Toby shiver with hatred. Their son was crushed

into the back seat, his head touching the car roof. 'I've been off the last three years. It's my turn.'

'Your turn. Your turn. You don't take turns, Rhys. You fix things so that you have a proper life, for fuck's sake. For God's sake don't tell Daddy you're not drinking. He doesn't need another excuse to be mean.'

Toby stared out of the car window. They passed a massive brown stone sculpture that seemed to be mostly buttocks. Algae greened its cheeks.

The air in the mansion was clean and stale. The carpets were fish-belly pale and walking on them was like walking on moss, except they sprang back so there was no trace of your footsteps.

The glass walls revealed the garden, dripping and decaying around the great stone backside. Paintings hung edge to edge on the walls, works by bankable artists, Francis Bacon, Lucien Freud. Tortured paint. Visceral abstracts. Slashes and stabs in stormy colours. The art was supplied on contract by the dealer.

This was the method of acquisition that Barbara's father favoured. 'At my time of life, you can't be bothered with people,' he said. Wealth protected him from human contact, ensured that all his relationships were commercial. In place of a live-in housekeeper he employed a contracted team of Filipino women who arrived daily in a mini-bus to clean and cook for him. A nursing agency supplied a carer as required. A florist renewed the flowers twice a week. A lawyer visited to suggest suitable charities for him to support. A private hire company supplied cars and drivers. Every morning, a barber came to shave him and cut what was left of his hair. When he went to the theatre the tickets were bought by a critic in his employ; when he read a book it was selected by an earnest small shop in Chelsea, delivered to the house, carried indoors, unpacked and placed in the right place on his segregated bookshelves, in the same way as his wine was chosen by a wine merchant and loaded into the racks in his cellar.

Toby had once suggested that his grandfather should forget his blood relatives and hire a family on contract. 'He could instruct them as to his taste and they would send people he approved of. It'd be much better.'

The old man greeted them with the facial twitch he used for a smile. He seemed to count them, one, two, three, and then looked in accusation at Rhys and said, 'Where is my only grand-daughter?'

'She's working today,' Rhys explained. 'Accident and emergency. She volunteered.' He was proud of her. Blood was telling. If he'd given up his own ideals and mortgaged his soul, at least he had passed something on to the next generation.

'I would not have allowed it,' the old man told them. 'No manners. There are always volunteers for these things. Someone without a family could have done it.'

They sat around the mahogany table laid with embroidered Italian linen and set with an armoury of silver cutlery while the Filipino crew carried in the courses. The chef, a man as tiny as a jockey and dressed in immaculate whites, appeared from the kitchen to announce each course, his voice metallic.

At the head of the table, the old man looked young for his age. He sat erect in his chair, as scrawny as his daughter was fat, and made the most of each opportunity for disapproval.

In this pastime Barbara was happy to join him.

'Ngeah!' The bowl of caviar, presented on ice, displeased him first. 'It's salt.'

'Much too salt,' Barbara agreed, loading a triangle of toast and stuffing it whole into her mouth. 'Is it Russian?'

The waitress paused, anxious not to offend, but they ignored her.

'It can't be Russian, they never put in too much salt. Must be Iranian.'

'Far too much salt. Leave it.'

'Yes, leave it.'

Toby and Rhys were in any case making a course from the chopped egg and onion. Years of visits to the pater familias had confirmed them both in the opinion that caviar was a tasteless, slimy, unnecessary substance and the greatest con trick in gastronomy.

With the caviar came an innovation: shot glasses of vodka set in ice. Barbara downed hers, and once her father had sipped and winced and sucked his teeth and muttered, 'Too cold,' she finished his as well. Toby threw down his allocation in a gulp. In sympathy, Rhys passed his son his own glass.

'Ngeah.' A ballotine of truffled mushrooms in a puff pastry shell offended next. The old man spat a mouthful into his napkin. 'Gritty.'

'Full of grit!' Barbara agreed, tearing a roll in half and swabbing the sauce with it. 'Can't have been properly washed.'

'Ruin your teeth.'

'Terribly dangerous. Don't eat it.'

'I'm not eating it. Certainly not.'

'You could lose a crown.'

'I know, I know. Only a few days since I last went to the dentist. Can't take the risk.'

Toby and Rhys demolished this course in two mouthfuls, finding it excellent. The waitress delivered a fresh napkin to the old man.

The grapefruit sorbet was waved away by both Barbara and her father. Rhys followed their lead but Toby, happy to eat ice cream in any form at any time, accepted his serving with enthusiasm. His grandfather watched his grandson's large hand wield the spoon. Two scoops and it was gone. Rhys winced for his son, for his innocent enjoyment and the doom it would surely bring him.

'It's too much,' the old man pronounced. 'Sorbet is too much.'

'He eats far too much,' Barbara agreed, looking at her son with contempt. 'He'll get fat.'

'I'm not fat,' Toby pointed out, 'and there was hardly any of it and it is Christmas.'

'As if that was any excuse,' said Barbara.

Pink discs appeared, disciplined mounds of tartare of wild salmon now swimming in a sea of cream sauce. The first of the wine glasses was filled. Toby ate efficiently and wiped his plate with bread as his mother had done a moment earlier, but she glared at him and flared her nostrils.

'Ngeah.' The old man stirred on his bony haunches. 'Fishy. Tastes fishy.'

'It's fishy,' said Barbara, flicking her portion about the plate with a fork. 'It must be farmed. Only farmed salmon tastes fishy.'

'He said wild, didn't he?'

203

'Yes, he did, but it was a lie, wasn't it? This has to be farmed.'

'It's too pink. It's slimy. It must be farmed.'

When the turbans of turkey with cranberry jus were placed in front of them, Rhys tried to break the hex.

'You're keeping well,' he suggested to his father-in-law, as soon as the old man had been supplied with vegetables.

'Don't insult me with that professional concern,' was the reply. 'I don't discuss my health at the table. Anyone's health. It's distasteful. Surely you should know that.'

The paintings; he would always talk about the paintings. Rhys scanned the wall in front of him for a topic of conversation. A canvas of grey stripes loured over the table.

'That's very powerful,' he suggested, nodding at the picture with the most positive face he could find to put on. 'Is it new?'

'I shan't keep it,' said the old man, as if Rhys's approval had made up his mind about the picture. 'It's too big.'

Facing him, Barbara choked and convulsed, her lips working frantically. When she had all their attention, she raised her fork to her mouth and disgorged a chewed lump of turkey meat. 'Ngearrh!'

'Ngeah,' her father agreed. 'It's tough.'

'It's all gristle. Turkey breast should be like butter.'

'It's like rubber.'

'You should be able to cut it with your fork; it should just melt in your mouth.'

'There's a joke about a man who goes into a Chinese restaurant,' put in Toby, who had cleared his plate in thirty seconds. 'He says, "Waiter, this chicken is rubbery," and the waiter says, "Thank you sir, I'll tell the chef, he'll be delighted."'

'Is that supposed to be funny?' demanded Barbara.

'You are not an odious American comedian in Las Vegas or some place like that,' said his grandfather. 'We don't want to hear your jokes. Jokes are not conversation.'

Not long to go now. Salad, cheese, dessert, freedom. Or at least permission to break the poisoned ring around the table and sit in the drawing room with coffee. After which they would usually be allowed to ask for a walk on the Heath while the old man took a nap. Then a short ordeal over petits fours and Earl Grey, and the final escape.

The salad was condemned as not really fresh and dressed with oil that was not properly filtered. The Stilton they called unripe. Barbara attacked Toby for taking two pieces of bread with his cheese. The smothered pop of champagne being opened was heard from the kitchen.

'*Fantasie de nougat glacé, cage au caramel, avec son coulis de framboises!*' announced the chef.

'Oh wow, cool!' A plate bearing everything that could be achieved with sugar, cream and artistry was placed in front of Toby. Over the ice cream was a dome of golden caramel cobwebs.

Toby picked up his spoon and smacked the dome. It shattered with a will. Chips of caramel scattered all over the table.

'My God!' shouted the old man, the force of his anger pushing him halfway up out of his chair. 'The boy's ruining the table!'

'Toby!' Barbara howled at her son. 'That's disgusting! What do you think you're doing?'

'I was only—'

'Whatever possessed you to do such a revolting thing?

Re–volt–ing,' she said, stabbing her finger at Toby in time to the middle syllable and raising her voice in a shriek of disdain.

Toby was very still, sizing up his mother as she poured out her scorn. Rhys saw his son's boyish expression of protest fade and a new, adult face replace it, a face of thunderous colour and vengeful intensity.

'I can hardly eat this stuff without breaking it, can I?' Toby said, going to work on the main body of the dessert. Calm but provocative. Maybe I'm reading that into him, Rhys tried to reassure himself. He's not trying to taunt them. He just wants to eat.

The old man was jigging in his chair and a red flush crept up his neck. His fingers began to scrabble on the table. 'Swinish behaviour. I won't allow it. Where on earth do you think you are?'

'Well, I presume I'm with my family. Since I've heard nothing but bitching all day, and everything I do seems to be wrong, and everything everyone else does seems to be wrong, and you're being as horrible as you possibly can, that would appear to be the logical conclusion.'

'How dare you take that nasty tone with your mother?'

'She dares take some pretty nasty tones with me. Maybe it's in the genes.'

'Hah! You're blaming me? You're actually blaming me, you great ugly pig?' Barbara was hissing now, her jaw rigid with rage. 'Well, you could be right. I tried, you know. I tried not to have you. Do you know that?'

'That's enough,' said Rhys. Was that going where he thought it was going? Was she that much of a monster?

'Oh no!' She spat back at him. 'Oh no! It's my turn. Why

should everyone else just spew up their feelings and we all have to listen, but when it's me, when it's my turn, I have to shut up? I'm tired of shutting up. I'm tired of being seen and not heard. I'm tired of being nobody in my own home.'

'Barbara . . .'

'I'll say what I have to say.' She turned on her son, and it had to be admitted her face was a labyrinth of pain, even though it was not the wound she was protesting that maddened her but an older, deeper injury she had carried her whole life, one that Rhys had once flattered himself he could heal. 'I tried not to have you,' she announced to Toby. 'I did everything. I went to every doctor in London. I asked them all, I said I'd pay them anything.'

'Barbara, stop it,' Rhys insisted, jumping up. What was he going to do, drag her out of the room by her hair? The old man raised a hand, finger upstretched to remind Rhys who was master. Behind him the waitress was frozen with embarrassment.

'Shut up!' Barbara was screaming. 'Shut up, shut up, shut the fuck up, you stupid selfish stupid worm.' A fork from the table was snatched up and thrown in his direction. 'I'm telling him, it's time he knew. Time you both knew. I never wanted him. I did everything to stop it. I went abroad, I went to Amsterdam. They said it was too late. The only way was to cut me open. I didn't believe it, I never believed it. Fucking cowards. They meant they were afraid of me.'

The old man was nodding, as if he'd heard the story before. The realisation went through Rhys's chest like 2000 volts. The old man really had heard this confession before. It was not news to him. Daddy's cheque book, the answer to all his wife's little problems. They had done that, the two of them, the two monsters together – they had conspired to kill his son.

'They were afraid I'd go mad. You were driving me mad, even before you were born. I took pills. They made me bleed. I took so fucking many I was in hospital.'

'They said it was a threatened miscarriage.' He remembered it well, the crisp young registrar, his professional colleague. So he too had been bought and paid for by the old man.

'So? They weren't wrong. They gave me stuff to stop it and I threw it in the toilet. I nearly killed myself trying to get rid of you. I wish I'd done it too. Saved us both the trouble.'

'Well, cheers, Mum.' There was Toby, smiling. A thin, cynical, lop-sided smile. His son was safe. The boy was muffled up in irony, snug and warm against his mother's freezing cruelty. Smarter than you. You're standing there like a spare prick at a wedding, just about ready to faint from the hate and destruction raining down all around, and your boy's doing fine.

Toby appealed to the waitress. 'Is there any more ice cream?'

Eh-eh-eh-eh. The old man began to laugh. A hard, shrivelled noise, more like a cough than anything to do with pleasure. Eh-eh-eh-eh. He twitched his hand to give permission and the waitress, slow with amazement, moved to collect the boy's plate.

Later, when they were alone together walking around the sodden turf of the Heath, not bothering to enjoy the view of the rest of London sprawling under a veil of vehicle emissions in the near distance, Rhys tried some damage limitation. 'She didn't mean that. Any of it. You know how she gets when she's with her father. They make each other worse.'

'I appreciate you trying to make me feel better.' He couldn't be as unconcerned as he sounded. Could he? Toby was speaking like an adult but acting like a boy, trying to slide on the mud on the path. 'But I think she meant it. She's been bottling it up for years. I suppose it had to come out some time. Christmas kind of catalyses these things, doesn't it?'

'She was distressed about something.'

'I'd say. But she's always distressed about something, isn't she?'

'I think she feels life hasn't treated her well.'

'Hard to understand, isn't it? Do you think she's ill, Dad?'

'Ill?'

'Depressed or mad or something. I mean, I know it's not an original question, but what do women want? We're rich compared to most people, aren't we? She's got us, we're all pretty good. I know I mess around at school sometimes, but I'm not out there doing drugs or mugging people or anything. And you're not running around drinking or having affairs – with other women.' Halfway through the sentence he lost confidence. Then he seemed to make a decision. He added, 'Not that I'd blame you if you were.'

Did Toby know? Had he found out? A boy could just implode emotionally if he knew his father was unfaithful to his mother. Now Toby was mooching along beside him, hands in pockets. Rhys knew that act. He'd worked on it himself. Caring detachment. Concerned but backed-off in a sensitive manner. Giving the other party space. So what – his son was just finessing, hoping for a confession. Was this the moment, then? Could he begin his new life here?

They drew breath together and turned to each other at the same time. Eyes locked, breath held. This was the moment. Then Rhys laughed, mostly with relief, and said, 'You first.'

'OK. Who's M, Dad? The M on your speed-dial. When you lent me the phone. M's the first number. I hit it by mistake. Just forgot it was your phone, pressed one.'

Sandbagged by anxiety, Rhys tried to bluff. 'I can't remember. I never use the speed-dial, I've forgotten how it works.'

'Well, I dialled the number anyway.' Toby looked dogged, as he had done in all those interviews with the sad-but-firm headteacher who suggested he should not come back to their school next term. 'I just made like a nice wrong number. I asked her name. So I know, actually. It's Mrs Ryder, isn't it? Who has that shop. I suppose what I want to know is who she is to you. But I know that, really. I just thought you might tell me.'

'Sorry.'

'Be my guest.'

'I've wanted to tell you for a long time.'

'It's been a long time, then?'

'Just over five years.'

'And are you in love?' Toby said it with such ridiculous solemnity, as only someone who has not yet been in love can.

'Yes. Well, I am.'

'You mean she's not?'

'It's not that simple. We are both married. Got families. Her husband is my friend. These things aren't black and white, Toby. We haven't talked about where we're going, we haven't made any plans.'

He looked disappointed. They were walking awkwardly along a steep slope and the path was too narrow for them to be side by side. Toby loped ahead, and when the track widened slowed down to wait. He was running on bursts of energy, starting and stopping like a stuttering motor, bright then uncertain, brave then timid, old then young.

'Obviously Mum doesn't know or it'd have been like Hiroshima.'

'No, she doesn't.'

'Are you going to tell her?'

'I want to tell her. We need to have that conversation. Mo and I.' There, he'd done it. He'd shared her name with another person, with his own son, even, and lightning hadn't struck him down. 'The time hasn't been right. We can't be together that much. It's sort of precious moments.'

'That's very Noël Coward, Dad.'

'Huh?' What the fuck had Noël Coward got to do with this?

Toby rolled his eyes and struck a pose. '"Strange how cheap music can be so potent".'

'I don't get it.'

'The song: 'When will I see you again'. The Three Degrees. The Philly Sound.' He went falsetto. 'Ooh, aah . . . '

'My son is a Diana Ross impersonator?' My son is a transvestite? My son is gay?

'No, Dad. Fear not. I just meant, precious moments. You know.'

I know that you can't possibly know. You whose life is largely made up of howling deserts of boredom, of teenage cafard, of endless, pointless, lifeless afternoons of not having anything to do; what do you know about precious moments?

Rhys's phone rang. On call, on call. Yes, I am a doctor, I have responsibilities, I must leave you now. 'This is Doctor Pritchard.'

'Rhys?'

'Andy.'

What the hell?

Smiley Andy, season of goodwill?

'Andy. Sorry, I'm on call this afternoon. I thought it was the emergency service.'

'No, I'm sorry. I've been trying to get you but you've been switched off.'

'We're up at my father-in-law's. But it's OK, I'm on Hampstead Heath, we're walking. Happy Christmas.'

'Oh yes. Look, there isn't an easy way to say this . . .'

To say what? This is Andy, just a mate in the band. I play the drums, he plays bass and sings. We have a few beers, that's it. Why can he possibly be calling me in those terms on Christmas Day? It's cancer. He's got cancer. That's why people do things like this. He's worried and you're the only doctor he knows. He'll want me to check out his specialist, go over the treatment, the usual story.

'No, please. I'm OK to talk. What is it?'

'It's George. He had an accident, a road accident.'

'He's hurt?'

'He was on his bike, of course.'

'So how bad is it?'

'He's dead, Rhys.'

'Oh. Well. Ah.' So what do you want from me? There isn't anything to say, is there? Don't lay your expectant silence on me, old chum. I'm not needed here.

'Killed instantly, most likely.'

'Well.'

'So he didn't suffer. He's not in touch with his family, of course, so I'm going to do what I can.'

'Good of you.'

'And I guess the band is the nearest to family he's got. In a practical sense. So maybe we can meet up, talk about arrangements.'

'I didn't know that about his family. Yes, of course we must do what's got to be done.'

'So maybe you can call me tomorrow or the next day. Think about it and give me a call. Or I'll call you, if that's easier.'

'Yeah. Yeah. I'll do that. Thanks for letting me know, Andy.'

A few more things to say, the verbal polystyrene filling up the space, keeping things safe. Then the end of the call. Toby was looking at him with large eyes.

'One of the guys in the band. Had an accident.'

'What band, Dad?'

'You know what band. I've always played in a band. Since I was a student. They asked me to play with them. They needed a drummer.'

'I'm sure I did know. I must have lost sight of it. Sorry.'

'That's OK.'

They were on their way back to the road now; only a few more yards of soiled city grass, then back to paving and tarmac.

'You must think I'm pathetic. About Mo.'

'I'm too young, I'm not there yet. I don't understand.'

'But you don't disapprove?'

'Oh no. I mean, it's your life. You can do what you want.'

'Now what does that mean?' Relief. We're back in the right roles, I'm the daddy and he's the son. No more of this uncomfortable precocious conversation. Back to normal.

Toby was no longer striding. He was dawdling, trying to stretch out the walk for as long as possible, putting off the evil hour when they would have to re-enter the concrete mansion. 'You know all those counsellors Mum made me see? They ended up saying the same thing, really. Not in so many words, they don't do that. But they all saw it the same way. They said Mum's the problem. They really went bananas trying to make me feel OK about hating her.'

'You hate her?'

'Well, yes, Dad. Don't you?'

'I wouldn't put it as strongly as that.'

'Well, I would. Even stronger, actually. I feel like I'm going to die when I'm at home with her, like she's going to crush me or smother me or something.'

Was this right? Was it normal? Goddamn it, he'd done a module in psychology at med school and he couldn't remember a thing.

'What I'm saying is, Dad, I'm not sure how long I can go on like this. I mean, if you aren't going to make a move, then I might have to.'

'You've been watching too many bad films.'

They were at the top of the street of mansions and his son was standing still, kicking a dead leaf about. 'So if you wanted to make a move, I'd be right behind you, Dad.'

'You're disappointed, then, that I'm not doing anything right now?'

'Well, I was kind of hoping . . . Anyway, look, I'm not

going back in there. I can't. I'll get a tube or walk home or something. Find a kebab, maybe. I'm still hungry. Don't worry, I'll be OK, I won't do anything stupid.'

'I'm glad we talked.'

'So'm I. Catch you later.'

It was time for Rhys to move. It was time to go back to his wife and her father, taking the smothering sense of a lost opportunity with him, while Toby took another road. He waved, a whole-arm wave, before they lost sight of each other.

Afterwards, in the half-conscious state in which he hibernated in Barbara's company, he wondered what Mo was doing and found that the Mo of his thoughts was a different shape now. She was dark, she was concrete, she was clearly defined, she was almost real. No more daydreaming of Mo like a child desperately pressing his face into a comfort blanket.

'I wanted to talk to you today.'

'Well, you haven't. You've talked to the boys in the band.'

'It had to be done.'

It is dangerous to be alone together after sixteen years of marriage. The festive meal was scheduled for six in the evening. Lily was giving the day to feeding the homeless in Soho and, as Andy should have expected, had crashed out of the house before dawn, leaving her stocking untouched. Daisy, unexpectedly and implausibly, had gone for a walk. In his stocking from her was a purple T-shirt with lettering that said: This isn't a bald spot, it's a solar panel powering a love machine. He had told her that he'd grow into it. Outside it was raining heavily.

Andy and Laura sat in their vacant living room, he at his desk, she flopped on a sofa.

'It didn't have to be done, Andy.'

'There's nobody else. He didn't have anybody.'

'Everybody's got somebody.'

'It seemed the right thing to do. I didn't like the idea of what's left of him lying in a morgue somewhere and all the rest of us having Christmas Day.'

'It was a nightmare when we had him for Christmas. He got so drunk.'

She was wearing the dress with the frilled hem. That dress had been around for a few months already. He didn't like it. In particular, the way it drooped around her knees. Fine if you were some sad girl in a small-town salsa class, but a bit of a joke on a woman adult enough and rich enough and still slim enough to be elegant. She'd always been elegant.

'I just thought I should tell them.'

'So did they appreciate it, your friends?'

'I don't know. Rhys was the worst. I suppose he's used to people dying.'

'So they were not greatly moved?'

'It's not the easiest call I've ever made.'

'OK.' She shifted around to sit square and businesslike. 'You wanted to talk to me. I'd like to tell you that I really wish you wouldn't do these things. Taking everyone's troubles on your shoulders. Living people's lives for them. I wish you'd just leave people alone and let them look after themselves. They don't care, Andy. You're the only one who cares and you can't make people feel the way you do.'

'We were like his family.'

'But we are your family, like it or not.'

'But you're never home, Laura. If you're saying you want me to give you more time, I've got time, plenty of time. Ever since I've been working for myself. But you're never here.'

'And you're always here. When I get home you're either sitting in an armchair or pottering around in the kitchen without any shoes on. That's not what I want.'

Into his mind popped a picture of the weather house he had bought for his mother on his first skiing holiday. A little wooden chalet with two doors, window boxes and a woodpile outside. If Mr Rain in his lederhosen was out, Mrs Sun in her dirndl was in. If Mrs Sun was out, Mr Rain went in. The best you could get was the two of them standing in the doorways, painted smiles facing forward.

'Is that it, then? What's gone wrong? Because something has gone wrong, hasn't it?'

She sighed as if the question bored her deeply. 'I suppose it has.'

Yes! The day wasn't going to waste after all. They could get somewhere.

'That evening with Pascal – you know I was just fixing the tap, don't you?'

'Do I?'

'Yes, you do. You know me, Laura. Am I more likely to be fixing someone's dodgy plumbing or giving their boyfriend a blow-job? Given the choice, all other things being equal, which one am I going to go for?'

Her mouth twitched. She was trying not to laugh. 'What do you want, Laura? Tell me. We can work on this.'

A shadow of annoyance passed across her face. Sod it, how dare she try to warn him off? They were drifting, had been for months, and not in the same direction. Time to pull back on course. 'If it bugs you that I'm at home, I could get an office somewhere. We're doing well, I'm sure it's tax-efficient. Shall I do that? Then I can go out to work every day like I used to.'

'I don't know,' she said. 'Don't hassle me for answers, Andy. You always think people are broken and you can fix them. It's not like that.'

'Do you want us to see someone? A therapist, maybe?'

'Good God, no. You're not that desperate, are you?'

There it was. The stab. She'd always been like that. Get too close and arrgh! Stabbed in the guts. Right in the guts, the major artery, the place you could bleed to death from. 'Fuck off,' he said. It came from somewhere deep, some-where near the wound. 'You cow. You miserable lousy bitch.' The anger threw him out of his chair and out of the room in an instant.

The result was a surprise. Moving as if someone else was pulling her strings, she came over and put her arms around his neck before he could move away.

She kissed him. Her hands were everywhere – she was hot, hotter than hell. And he was sad, and tired, and angry with her, and angry with Mickey, Rhys and Sam for being three cold bastards, and angry with George for riding a stupid motorbike and for being a washed-up flake and now, to top it all off, for being dead at Christmas.

He could have slapped her, if he was the kind of man who slapped women. And they had not had sex for weeks. Months, to tell the truth. And he didn't want it now. So he slapped her.

For the sake of acting like adults, for the sake of a good,

clean fight and not a childish shoving match, he made it a good one. And for the sake of not having to hit her again, he took it out on the dress, so that when she came back to hit him he took a good grip and ripped it. And for the sake of not getting into any embarrassment with that goddamn drooping frill, he made the rip a good one too.

So they fell over and hit the floor together. The mark of his hand came up red on her face. His brain left the building. She wanted sex; well, she could have it.

Afterwards, when they were still on the floor in the hall, sitting up against the walls on opposite sides, she took a breath to speak.

'Don't say anything,' he said. 'Whatever it is, I don't want to hear.'

She took another breath to speak.

'I said, don't do it. Good or bad. I don't want to know right now.' He got up, painfully, and went to the bathroom.

Much later, when he came out, she was in the kitchen in his apron and what was left of her underwear. Something was cooking. He had had plans for the meal. Marinades, stuffing, glazes. Not the moment, better let it go.

She came over and hugged him around his waist. 'I'm sorry,' she said. 'But it can't be that bad, can it?'

He accepted the hug. He folded his arms around her and gave her a coward's kiss on the top of her head. He did not answer.

CHAPTER 8

Keep The Faith

They met in the pub. The band had never been an indoor game, to be played in an environment that featured fitted carpets, a full fridge and a well-serviced mortgage. Band business had to be done away from home, after dark and out in the world of infinite potential.

Important to do it right. Andy got there early. George might have screwed up his life but they, who were surviving him, were not screw-ups and they would say goodbye to him in their own style. No trouble to stake out the usual table; the bar after Christmas was vacant and wiped-down, ready for the next big trauma.

He found himself blinking. Everything was high-contrast, high-definition, hyper-real. It hurt your eyes. He saw Mickey roll through the doors, shoulders braced in his leather jacket. Surprising how slight he was, how the empty room swallowed him. He walked over like a figure in a Japanese video game, legs jerking at each step, feet not quite touching the ground, and turned around to sit in the same style, skimping the three dimensions.

'All right?'

'Yeah, great.'

'Anybody else?'

'We're all going to be here.'

Rhys was next. Funny how Rhys always came into the bar as if he'd never been there before, looking around brashly, with a swagger, because he needed to show strangers that he was completely in control. To join them he came storming over like a soap opera doctor shouldering through hospital double-doors to deal with a cardiac arrest.

'All right?'

'Yeah, fine.'

'Sam?'

'Sam's coming,' Andy said. 'What are you having?' Sam had left his home. Alice had said that. Not the business of the day. Nothing to do with them, anyway, if one of them left his family. Can of worms, don't open it. Andy got up to get the beers in. When he got back, they assured each other that their Christmases had been good.

Rhys asked, 'Are we sure Sam's coming?'

'Andy says so. Sam's coming, isn't he?'

'Yeah, he said so.' He may have left his wife but he won't be leaving us.

Time yawned. The bar was not filling up. The fruit machine on the far wall glowed for no one. The clientele ran to a few sad bastards propped up in corners. And them. At the usual table. Early in the evening – it'd get busy later.

'Do we know where he is, Sam?' Mickey had the shortest fuse.

Confidently, Rhys answered him. 'He'll be coming from home, won't he? They didn't go away.'

'I heard he wasn't at home,' Mickey ventured, ignoring the warning sign: Minefield, danger, stay out.

'How d'you mean, not at home?'

'Mo got it from Alice. Bit of a domestic, or something.'

'Domestic?'

'Moved out.'

'I didn't know that.'

'That's what she said.'

Now the two of them were looking at Andy. He was on the spot. Say nothing. Do not disclose. Saying things would lead to opinions and opinions to argument and argument to fighting, feuding, murder, revenge, a vendetta, a war, Northern Ireland, Palestine, Kashmir, Macedonia. Don't go there, don't even think about it. Suppress, deny, ignore. It was the best way.

'He wasn't home when I rang,' Andy offered. 'I called back and got him later.' It was enough. The other two relaxed, satisfied that they had as much information as taste and decency required. To make sure the topic stayed closed, Andy unfolded his list.

'Oh God, look at that.' But Mickey was delighted, his grin unwinding around half his face. 'Trust old Andy, eh?'

'There's stuff to get through,' Andy protested. But he was pleased to be teased for his old-Andy-ness. Once it had been old George. Now, apparently, old Andy.

'Do we really need an agenda?' Rhys was serious. 'There can't be that much to discuss.'

'There's Sam,' Andy pointed out.

Sam was thrusting in their direction, snatching the skirts

of his coat around his knees as if the low environs in which he found himself might pollute his person. They appraised him without letting him know they were doing it, the sharp glance scanning for changes. Fatter. New clothes, expensive. Grand manner. But that was Sam; he could put on weight, he liked to spend too much and he enjoyed a good sneer when the occasion demanded it. No sign of any domestic. OK, a bit of purple around the left side of the face there, but maybe it was the light. No change, situation normal.

'All right?' they greeted him, sure of getting the right answer.

'Yeah, right.'

He took a seat, he asked for a scotch and Rhys bought him a large one. 'So,' Sam began, as if he had another meeting to get to and was already running late, 'what about George?'

'What exactly happened?' Just gotta get the facts. When Rhys read a book, he liked a classic mystery. Cadfael was his top favourite.

'The police think he ran out of gas and skidded. On the motorway, just before the Westwick turn-off. Thrown over the central barrier. There was a truck coming the other way. From what they can work out from what's left of the bike, the tank was empty.'

'Christmas Eve, eh?'

'That's right.'

'He was coming to see one of us, then.'

'Well, he wasn't going to Land's End.' Mickey raised an eyebrow to take the sting out of the words. 'Yeah, sounds like he was coming to see me to bum another fifty.'

Andy felt a prick of guilt. George had been broke and he

hadn't known. 'I didn't know he was that bad.'

'Must've been, if the bike was out of gas,' Rhys deduced.

'I'm not going that way,' Mickey declared. 'I don't want to talk about what kind of no-hoper he was. He was a great musician. The band would have died without him, we'd have been nothing.'

'Great's a bit strong.' Sam discarded his glass as if it was its own fault that it was now empty. 'He thought he was fucking Gary Moore and he certainly wasn't.'

'Have we got any tapes of him?' Andy asked.

'Tapes? We did a tape once, didn't we? What do you want a tape for?'

'He wants to play it at the bloody funeral. Don't you?' Mickey was probably still teasing.

'It's an idea,' Andy defended himself.

'Why do we have to have a funeral? Who's going to pay for it?' Sam clearly regarded this as a clinching argument.

'I just assumed . . . it's what you do when somebody dies, isn't it? Have a funeral. Get up and say what was good about the person you've all known. I was thinking – we all knew him as a musician. Maybe nobody else did. Just like nobody else in our lives really knows us as musicians. If you didn't know George the guitarist, you'd think he was a bit of a sad character, bit of a nutter, even. It'd be nice to play his music and maybe one of us say a few words . . .'

'Who's coming to this fucking funeral? It'll be one of us telling the rest of us what we already know. Why do we have to have a funeral? I'm asking again.' Sam was rolling his empty glass around in one hand and drumming the fingers of the other on the table. Time seemed to be running out on him.

'It'd just be a crematorium service. Ten minutes.'

'Exactly. And it'll be us and a couple of bike boys skiving on their deliveries. So why are we bothering? Do they still have paupers' graves? What happens when somebody dies and they haven't got any money?'

Rhys saw his way into the argument. 'People who're homeless or whatever, the council pays for their cremation.'

'Well, I vote we do that. Who do we have to call?'

Mickey said, 'It'd be what he'd have wanted, old George. I can hear him now, can't you?'

This was not the right conversation. Andy had been expecting everything he felt himself: loss, regret, compassion, nostalgia, guilt – horror, even, for a life lost, for a spirit extinguished, for a body they'd been seeing around all their lives smeared all over the road they'd been driving down all their lives, under a freezer truck full of chilled Christmas turkeys for the Magno supermarket at Helford. Surely there should be some feeling for the end of all those years?

'Fat lot of use to me, some scurfy old child-molesting vicar going on about me when I am deceased,' continued Mickey. 'That's what he'd say. He'd rubbish the idea, if he was here.'

'Exactly,' Sam pronounced with triumph, as if he'd tricked a devious witness into self-incrimination.

'You guys go way back with him. You'd know what he'd have wanted.' Rhys the traitor. So much for medical ethics.

Time to get to it. 'Is this just about what George would have wanted?' Andy held their eyes, a pair at a time. 'Or what he'd have said he wanted? Because it was all an act with him, wasn't it? All that eat the rich, burn the town, piss on the lawn crap. He just knew he couldn't hack it and he'd found a rationale, that's all. Let's face it, things went wrong with George. It wasn't that he didn't have the talent. He just couldn't make his life work, somehow.'

'Few strings short of a Stratocaster, if you ask me. Still, he was happy,' said Sam.

'No, he wasn't.' How could all three of them sit there, alive, well and prospering, and deny George's pain? Andy was indignant. 'He was pissed off. Every minute of every day, he was just in a rage that he couldn't get his life sorted.'

'Nah,' Mickey asserted. 'He was fine. Fine the way he was. He wasn't materialistic, George. He despised all that, he really did. He had exactly the life he wanted.'

Was this for real? He really was the only one who'd thought to look beyond the George act and figure out what was going on. But they did care, in their way. They must have cared. 'This isn't about what George would have wanted, is it? It's about what we want for ourselves. We've got to say goodbye. We're talking about how we want to do it.'

'No, we aren't,' asserted Sam. 'We're talking about how to sort out the mess he left behind because for some reason you feel it's your job to do that and you want to get the rest of us involved. And I, for one, I'm not buying into it. All that saying goodbye bollocks – he's gone, what's the point?'

'Like he didn't mean anything to us?' He could win this. Mickey was looking doubtful now. Rhys was uncomfortable, he could feel him fidgeting. Sam had cut into the heart of the matter, but brutally, so now the others were feeling guilty. 'He meant something to me. I'm not ashamed to say that. I've thought about it the last few days. He was like the stakeholder for all of us. We gave him part of ourselves, the part we were willing to risk, and he was holding it. He was keeping faith for everything we thought we could lose.'

Sam began to simmer with truculence. 'Andy, you talk such unbelievable fucking crap sometimes I can see what it was that ended your advertising career.'

No, no, no, my friend, you can't get me there. Solid scar tissue, hit me as hard as you like, I am invulnerable. 'That's exactly what I'm talking about. I remember you, Sam. You were going to make a pile and buy your own vineyard before you were forty. And I never saw myself in advertising. Nor did you, Mickey. You were going to be Tarkovsky or Jean Luc Godard or somebody and go to film festivals and win prizes. And I was just messing around at art school until some A&R man put a contract in front of my nose. My life was going to be in music. And you were going to Africa, Rhys – don't you remember?'

'Oh yes, I remember that.' Rhys folded his arms to defend his compromised heart.

Sam was scowling. Mickey hadn't moved. Careful, now. It could still go pear-shaped. 'And then it didn't happen. Maybe we knew we were only dreaming. You leave college, you meet reality. We had to get our lives sorted. We got jobs. Maybe we were challenged by the work we were doing, got good at it, made some money. We fell in love, we got married. We had our children and we loved them. We ended up doing things we never saw ourselves doing. Things we'd maybe despised when we were kids. But every month or so we'd meet up and play some music, enjoy ourselves, just like we'd always done. And there'd be George, and he never changed, and he never got a life. So he was keeping faith with the guys we used to be.'

'You really thought that was what was going on? You're speaking for yourself,' Sam insisted. 'I never thought that. He was just a flake. Sure, he was a laugh, but his life wasn't happening, was it? It was embarrassing being around him. I used to wish he'd get into one of his bloody solos and keep playing so I wouldn't have to listen to his endless loser conversation.'

'Yeah, but that was the point of him, wasn't it?' Thank God, Rhys was coming in on the right side, arms and legs twisted to screw up the courage for disclosure and that earnest professional face of his put on to make it all sound so official. 'Part of what we liked about him was that he was a loser. We've been at this a long time, don't forget. Over twenty years, with a few years off when we got married. As long as most of us have been married. It's not just the music, is it? Whatever was going on in our lives, problems with our kids or our jobs or whatever, we could get together and there'd be George, going nowhere fast, stuck in a time-warp from when we were all nineteen, and we'd feel better about ourselves. And we'd help him out and feel good about it because we were in a position to be generous.'

'Psychobabble. I don't believe this.' Sam rolled his eyes. 'We were in a position to be guilt-tripped and ripped-off, you mean. So go on, how many of you were lending him money?'

'I used to bung him the odd fifty,' Mickey confirmed.

'I lent him a fifty once,' admitted Rhys. 'We both knew he wasn't going to pay it back.'

Andy said, 'So did I, but when I left KKDW he stopped asking. I think I was more hurt by that than by getting fired.'

'I thought you were made redundant?' cross-examined Sam.

'Fired, redundant; same thing, isn't it?'

'No, not necessarily, not at all.'

'Yes, it is, Sam. Anyway, George stopped putting the squeeze on me after that.'

'He had a business,' Mickey reminded them. 'I lent him a bit more to get started.'

'What business?' Sam wanted to know.

'Growing weed.'

'Not exactly a business,' in Sam's opinion. 'A few Grobags here and there.'

'No, he'd found this derelict building and he'd gone into industrial production.'

'How much did you give him?'

'A grand. He said he had a thousand plants or something, harvesting in time for Christmas. He'd teamed up with this Australian girl. Nice kid, I met her, he brought her round.'

'A grand! Are you out of your tiny mind? You realise you've bankrolled a couple of drug dealers, Mickey? Do you know that could ruin my professional reputation? What the fuck were you thinking? Criminal associates! I'd be disbarred.' Now Sam was clucking like an apprehensive turkey.

'So he had finally got it sorted.' The poignancy of it all. Andy heard his voice falter. His voice, the symbol of his strength, like Samson's hair. 'He'd got a woman, he'd figured out a way of making some money, and then he gets unlucky with a truck on the motorway. Life can be a bitch, eh?'

'Yeah, that is sad, I suppose,' Rhys nodded in sympathy.

'I say, let's do the funeral. If you're worried about the

cost, Sam, I'll do your share. Or we can split three ways.'
Mickey raised eyebrows at the other two, who nodded, ves-
tigially, blank-faced, with hesitation, in order not to offend
Sam, because Sam in a sulk was an ugly beast.

'Fine by me,' the dissenter assured them. 'If that's what
you want to do . . .'

'Something happened to your face, Sam?' That was it with
Mickey – when he was in, he went all the way. They scruti-
nised Sam's features, noted the swollen nose, the purple bag
under one eye, the undeniable scab over a rather large cut in
his lip. 'What happened? You have an accident or something?'

Sam folded with no more argument. 'Let's split four ways.
Band decision, I'll abide by it.'

The relief! All that angst and persuasion, just to get them
to act like – well, men. To Andy, a man had broad shoulders.
A man took responsibility, a man did what had to be done,
a man observed the decencies. That was it – observe the
decencies! That petit-bourgeois circumlocution, that expression that went with pursed lips, paper doilies, lace curtains,
John Betjeman and raising the teacup with the little finger
crooked. George would have said it that way, and laughed
down the back of his throat the way he did.

'He'd be glad we've decided to observe the decencies,'
Andy suggested.

'Yeah, observe the decencies.' Mickey agreed, raising his
glass with his little finger crooked and pursing his lips
before sipping.

'Do the decent thing,' said Rhys, his tin ear for cultural
nuance working well. They winced, but nobody let it show.

'So, have we got a date? Isn't Christmas rush hour at the

crematorium, what with people topping themselves and everything?' Now Sam was impatient, eager to go. To get back to The Woman, whoever she was. He was fidgeting, looking at his watch. Why, the man was downright hag-ridden.

At last, time to talk numbers. Andy opened his PalmPilot. 'If we hold off until next week, say January third, it gives us time to make enquiries about his family.'

'What enquiries? What family? He despised his fucking family, for God's sake.'

'Observe the decencies,' Mickey reminded them. 'They've got a right to know how their boy ended. If they had a part in it, it might make them think.'

'If they're still alive,' Rhys pointed out. 'How many parents have we got left between us?'

'If they ever had the power of thought, which I doubt. Next Tuesday?' Sam had his small black legal diary open in his hand.

'Good for me,' Mickey agreed.

'I can get my duty covered for the morning,' said Rhys.

'Next Tuesday, then. OK, anybody want to come with me to sort out his place?'

It was the question-expecting-the-answer-no, probably the only concept he retained from Latin lessons in school, but it didn't get the answer it predicted.

'Yeah, I'm up for that,' said Mickey. 'This afternoon?'

'Let's do it.'

A strange number on the pager. The hospital exchange, an extension he didn't recognise. The assistant manager. Wondering if he had a moment to pop by. With any records he might have relating to the last month and also his diary, if that was convenient. Rhys smelled a rat. As George would have put it, there was a powerful whiff of rodent.

In six years he'd never met the assistant manager, or seen her around to notice. A woman in her thirties, pale, with large, slightly prominent eyes, eyes that accused expressionlessly, a fish on a slab. Matching silver metal jewellery, a pendant, a bracelet, earrings, all dangling little cylinders that might contain scrolls with her name and address. A grey suit, very long fingernails bent back by the medical record file as she opened it. 'Thank you for coming in.'

'No trouble. After Christmas, not a full schedule.'

'This is about an operation you assisted on in early December. Do you remember assisting Mr Debrosser when he did an abdominoplasty on Ms Serena Watson on December fifth?'

December fifth? The date was still smouldering in his memory, the Friday before the first Sunday in Advent. He had been eaten up with eagerness to finish his work and drive to France to meet Mo. Christ, had he made a mistake? He'd heard nothing, but it was Christmas, people were away. Now a one-to-one interview, a bad sign. Where was Debrosser? A witness, at least.

'Yes, I remember that one.'

'Can you remember the patient?'

'Yes, clearly. I've got my diary here.' It was an A4 book and her desk was already stacked with files. Rhys was forced to turn the pages with the diary balanced on his knees. Feeling awkward, unprofessional, incompetent. Yes, there it was, his note about Ms Watson. Thirty-seven minutes under, no signs of distress, no complications. He passed it over with a clear conscience but also a niggling doubt.

'The complaint is not about anything clinical.'

'It's not? What is it, then?'

'She says she heard you talking about her, making offensive remarks. Racist remarks.'

'She couldn't possibly. I'm absolutely certain we never said anything like that.' She was not a clinician, none of the managers were. He'd have to draw her a picture. 'Patients occasionally say they've heard things. They can dream as they're going under, although they don't usually remember because there's a degree of amnesia caused by the process. And there can be awareness under anaesthesia.'

'The theatre sister says her eyes opened. Would that happen with this awareness? I'm sorry, the clinical director of your department should be dealing with this but he's away for Christmas. This woman wrote to the boss and our policy is to respond within five days. I've got to make a decision today.'

'The patient retains a sense of hearing when all other signs of consciousness have gone. So they can hear you for the last few seconds as they go under, the first few seconds when they come back. Possibly. And in theatre, they can occasionally have some awareness if the intravenous is wearing off and the inhalation agents haven't taken over completely.'

'Would she have that all through the operation and still not report feeling any pain? She's saying you had a racist conversation about her but she hasn't reported feeling pain at all.'

'No, that would be really unusual. I've never heard of that, except rarely during Caesarean sections when you keep the dose low for the baby's sake.' Debrosser. Big, blond, red-faced, full of bounce. And young. Sensitive, like all the young. Debrosser would have died rather than distress a patient that way. 'I can't imagine Debrosser saying anything racist. Not at all. The last person. His language is,' careful, careful, 'exaggerated but he is extremely sensitive to racial issues. Given his background he's acutely aware of the possibility of giving offence.'

'Given his background, the patient feels she's got him bang to rights as a racist. Can you remember any conversation in theatre?'

Rhys thought back. Mo asleep in front of the fire. The bamboo chairs, the madness of the braderie, the sense of failure wreathed around a time he had planned to open his heart to the woman he loved, the anger that he'd allowed himself to be thwarted by events. Before that the high-adrenalin drive to the ferry, the stormy crossing, the vomit in the lavatories, the cold. Before that, the operation. Planning what he wanted to say to Mo? Had his mind wandered, had he failed to check his doses, had the numbers on the dials done some kind of do-si-do and taken each other's places? He knew it could happen, however careful you were. Ms Watson's eyelids had flipped up as if she had been a doll.

'He usually has some sport on the radio. Yes, I remember. It was the cricket. He was getting wound up about the cricket,' he recalled. 'Some decision the umpire made. I don't know what it was, cricket's not my thing.'

'No,' the administrator agreed. She seemed to have a working knowledge of cricket at least. 'I should imagine it was the Grenadian who gave Khan an out.'

'So she didn't hear all that he said? She got the wrong end

of the stick, thought we were talking about her? It's not racist to criticise an umpire, is it? I mean, everybody does it.'

The administrator flapped the papers in her hand. 'From what it says here, she thinks she had awareness through the entire procedure and heard the doctors having a racist conversation while they were working. She isn't claiming traumatic pain. But unless it's an anaesthetic-induced hallucination, she *was* able to hear during the procedure and now she's claiming you were giving her racial abuse the whole time and is threatening an action for – what is it? – emotional trauma and psychological damage.'

'What, she said that I was abusing her as well? Is that what she's saying? Because I'm sure I'd never do anything like that.' Rhys was outraged. He considered that he spoke PC pretty well. Unlike Sam, who just couldn't understand that it was a different language and brought with it a different set of values. Sam would argue doggedly against the notion that a barmaid would be offended if called 'love'. Or if called a barmaid at all. He actually enjoyed posing as a bigot. Maybe he was a bigot, no posing involved. And Sam enjoyed giving offence in what he considered was a good cause. But Rhys was not like that. Not at all.

Rhys was an immaculately reconstructed PC-compliant professional. He understood, humbly, that a person of his gender, colour, age and ethnicity had no hope of not developing discriminatory attitudes in response to his childhood conditioning. But he had evolved. He was sensitive, he had adapted, he had rigorously weeded out every incorrect thought and inappropriate attitude. Why, the way he'd been brought up to think disgusted him now. With a will he had taken on decimal currency, metric measurements, feminism,

EU regulations, cycle paths and patient-friendly dress codes, and he'd taken on post-colonial guilt with all the rest and mastered it with a will because he believed in the principles. When government forms had to be filled, he ticked the box for 'white' with a proper sense of shame. Not a racist word had passed his lips for ten years at least, unless you counted George's joke about the Irish contestant on *Who Wants to be a Millionaire.*

'This report has several paragraphs of conversation. Expressions like "witch doctor" and "monkey's fart". References to "natives". Obscenities and general abuse.'

'She's got it all wrong. She must have been drifting in and out, hearing bits and pieces. I never, ever, discuss a patient except in clinical terms. Nor does –' He checked himself. He could be called to account now. 'Nor has Mr Debrosser done so in any of the operations I've assisted at, as far as I can remember. He has never expressed racist sentiments to me in private – quite the reverse. One of the reasons I like to work with him is that he is a genuinely tolerant man, he's a man of principles, you might say, good, liberal principles. On this occasion all I can remember is him talking about the cricket. He is obsessed with cricket, Mr Debrosser. All sport, really. And all I said was "um" and "er" and "yes" and "no". Because I don't know anything about cricket so that's all I can say.' And I was thinking about my lover the whole time anyway. Please God they don't find that out.

'Look, Dr Pritchard, I think I know what's happening here. This is an opportunistic complaint being made in a culture of entitlement that's growing stronger every day. Patients have very high expectations, quite rightly. But in this case it looks like Ms Watson enjoys publicity. Since getting that slimming award, or whatever it was, she's had quite a lot of pictures in the *Westwick and Helford Times*.'

'Dangerous.' He could see the headlines. 'Love-Nest Doctor Killed My Daughter'. 'Dr Booze-Cruise And The Beauty Queen'.

'We have to recognise that she could be. You've both got spotless records. I can see Mr Debrosser played for his university team and the hospital eleven. And he's an active human rights campaigner – he's just organised the Christmas raffle for Amnesty International here and he stung me for a whole book of tickets. He's an extremely good surgeon and he should have a bright future. And you're a fine doctor with an exemplary career behind you and there's no reason your last years should be blighted by a thing like this.'

Last years? Career behind him? Well, she was only young, just a thoughtless kid, hardly older than Toby. A joke to make him feel better, that must be it. Maybe a bit of a patronising smile here, just to let her know he knew she was kidding.

'So what I'm going to do, if you can bear with me, is suspend you both and order an inquiry . . .'

'What!'

'Which will show the complainant that we are responding properly and taking her seriously.'

'But we've done nothing wrong, either of us. She's fine, isn't she?'

'GP says she's recovered really well.'

'So why penalise us?'

'It's not what happened, Dr Pritchard, it's how it looks. And how she feels. That's what's important.'

'No, it is important, what happened. What happened is not what she's accusing us of.'

She flipped into automatic negation. 'I know it's difficult to accept, Dr Pritchard, but the patient's perception carries greater weight here. I'll speak to the Clinical Director and most likely what we'll do, we'll make her a good offer of compensation straightaway and if she accepts that, well, that'll be it, it'll be all over then. If not, we'll invite her to attend the inquiry, and co-operate if she wants any publicity. That's usually what these people are after. The inquiry will be an internal one so hopefully there'll be no need for things to go any further. When the inquiry publishes its report, if she hasn't already settled, we'll repeat our offer. They usually do settle at that point.'

So young, so badly spoken, so world-weary. Still, he believed her. 'You've done this before?'

'I wish I could say no. Three times last year. These are the times we're living in now.' Just the faintest suggestion that he was not a man of those times. Just a chill oscillation of those cod eyes to let him know he couldn't be entirely right here, he was damned by his age and nothing would change that. Too old to be good. Guilty, and not capable of being found innocent.

He retreated into clipped propriety and got out of the office as fast as he could. From the car park he picked Debrosser's pager number from the speed-dial and sent a message. When the answer came, on his way home, he pulled over. Unthinkable that he, a man so punctiliously socially responsible that he parked to take a phone call, stood accused of racist language. Why had he devoted all his working life to a caring profession? He who had passed up the chance of real wealth, incurred the contempt of his father-in-law and the hatred of his wife, become a hermit in an emotional wasteland, just to keep on giving as much as he could to the society in which he was about to be victimised.

'Ain't this a bitch?' said Debrosser.

'Have you seen her?'

'Yeah, I've seen her. She's doing her best, poor cow. Can't blame her.'

'What are you going to do?'

'Do? They haven't set a date for this inquiry, have they? There's nothing I can do here. We're on suspension as from now, as I understand it. Until we're called by the inquiry. Have you got any notes?'

'I keep my own. I gave them to her.'

'Any idea what happened? How much did you give her? What was it? Is this a false memory thing or what?'

'She's not saying she felt anything. It could be she was aware, and her hearing persisted when she appeared to be unconscious.'

'That ever happen to you before?'

'Never, but I've heard of it.'

'Ever know anyone it happened to?'

'Nope.'

'You mean, you think she actually heard us say those things? I'd never use those words. I don't say that stuff. She's a gold-digger, she's making it up. She didn't say anything to me when I saw her afterwards.'

'Nor me. It was a couple of days.'

'She's got to be making it up. Her family have wound her up to do this.'

'You were talking about the cricket. She could have heard that.'

'Cricket?'

'Don't you remember? You were down on the umpire for some decision.'

'You mean she was actually conscious?'

'She must have had some awareness. No pain but some hearing . . .'

'Christ, Rhys, that's bad.' Decent, sincere sympathy. The kind of sympathy one schoolboy has for another who's about to be punished. He's sorry for me. Sorry for me because he's assuming this is my fault. I didn't anaesthetise the patient properly, therefore I am to blame.

'I gave her the correct doses at the correct time. It's all in the notes. And my own diary.'

'You keep a diary with that kind of stuff in it?'

'I've always kept one. In case of this kind of thing.'

'You mean you've run into this crap before?'

'Well, no, but . . . Anyway. I didn't make any mistakes.'

'Then how could she hear us talking? She couldn't possibly. You don't actually think we said what she's claiming, do you? Can you remember what we were talking about? Because I can't. It was nearly a month ago. Had that manager talked to any of the nurses?'

Neat and fast, just the way Debrosser worked on a patient. Two Zen-like sweeps of the scalpel, open the body, expose the disease. My fault because I remembered too well and spoke too soon and kept my own records as if I was expecting trouble. As if I was in the habit of getting complaints. Even with the records though, it would be Ms Watson's drug-induced word against theirs. Except he'd claimed to remember what was said. Eager to look on top of everything. Fool.

'She said the sister remembered Watson's eyes opening.'

'But not what we're supposed to have said?'

'I didn't ask.' How could I have been so stupid? He heard Debrosser sigh.

'Well, I've had it with England in winter, that's for sure. I'm going home tomorrow, see the family, catch the second series. See you at the inquiry, I guess. Take care, old chum.' There was nothing at all chummy in the way he said it. Old chum he may have said, bloody fool was what he meant.

He wanted to call Mo, but La Maison was shut until after New Year. But – aha! Mickey had gone over to George's with Andy. Speed-dial, indiscreet facility, join us together.

'I'm so sorry,' she said. Spooky. Gossip – Westwick was full of it. But hell, he'd only just left the hospital.

'How do you know?'

'Mickey told me. We were together when he got the news.'

Together! No, no, no. 'So he's there now?'

'No – Christmas Day, wasn't it?'

'Oh, you mean George. You're sorry about George. Yes, it was a bit of a shock.'

'You know, I think Mickey's quite upset. It's hard to tell with him. He's just very quiet. But he's been quiet for months. I don't know. What do you think?'

'What do I think?'

'About Mickey.'

I don't think about Mickey. I've loved you for nearly five years and I can only live with it if I don't think about all the bad things around us, including Mickey. Including the way

241

you're talking about him, too. He said, 'That wasn't why I called.'

'We haven't spoken since we got the news.'

'I haven't been able to call. You've been home all the time. At least, I assumed you were home.' She didn't really care about Mickey. She was bored, that was all, stuck at home with nothing else to occupy her mind. Next week she'd be normal again.

'So,' she was pulling herself together already, 'how are you?'

'Not the best.'

'Where are you?'

'Driving back from Helford. From the hospital.'

'Are you working this week?'

'No. They called me in. There's been a complaint.'

He gave her the facts and she said what he'd wanted her to say, but it didn't help. Yes, she gave him sympathy, but she'd given it to Mickey too. He didn't want to share. After all those years in the wilderness with Barbara, his heart was as thirsty as a dry sponge, a desert riverbed, a sun-worshipper's complexion; the dew of her attention sank in and vanished.

'Can you get out to meet me?' he asked.

'Maybe. I don't know where Mickey's gone. I thought he was still with you guys.'

'He's gone to George's place.'

'Where's that?'

'South of the river somewhere – I've never been.'

'There'll be a lot to do, I suppose. I can't imagine he left his life in good order.'

'Well,' Rhys said bitterly, 'what would be the point of

that? You can beat your brains out keeping your life in good order and you'll still get stuffed. He wasn't so dumb, old George.'

Swearing at the traffic all the way, Sam drove hell-for-leather back to Belgravia. He also swore at the band. Bunch of wankers who had endangered his precious moments with Elizabeth. Time they were out of his life. He was moving on, moving up, dumping the saddo tendency.

He had been honoured. Elizabeth said she was free for dinner. Most evenings she had to have meetings with her father's business associates. Her role in the UK end of his operations was vital; he trusted her judgement, he relied on her. As any wise man would. Her time was precious, Sam was impressed with himself because she wanted to be with him for several valuable hours. Unthinkable to be late. Insane to risk their relationship on account of this infantile band business.

It was getting clearer and clearer. The band was something he had done for the others' sake. It was a kid's game and they had kept it going for their own reasons. He, Sam, with his exceptional gifts as a musician, could give them that extra edge, and they had needed him. It would have been unfair on them to deny the band his input.

He'd been on the point of leaving for years, but it had been one thing after another. This time of life certainly sorted the men from the boys. Andy losing his job. Rhys with his stupid so-called conscience, putting himself under stress in the medical business when he already had a problem child to slow him down. And Mickey, stuck in the superficial world of advertising, running around the world thinking he was some creative genius when all he did was sell beer to yobs and cars to people who couldn't afford them.

The band was over as far as he was concerned. It was like the haircut you had when you were twenty, something you did because you didn't know any better. An embarrassment, best forgotten. Perhaps, if he was to be honest – and Sam considered himself scrupulously honest – it had served a purpose for him. Those wasted years with Alice, maybe they'd been harder than he realised. A bad relationship was draining, the band had been some sort of comfort activity. It had kept him together when he needed it, but now it was just like your old shoes or the teddy bear you had as a child, something fit only to be thrown away.

As the variegated bulk of the Natural History Museum loomed, and he approached Knightsbridge and the smart shops, the stucco crescents and the portered mansions among which he belonged, he saw that he had made up time. He was not late. In fact, he was going to be that chivalrous five minutes early that a woman of Elizabeth's status deserved. He would sit across a pink tablecloth from her, and order the waiters to bring her whatever she wanted. All around would be couples just like them, happy and rich, the women jew-elled, the men with their tax-haven tans. He would have that kind of tan soon. He was working on a scheme with some people in Andorra. Elizabeth would be impressed. Maybe her father, even, would be impressed.

'So, you can see me,' she announced as she gave him her cheek to kiss.

'Of course I can see you. And very lovely you look.'

So classy, the way she ignored compliments. So sexy. Oooh, there it was, that special tingle only she could start. 'I am being serious here. One day you will look for me and I'm not there.'

What? Was she planning to leave him? No. No. He was reading her wrong. Change the subject. Let it drop. You're fine. She's fine. Forget it. Distract her.

'Have you looked at the menu?' She was sitting in the restaurant like a woman who had been waiting a while. There was an air of expectation about her. A fresh packet of cigarettes was flipped open in front of her, with two missing. The little gold pentacle lay still on the foothills of her breasts.

'I learned something extraordinary today. Shall I tell you what it is?'

'Oh, yes.' A clever woman, well informed. Her conversation could be fascinating.

'I am chosen. Do you know what that means?'

'Chosen? No, I'm afraid I don't.' Chosen by me, of course, a man of exceptional discernment able to see beyond a mere business transaction and find a partner of the highest quality to complete my life's achievements.

'Soon I shall be working in the fourth dimension,' Elizabeth warned him, her eyes round and serious. 'I will only stay visible while I am working on this wavelength. That's why I say, one day you will look for me and not find me. I want you to understand what the effects of this will be.'

'I shouldn't like that. I should miss you,' he assured her. This was some flirtation game, one of her elaborate sex scenarios. She was full of ideas to keep him on his toes.

'What you like is not important. Soon it will be time for Horus to declare war on Set once more.'

Her eyes flashed and Sam felt the tingle in his belly burst into flame. Her eyes were now a cloudy violet, like the eyes of a Persian kitten. 'When do you think that might be?' he asked, playing along like the sophisticate he was.

'The Gods appear at regular intervals according to Earth's consciousness. We appear in every country of the world. Maybe I have to be here a hundred years.'

'Does this mean you are a goddess?' Best to proceed delicately. She could turn nasty if he said the wrong thing, and guidance on the right thing was hard to get. The flame in his belly was licking downwards. Shortly after dinner, he hoped to be on fire all over. 'You know I worship you, of course.'

She inclined her head. Yes, this was a new game. Splendid.

'So you have appeared in other countries?' he enquired.

'Only two of us will work in the fourth dimension. Harseisis has been working on earth for two hundred thousand years already.'

'That's a long time,' he commented, fishing for guidance.

A waiter came to their table. 'Have you decided what you'd like to eat?' Sam prompted her again. She seemed startled.

'The fish is always good,' he encouraged her. Exotic women often liked fish, especially sole off the bone with champagne sauce.

'Fish is cursed,' she informed him. She was playing with her necklace, letting the little gold star slither down the cleft between her breasts. The flames were roaring south. 'The fish of the Nile ate the member of Osiris.'

'Our fish comes from Paris,' explained the waiter, whose

English, thank goodness, wasn't good enough to get the reference. He was wafting beside the table, courteous, deferential, sensitive to the situation. Sam also fancied that the waiter was trying not to watch the necklace.

'Do you have grouse?' she demanded, suddenly clear-eyed and snappy.

'Yes, Madam. Fresh every day from Scotland.'

'It's not stinking?'

'No, Madam. The chef prefers not to hang the young birds.'

'Excellent. I want it with all the stuff, you know . . .'

'Game chips, toast, bread sauce . . . of course, Madam.'

Sam ordered the same. He still felt quite reckless, ordering without looking at the menu. But why bother, when you knew what you wanted?

'And some beautiful wine,' she specified. 'This is a special day for me.'

He disdained to open the wine list. Better not to count the cost, better not to spoil the moment.

'And cigarettes,' was the last demand. 'Tomorrow I will give up drinking and smoking. It's important that my body is completely pure. But I'm not sure that you are worthy,' she informed Sam as the waiter flourished away. 'Even for the Omega order. The consort of a goddess must be dedicated. You will not give yourself, and that is what's necessary.'

'It's not that I can't give myself.' The flames faltered and his heart flipped over. Not this again. No, no, don't displease her now. Not now when perfect gratification is right here under my fingertips. Women never understood men's problems, not even a woman as remarkable as Elizabeth.

'There's things happening in my life, that's all. My son's

247

taking it very badly, giving his mother a lot of trouble. And an old friend of ours has just died. That's where I've been today, I told you. Organising the funeral.'

'Pfff. You say one more word about your family, I walk out of here and you never see me again.' Now the eyes were cold and grey, forbidding as the North Sea in winter.

'Of course. I'm sorry. It wasn't appropriate.'

'I have been chosen,' she reminded him. 'I must dedicate myself, and you must dedicate yourself just the same. Otherwise you can't be with me.'

'All I want is to be with you, Elizabeth. Of course I'll do whatever is necessary. No need to worry on that score, I promise.'

'Good.'

He caressed her with his eyes. He'd been perfecting this move for a few weeks, having heard somewhere that women found it irresistible. Fix your eyes on hers, then let your glance stroke her body, lingering on the most sensitive parts. Oooh. Warming up nicely.

'Don't stare at me,' she ordered him. 'You should avert your eyes when a goddess is before you.'

'Of course,' he agreed.

When they got back to the apartment, she seemed to stop playing and locked herself in the bathroom. He waited forty-two minutes by the gilt carriage clock and then she appeared, swaddled in a towelling robe.

'You can't sleep in the same bed as me,' she announced, pushing him away. 'I must keep myself pure. You can go home now.'

'I can't do that. I mean, this is my home now. With you.'

248

'You are not worthy. I have rituals I must do, I can't have you around then.'

'Rituals?'

'Go, please. Now.' She was opening cupboards, pulling out candlesticks and arranging them on the coffee table. 'Go on. Get out. You're polluting my sacred space.'

'Are you all right, Elizabeth?'

'Haven't you been listening to what I've been saying? I have been chosen. I must keep myself pure. Go away. Or I'll call Security and have them throw you out.'

He gulped. Elizabeth was highly strung. She threw things, especially when she was having one of her moods. Or starting her period, maybe. Well, he was a sensitive man, he knew how to handle a woman. Be tactful, go along with whatever she said. Give her some space. Call her tomorrow.

The room smelled of old smoke, damp and sour milk. Andy took the stinking bottle to the bathroom on the half-landing and washed it out. Getting to be a right old housewife, thought Mickey. A real Auntie Nellie. He'd be wanting to tidy the place up next.

Something about the way stuff was piled up appealed to Mickey's eye. He climbed the platform and sat on the mattress. Don't think about how many years of desperate wanking that bed had seen. He let his gaze pass over the heaps of whatever and the dust over them and the little paths trodden in the dust from the bed to the heaps and back again. The light from the roof window fell hard on the dust; it looked pale and bulky, like new snow in the city.

A heap of clothes. A heap of gardening supplies – the least

dusty, well visited. A heap of old newspapers and another of bike bits. Broken china, old pieces of metal. Three dismembered guitars. A road sign; Danger: Men At Work, buckled as if a car had hit it. A stuffed seagull in a glass case. Most of a cast-iron Victorian fireplace inset with green and yellow tiles. A box of old records – LPs, 45s, even an old case of 78s, covered in fake leather with a white card envelope for every platter.

Stereo stuff was piled against another wall. Two old speakers the size of coffins and a stack of stuff between them, and cables tangled all over. The guitar he actually played had a stand in front. Here and there were lights glowing – orange, red, fluorescent green, digital displays, grimy dials. Where the cases made ledges and shelves, they were stacked with tapes. Neatly. In all the filth and accumulation, rows of cassettes were lined up in alphabetical order by artist.

Andy was back, overwhelmed by chaos, standing on a clear piece of carpet with his arms hanging. 'Did you know he lived like this?'

'You could guess, couldn't you.'

'I don't think I thought it was this bad.'

'He held it together pretty well when he had a job. Maybe it got worse the last few weeks.'

The man was determined not to spare himself. 'It's been like this for years. You can tell from the dust.'

'We're not going to find a nice PalmPilot with the memory full of all George's friends and family, that's for sure.'

'He had that little book he used to scribble in.'

'He always had that on him. Inside jacket pocket, wasn't it? The book will have had it.'

They fell silent and thought about blood, and George's notebook soaked in it, the pages stuck together.

Andy went to the wall of sound and began looking at the labels on the cassette boxes, turning his head sideways to read them.

'He had his music organised, anyway. Here's all our stuff.' It was the longest row, in date order. 'He's got a lot. It's like an archive.'

'I think he thought we were for real, at the beginning.'

'Didn't we all think that?'

'Nah. Well, I never did. I was just having a laugh. We all were.'

'Try this.' Andy pulled out a box from the middle of the row, opened it with careful fingertips and fed the tape into the deck displaying the most lights.

A hiss, then a few random guitar chords and the audience noise of a set in full flow, humming voices, clinking glasses. Then a long metal howl from George. Rhys coming in with a jackhammer beat. Finally the full band barrelling into a number he couldn't put a name to.

'When's this from?'

'Only last year. Remember it?' Smiley Andy, always smiling.

Mickey shook his head. Time had been getting funny lately. Last year seemed to take up the past five years, and before that was ages ago. 'Let's hear it.'

Nearly four minutes of it, steaming stuff. Then suddenly Andy's own voice, taking off the affable jazz maestro introducing his combo.

'Hi there, nice to be with you, glad you could stick around. Hope you've enjoyed the set.' A bit of noise from the crowd.

'Like to introduce – Rhys "The Gas" Pritchard, drums!'

Tss, tss, boom, boom.

'Come in – Mickey "Blue" O'Ryder, guitar!' Throb, throb, thro-thro-throbb!

'And – Sam "Fingers" Chudleigh, over there on keyboards.' Much tinkling.

'George K. Hodsoll, guitar – take it away, George.' Eeeowoweeeeowwww. Kreeeeeeeeeeeeeowwwww!

'I'm Andy Forrest, vocals. They call me Mr Fabulous.' Applause, warm and immediate.

'And say hello to big John Wayne, xylophone.' A few laughs from the audience, catching on.

'And Ralph Fiennes, guitar – Raphie, baby!' A good laugh that time.

'Richard Branson, spoons. Yeah!'

'And looking very relaxed, Adolf Hitler on vibes. Nice!'

'Bridget Jones on sousaphone – mmmmm.' Quite hysterical by this time.

'Introducing Liberace, clarinet.

'With Deepak Chopra, bass trombone.

'Buster Gonad, tap dancing. Go, Buster.'

Mickey remembered now. George had rescued an old synthesiser from a skip and spent weeks compiling a tape of effects so they could recreate the Bonzo's cult classic.

'In the groove with David Attenborough, violin.' Mweeeee-eee-ee.

'And Eminem on harmonica – cool, Em.' Shouts in the laughter at that point.

'Thank you, sir. Over there, Eric Clapton, ukelele. Sweet!' George had fixed up some falsetto take on 'Layla'. It went over well.

'On my left, Betty Boothroyd, bass sax – a great honour, ma'am.

'And specially flown in for us, the white rhinoceros on vox humana.

'Nice to see Darth Vader on euphonium.

'Drop out with Madonna on duck call. Quack! quack!

'Hearing from you later, Casanova on horn. Yeah!

'Digging Saddam Hussein on accordion. Rather wild, Saddam, thank you, sir.

'Roy Rogers on Trigger.

'James Bond on the bongos – James, do be careful.

'Count Basie Orchestra on triangle – thank you.

'Great to hear the Gallaghers on trombone, Noel and Liam!

'Back from his recent operation, Dan Druff, harp.

'And representing the flower people, Quasimodo on bells. How's it hangin', Quasi?'

Hooray!

'Wonderful to hear Courtney Love on euphonium.

'We welcome Richard and Judy as themselves. Hello there!

'Very appealing, Damien Hirst.' George had got the sound of a sheep bleating and whacked it up into a wail. 'Mmmn, that's nice, Damien.

'What a team: Hulk Hogan and Rolf Harris on percussion.

'A great favourite and a wonderful performer, from beyond the grave, J. Arthur Rank on gong.'

Bonnngggg. Ngggggggg.

'Goodnight, everybody!'

More applause, definitely less than rapturous, then an

angry rustle and the recording cut to tape hiss. The audience was puzzled, they hadn't got it. Mickey remembered clearly now. George had got well aerated. Later there'd been a fight.

Andy had turned away and his shoulders were up around his ears. The cassette case was still in his hand. He was going to cry. Big girl's blouse, sometimes. Move him on quickly, Mickey decided. He could cry at the funeral if he had to.

'Come on.' Mickey got off the bed and made for the door. 'I can't stay here with all this crap. We're not going to find anything.'

'You go.'

'I'm not leaving you here.'

'Someone's got to sort this.'

'The landlord can sort it. That's what he takes the rent for. Why should you do all this? You've got enough on with the funeral and all. It's not our bag. What's the point now, anyway? Come on.' He judged it to perfection. The voice that a thousand Russians had obeyed, at about a quarter of the volume. Andy pulled himself up, shook his head, rubbed his eyes as if he'd just woken up and headed for the door, saying, 'OK, you're right, let's get out of here.'

In the car on the way back to Westwick, Andy asked, 'Was there anywhere he went? A bar, a pub. You said he'd got a girl, she won't even know if we don't find her. She'll just be sitting there wondering what the fuck's happening.'

'I don't know,' Mickey told him. I don't want to think about all those evenings playing pool, all those nights in all those pubs, all those long hilarious conversations, all those loser scams, those adventures, those random ramblings.

Don't make me go there. Shut up. Just shut up.

'There was a bar in Soho, wasn't there?'

'I don't know.'

'Yes, there was. You said you'd seen him there sometimes when you were going to The Groucho.'

'Bar Italia. The couriers all go there for the footie.' OK, he'd let it out. Emotional catharsis had been achieved. Stop talking now. Just shut up.

So many questions. Did they want to see the body? Did they want an announcement? What sort of flowers did they want? Which model coffin would they like? Did they want to do any pall-bearing themselves. The undertaker was a woman in her thirties with wide hips and short hair. So many questions and none of them fitting.

Andy heard George's voice. 'I want to go like a gangster. Like one of the Krays or some'ing. I want a load of tarts with big blonde hair, with their mascara all running, and a load of big hard geezers walking along wiv the hearse. And a guitar done in flowers.' The guitar he could do. Marcia at Pot Pourri listened earnestly and said she'd have a go, she'd seen guitars in Oasis at Covent Garden and if he'd be happy with just carnations it shouldn't be too difficult.

'Do you want me to come?' Laura asked him. Question expecting the answer no. 'We've got a big presentation next week, so if you want me to come I'll have to get organised.'

'I don't suppose the other wives will be there.'

'Maybe Daisy can go with you.'

'She's a bit young, isn't she?'

'It's only a cremation, isn't it? You won't be doing all that side of the grave business, ashes to ashes, whatever it is.'

He wanted her to be there. He wanted someone to be there. Not Daisy, not the way his daughter should start to get acquainted with death. Just someone who wouldn't criticise, who'd just sit beside him on the chapel bench, someone on his side.

He went for an announcement in the *Musician's Gazette*. He fiddled around on the computer, printed out a small, black-bordered poster and went into Soho to persuade the manager of Bar Italia to tape it to his window.

In the end, thirty-six people came to the crematorium that was over the river in Mortlake, past the Beehive and down towards Richmond. Mo came with Mickey, and very fine she looked in her black trousers and pill box hat with a veil.

He counted the congregation while the duty priest of the day was talking from the notes he'd given him. 'George Hodsoll was an unusual man,' the priest began, and wondered why people chuckled.

Andy had fixed for George to play himself out with his own 'Parisian Walkways', while the coffin sailed forwards on its rollers and the mock-Georgian doors of a leprechaun's garage closed behind it. Goodliebylode, old chum.

Perhaps because he was standing there with his wife, people fixed on Mickey afterwards. Quite a few came and shook his hand, said it had been a good service, they liked the guitar, that George had been a good laugh, a bit of a character, quite a figure in Soho. Mickey heard himself saying, 'Come back to ours, why not. Have a couple of drinks, yeah?'

Certain realities are obscured by friendship. Realities including how rich Mickey was. In the band, this was never mentioned. He bought his rounds like all the rest, and, since

Mickey was a man of few words, it was natural never to mention any other wealth indicator, like the size of his tax bill or the newness of his car.

In Westwick, a man demonstrates his wealth by the size of his house; the size and also the marketability, meaning how much the interior looks like a cover picture for a newspaper property supplement. As they got out of their cars, Mickey's house loomed over them. Three storeys. Double-garaged. Conservatory. Blue shutters like some fucking French château. Rooms upon rooms. Five bedrooms, five bathrooms. Sitting room, family room, pool room, utility room.

Sam had heard of people with rooms for arranging flowers or wrapping personally selected presents or storing their matching Louis Vuitton luggage, the last word in spatial lavishness; Mickey's house might well have had ridiculous rooms like that. He shrank a little in his speckless dark coat. Along with the four of them came a few stragglers from the crematorium, skiving delivery drivers whom nobody liked to exclude. They fell silent and looked around at Mickey's magnificence as if it frightened them.

Inside, the décor. Ye gods, what décor. Everything painted the colour of clotted cream, sofas as big as battleships, antique twiddly mirrors, fur rugs from a Thirties movie set. Curtains big enough for a theatre, and not just one window, one curtain, but curtains upon curtains, draped and swagged, a dance of the seven veils at the Edwardian bay window that Rhys estimated was as big as one of his children's bedrooms.

And the bits. Bits beyond the vocabulary of a heterosexual British man. Metal bits, French bits, carved wood bits, old painted bits, china bits, bits with gold on them, bits of sculpture. Bits hanging from the conservatory beams and the kitchen ceiling. Bits on the walls, bits on the floor, bits on the tops of cupboards, bits on special little shelves built for showing off one's bits to admiring guests. Nice bits, Mick. Yeah, well – they're the old lady's department really.

Rhys had that conversation in his head. He didn't look too closely. Envy of Mickey was rolling him over like a giant wave tumbling an unlucky surfer. How could a man have so much? So many rooms, so many bits, and such a wife to devise it all. Quite possibly, Mickey had so much money he didn't know how much he had. Bank accounts he'd forgotten about, investments he paid experts to worry about. And all this blatant, outrageous, insulting wealth was Mickey's reward for persuading people to buy things they didn't need, and filming thin models who gave young women bad body images. Immoral, that's what it was.

But then, Rhys accused himself morosely, he'd achieved his own immorality. Adultery, breaking the seventh commandment, committing a deadly sin – he'd done that.

Worse, he'd done it with the wife of his best friend. The way she walked. The way she talked. The way she was in her own home now, *their* own home, the home that also belonged to Mickey. The way she melted away now, just disappeared to let them get on with it. The way he couldn't follow her.

The roaring in his ears stopped. Rhys found himself in calmer waters. How could loving Mo be wrong when her husband had got rich on the wages of sin? Suddenly he felt he was redressing the balance of nature. He was fine, he was OK; actually, he was good.

'You could fit three of our house into this,' said Rhys to

Mickey at last, slipping a matey stiletto in under the ribs.

'Nah,' Mickey replied, feeling uncomfortable. He held out a can of beer. Rhys took it and pulled the ring. Pfft, just like his dreams went.

'How long have you been here now?'

'Must be five years. Or six, maybe. Old lady'll be wanting to move soon, she always does.'

'You got a mortgage?' Sam demanded.

'No point really, now they've taken away the tax relief.'

'Money's cheap,' Sam pointed out. To him, a man not mortgaged to the limit of his creditworthiness was a man a few chromosomes short of a full pair of balls.

'Hangover from his upbringing,' Andy put in. 'Mickey's dad was like mine, thought borrowing was a sin. You never feel quite comfortable living with debt if you had Sunday lunch with Mr Micawber every week for your first sixteen years.'

'You 'ad Sunday lunch, lad?' Mickey fumbled for a Yorkshire accent. 'Eeh, you didn't know you were born. Sunday lunch in our 'ouse? 'Appen our dad would bring 'ome a sparrer an' our mum would roast it wi' a dab o' drippin' and then at table 'e'd carve it that fine it'ud feed six of us for three whole meals, wi' second 'elpings all round.'

'Eeeh! A table! Feather-bedded you were. We ate our lunch off t'floor. And you 'avin' drippin' in t'house an' coal ter spare ter roast a sparrer. Our dad – ah – 'e were a right 'ard man and 'e – ah – ah – er – oh fuck.' Andy suddenly found his brain bare. The half-inflated bubble of goodwill in the room began to collapse.

'Yeah,' said Mickey, misunderstanding. 'George ain't here so what's the point?'

259

'He was a good laugh, old George,' somebody said again.

For something to do, they moved towards the pool room, where Sam, in a show of bravado, rolled a couple of balls across the vastness of the table. Calling it the 'pool' room, they realised in awe, was a democratic understatement, a clumsy bid for a bit of cred. The room held a full-size snooker table with bulbous mahogany legs like carved pumpkins.

'You play?' Sam said to Mickey.

'George and I had a few games.' He was pouring drinks, followed by eyes glazed with envy. Beer, vodka or whisky. The man had a special fridge for his drink in his pool room. Now that was . . . wicked.

'Sign of a wasted life, snooker,' Rhys observed, and immediately wished he hadn't.

'That's what they say,' Sam replied, suddenly righteous with work ethic.

The others were some way distant on the far side of the green baize prairie, and Rhys needed to talk, because a feeling was swelling painfully in his throat and he had to give it a voice before it choked him. Any voice would do. He just had to say something.

'Everything all right at home?' he asked Sam.

'You've heard, I take it,' said Sam, feeling quite pleased that his move up to new heights of sex and prosperity had been acknowledged.

'I did hear something,' Rhys agreed, by then not sure what information he had or when or how he'd acquired it.

'I . . .' Sam groped for the words to describe Elizabeth and the financial stratosphere. 'I have met a lady,' he said finally. 'A very special lady. Special to me.'

'And she . . . ?'

'We feel the same way about each other. It's our intention to make a life together.'

'Good. That's good. And—' What was the name of Sam's wife?

'Alice? She's fine. Absolutely fine. Alice and I – we've always known it was just a phase in our lives, something that wasn't going to last. We've stayed together for the children, of course, but they've got their own lives now, they're not bothered about us any more.'

'They didn't mind?'

'I talked to them, of course. Made sure they understood. Melanie has followed me into the law, she has a very good take on the way things are nowadays. It's natural, I think, to move on to a new partner at this time of life, and of course they've seen that with other families.'

Rhys found himself enchanted by this vision of a man apparently fading out of his marriage in the same effortless way that Mo had just disappeared from this gathering, sinking out of sight without leaving a ripple behind. Could this be done with Barbara? Alice and Barbara, they were both women, but not the same kind of women. Alice, Rhys considered, was rather the startled rabbit, couldn't-say-boo-to-a-goose type. Barbara, before she turned into a monster, had once had spirit. Like Mo had spirit. Could you just fade out with a woman of spirit?

'How did you approach it?' he asked, trying not to sound too pointedly curious.

'Quite simple. I just explained the situation. I'm sure Alice had an idea what was coming, she used to think about things a lot, got quite obsessive at some points. She must have known. She was perfectly calm and sensible. I think she was quite relieved. She'd been living her own life for – oh, quite a while. I was getting in her way, really.'

'And then you left? And what, took a suitcase?'

'Well, yes, I took some things. Over a few weeks, moved my stuff out. All very – well – amicable.'

To Sam, this was the honest truth. He had edited his memory. Gone and deleted was the shameful sensation of hot clam chowder hitting his shirt-front. Gone and deleted was the hurtful sight of Alice's face crumpling up and turning both red and astonished, like a baby about to cry. Gone and deleted were the bonfire of his possessions – his shirts in flames, his music melting – his son's punch on the nose, his daughter's icy outrage. Deleted, recycled, gone and forgotten for ever. And his bizarre evening with Elizabeth, and the fact that he was dossing in a hotel around the corner. If cross-examined, Sam would have sincerely denied that these things had ever happened to him.

'Lucky,' said Rhys, trying not to sound wistful.

'We always believed communication was the secret,' Sam informed him. 'As long as you keep talking to each other, not much can go wrong between two people.'

'Barbara talks.' Rhys winced at the thought.

'Excellent,' Sam responded, with a broad smile of encour-agement. 'There's your basis, then. You can work on that. Why, are you . . . thinking of making a move?'

'Like you say,' Rhys answered cautiously, torn between wanting to jump on the snooker table and shout the truth and the blind terror of being found out. 'It is natural at this time of life, isn't it?' Information is power, he remembered. Never give information.

'I should say so. You've got someone in mind, I take it?'

'Yes, I have.' Especially not this information.

'Do I know her?'

Yes, you know her. You all know her. 'I'd rather not talk about it. Not at this stage.'

'Early days, eh? Well, good for you. I've often wondered . . .' Sam paused, weighing his words; he had always assumed Rhys stayed with Barbara for two perfectly understandable reasons – his inherent gutlessness and her wealth. He ploughed on. 'Well, I've wondered if you had a reason for staying with her. With your wife. You've never struck me as – completely happy together.'

The words came out of Rhys's mouth like vomit, an unstoppable gush from the guts. 'I'm fucking miserable,' he said, taking care not to make eye contact. 'And so are the kids. Well, Toby, he's still at home. I think Barbara's got . . . mental problems, to be honest. There. It's harsh but that's all I can think.'

Sam's face flickered momentarily with something that Rhys assumed was kindness. 'Good for you,' he murmured. 'I thought it was something like that. Good for you for getting out. You've given her – what? Twenty-five years or so. That's very fair. It's time to live for yourself.'

'Yes,' Rhys agreed.

'You won't regret it. Get out before it's too late.'

'Yes,' Rhys nodded, frightened at the sheer allure of the idea.

'It'll be the best thing you ever did. Believe me.'

'Thanks,' said Rhys, draining his glass. And they turned back to the rest of the group, both satisfied with their adventures into the wilderness of emotion.

*

263

Mickey found Andy by himself in the kitchen, pacing alongside Mo's stainless steel worktops, rolling his empty glass between the palms of his hands. Not crying, thank God, but there was still time. 'You all right?' he asked.

'Yeah, I'm all right,' Andy told him. 'Just wanted a minute to myself.' He smiled. Smiley Andy, he could even smile at a wake.

'Top up?'

'Cheers.' Andy held out his glass and Mickey poured, finishing the bottle. 'It's been a long day.'

'And it ain't over yet.' It was like a catechism. Comforting, meaningless, faithful to something they'd believed for so long there was no need to define it any more.

'Good turn out, after all. He did have some friends.'

'Yeah. Everyone's got friends, haven't they? Old George had a good life, by his own reckoning. If you'd asked him, he'd have said that.'

'Did you ever ask him?' Whoa! Steady! Questions off the hymn sheet, could be dangerous.

Mickey deflected the enquiry. 'He liked his freedom, George did. It really was important to him to travel light. He hated to be beholden to anyone. I saw that when I lent him money, you know. He hated having to ask. He couldn't cope with being fenced in and told what to do. Demanded of. He couldn't be demanded of, couldn't cope with people expecting him to behave a certain way or do certain things.'

'No, he couldn't,' Andy agreed.

'And I know how he felt.'

'Don't tell me you feel demanded of by all this.' Andy waved his glass to indicate the bits, the rooms, the house, the wealth and the wife who could just disappear at the right moment. A little twitch of bitterness there on the edge of his smile.

'No. Not really. I feel . . . see, I know what I've got. I've got a gift. A talent. Put it simply, I can make pictures that say things to people. I can do it really well. So I've got talent and I suppose that's what tells me what to do and where I feel demanded of.'

Fuck me, Andy said to himself through a thickening veil of whisky. The statue speaks. The kraken wakes. The worm turns. Mickey just said something significant about himself. Never done that before. Just stay quiet and see if he wants to say any more.

Mickey did not want to say any more. He considered he'd said too much already. Fucking weaselly words, sneaking out the minute you let your guard down. 'Funny things, funerals, eh?' He walked over to the far side of the room. 'You go to a lot?'

'Not yet. I suppose we've got that to come.'

'Not me. No offence, but I don't think I'm going to make a habit of this.'

'You don't have to come to mine. I won't mind.'

'Well, that's it, isn't it? A person's gone, they're gone. Flogging out to the suburbs to see the box taken away ain't gonna change anything.'

'It's for the families, really.'

Andy had a flash vision of his wife sighing with irritation as she put on a black hat. Mickey had a ten-second clip of Mo standing outside the crematorium chapel with another man, a large, faceless male whose essential quality was that he wasn't Mickey.

They both shivered. Without, of course, letting it show.

'It's one of those things,' Andy went on, hoping to ramble out of this cold dark wood. 'Things you've got to do.'

'Who says?' Mickey replied, his face creasing as he grinned. 'It's my life, I don't have to do anything I don't want to.'

'Oh yeah,' Andy kidded him. 'I remember now. I knew there was a reason we were in such a goddamn hurry to grow up.'

At the same moment, Andy and Mickey decided they needed another drink.

CHAPTER 9

I'm The One Your Mama Warned You About

Much later, when he got home, Andy sensed that the house was empty. Put on some music. Music will fill my home and my heart and my life. Music took care of those things before I had a home and a wife and children, and I feel as raw now as I did then, so music will do the trick. Andy found he wanted Vaughan Williams' 'Setting of the Mass'. Weird, but he definitely had a craving. Took a while to find it.

No Laura, no Daisy, no Lily; they were all out. Not that he expected anything, but one of them might have stayed around to talk to him. Not very Christian of Lily, even one of her sermons would have filled up the space a bit. Andy grinned at himself in the glass fronts of the kitchen cabinets. Grin and bear it. His dad had said that whenever something went wrong. VAT, devalue the pound, lose your job, out on strike, Margaret Thatcher as Prime Minister – whatever life threw at you, just grin and bear it.

Down in the kitchen, the glass door looked out at the garden. A night in winter, at the beginning of a year, and frosty. The air outside was crystallising into a white mist. Laura had had the Sands woman do the back garden as well, so he was looking out on a Tuscan-style terrace with roses tied to trellis pillars and box balls growing, if that was the right word, in urns posed on plinths.

He knew nothing about modern gardening except that Charlie Dimmock could invade his space any time, but he knew he didn't like what had become of his own garden. It should have been a place for kids to pitch tents and husbands to strim lawns. Not that he wanted to be that kind of a husband, but grass was good. More friendly than gravel. The weather was all wrong; you felt miserable looking at a rain-sodden vista that ought to be golden under the sun. Some of the roses still had flowers, gallant but exhausted, flapping petals from the ends of the arching runaway branches.

He decided to follow Mickey's whisky with some more. After a while he opened the kitchen door and went out to stand in the middle of the gravel sward. He had a tree, at least. The fight he'd had to put up for just one tree. Laura had given in in the end, with one of her side smiles, the sort that bared no teeth but tipped up her lips in one corner, tipping out something unwanted. She'd said, 'Oh well, if you really want a tree I suppose we can leave it.' At the end of the garden was an old pear tree, now as tall as the house itself, a few blackened leaves still clinging amid the spire of branches.

The alarm system turned on the lighting to greet him; it was artful, concealed, positioned to illuminate the features, Laura claimed. He wanted darkness so he turned it off. What remained was the lurid red glow of a city at night. What he really wanted was the star-kissed blackness of night in a field. Westwick might pretend, but it was really just another chunk of the filthy old metropolis.

'Is that you, Andy?'

Jesus! Who the hell was it? And where the hell were they?

'Hee! You don't know it's me. It's Pascal. I'm here on the wall.' Yes, there was a shadow moving in the shadows. And he picked up the accent, American-plus. Six feet above the ground, Pascal was walking along the top of their party wall, arms waving over his head to keep his balance. He was dressed entirely in black, a silhouette in the gloom, the Milk Tray Man.

'Wait, I'm coming over.'

Some tree branches shuddered. Lithe as a panther, not. Pascal fell to earth heavily, lurched sideways, lost balance, swore, got up, massaged his hand, picked gravel out of his palms. Then he leapt forward.

'How are you, Andy?' A hug. Arms around him, a chest pressed to his. Aftershave and the spicy flesh smell of Pascal. Andy stood firm; a gay man is hugging me and I'm fine with that, I shall not waver. Pascal was wearing a black sweater, high-necked, very soft. Probably cashmere. 'Well, you don't have to tell me how you are,' Pascal continued.

'I don't?'

'You're sad, I know that. You've had a sad day, I believe.'

'Well, yes.'

'Was it good, the funeral? If a funeral can be good. I think it's possible.'

'I suppose it was. It was a guy who played with us in the band, you know.'

'Laura told us. I didn't know that. You're a musician.'

'Not really. We just play a few gigs. Some people play golf.'

'No, but music – that's very good, I think. Music helps me when I'm not feeling so good.' A low wall ran around what was left of the flower beds and Pascal sat down on it with a bit of drama, just to make it clear that nothing conventional was to be expected of him in any circumstances. 'You can give me a drink if you want.'

Andy found he had carried out the bottle in one hand and his glass in the other. 'I'll get you a glass.'

'No need. We can share. Or one of us can have the bottle. Whatever.'

It was ridiculous to stand over Pascal while they were talking, so Andy flexed his unwilling knees and sat beside him. He poured two fingers into the glass and gave it to Pascal, keeping the bottle himself. Pascal reached over to toast.

'Absent friends. That's what you say, isn't it?'

'People who were in the war said it. My father did.'

'Tell me about your father. No, tell me about your friend. I want to know everything, but tell me about him first. This is his day, after all. And you did everything. Organised everything. Because he didn't have anybody, is that right?'

'Yeah, I suppose.'

'But that's a wonderful thing to do, Andy.'

'Anybody would have done the same.' Not true. Surprise of the year, that altercation about the funeral. Just what would have happened if he hadn't argued? Sam and Rhys, they'd have let the council take care of it. A pauper's grave. Strange how you could call people friends for years, decades even, and think you knew them, and be wrong.

'So your friend. What was he like?'

'George. Well, where do I start? He was mad, I guess you'd say. In an English way. Eccentric.' He reeled out the clichés pressed on him at the crematorium door.

Then a kaleidoscope of George broke out of his memory, a thousand images whirling past his mind's eye. George in a corner of a pub with a pint. George in his bike gear doing Darth Vader. George slowly pulling a bag of grass from his top pocket, humming the title music of *Hancock's Half Hour*. George's skeletal fingers on his guitar, curved at the neck, flat on the strings. George kicking a piece of equipment that had displeased him.

'He was a funny guy. He had a name for everybody. Like if you were Dave, he'd call you Dangerous Dave. Tall Paul. Big Bad John. He gave us all names in the band. Rhys "The Gas" Pritchard on drums. Sam "Fingers" Chudleigh. Mickey "Blue" O'Ryder. Andy "Mr Fabulous" Forrest, that was me.' In the dark, he sort of felt Pascal smile.

'I went to the place he lived in. Just a room. It was a tip. He was fascinated with tips, skips, rubbish, dustbins. Couldn't resist, had to look in, go through them, save something. He liked everything broken, bits of old china, plastic, buckets with holes in, chairs with broken legs. It was full of that kind of stuff, his room. Everything useless, thrown-out, rejected, out of fashion, he liked.

'He'd tell old music hall jokes that weren't really jokes. He'd say things like, "If it takes a one-legged duck half an hour to swim around in a two-metre circle, how long will it take a black beetle to crawl through a barrel of treacle?" Or about the man who taught his horse to live on air or the old lady visiting a shipyard asking a man if he was copper-bottoming or aluminiumming.'

Pascal giggled. 'I'm sorry,' he said, pulling his hand over his face as if he could straighten it out. 'It's funny, I don't know why.'

'Yes, it's funny and you don't know why. He was full of stuff like that. It was part of his life on the edge, I suppose. He could speak back slang, George could. You know what that is? It was the language of working class people, kind of a dialect, developed so they could talk without people in authority knowing. Rhyming slang, the cockney thing, that was part of it, but it was a whole language. He said he learned it from his mother. Sometimes if somebody annoyed him he'd start haranguing them in back slang. Sounded like Stanley Unwin. Complete gibberish. Mind you, he did Stanley Unwin too. He did it one time with this bloke who just piled in and hit him. We had to pull him off.'

'Who did he sound like? Who is this Stanley whatever?'

'You won't have heard of him. Where did you grow up?'

'Canada. Actually, I am Canadian. My family came from Algeria. I was studying in Paris when I met Charles. But my home is in Canada.'

'Well, you might have heard of him, but the most English things don't go abroad. The most English music, films, comedy. Nobody else gets it. Stanley Unwin was a comedian who spoke in funny made-up words. George used to imitate him. And Ken Campbell he liked. All those special loony English things, crazy stuff. Ivor Cutler. Peter Cook. Kenneth Horne. Ian Dury – you ever heard of him?'

He could feel non-understanding in the darkness. The boy was trying but he hadn't got the equipment. Rootless, homeless, sex-defined, modern. How could he understand? Still, he was trying. '*Carry On* films? The Bonzo Dog Doo

Dah Band. Neil Innes. Viv Stanshall. You won't know who they are. They were kind of before Monty Python.'

'Before Monty Python,' Pascal marvelled.

'Yeah, well, at the same time, maybe. An influence on our generation, anyway.'

'I wouldn't have thought that. Your generation. You don't seem . . . you're not like a person that old.'

'Well, George was a bit older than the rest of us. We hung out together at art school. He'd been thrown out of a few places, lost a few years. He said he was born on VE day. Victory in the East Day. Or Victory in Europe. Or VA day, Victory in the Atlantic. Or VP, the Pacific. Or VS, Scandinavia. Or maybe Switzerland. VM, VIP, VG, SVP, VSO, DSO, excuse me, gotta go PDQ, I'll say TTFN, and be orf to put on the DJ for the OBD.'

Pascal hugged his sides, hissing with amusement.

'People talked like that after the war. In the Army everything was all initials. There was conscription.'

'You did conscription?' Even in the half-dark he felt the great black eyes roaming curiously all over his shoulders and around his face.

'No, it ended years before I was old enough. But somebody older, ten, fifteen years, he'd have done it. Your father or your teacher or your boss, definitely. It was sort of in the culture.'

'That explains a lot.'

'Does it?' Feeling better. Feeling relaxed. Quite tired, maybe. But not cold, which would be down to the whisky. He refilled Pascal's glass and felt himself sway on the narrow wall. Steady. Taken on a lot today.

'Why people can be so cold, perhaps. You think they

don't care. I was surprised, you know, to find out you did those things for your friend. I thought everybody was the same here, that you all didn't look at each other on the street, didn't speak to anyone. Not you. You're not like that. I saw that at once.'

Perhaps he was in the mood for some flattery. One thing about working for yourself, you missed the day to day glad-handing that was part of being a bought man. The best part. In a remote office nobody schmoozed you, it was worth no one's while to kiss your ass. OK, that was all bullshit, but sometimes bullshit could work. Day in, day out, no good morning, not even a plastic smile from a receptionist. And you didn't get any medals for being a husband and father, that's for sure. And Pascal knew. He just knew. Sixth sense for the soft underbelly. He dived right in, talking on in his purring accent, looking Andy's way every second sentence although the look was just a gleam of eye-white in the darkness.

'I thought, here is a beautiful man. OK, you are as old as you are, but you're a beautiful man. And you are also a proper man. A proper man who has a heart in his body and who's not afraid to act like that.'

What do I say? Do I have to say anything? What can I say that doesn't sound daft?

'And I just felt when I met you that you were that kind of man, and you were unhappy, because all around you were people who were not the same, they were just machines, they didn't feel like you. And you were pretending to be like them. All the time, underneath, up here . . .'

Pascal leaned over to touch the top of Andy's head, right at the back, where the hair was thinnest. You're cool. You don't move. No reaction, all perfectly normal. Just because a gay man touched you. It's dark, maybe he won't notice where the hair is thin. 'In the very bottom of your mind, in the bottom of your heart, you know what you are. It's very exhausting to live like that, isn't it? Emotionally, you are always tired. You want to give but you're giving from nothing all the time. It's quite heroic, I think, to live like that.'

OK. Stop. Too much. True, maybe, but too much for a conversation. Especially now, after days of aching with grief in the company of three other men who wanted to pretend nothing had happened, now when intimacy felt like a warm bed. Still, the kid thinks about things. He'd assumed that Pascal never thought about anything except himself and causing trouble.

Pascal loomed close and kissed him. On the mouth. Held his face in one hand, put the other around his shoulders, pulled him close and kissed him. Whoah. No. Very nice kiss, soft lips, strong, cold, dry. A kiss full of intention, a kiss launched with serious thought, the kind of kiss you'd expect from a man with Bernini arms. Oh my God, here comes the tongue. Hot! No, no. Stop now, immediately; stop, just stop.

Andy found himself standing on the gravel at least six feet away from danger. He'd twisted a knee and his mouth was alive. More than his mouth. Don't go there. Whisky had spilled on the ground. He was still holding the bottle. He put it down, carefully, on a corner of a plinth.

'That was a mistake,' he said.

Pascal rose to join him. Worse than ever. Don't stand so, don't stand so, don't stand so close to me.

'No, it wasn't,' he said, very gentle. 'It was good. You

275

liked it. You like me. I like you, I want to make you happy. You're sad, I want to make you feel better. That's OK, isn't it?'

'I don't like you like that. I'm straight, I've never been anything else. I don't want to get into anything else. I'm happily married.'

Now Pascal was stroking his arm, trying to get Andy to hold his hand. 'That I do not believe. The happily married part. You aren't happy, I know it. She isn't happy, your wife.'

Shit, another can of worms. How did he know? Did they spend the whole day snooping on their neighbours? Did they listen at the walls with upturned glasses, hack into his computer, put bugs in his phone? None of their business.

'We've been married a long time. Sixteen years. You're not like young lovers after sixteen years.'

'Of course not. But she's into things you wouldn't believe. She talks to Charles, you know. They're as thick as thieves. I get quite jealous. You know what she's doing? She's going with other men. Did you know that?'

'I don't believe you.'

'That's your choice, of course. She's told Charles she goes out to have sex with men she meets through some dating agency. An agency for married people. All the time. Every week. She goes to a hotel with them, just for sex.'

Pascal is trying to cause trouble. Pascal is after my ass. This is all bullshit, this isn't true. 'That's crazy. Laura would never do anything like that.'

'It's what she said. I was there, I heard them talking. Anyway, he told me afterwards. It's unusual for a woman, I think.'

'This is a racket, Pascal. You're making this up, it's a

276

game. Don't play games with me, I don't like it.'

'It's not a game. I'm not making anything up, I promise. Ask her. Ask her what she does. She says it's safe. There's no emotion, so it's safe. No emotion for her, maybe. She doesn't think about you.'

'You're making this up to punish me because I don't want to have sex with you.'

'Well, it's true I'm disappointed and I want to have sex with you very much. Every time I see you I want to touch you.' His hand spanned Andy's arm like a bracelet and he tightened his grip, his fingers digging in. 'A man like you, a big man, a real man, it's very exciting to me. If you're not in the mood right now, that's OK, that's cool. What else can I do? But I'm not making up anything. You ask her. It's true. You really are kidding yourself if you think you've got a happy marriage.'

Andy pulled his arm away. 'Go home, Pascal.'

'You ask her, if you don't believe me.'

'Go home, Pascal. Now.' Don't push him. Don't touch him. No contact. Don't give him the excuse. Don't get into some shoving match with a younger, stronger man. Who wants to touch you.

Pascal held up his hands, palms out, a gesture of pacification. 'OK, OK. I'll go. It's cold out here, anyway. But don't go into your house and forget everything. I want to say I love you. This isn't just about the sex. You have a problem. I am the answer. I'm waiting, I'm the other side of the wall.' He pointed with one finger at Andy's chest, his whole arm extended, while he walked backwards a few steps, then turned and leaped at the trellis. There was enough light to see him now, light from the house shining out into the garden. A few branches crashed, the trellis cracked as he scrambled over it, and then he disappeared. Thank God. Safe at last. For the moment, anyway.

Andy went back to the house, his house, his family's house, the four walls that would protect him, and bolted the kitchen door.

'A bit late, aren't you?' It was Laura. She was standing at the end of the room, balanced fiercely on her heels, her back to the wall, her arms folded. It had been a long day and the sight of her hit him like a wet pillow. 'It's only Pascal. What do you think he's going to do? Break in and rape you?'

'You weren't here.'

'I was next door.'

'As usual.'

'Yes, as usual I was next door, talking to someone worth talking to.'

No feeling whatsoever. It was all happening the other side of a wall of glass. A man in a bubble, nothing was touching him. Why don't you ask her, if you don't believe me? She's going with other men. She goes out to have sex. With other men. She says it's safe because there's no emotion. For her, maybe.

They were in the middle of the room now, stalking each other in a circle, like boxers. 'What else, Laura?'

'What do you mean, what else? Charles and I were sitting having a drink when you and Pascal decided to entertain us.'

'You know Pascal. He was just trying to make trouble.'

'You didn't exactly push him away.'

'I didn't exactly grab him and stick my tongue down his throat, either.'

Gotcha. She sniffed and pulled her arms tighter around

278

her body. Once, he'd found that mannerism sexy. It pushed up her breasts, squared her shoulders, gave her a bit of attitude. Not that she was ever low on attitude. But it wasn't working for him now.

'He was telling me something about you.'

'About me? You were standing out there in the freezing cold snogging the face off some candy-assed boy and you claim you were talking about me?'

Well, that was Laura. Front up, stare 'em down, talk 'em out, never surrender. Now he believed. He was sure. She was doing it, she was . . . he hadn't got the words for what she was doing. But it was what she did when she felt threatened. She goes to a hotel with them, just for sex.

'Have you ever slept with anyone else, Laura?'

'Don't be melodramatic.'

'Since we got married. Have you been unfaithful?' On a high plateau somewhere, way above feeling. I ought to be gutted. What's going on?

'No. I haven't. Have you?'

'You've never had sex with anyone else, not since we were married?'

'Not so as it would matter, no.'

There's no emotion, so it's safe.

'What are we talking about here? What sort of unfaithful wouldn't matter?' Quite philosophical. I can't believe I'm acting like this. Why aren't I yelling blue murder, crying my eyes out, chewing the carpet?

'Well, if I'd had an affair with someone else. If I'd fallen in love or something. I haven't done that. In fact, since we're talking about it, I've had the opportunity. One of the guys I work with. I got rid of him. I wouldn't take the risk.'

She wants to tell me. I know that look, that terribly afraid look, and it means she wants to tell me. She can't live with it any more and I'm here so she's going to spill. I'm not paranoid, I know that look. That was why she told Charles, but it wasn't enough. Maybe that was even why she's doing it, so we can get to this point, and she can dump it all on me. That's Laura, that's her way.

They were standing opposite each other, on either side of the kitchen, Laura leaning against the draining board, Andy leaning against the Aga, the warmth of the great domestic mother ship thawing out his legs.

'You wouldn't take the risk. So what risk are you taking?'

'I suppose he's told you. Charles must have told him. Or he was lurking in the house somewhere. He's always lurking.'

'It's his home too, he's got a right. So go on, what risk are you taking?'

'I did it for us. For you. So there'd be no involvement.' Nausea starting now. Maybe the whisky to blame, but a seasick feeling at the centre. He held on to the Aga rail for support.

'Did what?'

'I answered this ad. In a paper. For married people. It's an agency, they put you in touch with people in the same place. Who're married, who're really committed to their marriages, but need something more.'

'So you meet these men and have sex in hotels. Is that really it?'

'Well, yes. Obviously we don't want to go home together.'

'I've got trouble with being really committed to your marriage and having sex with strangers in hotels. I mean, what would you say if I told you I'd been going with prostitutes or something?'

'I'd say it was the same thing. Almost the same thing.'

'You wouldn't be disgusted? Because I'm disgusted. I feel sick. Physically sick.'

'Like I felt watching you and Pascal.'

'You were seeing what you wanted to see. You know me, you know him. We've been through this.'

'But don't you understand?' She raised her voice, one of the master race telling the rest how it was. 'What else could I do? It was all I could think of. You were completely different when you lost your job. All the edge, the sharpness, the things I used to love about you, all gone. You were just this . . . this blob, slobbing about the kitchen in trackybums and no shoes. Some days I'd get home and feel like I'd rather die than have to fuck you.'

'Thanks.'

'You didn't think of me. You worked all hours, you fussed around with the girls, you didn't think of me.'

'I'm sorry.' Why? Why did I say that? She's trying to blame me, why did I let her?

'That's so easy for you to say. You've no idea what I went through.'

'I was the one who got fired. I was the one who had to keep paying the mortgage.'

'And didn't we all know it. I had to do something, Andy.'

'But why that?'

She shrugged. It used to look so elegant. 'It was the answer. I was going mad. Some women really don't like sex. I'm not one of them. I'm a physical person and playing more tennis wasn't quite what I needed to be doing.'

Just when you think you're home and dry. You think you've weathered the storm and it turns out it's only the eye of the hurricane. He was cold, deep down in his core, and the heat of the Aga was only baking his skin in a few places. Cold as if he was hanging like a carcass in a giant fridge, cold as if he'd fallen in a field of snow and been blanketed in a new fall. The cold that feels next to death. He realised he was gripping the rail of the stove very hard. When he let go, his hands were shaking. His arms were shaking, even.

The room was silent. No pipes hummed, no machines turned, the music was finished. He could hear himself breathing, unevenly. Death, sex and betrayal, all in one day. If he was a system, he'd be crashing.

'You do understand, don't you?' That cruel voice, the way it cut the air. No pity for him, no shame for her.

'No.' He pushed off from the stove and stood upright, preparing to make a move. 'I said goodbye to half my life this morning. I'm all out of understanding right now. Try me tomorrow.'

'Where are you going?' she asked when he was almost at the door.

He hadn't got that far, but since she was asking, he picked an option. 'To sleep. And I don't really want company, if you don't mind.'

'Well, where am I going to sleep?'

He didn't answer.

CHAPTER 10

Little Red Corvette

'It's different.'

'How can it be different?' A tampon is a tampon. To Mickey, the crucial thing about tampons was that they were not his thing.

'It's a different product. They want a different approach. Mould-breaking. New design, needs a whole new brand personality. The brief is the girl of twenty who'd die rather than use the same product as her mother.'

The idea of a girl of twenty had some appeal. He said nothing. Seven months and no work. Never take a job because you need it. George would not be dropping round for a game of pool. The account director from KKDW kept gabbling.

'You were a key part of the pitch, Mickey. They went apeshit when we said we could get you for this. The top creative thinks the piano was a work of art. Said it should be in a museum. Don't say you're going to let me down here.'

'Knows his art, then.'

'Really serious. One of those goatees who takes his kids to the Tate Modern every Sunday.'

Mickey had taken his son to an art gallery once. Joe had been about twelve at the time, old enough to take notice. He'd walked rapidly through the whole thing like a commuter walking through a station and then assumed they were going home. No artistic feeling whatsoever. My son, the alien.

Would Draco do this? Was old Draco into sanpro? Had old Draco ever gone seven months without a job? Draco probably knew more girls of twenty than he did.

'It's a huge market, Mickey. We'd really like to get in there.'

'OK. I'm in.'

'Great. Really great. The meeting's in Milan, I'll get the tickets biked over straightaway.'

On his mental screen, George came into focus, doing John Cleese: 'Rule One, no sanpro. Rule Two, there is no Rule Two. Rule Three, no sanpro.'

Beer. He drank beer, no problem. Cars, he drove cars, no problem. Financial products, he bought financial products, no problem. Sanpro. No data. He found Mo in the kitchen, drinking tea before she went to work.

'Would you have used the same brand of tampon as your mother?'

'I thought you didn't do sanpro?'

Information is power, do not give information. 'Well, would you? When you started?'

'Tampons had only just been invented. People thought they were immoral. If you could get one up it proved you were a slag.'

284

'What about later? Was there an issue about using the same thing as your mother?'

There it was again, the face he'd seen when she'd caught him looking her over by the pool. Shutters down, lights out, gone away somewhere, a place you can't hurt me. 'My mother died last year,' she said, in the super-sweet voice of an irritated teacher trying to keep her temper with an annoying child. 'And I haven't had a period for longer than I can remember. Ask somebody else, why don't you?'

'You must remember something about it.'

'My mother wouldn't talk about periods. When I started, she pretended nothing was happening. I thought I was bleeding to death from cancer or something. After the third time, I went to the school nurse and asked to go to hospital. Everybody went around sniggering at me because I was the first to start in my year. I was only nine. That help you?'

'In a way.'

You never knew what women were going to get in a strop about.

The following morning, in the orange glow of the Acorn Junction at 4 a.m., he pulled out of the Westwick slip and took the motorway to the airport. His car wallowed on its luxury suspension. The Corvette came into his head from nowhere. The classic Corvette Stingray, the early one, '64 or '65, before they James Bond-ed the design. A great car. Like Gazza before he lost it, like the young George Best even, the Corvette would have made the perfect move before you knew what was happening.

An empty road with no challenges. Reminiscence passed the time. Mickey searched his memory for the machine of his dreams. He found a clip of himself aged thirteen, standing by a bus stop on a gloomy street, kicking at bits of rubbish as a cover for keeping warm and yearning with passion for the new Stingray.

It was always there, that little Corvette, slipping around the corner of the street of his childhood. It rode high and cheeky, sort of duck-arsed, growling through its twin pipes, chrome winking, a slash of red in the teenage twilight. Definitely, he could remember that he'd wanted one.

Did he remember having one?

He must have had a Corvette. He had had most of the things he had ever wanted.

No. No memory of an actual Corvette.

Mickey's forehead crinkled. Not fair. He was disappointed. On his mental screen George came into focus, eyes rolling down, saying 'Disappointment is a dangerous age, Cynthia.'

Mickey had a name for his present car: The Thing. The Thing was whistling along the fast lane. The Thing had automatic transmission. It rode like a pregnant buffalo and it pissed him off. Surely he had driven a Corvette? Maybe he'd rented one on a shoot once.

One of the beauties of Westwick was that with a clear road and a need for speed in the fast lane you could make Heathrow in ten minutes. Away to his left he saw a jet low in the sky, a paler shape, a set of lights. The airport was coming up on the other side of the motorway, a white glare behind a grassy mound. He was going to Milan on a dark Thursday morning to talk about tampons.

One of the runways ended so close to the road that the plane had to fly right over the tall street lights. Right over The Thing's roof. Right over his head. Very Ridley Scott, the lights underneath, the orange haze, the street lights standing around on stalks.

Incredible how low the planes flew. Mickey thought he could almost put up his hand and touch the undercarriage. Look, darling, it's a can full of people.

Had he really had a Corvette? Had he sold it? Or wrecked it? Or had it nicked? Or only rented one on a shoot somewhere? No data matching your query. He didn't fucking know.

So the car of his teenage dreams had slipped past in his peripheral vision. The bullet that you don't hear kills you. The plane that you don't see crashes on your head. Mickey had caught his life in the act of sneaking away.

The Thing forgot its manners. The wheel twisted in his hands. They were lunging across the road. Mickey felt his heart race.

It was a blow-out. The bang had been drowned in the roar of the jet. He got control and pulled off to the hard shoulder, missing a couple of lorries. Stupid Thing. Smell the rubber. The driver of the last lorry turned a white face to him as he passed. Not a lot on the road this early.

He was heading for Milan. A job. Another job, another meeting, another client, another fee. Sanpro. A girl of twenty. A manic shoot, a shot of sex, a load of back-slapping, the big cheque and maybe an award. In the bag. Another break-through for award-winning commercials director Mickey Ryder. Award-winning millionaire commercials director Mickey Ryder. His life was supposed to be in the bag.

The plane he didn't hear was coming in.

Smell the rubber. A strip of black out on the road was what had been the nearside front tyre. Stupid Thing, stupid car. Mickey had clean fingernails and a new black leather jacket in something called peach-touch baby calf. He had a five-star emergency service contract and a nifty Motorola.

The Motorola had no signal. Maybe they blocked the mobiles because of the airport. He took his wallet out of his jacket and started walking along the roadside to the emergency call box.

His father had changed wheels. His father used to roll up his sleeves and leave his mother sitting in state in the passenger seat while his stiff, old fingers fumbled around with the jack. His father was long gone. No longer with us, as his aunts used to say. Never had been with us, in his son's opinion. Not Dad's fault, just his generation. Mickey felt silly with tools and he liked to have clean fingernails.

By the emergency phone he turned around and saw the plane he hadn't heard. Only a small one, sitting there in the sky above the stupid car like a chicken settling over an egg. A great image, that. OK, bit of a cliché, but basically great.

It was a Johnny Woo sequence. The nose wheel caught the neck of a street light and snapped it. Sparks showered when the hull grazed the stalk. The great mass of metal in the air foundered. It tipped a wing, then fell out of the sky. Just like a bird, graceful in flight, clumsy coming down. It fell on his stupid car. The noise filled his head, hurt his ears, shook his bones.

The trouble with Johnny Woo was he made too much of things and it still wasn't enough. Where the lower wing was dragging on the road it sent out a wave of sparks. There was that horrible sound of screaming metal. A hole opened up in the fuselage, near the nose, a door opening. A balloon of red fire burst into the thin dawn air. After it came stink-

288

ing smoke, dark over the lights. His stupid car was under all that.

Mickey got a flash of the piano. The piano was the high spot of his life. His creative life, anyway. If you've put a piano on a bridge you've got to push it off. He had obeyed the logic then and performed a miracle. There was logic in this now. His car had blown out, a plane had come down. If you've got a plane crash, you've got to be missing.

At the crash, there was a figure in a doorway of the fuse-lage for a second, then too much smoke to see any more. They'd got an emergency chute down. On the far side of the road, going the other way, a panicking lorry driver hit his brakes and the great rig jack-knifed in slow-mo and crashed over in two pieces.

Black smoke was pouring from the guts of the plane and rising up in a pillar above it. Mickey found he was running towards the wreck. He could hear squealing tyres behind him, more vehicles trying to get around the truck. In front of him was the smoke. In his hand was his wallet. He stopped.

He was going to Milan on a dark Thursday morning. His passport was in his wallet. He was still The Man and he did not do sanpro. Slow, tired, less, cease? Fuck that.

He took out his passport. He took out a card, the card he never used, the card for the account nobody knew about, especially not the Revenue. He took the wallet by one corner, pinched between finger and thumb, and frisbeed it into the smoke.

'I've got a sore armpit.'

'A sore armpit.' Dr Carman peered at Alice's chest. Dr

Carman, wife of the other Dr Carman, had new spectacles, thin-rimmed, Russian anarchist style, and a Bride of Dracula streak of white in her hair, right at the front where it waved off her forehead. Way back in the days of the Magpies Montessori, the consensus among the other mothers in the playground had always been that Rachel Carman was off the wall and now she looked downright mad. But who am I to talk, a woman who throws soup at people, who has one breast bigger than the other?

'I noticed it in the shower yesterday. When I washed under my arms with the soap, it really stung.'

'Have you always had one breast larger than the other?'

'I don't know. I've lost a lot of weight in the past few months.'

'How did you do that?' On top of the specs and the streak, Rachel Carman had always been rounded and now she looked like two giant bagels, one on top of the other. She was always telling her patients they were underweight and everyone knew there was no point asking her for the new wonder obesity treatments.

'I've been busy at work and we've had a few problems at home. You might have heard. Sam's moved out.'

Not a flicker. Dr Carman never wasted time on idle conversation. 'Do you examine your breasts?'

'I sort of feel them sometimes.'

A grunt. Rachel was not impressed. 'Let's have a look, shall we?'

Completely bizarre, standing there topless, having Rachel Carman, mother of the Terrible Twins, leaning over and squeezing her breasts. Then prodding around in her armpit. It was tender. No, it was painful. Then peering at her breasts and turning her reading lamp on them. On the right one, the bigger one, the same side as the sore armpit.

'Alice, you've got quite a lump here.'

'Oh goodness, have I?'

Rachel was whipping forms out of drawers and covering them with notes in dramatically large writing. 'I want you to go straight to Helford hospital, to the oncology clinic on the first floor. I'll call them and tell them to expect you.'

'I'm supposed to be at the shop. Someone's coming in with some door furniture.'

Over the top of the glasses, the stern look that had turned head teachers to jelly. 'What's more important, Alice – door furniture or your health?'

'But these lumps are usually benign, aren't they?'

'Let's hope so. I want you to go right now.'

'Can't it wait until this afternoon?'

'It can't wait one minute, Alice. Not one minute. The test doesn't take long. I really hope I'm making a fuss about nothing.' And she reached for the telephone and started talking to the clinic secretary, demanding that her patient be seen immediately. 'And put a bomb under pathology. I've got an emergency here.' Alice put on her bra again, the new bra with the smaller band and the larger cups, one of which she did not quite fill.

'Come back tomorrow,' Rachel ordered. 'I'll get the result by then. You're on BUPA, right?'

'Yes.' On BUPA in my own right. I pay my own health insurance. I'm really grown-up now. With a touch of pride, Alice put on her sweater again. She did not say, 'And how are Don and Benny these days?' Well, you couldn't ask Rachel about her twins. Jail and rehab, everyone knew that. But no comments about La Maison. Rachel usually had something to say about the price of Mo's antiques. None of the expected social chat of a Westwick woman. So it really might be serious. But Rachel was always inclined to be colourful.

What day is it? The day after George's funeral. That was the third of January. This is the fourth of January. Today is the day that Daisy goes back to school. It is eight-something. I should be in the kitchen seeing that she eats her Weetabix. I should get up.

Andy raised his head. He tried to raise his shoulders. Someone had filled the duvet with fishing weights and superglued his back to the sheet. Probably the same person who had stapled his eyelids together and screwed a steel bolt through the back of his teeth. Putting the saliva glands out of action, most unpleasant. And they'd nicked his abs as well. Nothing at all where he knew he used to have a decent six-pack, just temporarily covered where his love handles were trying to join forces.

Laura. My wife thinks she is saving our marriage by having sex with strangers. There is actually a club for people like her.

He sat up. That sent 2,000 volts through the bolt in the back of his teeth. He dragged his eyes open. A million tiny red Chinese fishermen grinned under a million tiny red trees. Toile de whatsit wallpaper. He was in the spare room.

Laura.

Whoever had set his knees in concrete too. Standing up was another challenge. He reached for the bed's ornamental footboard to get some leverage and half the twiddly carved rosebuds came away in his hand. Laura was not going to be happy. Well, fine.

Down in the kitchen, it seemed to be nearly 10 a.m. Never, since the first day he had worked from home, had he got up so late. Not in three years. Not over two Christmases past. Not one day, not even on weekends. His moral fibre was fraying, he had to get a grip.

Daisy was out of there, presumably. Should he presume that, given the deep, deep sleep of adolescence and the extraordinary ability to remain horizontal and motionless for hours on end? No. Best to check. He washed out his mouth at the sink, rubbed cold water over his face.

Such a long way upstairs. The steepness, the altitude; the Inca road over the Andes to Machu Picchu could hardly have been worse. Finally he made it to the top landing, the bolt through his back teeth pulsing with agony. Both the bedroom doors were ajar. No sign of habitation.

'Girls? Anybody home?'

He knocked, then leaned around into Daisy's room. Empty. She'd gone to school. Only slightly less devastation than Massari Sherif after the siege. Clothes, makeup and magazines. She seemed to have been drawing eye makeup schemes on some old KKDW letterheads, thick, glittering swipes of turquoise and orange. Where Cherokee, the coloured pony, had recently looked down from the wall above the little pink bed, a half naked pop idol was now scowling in ripped denim and an indecent quantity of baby oil.

He sat on the bed. By his feet sprawled a magazine, its pages flung wide in invitation. A word caught his eye. PENIS.

Dear Wendi

My friends all keep talking about 'tossing boys off' but I don't know what it means. I'm too embarrassed to ask them, so can you tell me?

Becci, 14, Newcastle

Fourteen? Daisy was fifteen.

Dear Wendi

I've been with my boyfriend six weeks and we're starting to get more intimate. He says he loves me but we will have to split up because I can't give him a proper blow-job. I really love him. Please help me.

Desperate, 13, Aberystwyth

Dear Desperate,

Boys love blow-jobs and having a good technique is a great way to get your lad really hot for you . . . penis . . . lips . . . gentle pressure . . . teeth . . . up and down . . . rhythm . . . foreskin . . . swallow . . . but remember that though it can be so tempting to let your heart rule your head when you are in love, you shouldn't let your boy talk you into doing anything you aren't comfortable with.

Swallow? She hadn't had her Weetabix.

Dear Wendi

There's this lush lad at our school who I copped off with two months ago. I know you can't get pregnant the first time you have sex so we didn't use anything.

Now my breasts hurt and I feel sick all the time. I
did three pregnancy tests and two were positive. I
tried to tell him but he won't talk to me. What shall
I do? I'm terrified.
Steps fan, 14, Portrush

Steps fan? No surprises there, then.

Was that me? Did I have that thought? I withdraw it
unreservedly. I apologise to Steps fans everywhere. Thank
Christ Daisy was never into stupid brat bands.

Evidence of what Daisy was now into shrieked at him
from every surface. A black satin thong on the floor. Pots of
violet slime and purple gunge littering the unopened school
books on her desk. An excrescence of bubblegum-pink lace
that turned out to be a bra on the chair. Not just a bra, a
Wonderbra. Hello boys. Yes indeed.

Hence the changes he'd hardly noticed, the phone calls,
the prayers, the long walks, the excitable flushes, the secre-
tive silences. Horses, hormones, horticulture. His little girl
was now in Phase two of an Englishwoman's life. Apparently
the same phase as her mother. And maybe also her father.

Pascal. Oh God.

Somewhere inside him, the lava was glowing, ready to
erupt, hotter than hell. It was Andy's weakness to be honest
with himself. No way around it. He fancied the ass off Pascal.

Just go. Get on a plane. The first plane to anywhere. A new
sky, a new horizon. Climb a mountain, walk on a beach, sit
under a palm tree. I am The Man, I am connected, I shall
obey my logic.

Getting into the airport was the easy part. Planes were

taking on passengers, air crew were checking boarding cards. Gotta have a boarding card to get on a plane. Buy a ticket. Deciding which ticket to buy – a nightmare. Mickey stood in the departure hall watching the monitors. Arrecife, Kinshasa, Malaga, Bologna, Dar-es-Salaam, Casablanca, Bordeaux, Malaga, Cairo, Amsterdam, Palma, Paris, Geneva, Prague, Dubai. Every flight a different airline.

He decided to pick a desk. Shuffling queues of passengers filled the check-in hall. The first desk without a queue was KLM. Excellent, Surabaya, Curaçao, even Amsterdam. And the Dutch would understand.

'I need a ticket as soon as possible.'

A nice lad, long and thin. 'Where to, sir?'

'Doesn't matter where to. Just the first flight to anywhere.'

'OK.' Just like that. Did people do this every day? A sale was a sale, that was it. They were trained to take the money and ask no questions. 'We have a flight to Aarhus leaving in about fordy-five minutes. I can get you on that.'

'Fine.' Hand over the card.

'We have economy or business on that flight, sir?'

'Business.'

He signed the credit card slip and exchanged it for a sheet of computer paper. 'They're checking in now, sir, Gate fordy-six. Have a good flight.'

Where exactly was Aarhus? Information is power, never look as if you need more information. I'm surfing my destiny here, I will ask no questions.

A small plane, a Boeing 737. It filled fast, a large group taking up most of economy. Young men, mainly. Strangely similar; short-haired, skinny and tense, brownish all over, wearing sports clothes, logos, flashes, stripes. Many of them had red T-shirts which read: Swindon Cycles: Two Wheels to Heaven. Only two other passengers in business, a man in a white shirt and a man in a blue sweater.

According to the pilot, the flight would be one hour thirdy-five minutes and it was snowing in Aarhus. The stewardess invited them to taste some real Danish pastry. The man in the blue sweater put down a folder marked 'Dansk Neuroforsknings Center' and started eating his pastry with the plastic knife and fork.

The man in the white shirt was reading a paper headed 'Lego Mindstorms RCX: Multiagent System Robotics'. No way around it: he was going to Denmark with a cycle club from Swindon, a robot engineer and a foreskin psychiatrist. He was heading for Geek City. He had joined the march of the nerds. This was not, from any angle, cool.

Forget all that. He was buzzing, on a high. He'd broken out, defied his enemies, struck a blow for Mickey Ryder. This was the bold leap into the unknown future, the random strike that would lead to glory. He'd broken through, he'd reclaimed himself, he was on a roll. Nothing else mattered.

Two hours later he tramped through six inches of slush towards the airport building, the wind slashing through his leather jacket and sleet stinging his face. The sky was the colour of ancient pewter. On the side of the building he saw a big sign with dabs of primary colours, red, blue, green, yellow. Poster-paint colours. Above the dabs, large black letters which read: WELCOME TO AARHUS – THE SMALLEST BIG CITY IN THE WORLD.

George was talking to him again. 'Aarhus, Gateway to the North. Here in beautiful downtown Aarhus, see the bright lights – red, amber, green; green, red–and–amber, red.'

I have not screwed up. I do not screw up. The Man does not screw up. This is not some low-budget John Candy vehicle. Let them wonder in Milan. Let Mo worry in that shop of hers. I am The Man and I know what I'm doing.

Through the window of La Maison, through their New Year scheme of an old swan-necked sewing machine, two inlaid Victorian work boxes, several skeins of blue and white embroidered French name tapes, an armful of mono-grammed pillowcases draped on a wicker cradle and a slipware bowl from the braderie at Saucisson-le-Mauconfit planted up with white hyacinths, Mo saw that the traffic was extraordinarily bad.

The traffic in Westwick was like an auto-immune disease. It flared up whenever anything was wrong. Westwick had its days. Sometimes remarkable things happened, remarkable anywhere, not just out here in the ultimate suburb where nothing was meant to happen at all, and you knew immediately from the traffic.

The night George had died, Christmas Eve, absolute chaos. Everyone trapped in a gridlock on their way back from shopping and out to parties. The day the eco-warriors hi-jacked the morning show at the Channel Ten studios, the first idea anyone had that something was wrong was when the Broadway stopped moving.

The Broadway wasn't moving now. She turned the radio on, surfed some stations. Sky High, the traffic reporter on the news at Metro FM, was gibbering. Give that girl a Valium, please. An air crash at Heathrow. All six lanes of the motorway closed. Closed in both directions. Avoid the West completely. Just stay away.

She found some serious news. A cargo plane with only four people on board. The crew all accounted for. Uncertain if any drivers on the motorway involved. Flight investigators searching for the black box. Pilot unconscious.

All that, and only a few miles away. Maybe Mickey had seen it. A city was such a strange place. You could sit happily in your house and have a dead person on the other side of the wall. Mickey couldn't be . . . no, no. Impossible coincidence.

Mo was doing another quotation for Ted Parsons. Ted was a happy man. Even in the lacklustre end-of-year market, the first show-home in the new development had worked a dream. Ninety per cent sold off plan. Now he'd bought an old soap factory in Helford, to be renamed the Acorn Studios. Gentrification was creeping down the river. She'd negotiated some billing for La Maison. 'Show-homes styled by La Maison of Westwick.' Ted's billboard over the Acorn Junction said so. Woad-dyed linen? So over. It was all velvet now, but if velvet was the new linen, what the hell did the new decorator do about fingermarks?

Alice would be late. Alice was going to hospital. And Mickey was working again. As a child Mo had always been the little girl who piped up with what everybody else was thinking but didn't dare say out loud. Guaranteed to turn any happy family gathering into a genocidal war.

As a woman, Mo had been called sassy. And sharp. And a witch, once or twice. She never knew why exactly. It was just her way to sit up and take notice, and say very little. Thus other people, rackety, unquiet people who were too wrapped up in themselves, missed things that to her were perfectly obvious. She'd got better as she got older. Maybe the early change made her see more clearly. Maybe fifteen years' parole from the hormone penitentiary actually gave you a kind of wisdom.

Mo didn't like the way Alice was looking lately, even allowing for the trauma of realising that your husband is a 22-carat arsehole. She was wonderfully thin but her hair looked tired. Mo didn't like the way Mickey had been looking since the funeral, either. He was chipper, he was perky, he was putting on an act and his eyes were almost hidden in the laugh lines.

She never prayed, she scorned even to make a wish. Take what was on the slate for you and run with it, that was her philosophy. But if she'd been a praying woman, or if she'd made a list for Santa, Alice and Mickey would have been at the top. Mickey first. Blood was thicker.

'You can't help a man, love. You can't say a word. You sit tight and you hold your tongue and you wait till he sees the light.' Her mother had said that every time her father was laid off and took to skulking down the pub at lunchtime and throwing furniture when he got back. It happened every two or three years towards the end. She'd taken the lesson. Nothing below the waist was her mother's theory. Not the kind of mum to take you off to buy your first Tampax. Not even the kind of mum to tell you how far to go on the first date. But in matters above the waist, the old bird was spot on. She missed her. And Mickey missed George. And life went on.

The search for the new linen wasn't holding her attention. Mo thought of Mickey when she'd first met him. Skinny, restless, bow-legged in his jeans. The hair! Long angel curls, most of the time dragged up in a rubber band because he thought, rightly, that it made him look older. He was seeing five or six films a week. He'd taken her to London, to the National Film Theatre for the all-night Joseph Losey screening, and somewhere on the South Bank before the dawn broke they'd managed to make a baby. Joe.

Then the mullet. Oh God, the mullet. The total, utter, complete full-on Kevin Keegan haircut. They'd moved to London. The agency was just Kaplan & Krieger in those days. He'd taken her to Edinburgh to see the preview of Ridley Scott's first movie and he'd vowed to follow in his footsteps and be a feature film director. Now he reckoned Ridley Scott had blown it. Mickey the mature seemed to be forever lecturing on the mistakes of the so-called great directors. They still went to the movies. Maybe once a month. Industry screenings at BAFTA. Networking opportunities: slap on the lippy and strap on the fuck-me shoes. People said the mullet was coming back, but they'd got it wrong.

Every time they said something was coming back they got it wrong. Once or twice she'd been to the V&A, to the fashion galleries, and looked at dusty old Terry de Havilland shoes in the colours nobody, but nobody, had ever bought. Samples, never even put in production, she'd bet on it. Whenever she heard Mickey going on about the film directors he had assisted and how they'd lost it, she buttoned her lip and thought about how she felt about fashion historians. Pretty much the same. Shooting was too good for them.

The phone rang and she answered it. 'Is that – ah – Mrs Ryder? Mo? We met last year. At the awards dinner. You won't remember.'

The new kid at KKDW, sounding twitchy.

'Of course I remember. What can I do for you?'

301

'I'm calling from Milan. I was expecting your husband.'

What time was it? Afternoon already. The meeting was at nine. 'Mickey left early this morning. His flight was around six.'

'He hasn't arrived here with us. I called the hotel, he hasn't checked in.'

'We have had some trouble at the airport here. A crash at Heathrow.' She felt the nose twitch. OH NO. No. Of course not, impossible coincidence. 'Do you know what airline he was on? I could call them and find out if the flight was OK. But he had his phone.'

'He had our number here, but you know Mickey. He was on AlItalia.' Keeping phone numbers was somebody else's work. He'd never even figured out how to programme his own speed-dial. That was what assistants were for. He'd have done the same for Ridley.

She rang off then and called AlItalia, talking eventually to a throbbingly sympathetic woman who clearly deduced that Mickey had run off with another woman. Yes, the flight to Milan had left on time this morning. No, it was impossible to confirm over the telephone that a specific passenger had checked in. But from the data she had she could perhaps say his name was not confirmed. Unofficial information, please not to tell anyone she'd said that.

She called The Groucho Club saying she had a message for him. He hadn't signed in, his name wasn't in the book for today. She called the new kid back in Milan and told him what she could.

'What's he having, a bit of a mid-life crisis?' the new kid said irritably.

'Well, you know how he felt about the product.'

'This is different. We're very excited about this account. If Mickey's going to bale, it'll be a disaster.'

Disaster for you, you mean. Not for my husband, who only took your dodgy job because I was on his case at home. 'He could actually be dead, you know,' she pointed out in an excessively reasonable tone. 'It said on the radio they were still clearing wreckage off the road.'

A no-frills live-work unit, that was a house in Little Chelsea at the time it was built. There are houses like them all over the former British empire. In Sydney, in Cape Town, in Toronto, even in the old parts of Singapore. The whole world knows them from the titles of *Coronation Street*: back-to-backs, artisan cottages, nineteenth-century workers' housing.

Once they were slums, now they are smart and architects rave about their logic. Two rooms downstairs, eating and sitting. Two rooms upstairs, parents and children. Kitchen and coal-hole out back. Outside space, created for throwing junk, drying washing and the original outside lavatory. To English taste, the minimal structure needed to raise a family, have a fighting chance of not getting TB and deliver a worker to the factory gates every morning.

The destiny of these houses has been the same all over the world, except in Singapore where the last three have been painted up and put on display as a quaint relic of the bad old days. Everywhere else, the unit built for a labourer, his wife, their six children and the dying grandmother is now highly valued as the perfect home environment for a yuppie couple.

The cheap, mass-produced cornices are picked out in shades of white, the rough pine floorboards are sanded and bleached, the coal hole becomes a conservatory and a New

Zealand tree fern from a sustainable source unrolls its fronds on the site of the outside privy. Come the first baby and the successful yuppie couple moves on to find a real garden and a second bathroom. Rhys and Barbara, not so successful, had found themselves trapped.

The Westwick property market roared around like a glittering carousel and never slowed down enough for them to be able to jump aboard. Rhys refused to compromise his conscience by doing more private work to make more money. Barbara refused to compromise her social life by agreeing to move to a cheaper neighbourhood. When Toby was three, and his sister refused to share a room with him any more, they increased their mortgage and built an illegal third bedroom in the roof. If you sneezed anywhere in the building, everyone at home heard it.

A man under a cloud, a man suspended from his job, a man suddenly forced to spend all day and all night in his own home, paces about a house like that with the desperation of a tiger in a zoo. Even a gentle man such as Rhys.

Of course, it didn't help that he was married to a witch. Now that Christmas was over, Barbara could get back to playing bridge every day, but she didn't get up until eleven, which meant she never left before lunchtime, so he walked on eggshells all morning.

He tried pretending to be a New Yorker and going out for breakfast. Sitting in the Quando Quando Coffee Boutique on the Broadway, trying to focus on the *British Medical Journal*, he felt the whole of Westwick watching him. There's Rhys Pritchard. He's been suspended from Helford Hospital, you know. Making racist remarks about a patient. And his son was expelled from St Nicholas's. Tried to set fire to the school. I mean, you have to ask. Have you seen the wife? Must be twenty stone at least. What goes on in that house? A doctor's family, you wouldn't think it.

Sitting in cafés successfully required more anonymity than Westwick could offer him. After a couple of days he tried taking a table at the back and buying a big newspaper to hold in front of his face.

He tried getting fit. The family membership of The Cedars Health and Racquet Club, optimistically taken out but mostly used only by Barbara on their bridge night, allowed him to use their state-of-the-art facilities every day. A man feels extraordinarily exposed on a treadmill. Rhys Pritchard. You know, the doctor. They suspended him, that's why he's down here all the time. There's going to be an inquiry. Did he kill someone? No, worse than that. Racist remarks. And you heard about his son, didn't you? That's his wife, she comes down on bridge night only. Surprised they let her in looking like that. It is a health club, after all.

After a couple of days he took to jogging on the towpath. His knees protested. Bursitis. The physiotherapists shared a waiting area with the beauticians. Was the whole of Westwick taken up with gossip all day? Tuesday's BodyPump instructor had moved in with the new crèche manager. Marcia's new spaniel was having puppies. The woman at La Maison, she'd lost her husband. The fair-haired one. Another woman, of course. She always looked kind of sad, didn't she?

Would they talk about him and Mo that way? The woman at La Maison, she's left her husband. The tall one. Another man, of course. She always looked kind of fabulous, didn't she? He missed her. Not a dull ache, an ugly, bleeding wrench. He missed her like he would miss that leg if it were suddenly twisted off like a drumstick. The physiotherapist applied ultrasound to his joints without conversation. Professional behaviour. He'd have done the same.

Would it be so bad to call in at La Maison? Just once?

There she was, sitting at the desk at the back, talking on the phone, the forever legs sheathed in embroidered jeans, the elegant feet hidden in red suede and snakeskin boots. Red boots. He could have cried with joy. His life was a wasteland and the woman he loved was wearing red boots. It wasn't irrational to hope.

She looked up as he came in, with a face he didn't recognise. 'If I get any news I'll call you,' she was saying into the phone. 'And you do the same for me, yeah?'

'Hello, Mo.'

No kiss. She was nervous and preoccupied. Maybe this hadn't been such a good idea.

'That was about Mickey. He was meant to be in Milan this morning. He never arrived. I know it's stupid, but I'm worried about that air crash, Rhys. The traffic piled up. I'm going to call the police.'

'What air crash?'

'This morning. At Heathrow. Cargo plane came down on the motorway.'

'So that's why the traffic's all fouled up.'

Wrong! Her whole face darkened. 'Yes, that would be the reason,' she said, dangerously ironic.

He looked for somewhere to sit and chose an old oak blanket box that was heaped with swatches. Unsmiling, she leaned over to move a pile of them to make room for him, dialling the phone with the other hand, implying that she was prepared to tolerate him more to maintain her own standards of humanity than because she actually wanted him to be there.

Mickey. She had feelings for Mickey. The factor he'd been screening out for years was suddenly obvious. The cold welcome, the frozen face, just meant she was worrying about Mickey. Over-reaction, probably displaced guilt. More worried about him because of what was between them.

Well, if she was worried, a caring man would empathise. He could do that, did it every day. From the phone, he heard the faint echo of an automated call system. He rearranged his head and tried speaking from concern. 'He can't have been involved in that, surely?'

'Why not? He was there. He was in the wrong place at the wrong time. First time in his life, maybe, but your luck has to run out one day, doesn't it?' She was short, snappy even. He wasn't coming over right. The police call system was playing Vivaldi.

'A man like Mickey wouldn't get mixed up in a motorway pile-up. He's a good driver.'

'Doesn't make much difference what kind of driver you are if a fucking airplane comes down on the road in front of you when you're going round the clock in the fast lane, does it?' The electronic Vivaldi gave way to a human voice. 'Have you got a contact number for people needing information about the crash at the airport this morning?' A unapologetic twitter. 'Well, can I talk to Helford Station then, please. Anyway, what do you know about the kind of man he is?'

'We go back a long way. I've known him as long as you.'

'Not exactly in the same way. All you do is drum along behind him and the others.'

'We talk.'

'If you call that talking.'

My, she was in a mood. Holding the phone, listening to a different automated tape now, keying in numbers with stabs of her forefinger. More reassurance, that'd do the trick. 'I'm sure he was nowhere near the crash. There's nothing to worry about.'

'He didn't get on his flight, Rhys. He's not picking up his phone. There's everything to worry about. What do you think was on his mind, since you guys do all that talking?'

'Well, that's my point. He was fine. I mean, he's immensely successful, you're fine, your son's fine, he's got nothing at all to be worried about . . .'

'You just lost your lead guitar. He was quite fond of George, you know.' Again, that deadly, gentle sarcasm.

'George? Well, they spent time together. They weren't exactly soulmates.'

'I'd disagree with you there. In some ways that's just what they were. I'd say he was pretty broken up, actually. And he hasn't worked for months, he's had to make compromises he didn't want to make. I wouldn't say he was fine at all, Rhys.'

'You don't think . . . ?' Us. A two-letter word. A two-letter word that filled his mouth so full he couldn't get it out. And he was breathless with jealousy.

'No, I don't think he knows about us. He's always been so busy making sure I don't know about his PAs and his makeup girls and whatever other handy little tart he's getting it on with, I don't think it's ever occurred to him that I might be seeing someone else too.'

'Surely not? Not Mickey.'

'This is hopeless.' No, she didn't mean Us. Mo threw the phone back on its console, got up and reached for her handbag. 'Look, I'm going to close up and go down there. Alice is still at the hospital. If she gets back she's got a key.'

She was hunting through drawers at the desk. Soon she found what she was looking for, the loopy-lettered sign that read 'Back in 5 mins'.

Slowly, still not understanding, he got to his feet. 'I can mind the store.'

'Don't be silly.' The sign was in the window already and she was holding the door for him. 'Come on.'

And they were out on the street and she was locking up faster than his eye could follow, saying, 'I told you, you don't know Mickey. I do. At least I think I do. Something's afoot.'

'Twelve inches?' It sounded lame as soon as he said it.

A kiss on the cheek. Terse, if a kiss could be terse. And she was heading for the La Maison Renault, saying, 'Call me later,' over her shoulder.

He walked back to his own car and sat in it for a while, meditating. Barbara would still be at home, not safe to go back yet. Obviously, it hadn't been a good time. He'd done the right thing, sympathy, support, being there for her. When she'd calmed down she'd think well of him for it.

So she thought that Mickey played around. PAs and makeup girls. He found that he was offended. Not a flattering comparison. Was it a comparison? Had she intended that? Was she trying to tell him that their affair was just her payback for what she imagined Mickey was getting up to? No. Just wound up, imagining this nonsense about the air crash. Displaced guilt.

Having explained their conversation to his satisfaction, and his wife still being at home, Rhys decided it was time to improve his golf. His golf, up till now, was a rarely indulged holiday pleasure. His handicap was pitiful. He paid all that money for membership of the Royal Richmond-on-Thames Golf Club. Time to do something about it.

Elizabeth obviously needed some space. She took her beliefs very seriously, such a contrast to Alice who was never the spiritual type. Sam felt he could understand. He called her every day. He offered lunch again but she said she was busy. His stay at The Westwick Hotel, a perfectly comfortable establishment on the Broadway, might have to be extended a few days.

The Westwick Hotel he knew well, since the owners were his clients, a Polish couple who made him very welcome. Their rules, which were only common courtesy to observe, stated that rooms should be vacated by 10 a.m. This was to allow for cleaning. Not because the establishment was just a painted-up bed and breakfast. Not at all.

At 10.05, therefore, Sam arrived at his office on foot. His parking space, he observed, was occupied by a white Transit van. Illegally parked, no permit displayed. He'd get the receptionist to get the warden to remove it straightaway.

Behind the reception desk, in the chair usually occupied by Pats, sat a tall man in a bulky padded jacket with a bad haircut, who was fiddling with the switchboard. 'Problems?' Sam enquired, wondering how much loss-of-business compensation he would be able to claim from the phone company.

'Are you Mr Chudleigh?' the man asked, getting to his feet surprisingly quickly.

'I am,' he admitted with pride. Sam Chudleigh of Chudleigh Estate Services. Having a business that bore his name had never lost its thrill.

'Take a seat, would you, sir?' The man tapped a couple of keys and spoke into the mouthpiece. 'Mr Chudleigh's here.'

'My office is through there,' Sam explained, moving towards his frosted-glass door.

'Sorry, sir. You can't go through there.' With astonishing speed the man left the desk and stood between him and the door. He was extraordinarily tall, and in the padded jacket impressively wide as well. Sam was forced to step back.

'That's my office and I certainly can go in there,' he protested.

'Afraid not, sir.'

Why was the phone engineer trying to stop him going into his office? 'Look, that's my office,' Sam explained again. 'It's where I work. If my phone's acting up, surely you can fix it while I'm working, like people usually do.'

'We're not fixing the phones, sir. We're the police. The Serious Fraud Squad.'

Serious Fraud? The glass door opened and the large man stood aside. Behind him in the doorway were two more men, one in a fleece and the other in a suit. 'That's right,' Suit confirmed. 'Acting on information received, we are investigating certain aspects of your affairs. Here's our search warrant.'

Suit handed him a document. As far as Sam could tell, it was indeed a search warrant. Having steered well clear of criminal work throughout his entire legal career, he had never seen one before. A scruffy little chit it was too.

'What's all this about?' he demanded, careful not to sound

as angry as he felt. Silly, of course, but he was feeling anxious as well. Angry at the intrusion, anxious as to the cause. Information received? From whom? Who would want to pull a prank like this?

Silly question. Look no further than his ungrateful, useless son, who'd always lacked any sense of appropriate behaviour. And who was now making a ridiculous fuss about Sam's new life with Elizabeth. Yes, this was Jon's doing. It'd all come out soon, then they'd be grovelling around apologising. Maybe it'd get as far as wrongful arrest. What would that be, ten grand? He'd look up the recent judgments as soon as they let him at his desk.

'I'd prefer not to say at this stage. If you'd like to take a seat, we'll be finished shortly. We're removing some documents for examination. You'll be given receipts for them all. We'll be wanting to interview you, in due course, and your employee, a Miss Patricia Green? Is she expected in?'

Pats? Why was she mixed up in this? 'My assistant. I took her on last year, when we bought another company. No, we're not expecting her. She's on holiday. In Barbados.' That should impress them. I'm a man of substance. Even my assistant can afford a Caribbean holiday.

'Barbados? You're sure?'

'That's what she told us.' They had moved out into the reception area, and through the open door Sam could see more men diligently packing files into brown cardboard document boxes. Another sat at Pats's desk, his face illuminated by the glow from her monitor. Pats. How dare Jon involve her?

Sam sized up Suit and decided he was probably a man of experience who would understand his position. 'Look,' he said, leading his listener a few paces across the reception area to a corner between the neo-Corbusier chairs where reasonable confidentiality could be created. 'I think I know what this might be about. Of course I don't expect you to disclose the source of your information, but it might be useful for you to know that I've recently split up with my partner. We've got a couple of kids in their twenties now, not little kids, nothing like that, but they're behaving very badly about it. The boy in particular, Jonathan Chudleigh. Or he might be using his mother's name, Waters. I've got his phone numbers somewhere, if you need to check them out. He's acted quite maliciously in the past few weeks, very resentful of the new lady in my life. I'm sure you understand that kind of situation.'

'Thank you, sir. As you say, we won't disclose the identity of our informant.'

Fleece, communicating with the men working in the filing room, called out, 'Ready to go, sir,' from the doorway.

'Right. We'd like you to come with us now. As soon as the stuff is checked in at the station we'll issue the receipts.'

'Of course.' Sam spread his hands wide, indicating that he had nothing to hide. Best to look blatantly co-operative. With a really juicy wrongful-arrest action on the cards, he'd play his part to the hilt. 'Happy to help the police in any way I can, Officer. You lead the way.'

Amazing how small a five-bedroomed Regency villa can be when the resident wife has taken against the resident husband and God and man respectively have laid claim to the resident daughters. Andy found himself alone in his four walls yet again, feeling miserable to the marrow of his bones.

Sixteen years of marriage and Laura was a woman he didn't know. Perhaps had never known, just imagined to lull himself into fake happiness. Had the whole thing been a fantasy? That she could wound him so deeply, so classically and claim it was for the good of their marriage: his mind couldn't get round it. The pain had frozen his circuits, he could not understand. Normally a bottomless well of empathy, and now he was dry. Every woman he had ever wanted, and she had never wanted him.

Forty-eight years in the same body and he didn't know that either. How could his own chemistry betray him this way? His atoms, his molecules, his proteins, his amino acids, his hormones. My God, his hormones. Pascal was running through his arteries like fire. Olive skin. Bernini arms. The Pascal smell, warm and aromatic, lingering in his memory.

Could he have been wrong all this time? Could he be gay, really? Could he ask for an independent opinion, say from Mickey? Or maybe Rhys? No. He thought of the party in the Pink Palace. No, he could make up his own mind. He didn't belong there.

How fragile was a family, even after all those years of building. The care, the sacrifice, the time, the thought, the work, the money: heap them all up, one year after another, until you're nearly there, the job is almost done, your children are mere months from adulthood, and a few casual words, a couple of selfish gestures, can blow the whole thing away like a pile of dust. Pfffff – gone! A moment of selfishness, a flash of lust, an ugly impulse lazily indulged, and it was all over. No more family.

Pain or rage, which one to start with? The pain was his

alone, the rage belonged to the others. Laura, so slick with a rationale for her betrayal. Sickening to see a fine mind put to such vile use. No heart, no values, she was their in-house psychopath who killed people to pass the time. And Pascal, with all his beauty and all his tenderness focused on getting his needs met, on filling the vacancy left by George. The wounds that won't heal, the broken life that I can't mend, my personal charity, that's what Pascal wants to be. And I'm so sad I almost believed him. Sad or horny, which? Maybe they're the same.

Sex. I just want sex. I'm dying here, I'm starving, I've got to have sex. Just a warm body to fuck and lie down with. Without any feeling, any feeling at all. Without having to feel disgusted. Without it changing my life.

All day he sat at his desk and went through the motions of working, blinded and deafened by unhappiness. When Lily came home from school, banged about in her room for half an hour and went out again without saying a word, he was hardly aware of it. The hours ran on with no meaning. He watched Laura come home from the office and go straight into the house next door. He imagined her commiserating with Charles. Well, let them. His conscience was clear. So far.

Eight o'clock came and went. He recognised that he was hungry and made himself a sandwich. No need to cook dinner, there was no family to eat it any more. Nine. He needed something to kill the pain. The computer had games. He beat his previous best playing Sonic 4. Since I'm feeling like an adolescent, I'll act like an adolescent. It was OK. The rule he'd made for himself was no games until after six. He'd stuck by it for three years. Good going. A desperate time, a desperate remedy was allowed. It was nearly ten. Now ten-thirty. No Laura. No Daisy. An inky, howling, January night.

Finally their iron gate banged. Daisy. Laura never bothered shutting the gate. He decided not to look out. If she was kissing anybody goodbye, he didn't want to know. Five minutes. Scuffling on the porch. Definitely more than one person out there. Ten minutes. Silence, still no Daisy.

Finally, after a good quarter of an hour, heavy feet jumped down the steps outside. That's the boy. Or the man. No peeking. Stay away from the windows. You don't want to know. He heard a key in the lock, the door opening and shutting.

'Hiya, Dad.' She looked around the drawing room door. Flush-faced, shiny-eyed, seething with hormones in her turn, his daughter was home.

'Hiya, Daze. I was wondering where you were.'

'Me and some friends went for a pizza.'

'Some friends and I.'

'Some friends and I.'

'You won't be wanting any dinner, then?'

'Not really.'

'You could have let us know.'

'Sorry.'

She wafted upstairs to her room, to consult the wisdom of Wendi about controlling parents, probably. No, here she was again. Coming down fast. Careful, don't rush and hurt yourself. There she was at the door, all the erotic bloom extinguished, looking mature and earnest. What proposal was coming now?

'Dad, you should look at this.' She gave him a letter, written on her own writing paper under the cheaply printed heading of dewy-eyed ponies. 'It was on my bed. It's from Lily.'

He read the blurry, cramped writing:

Dear Parents and Daisy
The Bible says that by the obedience of one to God's laws many shall be made righteous. So it is to save you all that I am going away now to follow a life with Jesus. Even though you are all the servants of sin, I can redeem you through obedience unto righteousness. I shall walk not after the ways of the flesh but after the ways of the Spirit and I will bring us all to light and peace. Do not worry about me, I shall have everything I need. Do not try to find me. If you want to worry, worry about yourselves because to walk after the ways of the flesh is death, but the gift of God is eternal life through Jesus.
Lily

Right there, right then. A couple of hours ago, his child had left home. Run away. And he hadn't even noticed.

Daisy said, 'I only looked quickly, I couldn't see what she'd taken except her backpack and her Bible. And she's taken all her posters down, so she must have them.'

'Did you know she was thinking of doing this?'

'Well, she was always saying we were sinners and she couldn't live with us any more. I didn't take any notice, really. I suppose it was you being gay that tipped her over the edge.'

She spoke with so little concern that at first he didn't think he'd heard her right. Should he let it go? No, he'd never let anything go again. 'What did you say just then?'

'She was always saying we were sinners and she couldn't live with us any more and I didn't take any notice.' Slightly uncomfortable now, avoiding his eyes.

'And after that?'

'Maybe it was you being gay that was what decided her.'

'Maybe you know something I don't, Daisy, but I don't think I'm gay.'

'You were kissing Pascal in the garden. We all saw you.'

All? The whole family? His skin prickled everywhere with embarrassment. The sensation of sliding helplessly from one disaster to the next, with every move he made just making things worse, was growing fast.

'That was all Pascal. Nothing to do with me. He was out of control, I didn't do anything. I just got rid of him as fast as I could without being unpleasant.' Maybe Wendi can help you understand.

'And Mum had a little talk with us. Like she does.' Laura's little talks. The edited broadcasts of her feelings, issued by way of propaganda in her own defence.

'I didn't know. What little talk?'

'Well, after she went next door with Charles and found you and Pascal together in the bathroom. She said she thought you were in denial about it all and that you might come out and we had to be ready and she wasn't sure she could share you with a man, actually she was sure she couldn't, and we might be leaving you and would we mind living in a smaller house. I think she was quite drunk, it was after she'd been having a drink with Charles one time. She wasn't very happy, anyway.'

He could see that to part of Daisy this was all theatre. She was enthralled by the drama that the large illuminated adult figures in her life were acting out in front of her. A real-life soap opera with a role for her. The other part, the part that was in the action, was just scared. 'Before Christmas, this was?'

'Yes.'

'Like she does, you said.'

'Well, she does. She gives us these chats sometimes.'

'What about?'

'What she thinks is going on. She started when you got fired. I think she does it because she wants to soften us up for whatever she's planning.'

'Look, sweetheart.' She was the picture of uncertainty, standing with her legs wrapped around each other and her arms folded, her head drooping so that her hair fell in her eyes, twisting awkwardly away from him. 'Come and sit down.'

'Oh no, not a chat from you too.'

'No, I want to clear this up.' Pouting, she flopped down on a chair. 'Whatever your mother thinks, I'm not having any kind of relationship with anyone. Anyone except her, that is. Pascal thinks he's in love with me and that's his problem. Your mother and I . . .' He was doing it. He was sounding like his own father. 'Well, whatever she'd say, we're having some problems.'

'That's what she's been saying. Anyone would know anyway, you hardly ever talk to each other.'

'I was thinking she was just working too hard. She never told me any of this. Until yesterday.' How much of a prat is it OK to look to your daughter? Suppose she took after Laura, started giving off that toxic contempt that seemed to be eating up her mother? 'So you might know more about her state of mind than I do.'

'I think she's just spoiled.'

'Spoiled?'

'Yes. She's like a spoiled brat who's always trying to make it everyone's fault if she hasn't got exactly what she wants the minute she wants it. I suppose she was quite beautiful when she was young and she got used to having everyone do everything she wanted, and when things went horribly wrong she couldn't handle it.' This was delivered with would-be gracious condescension, as if from a standpoint of all-knowing wisdom. At least she'd taken her hair out of her eyes and was looking squarely at him.

'She was very beautiful when she was young and I think she still is now.'

'Well, that's it then, isn't it? She says you don't turn her on any more.'

'What?'

'Lily was disgusted.'

'For once I'd say I agree with Lily.'

'That's no reason to get divorced though, is it? Unless you find someone else or fall in love or something. You know, Dad, you could tell me if you thought you were gay. I wouldn't mind as long as you were happy. I hate you moping around Mum trying to make everything all right by being nice. If you were gay and with somebody who really cared about you it might be better.'

He was about to tell her she didn't know what she was talking about when he remembered the world of Wendi. Very difficult to deal with a mind that had been stuffed with plastic platitudes before it was even fully grown.

Instead of knowledge, she had an instant supply of fake sophistication. Why, that caring little face she was putting on now was as phoney as a Bangkok Rolex.

'Charles says you don't have a choice about being gay, you just are, and the best thing to do is to come out.' Simple, really. Thanks, Wendi.

'Sweetheart, I appreciate you being concerned for me.' She perked up visibly. Yes, this was the way to go. Adult to adult, the winning approach. 'But I don't agree with Charles and I think he's painting things a bit too black and white. I really don't think there's anything to come out about here. I've been in love with your mother for nearly twenty years, how does that make me a closet gay? Pascal's just causing trouble because that's what people like him do.'

'He wants someone to look after him.'

'That's exactly what I think.'

'And he's rowing with Charles all the time. We can hear them, yelling at each other.'

'So he's trying to find another man to take him on. And I must have looked about ready to be suckered, with your mother round there all the time with Charles.'

'Pascal's hopeless, isn't he?' She giggled. 'I was watching him trying to open a window this morning, he couldn't work out how to do it.'

'And sometimes in life, people like that, if they are very good-looking, they know they need to be with someone who can make the world work and they don't have much trouble finding one, or moving on when they're rumbled. There's always another idiot ready to believe their story. But in this case, it ain't gonna be me.'

Daisy digested this and found it satisfying. Then she said, 'OK, Dad, I get it. Now what are we going to do about Lily?'

'You've really got no idea where she's gone?'

'She said the church took them all to see some community or something. I can't remember. I'm sorry, I just don't listen when she's going on about God and stuff. She's so aggressive about it, she's always telling me I'm a harlot. Why she can't say slapper and just come out with it I don't know. Not that she'd have any reason to say that.' She gave him both eyeballs, dead on and no smile. OK. Got you. Thanks for getting in touch.

'Has she got any friends down there she might be with?'

'I don't think so. This community, it sounded more like a cult.'

'I'd better go down to that church in the morning. Do they have things like vicars?' She shook her head and shrugged. 'They must do. And the police, I suppose. We can do that now. I'd better tell your mother first. Don't worry, sweetheart. We'll do everything we can. It'll be OK, I promise.'

He picked up the phone to call next door. All things considered, popping round for a chat wasn't quite the thing to do with Charles and Pascal any more.

Aarhus is a lively town with many cultural attractions. 'Why do I doubt this?' Mickey asked himself aloud, and heard the words bounce back from the walls of his hotel room. He reclined on the bed, reading the complimentary welcome magazine, waiting for the solution to his life to manifest itself. This would happen. He was The Man, God looked after him. All he needed to do was keep the faith, chill out and it would happen.

Outside, it was dark and snowing. Enormous flakes of snow were floating earthwards in clumps, as if God had ripped open a giant duvet and was shaking out the feathers. Nice. Not a cliché, this one. He stored the effect in his visual memory.

The town's attractive Concert Hall (Musikhuset) is the background for the great part of the larger cultural arrangements in Aarhus . . . The silence was deafening. He leaned over and fiddled with the radio. Merry Scandinavian pop songs, cloned contenders for the Eurovision Song Contest, spewed from the speakers. *There are several museums in Aarhus, including the Museum of Prehistory, The Ole Romer Observatory, the Danish Fire and Rescue Protection Museum and the Women's Museum.* Killing the radio, he got up and turned on the TV. *Friends* appeared, dubbed into Danish. The episode in which Joey blags his way into a dance audition and stands there waving his arms around like an orang-utan. *An ideal way to see the town is by cycling. Look out for the special cyclists' routes (cykelruter).*

It was snowing harder. The air outside was more white than dark. Lights from the buildings around were almost blotted out by the snow. There was another magazine, *Welcome to Denmark. Children from all over the world love to visit Denmark's famous Legoland attraction.* Pictures of plastic castles in primary colours, knee-high to shiny-faced eight-year-olds.

Lego was rubbish. Meccano was the all-time greatest construction toy. Meccano was little green metal bars fixed together with real nuts and bolts. With Meccano, his father had said, a boy learned to thread screws right and work out stuff like payloads and mechanical advantage just by instinct.

He had been crap at Meccano. He remembered being bored senseless while his father built the ferris wheel, spending an entire Sunday with the kit and the instructions, patiently assembling every section, then putting the whole thing together, wiring up the little motor which turned the wheel and worked the lights, his face glowing with pride when they flipped the switch and it all worked. 'There you are, son.' Pride he couldn't share with anyone because all his son wanted to do was get back to the TV.

No longer made in Britain. Japanese bought the company. Old Meccano sets were sold at auction as collector's items, up there with the wooden rocking horse and the china doll. And kids fiddled around with Lego and thought that was something. Joe had been Lego-mad. For years the house had been littered with lurid morsels of plastic, lurking, waiting to stab you in the toe when you got up in the dark for the bathroom. Disappointing your dad, maybe it ran in the family.

Now there was a storm raging. The snowflakes were blowing past the window about ten degrees from horizontal, moving so fast they blurred into white lines against the black sky. A TV snowstorm in real life. Curious at last, he went to the window and looked out at the white inferno. The hotel was taller than the buildings around it, and his room was on the top floor. Look up, look down, look left, look right. All you could see was snowstorm. Flakes large in the darkness, flakes smaller near the lights, flakes driven before the wind, flakes pelting into buildings, flakes eddying around street corners, flakes drifting upwards in chimneys of calm air. All in silence, beyond the triple glass of the window. Pretty goddamn strange.

He found, from the TV, that he had watched the storm for more than an hour. Two earnest men seemed to be discussing the impact of EU policies on Danish pig farming. Their speech pattered soothingly in his ears. He got a beer from the mini-bar, a Hofburg, wouldn't you know. Not bad beer at all. And on the top of the mini-bar, in the space between the little fridge and the birch-veneer Biedermeier-style mini-bar cabinet that concealed it, placed there by God to point him in the right direction, was a book. In English.

Mickey read books. Not many, but when the time was right, when there were hours to be killed and no other way of doing it, when he'd left home without his DVD or his Discman, when he was marooned in a snowstorm in a high-rise hotel in the style-free hell of a small town in Denmark, when he had probably assassinated his own career and aliens had taken away his perfect body and substituted some dys-functional humanoid that kept cracking up, then, if not before, he would read. So he read.

And in the morning, having not slept at all, he called the airport for the first flight home. All flights at Aarhus being grounded on account of the storm, he hired a car and set off to drive through the eternal snow to Copenhagen, pulling off at a truck stop just before he fell asleep at the wheel to take on coffee and some globally branded anti-congestant capsules which were known to be strong enough to keep a cow wired. All he really needed to be was conscious. His brain was driving automatically. Most of his mind was running a movie. The film of the book. His film. He had the opening shot already; a long pan around a room like George's.

A few hours later, waiting on a dockside for a ferry, in an out-take from *Babette's Feast* in which everything was grey and everyone was miserable, he thought of Mo. She could be useful here. An ace fixer, never lost her skills. 'How are you?' he asked when he finally tracked her down on her mobile.

'How are *you*?' she countered. 'Everyone's been going apeshit.'

This seemed to have no relevance so he ignored it. 'I'm on my way back but there's a fucking blizzard here and it's going to take me a couple of days. I want you to get on the phone and find out about the rights to a book, OK? And if somebody has already got them, find out what the score is and what they want for them.' He gave her the title and the author's name.

'Are you OK?' she said again.

'It's fucking freezing,' he realised. Where the hell was a hot flush when you needed one? 'Never been better,' he assured her.

Mo. His wife, the girl with the forever legs. The coolest woman in the universe, bar absolutely none. Somewhere behind the images generating themselves spontaneously in his brain was the picture of her sitting in a chair the way she always sat, looking at him the way she always looked at him. Her existence was a wonder.

Nowhere in Mickey's overactive consciousness was the idea that his actions might have created any feelings in his wife, or that those feelings might have been negative. Worry, anxiety, fear – no sign of those boys. Nor did he have any shadow of guilt or shiver of remorse. Nothing to be guilty about. The thing about Mo was, she was Mo.

He found himself dialling her number again, and when she picked up he said, 'Hum. Er. I just called.'

'To say I love you?' she suggested. Her voice sounded a bit shaky, but that was probably the line.

'Yeah, that's the one.'

CHAPTER 11

The Blues, Real Bad

A woman and a man sat in the bar of the Ritz hotel. The maître d' had shown them to a table in the thick of things, where they were brushed frequently by passing waiters.

She had asked for champagne. It was that time in the early evening when the yammering *jeunesse dorée* who have met for tea give way to the disoriented hotel guests herding together for cocktails.

He said, 'Have you used them before, these Table for Two people?'

Laura smiled at his question. 'No, this is my first time. I suppose I'm sort of testing the market. What about you?'

'First time for me, too.'

Was that a lie? She'd have to finesse a bit. 'The ad says "Serious Introductions for Serious People", doesn't it?'

'I suppose that's their way of saying no timewasters.' He cracked a meaningful grin as he raised his glass. A bit tight around the jaw there, a bit repressed maybe. 'So what exactly are you looking for?'

'Oh, a relationship, definitely. A partner, I hope. I couldn't do a casual thing.'

'Nor could I,' he assured her quickly, wondering how old she was. He'd given the agency a wide brief: slim, professional, anywhere in the thirties. Disappointing to get someone older. Well-preserved, nice figure for her age, nicely dressed, but she had that hard-edged manner an older woman developed. Confident, almost brash. Didn't do much for him.

In Laura's eyes, he was attractive in a rather old way, grey-haired, solid, certainly not fazed by the ormolu and chandeliers, quite happy to buy champagne. Sun-tanned, kept himself fit, not bad looking, maybe a bit short of the old factor X. Amazing, really, how many acceptable men there were around, looking for women. And it was all so painless. Make a phone call, answer a few questions, get out the credit card and there it was, a whole new life. This one didn't exactly turn her on, but he'd do. Perhaps. 'What's your history?' she asked, remembering to smile.

'I've worked in the Middle East all my life. Engineering, oil business. Well paid, quite comfortable. Time to come home now and start enjoying myself.' Not exactly trying to sell himself.

'Family?'

'No. Not much opportunity, out there. Not many European women, mostly married already.' He answered with an offended edge, as if he wasn't entirely sure her question was reasonable. 'And what about you?'

Holding back, definitely. Well, this was a different ball game. She did her best to melt a little. 'I was married quite young. Too young. We have a couple of children. They're grown up now, really.'

'So where are you living?'

'We're still in the same house. Until it sells, then we can divi up and move on. It's pretty awful. I mean, you can both agree to an amicable separation but there's always an atmosphere, isn't there?'

Wrong, wrong. Don't talk about pain, never mention unhappiness. Smiley person, problem-free, that's what you've got to be. At all times. Take me, I'm happy. He was looking downright anxious now. He said, 'I wouldn't know.'

Silence is golden. Rig out another smile, sit tight and wait for him to make the moves. The cocktail pianist tinkled. She sipped from her glass. Shiny, happy, problem-free, not at all worried. The last of the tea tables got up to leave and eager waiters swooped on the debris.

He said, 'You know what I do. What about you?'

'Marketing. I'm a partner in a small company.' No reaction. Just sat there like a lump, frowning slightly, looking at the top of the table.

After a pause, he drew a fresh breath and said, 'Successful?'

'Oh yes. We do pretty well.' The information sank without a ripple. Maybe he didn't believe her.

'So you work quite long hours, I suppose?'

'Sometimes. Success is a challenge in its way. When you're hot, you're hot, you know. Sometimes you have to go with it.' Again, no response. He'd made a list. He was working down his specifications, ticking off one item at a time. One man she'd seen yesterday had actually got out the list in front of her.

'And whereabouts do you live?'

'We're in Westwick.'

'Westwick? That's where this house is? Where you're living?' He sat forward, suddenly animated, and poured her more champagne. 'It's meant to be pretty nice, isn't it?'

'I suppose it is a nice area.'

'So you're selling a house in Westwick?' From the silver dish beside the bottle, he grabbed a handful of salted nuts.

'Yes.'

'And what, you get half of it?' A cashew, pop. An almond, pop. Crunch, crunch, grin, grin. Now he was interested. Almost human, even.

'I suppose so. At least. It was my capital in the first place.' Don't mention the children, remember you're problem-free. But it would be a lot more than half, if the children came with her. She hadn't quite decided what to do about the girls. Daisy was coming along now but Lily was going to be more trouble than she was worth for years. Andy liked messing around with them, it might be best if they went with him. But the lawyer had said she could go for two-thirds to three-quarters of the house if she got the kids. Two or three years, boyfriends of their own, who knew what might happen? She kept smiling. He was smiling too. Much better.

'So you're selling a house in Westwick, eh?' Smiling and rolling back in the awkward Rococo chair, looking like a man who'd just picked the winner of the Grand National.

'That's right,' she said. And checked her watch, because all this sudden interest was just a tad spooky.

'Time to go? I haven't offended you, have I?'

'Oh no. Not at all. You mustn't think that. But I think an hour's enough, don't you?'

'For a first meeting, yes. Ideal, I think. Shall we do dinner next? I'd like that.'

She told him to e-mail her at work. 'That's quite safe, nobody can read them except me.'

He kissed her hand. Argh! The dry print of his ingratiating lips right there on her own metatarsals! Disgusting! Thank God they were close to the door. Propelled by outrage, she shot through the revolving panels and out on to the pavement like a frightened deer. A taxi, quick. Her heart was beating as if she'd run a mile.

Laura rubbed her hand on the seat, rubbing off the feeling of his kiss. By the time the taxi was crawling through Knightsbridge, her pulse was steady and she was evaluating the information. Not keen, in the beginning, then suddenly all over her like a rash.

Only one thing to think, really. Having a house in Westwick was the most attractive thing about her. Nothing else in the package had interested him at all. In which case, should she give up on a good thing? Or keep looking, see some more men, try another agency? These guys couldn't all be weird. Could they?

'Your son is completely out of control,' Barbara accused Rhys. She was standing in the kitchen, filling up most of that tiny room fashioned from the former coal-hole of their cottage in Little Chelsea, holding a letter in one hand and with the other dunking a half-eaten bagel into a kilo jar of strawberry jam. A fair amount of jam was spread around her mouth, giving the impression that she'd been devouring a bloody carcass. 'He's having a breakdown. Look at this rubbish.'

Rhys took the letter. He should have recognised Toby's writing, his son's traumatised hieroglyphs. 'He says he's not coming home,' he deduced, moving into the living area to find his glasses.

'That much I can understand. God knows what the rest of it's about.'

Read with his spectacles, the writing was larger but not much easier to decipher. Finally Rhys got one sentence straight. *Susie, who you know as Miss Sweetling, has got another job now so the school should be OK with everything.*

What exactly would the school need to be OK with? In another five minutes he worked it out. 'He's fallen in love with one of the staff.'

'I got that much.' She spoke through a mouthful of food. 'The girl must be mad. She's got problems, must have. How on earth could anyone like that get a job with children?'

'He's sixteen now. It's not actually illegal.'

'Well, it should be. Dirty bitch.'

We will be living together at this address, which is close enough to the school for me to become a day pupil, which will save you quite a bit on the fees.

His uppermost feeling was a degree of pique. All the time he'd devoted to Toby, all the sensitively handled talk, the intimacy he had contrived with the wealth of his experience with people, and now the boy had written to his mother, not to him. The envelope clearly said *Barbara Pritchard*. His final stake in fatherhood had been lost and he had to get the news from her.

'Well, he can't do this, of course. He's not eighteen, he's underage. We're legally responsible, we can go and get him back.' Pique, then envy. His son and that exquisite girl. His son in the hectic certainty of first love. His son setting up a home that would be full of sex and laughter and sunlight, and nothing else, no baggage, no bills, no in-house psychopath spewing bile as she stomped from room to room.

'It looks to me as if he's thought of that.' Barbara stuffed the last of the bagel into her mouth and pulled another one out of its packet. 'Keep reading. Over the page.'

. . . you will have the time to work out your own lives without the excuse of staying together for my sake . . . Following that was an orderly paragraph explaining that *my father has consoled himself with an affair for several years.*

'Well?' Barbara demanded, her jaws never pausing until the last of the second bagel had been chomped and swallowed, after which she took a swig from her mug of coffee and then waved it at him to demand a response. 'Well?'

'What do you mean, "well"?' Rhys prevaricated.

'I mean, is it true, you arsehole? Have you been,' she pulled a derisively dainty face, '"consoling yourself"?'

A new world beckoned to Rhys. A gentle, smiling, honest world where he could tell the truth and stand tall, and be free of Barbara for ever. The door to this new world was open. All he had to do was step over the threshold. Could it be that easy, after all this time?

'You could say that,' he told her.

She sighed heavily. 'Look, yes or no, Rhys? Are you screwing around?'

'I am having an affair,' he replied, lunging for maximum dignity.

'What kind of an affair?' she demanded, draining her coffee to the dregs and slamming the mug on to the worktop.

'Toby knows about it. What he's saying is right. It's been a long time.'

'How long, for fuck's sake?' She wiped her mouth on the tea towel and her hands on her trousers.

'Five years.'

'Bastard.'

The jar of jam flew through the air and smacked him hard on the forehead, knocking him flat to the floor.

'I'm going to get a divorce,' she yelled over him, reaching for her handbag as if divorces were on special offer at the supermarket and she had to hurry while stocks lasted. 'You're not getting a penny of my money, not after this. Or your disgusting children. God, what a waste of my life.'

Skirts flapped past his head, the floorboards shook, then the door slammed. Rhys felt as if his heart was swelling in his chest, filling up with daring and potential. He'd done it. Free at last. Or as good as free, anyway.

'So, is it?' La Maison was closed for lunch. Mo and Alice had gone to hide from life with a pair of cappuccinos in the depths of the Quando Quando Coffee Boutique.

'Yes. Oh, Mo, it's enormous. I saw it on the X-ray.'

'Tangerine, lemon, orange, grapefruit?' Tumours were always citrus-sized. Another mystery.

Alice looked down unbelievingly at her breasts. They looked perfectly OK. Just that the right one was a little bigger. Nothing you'd notice. She'd never been well-endowed. Put them both together and they'd hardly make a grapefruit. How big could this thing be?

'Orange, maybe? I don't know. Big for a tumour, anyway.'

'My God.'

'I know. He said he will try to save the breast, but he didn't look very positive about it.'

'And when are you going in?'

'Well, they didn't want me to come out now. They were going to send me straight up to a ward. That wretched insurance, I'm so glad I paid it.'

Alice was as poised and calm as if she were sitting in the shop filing invoices. Almost. Only someone familiar with her dash and squeak reactions would have found it truly strange to see her so still and quiet. Only Mo, with fine-tuned antennae and a few years of close contact to advise her, would have noticed the lethargic falling-off in all her gestures. The strange tranquillity of deep shock.

'But why didn't you do what they wanted?' And so unlike Alice to rebel, let alone against an authority figure like a doctor.

'All those things you've been on at me about, Mo. The house and the locks and my will and things. I've got to do them, haven't I? I mean, if I don't come out of hospital ever, what about the children? I rang Mel and she's coming down tonight to help me. Thank God for the children.'

'Have you told Sam?'

'Well, that's part of it, you see. I didn't really want him to know. But I tried to call him. His mobile's off, nobody's picking up at the office and – Mo, you're not going to believe this. I went round there and there's police tape everywhere, it's all locked and there's a notice on the door saying it's a crime scene and no entry. And they've been to the house, too. They took everything of his, all the phones, everything.'

'Bloody hell.' But she wasn't surprised. And nor, even allowing for her wiped-out condition, was Alice.

'And do you know, I'm not really bothered? I mean, the

whole thing seems so trivial. He seems so trivial. What did Charles the Second say? Dying concentrates the mind wonderfully? Was that Charles the Second? It was one king or another, I know it was. Anyway, if this is the last day of my life, I don't want to waste one minute of it thinking about some stupid man following his stupid willy into some stupid mess.'

'Alice, this isn't the last day of your life.'

'Well, it could be. I've got to take care of Mel and Jon at least. If Sam's gone and got himself into trouble, I've got to protect us, haven't I?'

'He was always so greedy. What could he have done? It'll be some scam, I bet. That outfit he took over, the One-Stop Property Shop. Didn't the guy who started that do a runner?'

'Well, yes, now I think about it, he did. Sam was so pleased about that deal, too.' She giggled with satisfaction, then checked herself.

Mo reached over and held her friend's narrow wrist, feeling it warm and full of beating blood vessels between the sharp bones. 'I'm so proud of you,' she said.

'I'm so proud of me,' Alice agreed, adding her free hand to the pile. 'I could never have done this six months ago. Isn't it crazy that I could be on the way out now – now, when I've just found out how life really works?'

Then they both teared up but Mo managed to growl, 'I will not have this loser talk, Alice.'

'Anyway,' she rallied brightly, 'what about you and Mickey? Any more news?'

'Well, like you say, some stupid man with a stupid willy. But not too stupid to use his credit cards, anyway.' Mo's visit to Helford Police Station had embarrassed the officer in charge. A burnt-out car, Mickey's car, as it proved, but no human traces.

At this news, Mo's instinct made a prediction which, after a couple of nail-biting hours on a hard bench in a corridor, proved to be correct. One of the cards was being used. A card she didn't even know he had. Much spelling and re-spelling of his name and address. The card had been used first at the airport, then in Denmark. Then the phone call.

'He should be back tomorrow,' she said with the complacency of one who had been right in a crisis. 'He couldn't have made today's flight from Copenhagen. I think he wants to change direction now. Do a feature. Be a film director.'

'I thought he was already.'

'No, features not commercials. It's what he's always wanted to do. He lost sight of it. When everyone's making you into a big hero, it's not so easy to keep moving, I guess. You tend to want to stay and collect on it all. He'll probably want to put the house on the market.' She said this with a touch of eagerness. Mo was ready to move on.

'Your lovely house! But why?'

'Well, he'll have to start looking for finance. It must be worth a couple of mil. We hardly need it. I mean, we'll be lucky if we see Joe once in five years at this rate.'

'But you've made it so beautiful, Mo.'

'It's only a house, isn't it? I'd like to keep working, anyway. We're not going to starve. It's the right thing for him to do, I've got to get behind it.'

'Weren't you worried sick? I would have been.'

'Yes and no. We've been married a long time. When he got to the place he was in, he was always going to do something. Break out, kick over. He's not the sit at home moaning type, or the go out and get pissed type, thank God. I know my man.'

'Well, I certainly didn't know mine. Just as well, maybe. I've got two wonderful children.'

And a tumour the size of an orange, they added mentally, saying nothing. Astrology, Feng Shui, the emotional causes of cancer – they were feeling too mature to invest in any of it.

The far north of Helford was covered with cul-de-sacs of grey-roofed pebbledashed semis, public housing from the 1930s, some of them cheaply embellished with half-timbered bays or false Georgian porches. A few old cars sat outside them, a few vociferous dogs barked from the windows. It was Saturday and people were walking back from a small cut-price supermarket carrying their shopping for the weekend in plastic bags.

This house was different in that it had no satellite dish. Instead a plastic banner hung from the upper windows proclaimed COMMUNITY OF CHRIST IN GLORY. Dead centre in the dripping front garden was a rotting bird table with half its roof missing.

Not knowing what they were going to encounter, they had dressed to look normal, Daisy in her school clothes, Andy in jeans and a new grey fleece. Not too bourgeois, in case they were going to meet underclass triumphalism, not too scruffy, in case old-style material judgements were going to be made, but just right. We're a nice family, don't throw the first stone at us.

The man who answered the door had hair as short as Andy's but was perhaps twenty years younger. He glared directly into their faces, first Andy, then Daisy, as if searching for the tell-tale signs of sin. 'You are the family,' he told them, scrutinising Andy again. 'We spoke on the phone.'

'Andy Forrest, I'm Lily's father. This is her sister.'

'Hi, I'm Daisy.'

'We welcome a visit from the family at the beginning. They're always afraid that we're some kind of cult. I'm sure she'll be happy to see you.'

The hall had woodchip wallpaper and tiny pictures of flowers in tacky filigree frames. They passed a room furnished with bean bags and a kitchen that smelled of frying, in which two girls of twenty or so were making tea. Daisy openly peered through both doorways. In the furthest room, where there was a desk and some wooden chairs, Lily was standing with her back to the window.

'I don't need this,' she announced. Andy thought she looked fatter, in a loose, pale, unhealthy way. He didn't recognise her clothes, a matted sweater and leggings. She had more spots, too, and a new stud shone from a new piercing in one of her nostrils.

The staring man focused on his new acolyte. 'We consider the needs of others,' he said.

'They're trying to take me away,' she answered, eyeballing each of them in turn in enthusiastic imitation of him.

'We just want to know you're OK,' said Daisy, sweetly patient.

'I told you, you don't need to worry about me. It's me that needs to worry about you. Everybody is praying for you. Where's Mummy?'

'She didn't want to come. She's pretty upset.' Daisy said this in the level tone of a daughter trying to conceal her mother's deep emotional trauma, so only Andy was aware that she was colouring the picture. Laura was showing no sign of distress on Lily's account. Her own affairs were taking up all her mind space. When she had read Lily's letter, she said, 'Well, she's made her decision. It's her life. We can't do anything about it.'

There was a shade of reaction from Lily, the merest waver in her new earnestness. 'I shall pray for her especially,' she rejoined, as if it was the answer to a question. 'God sees how we suffer because others do evil against us.'

Still wrapped in a blanket of betrayal, Andy could think of nothing to say. There was no satisfaction in imagining Lily's reaction if she knew the truth. Not that she ever would. Nor would Daisy. How could he begin to tell their daughters how their mother had decided to shore up their marriage?

'You're still going to school,' he said. This her teachers had told him, in the nervous tones of people who didn't reckon to deal with anything their pupils did outside school premises. 'That's good.'

'Of course I'm still going to school. This isn't some evil cult, Dad. This is just a community of people who want to live with Jesus. I'm not going to bury my talent in the ground. I have to achieve my full potential and use it for the glory of the Lord.'

'Normally, what we do in these cases is apply to take the role of foster carers,' put in the staring man, as if talking about an application for a parking permit. 'Lily is seventeen, isn't she? Then the council will agree a level of support. Otherwise, some of our young members are self-supporting. Saturday jobs, things like that.'

This was clearly a new concept to Lily, who started and then smothered her surprise in a nod and a daffy grin.

'I think we would oppose that,' Andy told him. 'There aren't any problems in our family which would make us unfit parents. We have a good home.'

'I'm sure you do,' the staring one replied, with the righteous emphasis of a person who considered that a man who was concerned to put a roof over a family's head was self-evidently a moral bankrupt. And double that for a beautifully restored roof in The Terrace, Westwick's Georgian Gem. 'But it's not about material things, is it? What matters to Lily is the life of the spirit. That's what matters to us all.'

'I didn't mean materially good,' said Andy patiently. 'And I think you may have got some funny ideas about our family.' He drew a deep breath and continued, 'As her parents, we are legally responsible for her. That means we have to agree to let her stay here. In fact, we have to be satisfied that you are the proper people to look after her.'

Lily and the staring man exchanged glances and he took up a position behind the desk as if to defend himself better. 'As a Christian, Lily has chosen the way of the truth. We believe what she says.' The staring was redoubled.

'As she is also a child, I think it would be wise to take into account that she may not know the entire truth of what she's been telling you about us.'

'You and your wife are getting divorced so you can pursue a homosexual relationship. Isn't that it?' This was delivered with a smirk that he tried, too late, to suppress.

'Not as far as I know,' Andy assured him. Lily let out a hiss. Daisy rolled her eyes with annoyance.

'As far as you know.' Now the man was staring as if he hoped to achieve X-ray vision with just a bit of practice.

'Oh, Dad, you're just evil.' Lily stamped her foot as theatrically as if she'd been told to turn off a soap opera and get on with her homework. 'You know what you did.'

'Yes I do, and you don't,' he pointed out, struggling to flatten the bubble of guilt that was swelling up in his normally flawless conscience. Beside him, he felt Daisy seething like a kettle about to boil. 'I have done nothing that anyone could consider wrong on any grounds and your mother and I have never even discussed divorce. I've been there for you twenty-four hours a day and if you'd been worried about anything or upset about anything—'

'You're only around because you're unemployed.' Lily was panicking now, leaning back against the windowsill like a boxer on the ropes. 'You got sacked and you can't get another job. You're just playing with your computer, pretending to start a company, and it's all a fantasy.'

Daisy suddenly let out a scream of frustration. 'How can you be such a little bitch? When Dad's been working so hard to look after us all—'

'No he hasn't, it's all a lie,' screamed Lily back, pointing the finger.

'You're the one who's evil! You're just making up this stuff to justify what you've done.'

'Mum told me. She should know.'

Andy was not good with screaming, especially from women in his own family. Above a certain volume, every word slashed a hole in his mental equilibrium. 'Your mother knows exactly how real the company is and exactly how well it's doing. So could you, if you asked. Last year's accounts are lying around in the office. You could have read them any time.'

'It's not your office, it's just the sitting room. You're just evil, telling lies,' Lily insisted. 'You're having delusions. Mum's going to leave you. Why isn't she here?'

Daisy shouted, 'She's not here because she doesn't care, you stupid cow. She said you'd made your mind up and you could do what you liked. We're the ones who care. That's why we're here.'

The staring man had been staring at the door as if he expected a miraculous vision to drift through it and pronounce words of divine wisdom. Now he swivelled his head and looked at Lily. 'It seems to me we have to consider the good of our community as a whole here,' he suggested in a newly worldly tone. 'If Lily's got a bit confused about things, maybe you should all sit down and have a talk with her. We could send somebody from the house to mediate, if you would accept that. Some of us are trained family counsellors.'

'Fine,' Andy agreed at once. Lily looked as if he'd spoken only to annoy her.

'It's not fine with me,' she insisted. 'I want to be fostered with you like you said. If you talk to them, they'll just twist everything to make out there's nothing wrong.'

'There isn't anything wrong,' Daisy snapped at her sister. 'Only your head, that's the only wrong thing here.'

'That's unkind, Daze.'

Lily suddenly flung herself across the room, smashing into a filing cabinet and dislodging a pile of paper from the desk. When she hit the wall she whirled around, waving her arms. 'I knew this would happen. I told you and you wouldn't listen. They always twist everything round so they're right.

They won't let me do anything I want to do, even if it's giving my life to God. They've tried to stop me going to church . . .'

'No, we haven't. We've never stopped you doing anything.'

Lily was still twisting, turning clumsily on the spot, hitting the furniture as she lurched around.

'Even when Granny died and left us each a hundred pounds and you gave that to the church, nobody ever stopped you,' Daisy pointed out. Andy tried not to show surprise. In his mind, his mother's little legacy to her grandchildren was still safely in the bank. If he'd known Lily wanted to give it away, he might have had something to say.

The staring man twitched. For a spiritual leader, material matters seemed to press his buttons very effectively. What their presence, their manner and their concern had failed to communicate, the idea that the church had received a hundred improper pounds achieved immediately. 'We don't want to lay ourselves open to accusations here.' He raised his voice with anxiety. 'I think it's best, Lily . . .'

Lily threw herself backwards on to his desk, tossing her arms from side to side and babbling like a baby. As one person, they stepped back out of her way. To Andy it seemed like a ridiculous pretence, some kind of seizure faked by a cosseted child who got her ideas from *EastEnders* and who'd never seen a moment of genuine cerebral disturbance in her life. Daisy was looking on with supercilious contempt.

'Get up now, Lily,' the staring man ordered her, his voice rising in volume and sinking in pitch.

Lily babbled louder. The staring man appealed over her flailing arms to Andy. 'Does she do this at home? She doesn't have fits, does she? She's seen people speaking in tongues at our meetings.' He mugged at them, his face twisted in a confidential leer. Get her out of here.

Andy suddenly saw the situation from Lily's perspective. All this drama, and no way out of it with her dignity intact. Unless he found her a hole in the fence. John Wayne, here I come.

He stepped forward, grabbed Lily by the arms, dragged her upright and shook her. 'Shut up,' he said, not loudly enough. Her legs were bearing most of her weight, but she was babbling in an idiotic crescendo. He tried again in a louder voice, 'Shut up, you stupid girl.'

Lily burst into histrionic sobs and sank back against the desk. She was not, he could see, going to push her luck and collapse on the floor. Just as well, since his knees wouldn't welcome the opportunity to get her on her feet.

'Lily,' fussed the staring man, 'don't be upset. We must render unto Caesar, Lily. We mustn't break the law.' He flapped around her, conscious that for the sake of seeming caring he needed to be close but more aware that an inappropriate touch might be far more trouble than it was worth at this point. 'Go home with your dad now,' he urged her. 'You can come and see me on Sunday after the service. Come back for a witness meeting if you like.'

Hearing herself rejected, Lily started to cry for real. Daisy reached for the door, saying, 'Can we go now?'

'A donation to our work would be appreciated,' the staring man said as he followed them down the hallway, holding out a dirty anorak. Shamefaced, Lily grabbed it and shrugged it around her shoulders. It was on the small side.

'I don't think so,' Andy told him firmly, sweeping his

miserable daughter over the doormat and out into God's fresh air.

'What I don't understand,' Daisy said as she sank into the sanctuary of the back seat of the old Volvo and draped a hand over her eyes, 'is why being Christian means everything has to be so totally cheesy. Haven't they ever heard of white paint? I mean, why do you have to look like Waynetta Slob, Lily? God made you quite pretty, when you try.'

Lily let out a mutinous snuffle. As Andy turned south to head back to civilisation and The Terrace, his mobile phone rang. The landlord at the Beehive.

'I was wondering if you could help me out, mate.' Question expecting the answer 'yes'.

'Try me,' Andy suggested. 'Happy to help if I can.'

'Friday week. Had a cancellation. Wondered if you guys would care to step in at short notice. I'd up the money, obviously.'

Like an extra tenner was really going to clinch it. But what was the band, without George? 'I don't know,' he said. 'You heard we had a bit of a tragedy, didn't you?'

'No, I didn't. What—'

'Our lead guitar. Road accident just before Christmas. We haven't played since then.'

'Very sad. I'm sorry, I had no idea. Was that the – er – bloke with the teeth?'

'That was him.'

'But surely . . . I mean, you're the draw, Andy. You're the one people come to hear. There are plenty of guitarists. I could ask around, if you like.'

'We've covered for him before. Let me get the others together and put it to them,' Andy suggested. Mickey could

347

take lead, if he had to. Truth to tell, he could be pretty good. If he was in the country. If he was in his right mind. You never knew, nowadays.

A gig. Get up and make some noise, play some old songs, give the punters a good time. Sing about love and sex and death and pain, have a bit of a laugh, do a few beers. No wives, no daughters, no business. Well, why not? Just for a moment there, for a few golden seconds, he remembered how it felt to be Andy 'Mr Fabulous' Forrest.

Later, after he'd seen Lily to bed and sat up talking with Daisy for a while, Andy decided to take a shower and wash off the memory of the staring man, the well-worn bean bags, the smell of old bacon and the whole self-consciously poxy aesthetic of the Community of Christ in Glory.

Consideration was an ingrained habit with Andy. He showered downstairs, in order not to wake his sleeping wife. In the bedroom, however, Laura was still awake, starfished over their bed, listening to her gut. Her gut was telling her there was no point in testing the market for men any more. The guys out there were all like the ones she'd already met.

Some people, faced with information they don't like, delay making a decision in the hope that the facts will change to something more congenial. Laura made decisions very fast.

'The charge of fraud is a serious one, but since you are of previous good character I'm minded to disappoint the police on this occasion and release you on bail, on your own recognisance of two hundred and fifty thousand pounds.'

'Thank you very much,' said Sam, meaning every word passionately. Thank God the magistrate had recognised another professional man when he saw one. The distance from Westwick to Helford was only a few yards in reality but in culture it was another universe.

The once-white court building was a grimy exercise in municipal fascism and looked like the mausoleum of a Balkan dictator, with the bodies of his opponents concreted into the foundations. Its corridors were crowded with grey-faced, surly underclass and the earnest stewards of their deprivation, the social workers, the probation officers, the police, the criminal law.

Sam did not belong here. He belonged in Belgravia with pink tablecloths. It was all a shameful miscarriage of justice. He'd be suing, big time, no mistake.

It was all down to Pats. What a snake that woman had turned out to be. The business she'd brought in, that room stuffed with files, those new clients, twenty, thirty, sometimes forty a week? Fake. Every one. Almost every one – she'd been clever enough to send through a handful of genuine cases. But most of the fuel he'd trusted to propel him into the financial stratosphere had been nothing but a fraud.

She had negotiated mortgages for properties that didn't exist, owned by people who didn't exist, and inspected by surveyors who didn't exist. A room full of bogus business, that was all she'd brought him. The banks, the building societies, it was all their fault. Greedy bastards, they'd processed the paper and written the cheques and never asked the questions they should have asked. The name of Chudleigh Estate Services had reassured them, obviously.

The cheques had been paid into dozens of different bank accounts, the repayments had been made by dozens of direct debits, the system had ticked over for months without a hitch. Pats's old boss, founder of the One-Stop Property Shop, had done a runner to the Cayman Islands and set up a company there. Nobody suspected, nobody questioned it. Another Westwick man having a mid-life crisis, that was par for the course, just business as usual.

They'd planned it all, obviously. Just before Christmas Pats had transferred the thousands, the hundreds of thousands, the fucking bloody millions, to the Cayman company and closed all the accounts. Then got on a plane to follow the cash in person. Holiday period, the whole supposedly Christian world at home eating and drinking, leaving all the work to the computers. The flickering numbers, disappearing here, reappearing there, passing through filters and fire walls, triggering nothing, unsuspected. Until the first repayments of the new year fell due, the red flag went up and somebody, finally, twigged. That was what banking was down to nowadays. First class technology, fifth class employees.

A vicious wind blew sleet in his face while he stood on Helford High Street, restoring his personal effects to their appropriate pockets, seeking the fastest means of escape. No sign of a taxi. Obese women waddling after their skinny kids, young men drifting about in idle groups, huddled in their jackets against the cold, kicking cans and flicking their cigarettes. Not much on the street except for buses. He got on a bus. The first time for years. Decades. The smell, disgusting. They expected you to have change for the fare.

As they ground slowly into Westwick and stop-started down the Broadway, he sank down in his seat in case anyone recognised him. Sam Chudleigh on a bus, God forbid. It was going to stop right there on the street, how could he get off without attracting attention? Past the school, past the church, past the shops on Grove Parade, past Maple Grove. At last the bus turned north and he got off at a request stop in a side street.

Walking back, he called Elizabeth. The voicemail. Their relationship was obviously entering a new phase. More adult, not so intense. She hadn't left him any messages while he'd been . . . away. The word 'custody' just couldn't enter his thoughts. Let alone the word 'jail'.

Good timing, obviously. Until this business was sorted out, he'd have the opportunity to be with his family more. Give the children some attention. Sort out his affairs, which Alice had no doubt messed up. It was the right thing to do at this point. Hold things together for a while. For the sake of the children.

His ears stinging with the cold and his feet aching from the walk, he finally reached the sanctuary of Maple Grove and located his house. The garden looked neglected, Alice obviously wasn't on top of things at all. He reached the front door and tried to put his key in the lock.

The key did not fit. Sam went back down the path and assured himself that he was at the right house. Yes, this was the place. And his key wouldn't open the door. Alice was playing silly buggers. Right. He'd better sort this out immediately. Go round to that shop, ask her what the hell she thought she was doing.

At La Maison, a decorative old French shop sign hung on the door, saying '*Fermé*' in curly letters.

Golf probably wasn't the ideal winter game. Rhys could see no one on the course. The clubhouse was deserted, except for the lone waiter who brought him some coffee. Rain was driving thickly across the fairway and the first tee was barely visible. In any case, he felt too tired to try more than nine holes. In fact, he felt too tired to swing a club at all. It had been a challenge to drag himself out of bed.

This was not how he had imagined life without Barbara. She had run back to Daddy in his concrete mansion. No doubt they were abusing him, he could almost hear the echoes of their vile conversation broadcast over London from the intellectual height of Hampstead. No matter. The house was his for the meantime. His life was his for ever after.

He had expected to feel relief, maybe even joy. Instead he was weighed down by a blanket of – what? His feet were leaden, his bones ached. All he wanted to do was sleep. Everything was a supreme effort and nothing was worth it. Even Mo, the Mo of his daydreams, even she seemed somehow tarnished, as if he were seeing her reflection in an old grey mirror.

The inquiry hung over him like a thunderstorm. His insurers had sent over an assessor who had, courteously and sympathetically, talked him through every detail of Ms Watson's abdominoplasty. 'I'll be cleared, won't I?' he had to ask. 'We certainly hope so,' was the best he got in reply. Debrosser was still in Cape Town. No reason for a young man like that to blemish his career, nowhere was it written that he should be a sucker for punishment. It seemed likely Rhys would be facing the inquiry by himself. No date set yet.

At a table by the window, he sat drooping over the morning papers, reading of rape, murder, abduction, riots and global warming. Should he have brought his children into

352

the world, to live with all that? To live with Barbara as their mother? Better, surely, for a man to be sterile and impotent in this horrible world.

His phone rang and Mo spoke to him.

'Darling, I need to see you.'

She'd never said that before. Why didn't his heart leap? Why, instead of happy anticipation, was his heart dark with anxiety? She needed to see him. Wasn't that good?

'Good,' he murmured, turning away from the empty room.

'Where are you?'

'The golf club.'

'You don't play golf, Rhys. Do you?'

The woman he loved and she didn't even know if he played golf. 'Not really. Not today, anyway. It's raining.'

'Stay there. I'll meet you.'

He told her the way. So handy, Westwick. Encircled by satellites of affluent amusement, surrounded by golf clubs, country clubs, rugby clubs, tennis clubs, dry ski slopes and places where the hardy and determined could learn to wind-surf on a flooded sand quarry. She appeared in less than twenty minutes looking, to his eyes, old. Not like herself.

'To what do I owe the honour?'

She winced. Was that too Knopfler again? He never knew. 'I thought we'd better talk, Rhys.'

'About us?' He had rehearsed this a million times, so how come it went over all wrong?

'Of course about us. And Mickey.'

'How is Mickey?'

'Why are you being so sarcastic, Rhys? It's not like you. Don't you want to know how he is?'

'I know he's alive. I know he upset you, taking off like that. What else do I need to know?' This wasn't how it was supposed to be. She hadn't kissed him. She was speaking from some parallel universe, he couldn't reach her. And he was saying things he didn't want to say. The whole event was totally out of control and all he could do was watch it fall off a cliff.

'Rhys, I'm very fond of you.' There ought to be a song called that. Very fond of you. The long way to say goodbye. 'But Mickey's going through some stuff right now and I don't want to make it any worse. I feel bad we've gone on so long. I've been meaning to say this for quite a while. You're so sweet, always, I could never quite do it. But we've got to stop now.'

'Fine,' he said, his voice tight with anger.

'Mickey wants to set up a feature. It's a big step for him, I can help a little. It'll be a gamble, of course. Films aren't easy to finance. We've had some wonderful times, haven't we?'

Yeah, yeah. We will always have Paris.

'You know Barbara's left, don't you?'

'Then you're really free to find someone as good as you deserve, aren't you? I used to wonder, you know, if it was the right thing for you. Seeing me meant you could get along, but what you really needed to do was end it with her. She's an unhappy woman, she's got her own issues, you can't help with them. I do want you to be happy, Rhys.'

'I don't know I can help you there.'

She started to say something but pinched her lips on it. 'It's better if I go now. You're not in the best place to hear this, I guess. I'm sorry.' And she had gathered up her handbag, just the way she always did, slender fingers over the top, pulling it to her, and she was getting up, unfolding the forever legs, standing on her lovely feet, getting ready to leave.

Where was it, the one thing he could say to make her stay? He scanned desperately for inspiration but nothing came up except bitterness and hate, so he shrugged and turned away and said, 'You're right. It's not a good time.'

Goodbye? Au revoir? Catch you later? *A la prochaine fois?* There must be something better to say but his mind couldn't locate it. And she was gone. A huge empty hole in front of him, filling up with blood. Nothing beyond it. No future, no hope, no life.

The weather was really getting with the programme. Rain was falling in savage bursts, battering the shrubs outside the window, raising puddles on the fairway, lashing the trees. Less and less light struggled down from the murky sky.

His phone rang. She was calling to say she didn't mean it? Fat chance. He let it ring. Who could possibly be calling that he'd actually want to speak to? Probably a wrong number. The waiter, pottering at the far end of the empty room, looked over in his direction.

The phone was silent. Rhys appreciated that he must look like a nutter. Maybe they'd throw him out. In the cold and rain. Cancel his membership. That's Rhys Pritchard, the doctor. You know, the one who got thrown out of Royal Richmond-on-Thames Golf Club for going mad in the bar.

When the phone rang again, he searched around in his golf bag, tried to pretend he had trouble finding the thing. And then there was nothing to do but answer it.

'Dad?'

'Toby.' Now what?

'Don't worry, Dad. I just called to see how you are.'

'I'm fine.' No need to ask how Toby was, tucked up snugly with little Miss Sweetling, nothing in the world to worry him except getting his coursework finished by the end of term. Great to be sixteen and know nothing.

'You sound a bit down.'

Uncanny, the things children picked up. 'It's a lousy day and the golf's rained off.'

'Must be desperate if you're down to golf, Dad.'

'Yes, well.'

'You're depressed, I can tell.'

'How can you possibly tell, Toby? You're just a kid.'

'I can tell because I've been there, Dad. It's just the hormones, isn't it? Stopping or starting, must be the same, they mess up your head. It's not a nice smooth transition, it's just chaotic. Like when they started with me and I got all these feelings. If they're stopping with you, you'll get feelings too.'

Stopping? What did the kid mean, stopping? 'The hormonal system isn't quite like that, Toby. It's very complex and finely balanced—'

'Yeah, but it doesn't actually work very well, does it, Dad? There you are, just minding your own business, and then one day this wall of stuff hits you, you feel like shit, you can't get out of bed, the whole world hates you, your head's full of garbage and you start saying things you don't mean and making bad decisions.'

I am your father. I may mess up a conversation with my lover on occasion but I do not make bad decisions. Wait a minute, wait a minute. Is he talking about himself, here?

Maybe I should be listening. That's it, listening mode. Show you care, see if he wants to talk.

'Is everything OK your end?'

'Logically speaking, yes, Dad.'

'You haven't had a row with . . . Susie?'

'Not really. I suppose I'm feeling a bit hormonally challenged this morning. Have you had a row with . . . Mo?'

'Not really. We've agreed to cool it for a while, that's all. Her husband's had a bit of a mid-life crisis. I suppose that's what you'd call it.'

'I've got some Prozac, if you want some.'

'They're not sweets, Toby, you can't just hand them around.'

'Well, people do. Anyway, that's my best offer. Unless you want to buy me lunch or something. Susie's at work and it's my half day.'

Quite an offer, when you looked at it. Visit our love nest, go out and drink beer together. The boy was wanting to bond. Important to roll with it, the way they were super-adult one minute, clingy and babyish the next. This was going to be a new phase in their relationship, obviously. Toby still needed him, but in a different way. Well, fine. As it should be. He could relate to that.

The sky seemed a trace lighter, the rain a little less of a downpour. He found he had at least enough energy to think about driving over and giving his son the support a boy needed at an awkward time of life.

'So where is it, exactly, this place of yours?'

Alice hated supermarket flowers. She'd never understood why, when Marcia at Pot Pourri offered the most exquisite English cottage garden blooms that were ever raised in a polytunnel in

Kenya, why anyone with any taste would bother with the vulgar bunches that wilted in buckets in supermarkets. The gerberas that couldn't even hold up their heads on their own stems, the roses that weren't going to open ever, and the chrysanthemums – ugh, the chrysanthemums. Cemetery flowers; she felt depressed just looking at them.

There was a bunch of supermarket flowers at the end of the bed. Corseted in cellophane, the gerberas were custard yellow, the rose buds were screwed up as if they didn't want to see the world and the chrysanthemums were a revolting dried blood colour. Through the sickening mist of her drugs, she heard the flowers rustle and saw Sam's face appear coyly at one side.

'Hello,' he said with a roguish flash of his eyebrows.

Sitting up was a performance and she wasn't going to bother for Sam. Speaking would be a waste of good breath, too. The wonderful thing about being ill was that you had so many excuses to be rude.

'How are you?' he asked tenderly, advancing along the side of the bed. Alice felt a little anxious. Mel was still around somewhere. There was a handy red button to press if she needed the nurse.

'I've had a terrible time finding out where you were. Why didn't you tell me you had this . . . problem? I had to track down Maureen. She's doing too much in that shop, she's got no idea of customer care.' The garish bouquet was lowered to her table and he looked around for a chair. The only one available was a low vinyl-padded armchair that left the visitor's head about level with the mattress. He perched on the arm. She observed that his suit was crumpled and his backside about fifty per cent fatter than when she last had cause to notice.

'How are you, Alice? They wouldn't tell me anything

because they claimed I'm not next of kin. You'd think when you were paying people would at least be polite.'

How exhausting it was just having him in the same room. She'd never noticed it before. Just think, years of living with him, having him drain her strength like this every day. Did she want someone to come and take him away, or could she manage to get rid of him herself?

'Go away, Sam.' She thought her voice might not have been loud enough, so she tried again with more volume. 'Go away, Sam. You make me feel worse.'

'Is it very unpleasant, this treatment?'

'Not as unpleasant as you. Go away.'

'You must be feeling awful, Alice. I do understand.'

'No, you don't. Go away.'

'I'm going to come home for a while. I've been thinking about it. For the sake of the children. And now, of course, there's you. I've got a duty to my family.'

'You're a bit late, Sam. We're better off without you.'

'You're not well, Alice. We'll talk about it later.'

'I'm well enough. Just go away.'

His eyes shot left and right as he formulated his next question. She knew the expression of old. He was calculating, working out his advantage. Why, he wants to know if I'm going to die, because if I am, he won't need to make so much fuss to get the house. Which is probably all he's got left now. Or will be if his business goes under because of this fraud thing. Well, bad luck, Sammy boy. I'm doing fine. I'm going to be OK. I'm making my doctors happy. Six weeks of this shit and I'll be clean and clear.

'Haven't you got anything to tell me, Sam? I've been round to your office. It seems to be shut.'

'Just a misunderstanding, nothing to worry about. I'm co-operating fully with the investigation. There'll be damages to go for when it's all over. Oh yes.'

'And how's your girlfriend? Doing well, is she? Going out a lot?'

He got off the arm of the chair and stomped back to the end of the bed, where he stood holding the foot-rail, struggling for the best way to reclaim the conversation.

'I'm worried about you,' he announced at last. 'You're not acting like yourself.'

'I'm not acting at all, Sam. I'm more myself than I've ever been. Will you please get out of here now?' Perhaps she should have sat up. Easier to give orders when at least part of you is upright.

'All right,' he conceded, 'if that's what you want.' But he was standing his ground. He had this funny way of puffing up and swaying when he was angry, looking like an irritated balloon tied to the end of her bed.

The wound in her chest was throbbing again, she really wanted to stay as she was. Alice pressed the bell for the nurse, and when she came said, 'I don't think I'm well enough for visitors at the moment. Except my family. And Mrs Ryder. Will you stop everyone else coming up?'

'I haven't got anywhere to go,' said Sam suddenly. 'You've locked me out of my own home.'

'And the police have locked you out of your own office. You haven't managed things very well, have you? But that's not my problem.'

'Don't you have any sympathy?' he demanded, throwing out his chest again, struggling for self-importance.

The nurse quivered with outrage. 'Sir,' she said, 'Miss Waters wants you to leave.'

'Who's Miss Waters?' he demanded irritably.

'You're not doing very well, Sam, are you?' Alice asked, choking down the laugh that was going to make her stitches pull. 'I'm Miss Waters, and I want you to leave.'

'I can call security,' threatened the nurse.

'All right,' said Sam. 'All right. I'm going. There's obviously no point talking to her in this condition.'

He vanished from Alice's vision and she saw the top of the door open and close. What remained was a calming view of the window, the ceiling, the upper half of the nurse and the bedside table. 'Would you be kind enough to take the flowers away?' She pointed at them and the rest of the nurse came into view, smiling. 'They make me feel worse.'

At the window, white blinds and triple-glazing sealed out the world. Her room was quiet and white. Melanie was arranging everything, she'd got a lawyer drawing up the separation agreement. All she had to do was get better. Alice thought she could manage it.

CHAPTER 12

Rehearsed Encore No 1

'I don't know what you were worried about,' said the land-lord of the Beehive, handing Andy the last of four pints. 'I'm gonna have one wild night here. No, don't worry, these are on the house. Mark of respect. And I'm very grateful.'

An inferno of noise. Vibrations still bleeding from the speakers. Powerful, aggressive, the set had been up there with the greatest in the band's history. They'd played like rock and roll legends. Well, almost. Two hundred happy punters, shaken around like rag dolls, had forgotten their shitty weeks and let the sound of shredding metal carry them away to happiness.

Even Intro/Outro had gone over well. Maybe the audience was getting trained in the ways of the Bonzos. Carrying the beers back to the table, Andy's biggest problem was so many people thumping him on the shoulders and yelling 'Awesome!' in his ear.

'That was one for old George, all right,' Mickey said, pleased with himself, cracking his startled knuckles. When he let go, he was one hell of a noisy guitarist. Put together with the heavy bass sound Andy had come up with, there wasn't room for much else.

'He'll be listening, up there,' Sam agreed. Very satisfying, that exercise in tense and release dynamics, getting an insidious little groove going. He should have a music room in his new flat. A baby grand, at least. And a trip to Bang & Olufsen seemed to be on the cards.

'Here's to George,' Rhys proposed, raising his glass. God, his hands were sore already. Torn muscle fibres repairing themselves, trauma to the phalangeal joints. Amazing, the body's power of response. No slowing down of the healing process yet.

They raised their glasses and gulped. Andy gulped deepest. God, his throat was rough. That's what you got for a couple of months without singing. Use it or lose it. He'd go for the first one.

'So are we doing this again?'

'Do bears shit in the woods?' Sam demanded.

'No, seriously. You were the one saying it was time to knock it on the head and we were getting too old.'

'I never said anything of the sort,' Sam protested. 'You're making that up.'

'I'm planning to be around a year at least,' Mickey announced. 'Getting finance together, pre-production. No more travelling for a while. I'm up for it. I mean, everyone else is still out there embarrassing themselves. Bob Dylan must be sixty, for fuck's sake. Why should we worry?'

'I'm with you,' Rhys agreed. 'If Mickey's in, I'm in.' Friendship, that was the most important thing. Thank goodness he'd never gone so far with Mo that it threatened what was between him and Mickey. You had to respect a man who took risks like that. 'We can rehearse at my place, if you like,' he suggested, remembering his empty house.

Since they'd done good, they went for another two rounds, with vodka chasers, then loaded the gear into Andy's old Volvo and went their separate ways into the cold and rain.

One of the many beauties of The Terrace was that it looked out over the historic Burnham Green, where Cromwell had camped the night before the battle that had won him and his Roundheads control over London. Across this pleasant public space, now attractively planted with cherry trees, passers-by had a clear panorama of Westwick's Georgian Gem, twenty-two Regency villas whose pastel-painted stucco gleamed sickly under the street lights.

An instinct made Andy slow down as he approached. Loaded car, wet roads, poor visibility, Captain Sensible at the wheel. Light blazed from every window of Charles and Pascal's house. All those state-of-the-art blinds and they never did close them.

The traffic light was against him. While he waited, ready to turn right towards his home, the door of their neighbours' house opened violently. A man ran down the steps and didn't stop running until he reached the street. Slender, dark, supple. Pascal. Dragging a barrel bag, then slinging it over his shoulder like a sailor.

Someone slammed the door behind him. Bang. Even through the sluicing rain, Andy heard the noise. Good riddance. And don't come back.

Pascal was at the kerb, twisting this way and that, shivering with emotion. And cold. Wearing just a T-shirt, no coat. He let the bag fall to the ground and looked up and down the street. A car crossed the lights in front of Andy and Pascal attempted to flag it down. The T-shirt flapped, he was getting soaked to the skin. The car did not stop.

The lights began to change. Andy decided to take a left. Round the block, come into The Terrace the other way. Pass by on the other side, the classic Westwick manoeuvre. He had enough trouble in his life already. Somebody else could take on Pascal.